Emyr Humphreys was born in the Welsh seaside resort of Prestatyn, the son of a Flintshire schoolmaster. He was educated at the University of Aberystwyth, where he began to develop his lifelong interest in Welsh literature, language and politics. He has worked as a teacher in London, as a radio and TV drama producer for the BBC, and as a drama lecturer at Bangor University.

Winner of the Hawthornden Prize and the Somerset Maugham Award, his highly acclaimed novels include: *Flesh and Blood*, *Salt of the Earth*, *A Toy Epic* and *Jones*. He has also published books of poetry and non-fiction in Welsh and English, and in 1983 he won the Welsh Arts Council Prize for *The Taliesin Tradition*, a book about the Welsh character. He lives with his wife in Anglesey.

NATIONAL WINNER

Emyr Humphreys

SPHERE BOOKS LIMITED

A SPHERE BOOK

First published in Great Britain in 1971
by Macdonald & Co (Publishers) Ltd, London
Published by Sphere Books 1990

Typeset in Baskerville 10/11 by Selectmove, London
Reproduced, printed and bound in Great Britain by
Cox & Wyman Ltd, Reading

ISBN 0 7474 0611 1

Sphere Books Ltd
A Division of
Macdonald & Co (Publishers) Ltd
Orbit House,
1 New Fetter Lane,
London EC4A 1AR
A member of Maxwell Macmillan Pergamon Publishing Corporation

Contents

Book One   1

Book Two   125

Book Three   218

Book Four   308

Book Five   402

BOOK ONE

1

The two girls were out of breath as they climbed the third flight of stairs and the smaller one cursed aloud as she caught her heel in the loose linoleum. From the landing of the second floor a large man wearing an M.A. gown, with close cropped red hair and gold rimmed spectacles, watched their ascent, grinning cheerfully and pressing down his double chins.

'We are looking for Mr P.C. More,' the first girl said.

'Then you've come to the right place!'

The large man appeared to have the extensive leisure necessary for going about looking for amusing situations. He spoke with a rich and amiable West Country accent.

'In fact I shall guide you there,' he said. 'A personally conducted tour. Mind how you go now. This building isn't too safe. And I'm not joking. But never mind, my dears, the building programme is well in hand. Even now the plaster is drying on the walls of my new room.'

He was about to knock on a door which had been painted crimson in the hope that this would brighten a dingy corridor. In a small brass frame a visiting card gave the name *P.C. More, Department of Social Analysis*. He turned to look at the two girls and made a roguish face.

'Are you sure you wouldn't prefer to come and see me? Next door. Pure Mathematics. Much more exciting.'

He wriggled his eyebrows confidently and won a smile from the taller of the two girls. The other was still examining the state of her heel. He tapped the door and opened it wide enough to put in his head.

'Hello there, P.C.,' he said. 'Take off your helmet. Two friendly females approaching! Are you at home to visitors of the fair sex? Because if not, they can travel another couple of yards and I will entertain them in my mathematical boudoir. Together we will make a volumetric analysis of the Blue Grotto of Illicit Love!'

'What do they want?'

With guilty speed the solitary young don was putting away a small bellows he had been using to blow away the film of soot which covered the mass of papers on his desk. It was a back room that never saw the sun. Outside was an old railway yard now used for an industrial process which involved a large oil burner at unpredictable hours.

'Ah ha,' the large lecturer said. 'I see you've left your window open again, Peredur! It doesn't pay to be a fresh-air fiend in this neck of the woods you know!'

Peredur dropped the bellows in the bottom drawer of his desk and then clasped his thin white hands together in innocent passivity. Nothing his jovial neighbour said amused him. His callow face below his bushy black hair was pale with pain and anxiety and his lips were pressed tightly together over his teeth which protruded slightly. He had a boil on the back of his neck which obliged him to hold his head forward with unnatural stiffness. The taller girl was peeping in around the shoulder of his colleague. She was breathless but jolly, taking her cue from the friendly reception the other lecturer had given them at the top of the stairs.

'Oh dear!' she said in a high pitched excited voice.

2

'We're from *Nimrod*. We'd like an interview if you could just spare us a few minutes of your time.'

Peredur drew back in his chair.

'Well, well,' the large lecturer said. 'You are doubly honoured, Peredur P.C. You'll make the headlines yet.'

He chuckled and stood aside to let the second girl pass. She seemed very small alongside his great bulk. She was peering short-sightedly at the floor as though she was searching for some small object which she had lost. She wore large round spectacles with tinted lenses which on her small face looked like a disguise. Her features were delicately beautiful in an old-fashioned way and the spectacles seemed a desperate attempt to transform this beauty into something more contemporary. As she moved she put one foot in front of the other with noticeable care and her efforts to be unobtrusive drew Peredur's attention.

'The thing is,' the big girl said. 'If you have been correctly reported, which is always in question I admit, this could be a very big issue . . . oh sorry . . . by the way we are the Features Editors. This is Maxine Hackett and I'm Denise Rowley.'

She stood between the window and the desk, and the room darkened with her presence. With some difficulty Peredur lifted his head to look at her face which had the bland cheerfulness of a rising sun design on the face of a grandfather clock. She chattered brightly.

'Maxie is the brains and I'm the brawn. We should be on Teaching Prac really but we both feel *Nimrod* is more important and we've got a deadline to meet so we won't keep you, Mr. More. Do you mind if we ask you some questions?'

She produced a shorthand pad out of the briefcase she was carrying.

'I'm not saying we can give you instant fame,' she said, looking about her for a chair to sit on. 'But oak trees grow from acorns. Or so they tell me. And it could

3

be that yours is the message the whole world is waiting for.'

The small girl spoke unexpectedly.

'Denise,' she said. 'Don't talk like a bloody wet.'

In the doorway the large lecturer who had been watching the smooth invasion with amused curiosity broke into loud laughter. The small girl turned to give him a look of malign sweetness.

'Well I'll leave you to it,' he said and closed the door, dramatized his departure a little with a quick bow and another wiggle of his eyebrows.

'The man is a fool,' Maxine said.

Her voice was quiet, but her Birmingham accent was so pronounced it seemed aggressive, as though she were a foreigner who had learnt fluent English but spoke it with reluctance. Peredur had pressed against the back of his chair in order to discharge a protective fluid of hostility into the atmosphere but he could not help himself becoming interested in Maxine. His narrow nostrils distended as he caught the full impact of the perfume the tall girl had brought into the room. She had been considering sitting on the window sill. Ostentatiously she drew her finger along it and studied the black spot on her finger with exaggerated distaste.

'Don't make such a fuss, Denise,' Maxine said. 'Let's get on with it.'

Denise smiled at Peredur, apparently confident that he had been won over by her innate charm and friendliness.

'She bullies me,' she said. 'It gets quite dreadful at times. And she looks so innocent doesn't she? As if butter wouldn't melt in her mouth.'

Peredur looked at Maxine. She had found a chair and was examining the contents of a green and white Greek shopping-bag she was carrying. It was full of books and she rummaged about with a cool smile on her pretty pale face.

'It's this business of Mental Pollution,' Denise said. 'We'd like to ask you about it, if we may?'

She waved her pencil about encouragingly.

'Would you care to utter?'

Peredur unlocked his thin fingers and used them to give the papers on his desk a flick and a push. Denise smiled patiently but he preserved his sphinx-like silence. Only the presence of the second girl seemed to disturb him. Had he been able to fix his stare on Denise alone quite possibly he could have driven her into an early retreat.

'Of course, we could have got it wrong,' Denise said. 'And it wouldn't be the first time. But if you could help us we'd be ever so grateful.'

Peredur gave a characteristic double cough.

'How?'

He had spoken for the first time and it seemed like a statement that he was prepared to stand by.

'Well tell us in simple language what it amounts to.'

Denise spoke in imploring tones.

'What what amounts to?'

Stiffly he seemed inclined to play the first shots of a familiar academic game.

'You could always write it yourself,' Denise said, anxious now to please. 'Just fifteen hundred words. If you'd prefer it to an interview.'

Peredur put the tips of his long fingers together. Maxine was looking at him with a certain disapproval.

'You are worse than we are,' she said.

'Maxie!'

Denise sounded suddenly very childlike in spite of her size: a good girl in the playground reproving a naughty friend.

'If you'd got anything worth saying,' Maxine said, 'you'd say it.'

Peredur was blushing. He had allowed the girl's

physical beauty to make him neglect his defences and it was deeply annoying.

'I never invited you here,' he said. 'Desmond let you in.'

He seemed to stop himself saying more because the high-pitched indignant note in his own voice displeased him. Denise was eager to be a peacemaker.

'You said the world is being inundated with cheap electronic fictions so that children's imaginations are being polluted just the same as the rivers are being polluted with industrial waste. That's what we want to ask you about. I'm sure you're right anyway, but if we're journalists we have to maintain a kind of objectivity don't we?'

'That seems pretty obvious anyway.'

The smaller girl was relentless and Peredur was obliged to defend himself. He jerked his head in Maxine's direction and the pain from the boil made him wince.

'That's not what I said.'

'Well what did you say?'

There were white patches at the base of Peredur's nostrils.

'Do you think I'm afraid of you? Some stupid little student rag . . .'

'Ah,' Maxine said. 'I can see you're a snob as well.'

Denise wanted to leave. She was embarrassed by her inability to check the hostility between the other two. It distressed her so that she moved about in her confined space and made appealing gestures, first in one direction and then in the other.

'Why should I allow you to pester me with your half-baked notions for a half-baked . . .'

He just prevented himself from saying 'student rag' a second time.

'It's *your* notions we came to inquire about,' Maxine said.

He was both fascinated and repelled by her self-control.

'Am I obliged to defend myself?' he said. 'Is that what you're suggesting? Just because of an interview on television?'

'Well we could ask you about that if you like,' Maxine said. 'How did you come to appear in a medium you so much disapprove of – that sort of thing?'

Peredur wanted to shake his head but he couldn't because of the boil. Denise was anxious to explain something.

'It was the essay,' she said. 'Not the interview. In the *Left* – thing – *Review* – thing. Maxine read it.'

She pointed at Maxine in order to establish both her elusive identity and her remarkable gifts for reading out of the way magazines that most good-looking girls wouldn't dream of opening.

'Haven't you got a brother that works in television?' Maxine said. 'Would you agree that the medium tends to be structured by an equation of blood-relationship and class-power, like newspapers or publishing?'

'What do you mean by "structured"?' Peredur said defensively.

'What I say. You can look at its structure and you see that it is organized like a civil service. It exists as an organ of government and its first purpose is to perpetuate the existing power structure.'

'You have the basis of an argument.'

Peredur nodded wisely. Denise stared at her friend with a kind open-mouthed admiration that inspired Maxine to a further outburst.

'So all this stuff in your essay about polluting the youthful imagination and so on is an acceptable criticism to the power structure because it creates a pastoral mirage for everybody to feel nostalgic about, in between prolonged bouts of viewing and total acquiescence to the existing power structure?'

Denise's mouth quivered between devout seriousness and a smile. She stared openly at Peredur waiting for his response to the challenge. But Peredur had withdrawn into himself. He stretched his arm to open the bottom drawer of his desk and glance at his bellows.

'I'm sorry,' he said. 'You must come again. My mind is on something else at the moment.'

'Yes of course.'

Denise was very willing to leave. Maxine did not appear overpleased with her victory. She moved to the side of the desk to take a closer look at Peredur's boil.

'You'll want to do something about that,' she said. 'Have you tried bathing it with very hot water?'

2

Peredur sat next to his large neighbour, Desmond, the lecturer in Pure Mathematics, at the rear of the small audience in the new lecture theatre. The seats were steeply raked and the audience was easily accommodated in the centre of the lower rows. The lecturer's desk was also a control panel for visual aids and it was situated to the left of an ample screen area, now concealed by tasteful velvet curtains. Desmond had folded his arms in an attentive attitude but he was muttering impatiently.

'God,' he said. 'The man has said all he's got to say at least twenty minutes ago.'

Peredur concentrated harder. The lecturer wore a dark blue shirt and a light blue tie and he held out a conspicuously white handkerchief into which he peered from time to time as though it contained a store of invisible notes. He cleared his throat with care and he was obviously concerned about the husky state of his voice. The acoustic properties of the well appointed lecture theatre were deadening and added nothing to his near whisper which floated about to be picked up by the more attentive members of the audience and lost by the rest. He was saying:

'If the evidence suggests that no amount of planning or pre-planning – whatever the vile phrase may mean . . .'

'You tell us, mate,' Desmond muttered discontentedly.

'Does in fact alter the fundamentally uncontrolled nature of events in human history, does this mean that all critical effort is wasted in the same way as the efforts of those who imagine themselves to be in the driver's seat?'

'He's said *all* this before.'

Desmond shifted his bulk in order to mutter in the direction of Peredur's left ear while the lecturer paused to contemplate briefly the interior of his white handkerchief.

'In other words, are we in fact reduced by Technology to the passivity of Pharaoh's slaves, building a vast Pyramid the sole function of which from its very inception is to be a massive monument to itself and nothing more? Does Technology exist for its own sake in the same sense as Power exists for its own sake? You remember that we attempted earlier to demonstrate that the first obligation of Power was not to order events in any rational or predictable sense but simply to be Powerful. Should we also now create some sort of an adjectival substantive which would describe the abstract state of Technology functioning, being its own essential self, doing its own thing?'

9

'If he asks one more rhetorical question,' Desmond said, 'I'll throw up.'

Peredur became aware of the softened thud of a door at the back of the theatre opening and closing. His large colleague consciously exercised the enjoyable prerogative of sitting at the back and without unfolding his arms turned around to check on such a late arrival. It was a tall student who immediately beckoned in their direction. The pure mathematician shook his head and pointed towards Peredur.

'You're wanted,' Desmond said. 'Lucky sod. You've got a let out.'

He nudged Peredur who turned cautiously so as not to disturb the dressing on his neck.

'That's Roebuck,' he said.

'It's you he wants, brother . . .'

Peredur gave the lecturer all his attention.

'The purpose of critical effort of course is a subject in itself, but in this context let me offer very tentatively, some suggestions about the creative exercise of the critical function inside the apparently inflexible structure of Power-driven Technology.'

'Here we go.'

Desmond was deeply sceptical.

'And why you don't go while you've got the chance I can't think.'

'Such questions must have a direct bearing on our institutions of learning and higher education and it is important therefore that we should be among the first to ask them, not only because we profess a vested interest in the principles of verification, but in order that we may preserve that small share that we hope to have in guiding our own destinies . . .'

'At last,' Desmond said. 'He's getting down to it.'

The student called Roebuck moved crab-wise down the row of empty seats until he was immediately behind Peredur. His face was narrow and vaguely handsome but his eyelids were stuck together with a sticky mucus so that his eyes were red with irritation. His long yellow hair was plastered against his ears in a conscious attempt to make his head even more theatrically narrow. His lips were thick and pale and his complexion waxy.

'Could you come, Mr More?'

He was tapping Peredur insistently on his shoulder.

'Come?' Peredur said. 'Come where?'

It was clear that he distrusted the student. Desmond was showing, at last, a keen interest in the lecture and he had put his elbows on the narrow desk in front of him. Ostentatiously he put his stubby fingers behind his ears.

'It's Coothe,' the student said. 'Maurice Coothe. He's going out of his mind. You're his tutor. He needs you.'

Peredur's suspicion was easily aroused.

'Where is he?'

'He's on the roof of the new study-room tower. The very top bit. He's threatening to kill himself.'

Peredur shifted quickly from his seat like a man who suddenly hears a summons. Roebuck had to hurry to keep up with him. Short as he was, Peredur's stride was long and he swung his left arm vigorously while holding his right fist against his waist to prevent too much movement of his neck. It had been raining but he made no attempt to follow the complicated pattern of concrete paths from one precinct to another. He plunged through the muddy clay by the shortest route to the construction site and Roebuck followed him. At the foot of the Tower a group of students stood around a small exotic tree which was struggling to grow inside the cylinder of chicken wire placed there to protect the tender bark from the marauding sheep which still strayed around the site. Peredur recognized Maxine who was holding a crash-helmet by its straps. It

11

had been painted gold but now there was mud stuck to the crown where it had fallen.

'Look,' Peredur said. 'Is this serious?'

Maxine was disturbed and resentfully frightened. She shrugged away Denise's hand when she tried to put it on her shoulder to comfort her.

'Is this serious?' he said again.

'I thought it was a joke at first,' she said. 'He was wearing this silly crash-helmet and he had nothing on his feet. He just looked ridiculous. He liked looking ridiculous.'

Peredur stepped back into the mud to get a better view of the top of the tower. The work was nearing completion. The scaffolding was still in place and there was a primitive outside lift still in operation to carry materials up to the roof. Denise pointed up.

'He was sitting up there,' she said. 'On the edge of the scaffold swinging his legs. It was awful.'

'Get to a phone,' Peredur said to the nearest boy. 'Quickly. Dial 999 and ask for the fire brigade. Make sure of them first. And then ask for the police. And try and telephone the site manager or his foreman. The switchboard will have their numbers. Hurry.'

He had taken command of the situation, aware now that it was no hoax. Their alarm made all the students look younger. Both the girls were frightened and Roebuck, who was normally full of confidence, looked guilty. Peredur said to him.

'I need more information.'

'He's worried about his work,' Roebuck said. 'About the Finals. He told me last night he thought he was going to fail.'

'You share digs?'

Peredur kept his gaze close on Roebuck's face.

'You are his best friend?'

The sharp questions upset Roebuck. He looked around for somewhere to sit down. All the strength

12

had gone out of his long legs. Nearby was a heap of planks. He sat on them and held his head in his hands.

'What is troubling him? I must know.'

'It's me,' Maxine said. 'I gave him up for that one.'

She nodded contemptuously towards Roebuck.

'It's my fault. I'll go up and get him. I'll go up myself. I will.'

The rain had begun to fall and it ran down from her wet hair like tears over her cheeks. Peredur marched purposefully to the base of the scaffolding. Briefly he studied the lift, but could not discover how it worked. The temporary entrance to the ground floor was locked. Pale but determined and frowning from the pain in his neck he began to climb the system of ladders from one level of scaffolding to the other.

At first he made good progress. He kept a good balance, not bringing his knees too close to the rungs of the ladder, looking steadily in front, examining the condition of each rung, and breathing with measured regularity. At the sixth floor he paused on the scaffolding platform for a rest. Up to this stage the rooms of the building had been in an advanced stage of preparation and most of them had been fitted with windows. When he continued the climb the structure was more skeletal. He was able to enter the tower through an open window space and move up concrete stairs which went up around the deep well of what would become the central lift service.

He caught his first glimpse of Maurice Coothe lying on the edge of the top of the staircase. His feet were bare. They were large and red and very sore. His body looked abnormally long because his arms were stretched out above his head. His face was turned to the wall and his eyes were closed. Peredur moved quietly within natural talking distance and then stood absolutely still. For the first time he seemed concerned

13

about the height. He spread the palm of his left hand against the concrete blocks of the inner wall. His thin fingers trembled a little and their tips pressed into the rough surface as though they wanted to reassure themselves that the tower was a firm structure and would not start rocking. He took time to control his breathing. He was obliged to speak, but what he said would need to be correct and effective. He licked his lips and said.

'Maurice. I'm here. They told me you wanted to speak to me.'

The student had the beginnings of a beard. His spectacles were jammed on his furrowed forehead. His hair had curled in the rain. He opened his eyes and lifted his head to look at Peredur. In such an outstretched length his face looked small and squeezed up and asymmetric. His ears were pushed out by the curved shafts of his spectacles.

'It's me,' Peredur said. 'Your tutor. Peredur More. I'd like to talk to you.'

With great self-discipline Peredur took his steadying hand from the wall and walked the last stretch of concrete steps until he was alongside Maurice Coothe. At such a height with nothing around him to cling to, he was relieved to sink to his knees.

'That last essay of yours, Coothe,' he said. 'It was very good.'

There were tear stains on Coothe's cheeks and his nose was running. He drew down his arms with care and pushed them between his legs.

'Mind you, those foolscap sheets of flimsy paper were hell to read. And your writing is pretty awful. But the stuff was good. Sound. Well prepared and well argued. If its Finals you are worried about you can stop worrying.'

Making sure of his balance, Peredur raised a hand. Then he hesitated. Some deep reluctance to touch a stranger had to be overcome. Coothe saw the hand.

14

With a hungry movement he snatched at it. Peredur
allowed him to hold it even when he drew it up and
laid it against his tear-streaked cheek. Coothe squeezed
the cool hand in spasms that were like sobs. The surface
of his cheek was hot and soft and wet in contrast to
the grubby hands which were hard and clammy. The
longer he held on to Peredur's hand the greater became
the responsibility of the tutor for the student. Judging
by the look of dismay on Peredur's face it was not a
responsibility he welcomed. Coothe was moving his
cheek against his hand in a way that already showed he
would have liked Peredur to stroke his hair and mother
him a little. When he spoke his voice was incongruously
deep and Peredur listened as though he were hearing
it for the first time. It was the sound of a large mature
male but the sense and the expression were childish and
petulant.

'I really wanted to kill him. You know, kill him.
Choke him to death or something. I know I'm stronger than he is. He pretended to be my best friend so
that he could share rooms with me and get at me and
torture me. He didn't really want Maxine. Not really.
He just wanted to take something I valued from me.
Typical of Roebuck. It was worse than spite. And he
used his wealth. That's what I couldn't stand. He used
his wealth. He just pretended to be one of our group of
the Left. It was just a pose. He was never really one of
us. I hadn't the courage to kill him. I wrote him a letter
you see. I said if I see you with Maxine I'll kill you. I
meant it. And then he brought her in to our room. And
she let him use her as a weapon against me. She's clever
of course but she never understands anything. I should
have killed him. I wanted to kill him. But I couldn't. I
just couldn't. So I just stood up and began shouting that
I was going to kill myself. When I came up here I was
determined to do it. But I couldn't. I just couldn't.'

Peredur tried to withdraw his hand.

'Come on now,' he said. 'Let's go down.'

'Don't leave me. Please don't leave me.'

Maurice Coothe clutched his hand and would not let it go.

'No I won't leave you,' Peredur said. 'And everything will be allright. You'll see. You mustn't worry about it any more. Now come on. I can't stand heights. We'll take the descent very gently.'

3

The Professor was slumped in his chair behind a new desk that still had to be used for the first time. The walls of his room were barely dried out after the plasterers and painters. The staff of the Department were present, seated in new chairs that had been carried in for the meeting. The bookshelves were in the first stages of being put up and the contents of filing cabinets were stacked against the wall. Peredur had his knees drawn up to avoid knocking over a stack of gramophone records precariously near his feet. Locks of long grey hair flopped over the Professor's ears and he fumbled about in the pockets of his velvet jacket for his large packet of cigarettes. He wore gold-rimmed half spectacles and his fingers were deeply stained with nicotine.

'Well,' he said, and his voice trembled as he spoke. 'Am I to take it that I am about to be betrayed by my own Department?'

A lecturer stood by the window and looked longingly at his sports car parked in the temporary car park below. He was a balding bachelor with fluffy hair that grew luxuriantly over the back of his jacket. He was dressed ready to go away for the weekend. Opposite the Professor the senior man sat upright in his chair with his hands placed in a Johnsonian posture over the head of his stout walking stick. He had been stretching his jaw for some time hungry for verbal action.

'Let's keep off emotive expressions, Hugh,' he said.

He was the oldest man in the room and enjoyed the advantages of his seniority, playing the elder statesman, privileged to address the Professor by his Christian name. His voice was deep and sonorous and he liked to wag a thick forefinger and pull hard at his narrow chin. Next to him sat a handsome don in his early thirties with an operation scar on his neck. He demonstrated open support for the elder statesman. He made a noise through his nose which the Professor quickly registered as a hostile snigger.

'The feeling of the majority is against Roebuck,' the elder statesman said. 'I don't see why you can't accept that.'

The Professor heaved himself up in his chair and looked reproachful.

'I have always welcomed the maximum freedom of expression in the Department,' he said. 'But I can't be expected not to take a stand when my authority is being flouted.'

'Oh really . . .'

The elder statesman made a token effort to suppress a smile and the handsome don sniggered again, more loudly this time.

'A lad . . . a man . . .'

The Professor struggled to control his emotions.

'. . . this man. His whole future is at stake and some of you can barely spare the time to discuss it. Is that being responsible?'

The man at the window became embarrassed and

17

looked around to demonstrate that there was nowhere where he could sit anyway. He rubbed his right ankle against the calf of his left leg and inadvertently displayed a child-like pair of white socks. The elder statesman rumbled on unperturbed by the Professor's disturbed state.

'My dear Hugh,' he said. 'You mustn't be unfair. We have discussed it. In great detail. Roebuck is at best an industrious cataloguer and at worst a shameless plagiarist. That is the general view.'

'It is not my view,' the Professor said. 'And I take it that it is not your view, Gilbert?'

He turned to a grey-haired anxious looking man who sat at his right hand drawing hard at his large pipe. He sat at an angle with his thin legs entwined trying to look profoundly judicious and at the same time loyal to his Head of Department.

'He's always been very keen,' the man called Gilbert said. 'Never indifferent. Put it that way.'

It was qualified praise but the Professor accepted it greedily.

'There we are,' he said. 'The lad is keen. Why should we stand in his way? He may have a real contribution to make. All I ask is that we err on the side of generosity and make it possible for him to get the grant he needs to work for a higher degree.'

'We've been over all this.'

The elder statesman's deep voice was ostentatiously long suffering.

'We've been over this ground before. His father's a rich man anyway, so the point about the grant is pretty irrelevant.'

'Why should it be?'

The Professor was not inclined to give in.

'Why should it be? Hasn't the boy got any right to some independence, and self-respect that goes with it? This is a vital principle which I take it

18

we all accept. I would say the irrelevant point is the father's wealth, which in any case is mere hearsay.'

'Well you know him well enough, Hugh,' the elder statesman said.

He spoke in a tone of urbane amusement but the Professor reacted as if he had been insulted.

'What do you mean?' he said. 'What exactly do you mean by that?'

'Nothing offensive I assure you'.

'I very much doubt that. Let's have this out in the open.'

A junior lecturer had raised his hand and hopefully Gilbert pointed his pipe in the junior lecturer's direction.

'I think MacMaster wants to say something,' he said.

He nodded two or three times, pleased with the neatness of his intervention. The Professor and the elder statesman had begun to glare at each other with open hostility. With elephantine circumspection each was preparing himself to clash with the other in front of their colleagues on ground of his own choosing. MacMaster had untidy fair hair, bright blue eyes and a piping voice that sounded practised in protracted argument of a completely impersonal kind.

'I just wanted to say that in my opinion a Two-two is erring on the side of generosity. As far as my part of the course is concerned he's never been any good. And he's never worked either. The few essays he deigned to complete for me were mostly incoherent and often illiterate . . .'

Two or three of his colleagues laughed outright at this point but MacMaster waved at them briefly to show that he had not finished.

'. . . He seemed to be under the impression that since I was a junior member of the department he could treat me pretty well as he liked. He was a fearful nuisance in

19

his second year. He used to eat chips during my Tuesday morning lectures.'

There was more laughter and MacMaster blushed and began to grin as though he had just seen the humour of it for the first time. The Professor refused to smile.

'You should have stopped him.'

His voice was firm and fearless.

'Well I did ask,' MacMasters said. 'And in return he asked me if I would prefer him to finish his breakfast at home and miss my Tuesday morning lecture.'

'Students have to be handled,' the Professor said.

He spoke with great strength of character, as a man who had handled generations of difficult young people with conspicuous success. MacMaster was stung to a brief statement in his own defence.

'After all,' he said. 'It was my first year.'

'You could have sent him to me.'

'You were away, Professor. In America.'

'To Mr Sable then.'

The Professor pointed briefly at the elder statesman who was frowning down at the top of his walking stick.

'He was in charge during my leave of absence. In any case are we going to hold these youthful expressions of high spirits against this lad?'

Mr Sable spoke in a grave voice.

'By no means,' he said. 'But you should know I was not unaware of Mr Roebuck's boisterous behaviour. It is on record, if you choose to look it up, that our young friend was nearly sent down for attempting to black out the old Women's Hall of Residence.'

Again the room echoed with subdued laughter. Mr Sable allowed himself a tolerant smile and then turned suddenly to face the Professor.

'Look here, Hugh,' he said. 'This has gone on long enough. The fact is Roebuck is damned lucky not to get a Third. You must accept this.

There was an uneasy silence. The Professor lit a cigarette and sprawled forward over his desk. He was a tall man who liked to occupy as much of the surrounding space as possible.'

'Does any one else want to say anything?'

He looked around the room. He seemed to be making a silent appeal for support, which could also be interpreted as a threat. Younger members of staff largely dependent on his recommendation for their opportunities for advancement and promotion, tried to avoid his gaze which at the moment was as malevolent as that of a medieval warlock. Peredur sat up like a man obliged by an inner compulsion to accept a challenge.

'I have found Roebuck a thoroughly objectionable character,' he said.

This was all he said. His face had become so flushed that the marks of old acne trouble stood out in faint white scars on his cheeks and forehead. The Professor took his chance to reply sharply.

'I hope we shall never be reduced to basing our judgements on such open personal bias.'

'If he were to return next session,' Peredur said, 'I would not be at all eager to supervise his proposed M.A. thesis.'

'In other words,' the Professor said. 'You want this lad barred. I was quite right.'

He looked at Gilbert triumphantly and his loyal friend ventured the briefest nod and then looked about him quickly in the hope that many of his colleagues would not have noticed.

'There is a definite animosity against Roebuck. An open determination to bring him down. I'll be perfectly frank with you and I'll tell you quite openly I find this quite shocking and quite unprofessional.'

Peredur began to stand and then sat down again.

'I'll just tell you this.'

His voice was unsteady with indignant anger.

'He came very close to causing the death of one of my moral students. I have ample proof of this. I mention it now because the department should know that he is not only intellectually dishonest. A point which has been made over and over again. But also totally unscrupulous and selfish.'

The Professor leaned back and opened out his arms as mildly as he could.

'Are we now to set ourselves up as arbiters of moral worth and social behaviour? Is that part of our task? Is it?'

'Oh come off it, Hugh.'

Mr Sable was losing his patience. He spoke as if he had stopped circling at last and was lumbering forward through the dust in direct attack.

'You are making the mountain. Let's just measure the molehill. Five of us are agreed on a Two-two. You and Gilbert want to give him a Two-one, in order that he can start doing research in this Department. Put your cards on the table. That's what you're after. Very well. Why, we'd like to know. Has his old man been nobbling you or something? Is there a chance of a Roebuck Foundation or a Roebuck Visiting Fellowship or what have you? Put us in the picture.'

'That is monstrous,' the Professor said. 'There are times, Sable, when I believe it is your avowed intention to force me out of this chair. Well you won't, you know. No matter how hard you try.'

The Professor sank back in his chair, thrusting out his feet, exhausted with the struggle.

'You will dramatize things,' Sable said. 'I don't dramatize. I go by the rules. Rules and Regulations and thank God we've got to stick to them. It's six against two, Hugh, and you may as well accept it.'

'Six? Who's the sixth?'

'The External of course.'

The Professor waved his arms about.

'Rules,' he said. 'Rules and Regulations. It makes you despair doesn't it?'

He gazed appealingly at Gilbert who just managed to avoid responding by lowering his eyes to examine closely the content of the bowl of his pipe.

'Thank God for them,' Sable said.

His voice was deep and rich with impending triumph.

'Otherwise the whole of humanity would sink out of sight in one big emotional morass.'

'One tries to be liberal.'

The Professor sounded as if he were still looking for a way out.

'God knows one tries.'

'That's the biggest mistake,' Sable said. 'I've always thought that. We can't afford to be liberal. By definition we are a breed of logic-choppers. We've still got angels to count on the top of a pin. You can't be a liberal when you're counting angels on top of a pin.'

Sable was chuckling with appreciation of his own humour and the don with the scar on his neck was snorting obligingly alongside him. The Professor glared at Sable.

'The truth is Sable,' he said. 'You don't like people in general and students in particular. The truth is you'd fail every one of them if you could.'

A lecturer with close-cropped hair who sat by the door and so far had said nothing now spoke up.

'If we could have a decision, Professor,' he said. 'The time is getting on.'

The Professor picked up his heavy fountain pen and pushed about the paper with the list of names.

'Roebuck, Charles Lincoln Frederick,' he said. Two-two.

4

'Hello.'

When he heard her voice he stood at a file-index cabinet at the end of the top floor of bookshelves in the New Library. Behind the wooden cabinet there was an outside wall chiefly of glass which gave almost an aerial view of the building site and the twin towers of study rooms. It was the middle of the morning and work on the site was in full swing. Even in the New Library the air throbbed with an insistent roar and rumble of engines, bulldozers, concrete-mixers, tractors and lorries.

She had seen him through a gap in the lower shelves. She was smiling and he had not seen her smile before. Also she had given up wearing her outsize spectacles. There were minute dimples near each corner of her smiling mouth. She was wearing a purple dress of vaguely oriental shape, black trousers and a string of elaborate white beads.

'Is it better?'

Maxine raised her finger to her own neck to indicate the position occupied by the dressing on his neck. Peredur did not speak. He just watched the girl with acute suspicion.

'Have they done something to it?'

He looked as though he were about to ask her what she meant by the expression 'they'; but something serene in her face seemed to restrain him.

'Just lanced,' he said.

'You poor thing,' she said. 'I'm sorry you weren't able to come to our party.'

Peredur lifted a warning finger to his lips.

'Am I making too much noise?'

She emerged from between the shelves and tip-toed towards him.

'Are you cross with me?'

'No of course not.'

'I wouldn't blame you if you were. I behaved very badly?' Her complexion was as fresh as a small child's. Her manner was openly appealing and he began to blush at his own defencelessness. She paused to gaze meaningfully at the study-room tower which was still surrounded by scaffolding.

'Are you very busy, Mr More. I would be very grateful if I could have a word with you.'

Peredur made an effort to become decisive.

'Let's go this way then,' he said.

They walked briskly to the rear of the library to a narrow lift which they entered together. Maxine looked about her with interest as if she had not known of the lift's existence before and she allowed Peredur to look after her in an old-fashioned sense. This seemed to bring out in him an instinct for command and leadership: small as he was, he was a few inches taller than Maxine and this simple fact was in itself a source of satisfaction. He shepherded her safely into the lift and once inside stared sternly at his own dull reflection in the shiny metal doors.

'It was an awful party,' Maxine said. 'You were so right not to come. Roebuck turned up. He said it was my fault about Maurice. He said I ought to be publicly exposed. Whipped in public he said. He was drunk and it was *very* nasty.'

She moved inside the lift in order to be able to look into his eyes. Peredur lifted his hand to indicate that the door of the lift was about to open. He showed her the way down a corridor to a row of Research Rooms. He opened the door marked, *Social Analysis Research Room iii*, peeped in to make sure it was vacant, and then stood aside to allow Maxine to enter.

'Denise wrote the invitation,' she said. 'But I told her to do it. I wanted to talk to you so much. Not just out of gratitude for what you did for Maurice. Not just schoolgirl hero-worship either. I just wanted to talk. I knew I had some important things to learn from you so I thought if we could meet socially we could become friends. I could make up for that awful interview for *Nimrod*. I was unbearable, wasn't I? I was so determined to show how much I knew and pull you down a peg or two.'

Maxine sat on a chair in the corner and Peredur sat awkwardly on the corner of the writing table, unnecessarily pushing aside a wooden lectern that was not in his way at all.

'How is Maurice Coothe?' Peredur said.

His voice was quiet and determinedly correct.

'Oh he's fine,' Maxine said. 'I went to see him. The psychiatrist says he's not bonkers. He's just staying in for rest treatment. And the psychiatrist says it wasn't all my fault. It could have happened with anyone. He says I was just the psychogenetic trigger.'

She seemed to imagine that he was listening to her accent and trying not to show open amusement and she gave a little laugh to show she would not have been offended if he had.

'That cuts me down to size doesn't it?' she said. 'That's all I am really. A psychogenetic trigger.'

She giggled again at the way she enunciated the term and Peredur smiled a little unwillingly.

'My trouble is,' Maxine said. 'I've got absolutely no background. I come from the bottom you see. The absolute dregs. You think I've got an accent, well, if I really talked the way I do at home you wouldn't understand a bleeding word and that's a fact. That's what I am. I'm clever in a nimble-witted sort of way, but I've got no background. That's why I'm so aggressive.'

Peredur said nothing. He gave her polite attention.

'I need somebody like you to advise me,' Maxine said. 'It's been in my mind for ages. Even before you were so

26

marvellous with Maurice. That's why I tried to organize that awful interview. He's the one that's really got something to say. P.C. More. That's what I said to Denise. But when we got in up there I made a right mess of it. Now you must think I'm chasing you.'

Peredur smiled rather sourly and folded his arms with a certain care.

'That's one thing I'd never think,' he said.

'But why?'

She was instantly alert. He had said something and she was prepared to cling to it like a scrambler in unfamiliar territory pulling himself up by grasping the roots of a stunted tree.

'I know just how ugly I am,' Peredur said. 'I have two good-looking brothers.'

His cheeks creased in a smile but he could not altogether prevent patchy blushes from invading his face.

'That's ridiculous,' Maxine said. 'I've seen your brother on telly. Or at least I think I have. He's too smooth. He's not half as attractive as you are. You know what I think? I think you spend too much time by yourself.'

Her diagnosis was firm and final.

'It's a discipline.'

Peredur lifted his folded arms and resettled himself on the edge of the table. He appeared to be reminding himself that he was in a professional relationship with a student who had asked to speak to him. He was prepared to be patient and to be informal, but sooner or later she would have to state her business.

'I wanted to speak to you for another reason,' Maxine said. 'I'm applying for a job. As a research assistant. I know you don't know me really but do you think you could give me a testimonial?'

'What kind of research assistant?'

He was still cautious.

'On telly I'm afraid. I know I shouldn't. It's against all my so-called principles. But I don't really want to teach. That was only an excuse for staying on a fourth year. I'm a pretty horrible type really.'

She was looking at her feet so Peredur was not obliged to shake his head.

'I'm a show-off. I've got this urge to be seen. It's awful really. I'm quite ashamed of it. I always want to show how clever I am and afterwards I feel so ashamed. What should I do about it, doctor?'

She giggled in case there was any danger of him taking her question seriously. He was staring at her critically and she was moved to defend herself by attacking him.

'What about you?' she said. 'Why do you stay in a place like this? A place like this cuts you off from Necessity.'

'What do you mean by that.'

'What do I mean? I mean Life I suppose. Real living. This place is just a sequence of intellectual septic tanks.'

She looked pleased with what she had said but he took it seriously and tried to defend himself.

'I work,' Peredur said. 'I work hard.'

'Oh I know you do. But you're not part of anything are you. You are like a bachelor demi-god leaning over the edge of your cloud and watching the human ants messing about on ground level.'

'I've got things I must do,' Peredur said. 'This gives me a chance to do them. I'll give you your testimonial.'

Maxine jumped to her feet and showed her delight.

'Will you really? I knew you were marvellous. You've got that secret thing about you. That smouldering inside. Would you mind if I kissed you?'

Peredur licked his lips hastily like a housewife tidying up before answering the door to an unexpected visitor. Maxine gave her infectious laugh and kissed him quickly on the lips.

28

5

'I live alone,' Peredur said.

He stood behind Maxine in the doorway of his large living room.

'I can see that,' she said.

The room looked empty. Against the bare wall was an oval table which was surfaced with a blistered veneer of walnut. A chintz-covered settee of great age and bulk stood on the centre of a square brown carpet. It might have been on display or for sale. It was so unrelated to anything except itself. Then in the bay window there stood a single uncomfortable looking armchair. The room was very clean. There was a mirror over the mantelpiece. Maxine walked across to take a look at herself. She moved her head to admire her velvet peaked cap and pressed a finger against the button on the crown. Peredur found a box of matches on the mantelpiece and knelt down to light the old-fashioned gas-fire.

'You've got no books in here,' Maxine said. 'What do you do? Sit here thinking?'

'Thinking is important,' Peredur said.

'Do you lie on the mat and worry it with your teeth?' she said. 'You ought to you know. I'm sure it would help. When you're thinking.'

His unease seemed to give her greater confidence. She walked around the room with wide strides and then began to rock on her heels.

'I'll sit there,' she said pointing to the settee. 'Like an advert for *Homes and Furnishings*. And you'll sit there.' She pointed to the uncomfortable chair by the window.

'Like a philosopher.'

She took off her long coat but left on her cap.

'God this thing is huge.'

She left her coat at one end of the settee and curled up at the other end herself.

'I'll just have to make myself look small and loveable,' she said. 'Go on. Go and sit over there and be the Spinoza of the launderette. Come on. Let me hear you thinking.'

'It's an arid room,' Peredur said. 'To reflect an arid man.'

'It's wrong to think badly of yourself.'

Maxine spoke promptly and waved her finger. It sounded almost like something she had said before, and on more than one occasion.

'If it's false, it's just a disguised form of self-pity. If it's true, you should have done something about it long ago.'

Peredur smiled. He moved back to the fireplace and took down a wooden box with cigarettes in it from the mantelpiece. He opened the box and held it out towards Maxine.

'Would you like one of these? They look a little dry I'm afraid.'

Maxine took a cigarette and Peredur brought her the only ashtray in the room and took out a box of matches from his tight jacket to light it for her.

'You always look hungry,' Maxine said. 'Did you know that? I've noticed it before. And you prowl about. All black and Celtic. Did you know that? Like a general who's lost his army.'

Peredur returned to his chair by the window and said nothing. Maxine stubbed out the cigarette on the ashtray he had given her. The cigarettes could have been intended for guests who were never invited or never came.

'Sorry,' she said. 'But they're very stale. You ought to throw them away you know.'

They stared at each other for some time and Peredur was the first to look away. He studied the stream of traffic grinding endlessly up the hill. There were traffic

30

lights at the top which controlled the flow.

'I wish there was some way of communicating without words.'

He sounded unhappy and uncomfortable.

'Well there is, isn't there. Or so they tell say.'

Maxine laughed cheerfully. Peredur looked at her, puzzled and deeply absorbed by the fact of her presence in the very centre of his sparsely furnished living room.

'You've completely disturbed me,' he said.

'Have I really?'

'Completely.'

Maxine moved restlessly in her corner of the sofa very interested in what she was hearing.

'You've said things . . .'

He spoke slowly.

'What sort of things?'

She was anxious to hear.

'I don't know how I feel . . .'

He pressed his fists together until the knuckles shone in the evening light.

'I don't know whether it's love or infatuation.'

He shook his head, unable to solve the problem.

'You can see I'm emotionally stunted,' he said. 'You can see that can't you? You asked me why I was here. In this place. I came here for solitude.'

'Well you've certainly got it.'

Maxine looked around the comfortless room.

'I came here like a janissary.'

'What's a janissary?'

'A royal guard in old Turkey. Composed of children picked out from subjugated Christian communities. Tributary children. Except in my case I contributed myself. I thought there were problems I could solve if I gave my whole mind to them in this impersonal English atmosphere.'

'What kind of problems?'

31

'Problems about the individual in the industrial conurbation. Tensions and Fields of Force in Social Structures. That sort of thing.'

'And now I've gone and spoilt it all.'

She could barely help looking pleased.

'I think you might have.'

'How?'

She lifted her knees to her chin and looked as though she longed to know.

'It's not easy to say. It's more than just physical beauty and the romantic dreams that go with it. You set out to disturb. From the very first moment. That's what I find difficult to explain. Why me? That throws my whole view of myself out of perspective. Why should I be worth it. What am I to you?'

'What's anybody to anybody?'

'Exactly!'

Peredur jumped to his feet and moved about the room with his thin hands in his jacket pockets.

'You've got this remarkable instinct for putting your finger right on the sore point. This ridiculous random factor that makes solitude meaningless. This is what upsets.'

Maxine patted the sofa.

'Come and sit here,' she said.

She could have been giving comfort to some large pet dog. Peredur stood as though he were rooted to the floor.

'You are a perfectionist,' she said. 'I think that's what I like about you. Come and sit here and talk. I love to listen to you talking.'

'You can see how shy I am,' Peredur said. 'It's because I'm so ugly.'

'You keep on saying that,' Maxine said. 'That means you want to be ugly. And that's altogether another problem. Come on. Come and sit down.'

'Will you come to bed with me?'

The question burst out of Peredur's mouth like an angry challenge. Maxine opened her eyes wide and then laughed in a friendly way.

'Here?'

'Anywhere. You're not a virgin are you?'

'Should I be? Are you?'

Peredur shook his head.

'I'm sorry if I make such a neurotic noise,' he said. 'It's just that I like to know where I am.'

'I can see that.'

'I'm not interested in inventions and fictions. I can understand the need for them. Most people need things dressed up, disguised, falsified in some way or other. I don't. Or at least I try to do without it. And one of the things that excited me about you right from the first was that you had the same attitude. I could be wrong of course.'

'You can always be wrong,' she said.

He smiled grimly as though she had made a species of gallows joke.

'I try to be charmless,' he said. 'And I pretty well succeed, don't I? I have a charming brother you see and a charming mother and I suspect charm. This could of course be due solely to the fact I haven't got any.'

He sat down and took her hand. She moved to look at him closely.

'What is it you want most in the world?' she said.

'Visions.'

His answer intrigued her deeply. She came closer to him and touched his face. He tried to kiss her but he was clumsy and unpractised. She rose to her feet and began to explore the remainder of the flat. He stood watching her with his hands in his pockets. Her inspection was critical.

'I'm fussy, aren't I?' she said.

'I like that.'

He smiled grimly and wriggled inside his shiny suit.

6

At half past nine in the morning the traffic up the hill was heavy, moving sluggishly in the June sunlight. Peredur studied his watch and then stared down at the street below. From the basement door to the low gate there was a row of dustbins and on the other side of the path the square patch of garden had run wild. From the window of the top flat, the surface of weeds and shrubs undulated in a solid green sea heavily sprinkled with dust. The same dust weighed down the leaves of an avenue of solid plane trees that grew at intervals up the hill on the edge of the wide pavement. A white sports car with the hood down disengaged itself from the inside lane and drove into a space on the pavement between a request stop sign and a bulky plane tree the bark of which was scaling off in irregular patches. It was driven by Maxine who had a diaphanous scarf over her hair and wore dark glasses. She was wearing white trousers and a red sports shirt and she lifted her arm as she looked up to the window as though she knew beforehand that he would be standing there waiting for her. Within a matter of seconds a passer-by, an ageing man still spruce in clothes of a style that had not been worn generally for some fifteen years, halted near the tree and pointed at the bonnet of the car with a folded newspaper he was carrying.

'That's not legal, you know.'

He spoke boldly, trembling slightly so that his wide trousers trembled also above the brilliantly polished toe caps of his brown shoes.

'As I say, you can't leave it there.'

As if she were being photographed, Maxine removed her dark glasses and gave the passer-by a gracious smile, followed by a little shake of the head that indicated that she could not hear. The passer-by edged nearer. He was nervous and his head jerked about. He could have been looking for support, calling up other units of his species to repel this white intrusion into their territory.

'As I say, it's illegal,' he said in a sharp voice. 'The pavement is for pedestrians. Cars are not allowed on the pavement. I was a civil servant you know. I know the law.'

'I quite agree with you.'

Maxine smiled in her most disarming manner as she held on to the steering wheel.

'You are absolutely right. Isn't it a beautiful day?'

She looked about her, admiring the sunlight and the blue sky.

'I'm waiting for a friend,' she said. 'From up there. He should be down any second.'

The passer-by was not to be influenced. He shuffled nearer anxious to press a winning case.

'Its not allowed,' he said. 'It shouldn't be here.'

'I've just told you,' Maxine said. 'I agree with you. I'm a pedestrian myself. I'll be off any second. This isn't my car anyway to tell you the truth.'

'Well there you are.'

At last the passer-by allowed himself a limited smile.

'You shouldn't be here, should you? Move.'

He made a masterful gesture with his folded newspaper.

'I am moving,' Maxine said.

The passer-by scowled at the wheels of the sports car. There were polished chrome wings on the hubs.

'No you're not,' he said. 'You're lying. Go on. Move!'

Maxine raised her hand and then put it on the door handle. She considered whether or not she should get out to deal with the man. He shuffled closer to the door so that she she could not open it without knocking the door against his legs.

'You just get moving,' he said. 'I've told you more than once.'

Maxine looked up at him. Her lips were pale.

'You're nothing but a bloody little power maniac,' she said. 'That's what you are.'

'That's the young people of today speaking,' he said.

He sounded pleased to have his deepest suspicions confirmed.

'That's what you all are. Loose and foul mouthed. And the women are the worst.'

'Bugger off,' Maxine said.

She was cross with herself for losing her temper.

'There's a policeman coming,' the passer-by said. 'He'll deal with you.'

He stepped hastily to the middle of the pavement and waved his newspaper to attract the attention of a policeman who was some distance away making his way slowly up the hill.

'He'll book you,' the passer-by said.

He licked his lips and smiled.

'The law's the law in this country you know.'

Peredur appeared at the small garden gate. Maxine saw him and waved urging him to hurry. She leaned over to open the door on the passenger side. Peredur was smiling in an abstracted sort of way. He placed his travelling bag on the narrow back seat.

'Hurry up, for God's sake,' the girl said. 'I'm being attacked by a power maniac.'

'Is that what he is?'

Peredur tried to sound detached and light-hearted.

The passer-by had returned to examine Peredur.

'You can't go,' he said. 'You've committed an offence. I warned you about it, didn't I?' I warned her.

The last sentence was addressed directly to Peredur who had become suddenly embarrassed and couldn't bring himself to say anything. There was a momentary lull in the flow of traffic. Maxine seized her chance and the white sports car bumped straight off the pavement into a space on the inside lane. There was a sudden indignant blowing of horns. She turned around to swear at the cars behind her, tapping her fingers impatiently on the steering wheel as she waited for the lights to change. The passer-by was making desperate semaphore signs to the policeman with his newspaper. With measured strides the policeman drew nearer. The red light was slow to change, but change it did before the policeman arrived on the scene. The car shot forward, Maxine shouting with relief, and Peredur looking back.

'I think he's giving the policeman your number,' Peredur said.

But Maxine was elated with the joy of escape. She laughed and sang and drove very badly through the outskirts of the conurbation.

'Can't you sing?' she said. 'I thought all the Welsh could sing.'

Peredur did not answer. His hands hung between his knees. He was pale and nervous but determined not to complain.

'And did those feet . . .'

Maxine sang tunelessly, making operatic faces as she crashed through the gears and took the occasional careless glance into the driving mirror.

'Are you hungry?' she shouted. 'I'm always hungry when I get in a car.'

'Whose car is it?'

Maxine turned her head to smile at him.

'Do you like it? I've borrowed it for the weekend. The week if I like. As long as I like! Isn't that great?'

'Who from?'

'It belongs to Roebuck's big brother. He's gone off somewhere. America. On a sales tour. Isn't it a smashing car?'

Peredur pulled an unhappy face.

'I'm getting used to it,' Maxine said. 'It was a bit strange at first. It can do a ton without turning a hair.'

'Don't try.'

Mischievously she pressed the accelerator and the car zoomed forward with alarming suddenness. Peredur closed his eyes and did not open them again until the speed decreased.

'Are you scared?'

'Very.'

She reached out to touch his hand affectionately and the car gave a sickening swerve.

'Be a good girl,' Peredur said. 'Concentrate on driving.'

She drove with the main stream of traffic moving westwards. As her confidence increased she adopted a role of some importance on the road, practising hand signals, nodding and saluting the drivers of other vehicles, playing the part of a leading motorist with a share of the road to look after, attending to urgent business with speed and precise efficiency striving to achieve a definite destination by a definite time.

'Where are we going?'

Peredur had relaxed a little. He leaned back in his seat and allowed the wind to pull at his hair.

'I want to see where you come from.'

He looked intensely pleased and yet apprehensive.

'Why?'

'Why? Proper little fisherman aren't you? Because I want to understand you of course.'

She waited for him to speak. He lifted his hand to his chest and breathed deeply. He turned to look at her and his eyes were filled with water so that his vision of her was completely blurred.

'Are you all right?'

'It's the wind,' he said. 'I ought to have goggles or something.'

He smiled at her and they nodded at each other approvingly.

'We'll stop and buy some.' Maxine said. 'And we'll buy some food and something to drink. And we'll have a picnic in the country. And we'll drive right on and on, into the mountains of Wales. Isn't it marvellous. Oh I'm so excited. I haven't been so excited for years.'

She had begun to make gestures. The car swerved and there was indignant hooting from the car behind. They both laughed happily and Maxine drove with greater care.

7

A tilted outcrop of rock was shot through with mysterious veins of white quartz. Peredur was carrying the picnic basket and Maxine led the way towards the rock along a sheep track through ferns that were reaching towards their full height. The weather was cooler and a stiff breeze sent the high white clouds sailing north east across the blue sky. When they reached the table rock, they turned to look at the view of the dark blue waters of the bay and over to the north west the ruin of a medieval castle on a promontory. Inland, rocks in strange shapes thrust themselves out of the damp ground. The lowest lying areas were marshy, sprinkled with cotton grass and bog orchids. But there were also patchworks of small fields carefully marked out with dry stone walls and connected with neat stone farmsteads that stood appealingly small and human in the rugged grandeur of their setting.

'This is where my father came from,' Peredur said.

He put down the picnic basket and Maxine raised her fists to blow an imaginary fanfare.

'This is the place that shaped his sensibilities. The cradle of his imagination. I wanted you to see this first before we go to Brangor. What do you think of it?'

Maxine pulled a face to suggest she was hard put to it to make any worthwhile comment.

'The land of your fathers is on the rocks,' she said. 'From up here anyhow.'

'I am completely irrational about it,' Peredur said. 'It's the most beautiful place in the world to me.'

'That's just how I feel about Walsall. Dead romantic.'

She began to lay out the contents of the picnic basket on the rock. She became intent on her work and she looked as childlike and as innocent as a small girl playing some domestic game with dolls out of doors. Peredur stared at her, lost in admiration for her beauty. She was a pretty sight kneeling above the white cloth she had laid out on the close-cropped grass. The rock itself was too uneven and exposed to make a satisfactory table after all.

'I wish I could put into words what the place means to me . . .'

'You write the words and I'll write the music,' Maxine said.

She lay on the ground and pushed half an egg spread with mayonnaise into her mouth. She enjoyed the food and licked her fingers in a leisurely fashion before getting up to reach for some more.

'Come on, Lloyd George,' she said. 'Eat something or you'll waste away.'

Peredur lifted his head with the motion of a nervous mountain pony.

'Why did you call me Lloyd George?'

'Why do I call you anything? It's just a name. It's just a name. It's Welsh isn't it? Won't it do?'

Peredur sighed deeply. He looked to sea and pointed at the ruined castle on the horizon.

'"The British Empire will go the way of Pharaoh's chariots"!'

He raised his voice in a poor imitation of pulpit oratory but it was such a raucous shout that Maxine was frightened.

'What the hell are you on about?'

'I'm casting a spell,' Peredur said. 'I'm trying to connect you with this place. Really connect. I heard a man preaching when I was eight years old in a chapel down there. I think he was a friend of my father's. I assume he was. I connect him with my father. And I think he baptized my brother Bedwyr. And I just remember that sentence. It's stuck in my mind all these years. So you'd better not connect me with Lloyd George.'

'Instruct me, sage,' she said. 'Unfold the entire contents of your remarkable Welsh mind. Spread it out before me like an intellectual picnic. I am hungry for enlightenment and thirsty for wisdom. You should never let a woman get bored. Especially a bright one like me.'

Her mouth was full again and she passed her little finger delicately around her lips.

'You say I'm always taking things too seriously.'

'Well you do, don't you?'

Peredur looked around as though for inspiration that would give him the power to make his person and character more acceptable to her.

'See that rock,' he said. 'The one casting a shadow. A man hid there holding a spear that had been made during the length of the Mass, on fifty-two successive Sundays!'

'Are you trying to tell me a story?'

She showed enough signs of pleasure to encourage him to go on.

'This place is thick with legends,' he said. 'And it's not surprising is it really when you look at it. So mysterious and so beautiful. It doesn't give the imagination a moment's peace.'

'You can skip the lecture and go back to the story,' she said. 'What about our friend behind the rock?'

'He was infatuated with a woman made of flowers.'

Peredur stared at Maxine and forgot to smile.

'Cor. You must mean me,' Maxine said. 'What flowers were they? Give me the recipe. No, pa! No, ma! Let's try it.'

'All local materials. Oak, broom and meadowsweet.'

'Pipe dream of a feudal economy. Local monopoly!'

'Well there are other versions that include primroses, gnat's wings and the water of a ninth wave.'

'That's more like it.'

Maxine found some cake and began to munch it appreciatively.

'You will notice that no steps were taken to provide the lady with a conscience.'

'Quite right too.'

'But she was baptized.'

'By the same old boy that baptized your eldest brother I have no doubt.'

Peredur jumped to his feet. He shouted.

'Are you going to listen?'

Maxine put the palms of her hands together and nodded with mock humility.

'Yes, daddy,' she said. 'Yes, my lord.'

'Only in order to give her a name. Baptism strictly for linguistic purposes. Names are important. She was baptized *Blodeuwedd*, which being interpreted into your heathen tongue means literally, Flowerface.'

'Lovely,' Maxine said, clapping her hands. 'I love that. The original Flowerpower. Good old Blod.'

'You are not taking my story seriously,' Peredur said.

'I swear to you I am.'

'Long version or short version?'

'Both.'

She gave him an encouraging smile that made him anxious to capture more of her approval.

'She was given in marriage to an ice-cold man doomed by his mother to live without power and without love. His uncle was a magician and he had provided him by a series of sharp practices with arms and a kingdom and with a wife made of flowers, but this didn't really help him to avoid his Doom. The woman made of flowers entertained a hunter in their castle when the husband was away on state business and they became lovers possessed with and driven by an irresistible passion. After three days they decided to find out how to get rid of the husband. Flowerface soon found out how it could be done. When the husband came back to the castle, she was most loving and welcoming because the hunter had now taught her how to love and then in the night when he was dying to talk she pretended to become very worried and very silent and he asked her what was on her mind and she said that she was anxious to know how his death could be prevented so that her mind could be at rest in the knowledge that he would never die before her. She expressed it much better than that of course. She had been taught to speak by a magician. He was very touched and he told her not to worry. He could only be killed in the open air next to still water with his left foot balanced on the back of a wild goat and the right foot standing on the edge of a wooden water trough. And the only wound that could kill him would be a wound in the back from a spear with a poisoned tip forged at the hour of the Mass on fifty-two successive Sundays. Could there be anywhere in the world a narrower gate to let in the sudden death?'

Maxine sniffed the air and lifted her hand.

'Tell me no more,' she said. 'I can see it all happening. Right in front of my eyes. She persuaded old Chilly-feet to ⸺stand in the rare correct position while lover-boy hid behind the rock over there with his specially made spear all nice and handy. And because he was a hunter, he couldn't miss. Correct?'

'Brilliant.'

'And Flowerface and the hunter lived happily ever after!'

'By no means.'

'Oh dear.'

Maxine pulled a sad face as she searched in her handbag for a packet of the cheap cigarettes she liked to smoke after meals.

'Well go on,' she said. 'Tell me the worst.'

'The magician went looking for the corpse. It was nowhere to be found. He tramped all over the country looking for it.'

'No corpse, no crime,' Maxine said.

She gave a worldly-wise wave with her cigarette lighter in her right hand.

'Maybe,' Peredur said. 'Other places, other customs. One day he came to a serf's cottage not more than three miles from this very spot.'

Maxine moved her head admiringly.

'That's what I like,' she said. 'The documentary touch. Authenticity. Actuality . . .'

'Not so much a serf as a farmer tied to his land. A local. A native. Now this farmer had a sow which behaved very strangely. Now Gwydion – for that was the magician's name . . .'

'Oh no!'

Maxine exaggerated her surprise in a way that made Peredur laugh happily.

'Not your brother? The name's the same?'

'"The name's the same,"' Peredur said. 'That's what comes of having a poet for a father. You get landed with the outlandish. How much nicer to be Tom, Dick, and Harry – except I'd be Harry.'

Maxine kept her mouth open prettily and he waited, assuming that she wanted to make a joke. At last she frowned, shook her head, took a puff of her cigarette without inhaling and told him to continue.

'This Gwydion had in fact once been a wild boar – as a punishment for unbecoming behaviour at court involving rape – so he had no difficulty in tracing the sow. None whatsoever. They followed the course of a river upstream, not so far from here, until they came to a large oak tree. Like that one down there. And when he came up the tree Gwydion saw that the sow was grazing food that fell from the top branches of the tree. But not acorns. The sow was eating lumps of decaying flesh alive with maggots.'

'Ugh.'

Maxine pulled a face and shuddered.

'Just after my lovely meal. Have some respect.'

'He looked up and saw an eagle perched on the top of the tree and this poor eagle was moulting flesh instead of feathers. Now Gwydion tamed the eagle by reciting a series of three magic verses. And just as though to demonstrate the power of poetry, the eagle fell into his lap. He tapped it lightly with his professional wand and there lay the saddest bag of bones you ever saw, all that was left of the husband. Bright Boy with the Skilful Hands – or Chilly-feet as you call him.'

'Alive or Dead?'

'Gwydion collected all the doctors of Wales and they worked on him for a year.'

'Heart transplants and all,' Maxine said.

'And they brought him back to life. A sadder but a wiser man.'

'And what happened to Flowerface?'

'Well there you are. She tried to make a run for it. But Gwydion caught her on the shores of a lake. All her maidens fell in the lake and were drowned. As for her, he turned her into an owl. A night bird never to show her face to the light of day. Obliged to hide her shame. Hated by all the birds. A feathered outcast with a woman's face.'

'Do owls have women's faces?'

'Flowerfaces. You look at an owl very closely next time you meet one.'

'And what about Lover-boy?'

'He was invited to stand with one foot on the back of a wild goat and the other on the edge of a wooden water trough . . .'

'Say no more. And poor old Chilly-feet?'

'He ruled this land for ever after. But with the sad face of a man who had lost a dream.'

Maxine threw away the stump of her cigarette. She climbed on the rock and shaded her eyes to look at the mountains.

'They are mysterious aren't they? Such funny shapes. So hard and so green. Look at the slope over there. It's like a mad billiard table.'

Peredur tried to find a foothold on the rock where he could stand alongside her and perhaps hold her in his arms.

'Are you still curious?' he said.

He sounded eager to please her. She gripped his arm to maintain her balance.

'Oh very,' she said. 'Come on. Now you can show me the gingerbread house where your mother lives. She is a witch of course?'

They jumped down laughing and she ordered him to help her pack the picnic basket.

8

They left the white car pointing awkwardly into the un-
cut grass of a lane that seemed to peter out in a mass of
brambles. The lane was on the fringe of a wood of short
oak trees that spread up the side of the hill.

'Gosh isn't it quiet?' Maxine said.

'Not really. Listen.'

There was a lark singing. And far away a concerted
bleating of sheep being washed in a distant stream.
Closer at hand insects clicked in the long grass and
bees explored the honeysuckle in the hedgerow.

'Do you like it?'

He sounded anxious that she should. She stood still
in her bronze coloured mini-dress, bending her head
to listen. She shook her head gently.

'I don't know. I'm a slum girl you know. The country
frightens me a little. I know I'm supposed to like it and
when I don't I feel guilty.

They stopped talking to each other and moved
apart, advancing towards the old churchyard along
divergent paths. Like scientists who submit elements
to new environments in order to discover more about
their true nature, they seemed to wish to observe each
other at a distance. Maxine loitered by the long grass
and filled her small fists with seeds pulled from the
dog's foot that grew tall in the shelter of a hedge.
She examined the seeds and smelt them, crushed one
between her teeth and then spat it out. To Peredur
nearer the gate, she was half hidden by the green
haze of the long grass and he was glad to wait and to
watch her move; a small slum figure, very sophisticated
in such rural surroundings, very young, habitually
on her guard and ready to protect herself with a
surface manner that she had cultivated to repulse

47

or charm, and underneath, perhaps, a reservoir of fear.

When she, in her turn, began to watch him, he showed a deep interest in the inscriptions on the older gravestones. He moved about with a neat intensity, pale and withdrawn, even now not really at ease. He was too frail to be athletic but the desire to be athletic was there. His clothes were shabby and old-fashioned: an opened-necked white shirt, a tweed coat with leather elbow patches, a pair of baggy trousers that hung down over his heels. The tense stillness of his body among the slate gravestones suggested a continual state of expectation.

Because he was so interested in the tombstones perhaps, she decided to make the little church her own area of discovery. It was a low squat 'L' shaped building where half the congregation would be concealed from the other. The stone pulpit close to the altar commanded a view of both. Each half had its own entrance, but one was longer in order to accommodate a modest bell-tower. Maxine explored the building thoroughly. It was cool inside in spite of the hot sun. The prayer books smelt damp and the brass eagle of the lectern needed polishing. She removed the wooden lid over the font. There was still water at the base of a damp oval patch. She walked through to the further door. It was not in use but the large key had been left in the lock. Maxine turned the key and opened the door. She pierced a cobweb that hung across the opening with the sharp end of an enamelled fingernail. The porch was in decay. Its beams were bent precariously. There were ledges on either side. One was covered with a single stone slab on which was carved the faint image of a long fish. Opposite was a slab which had been a tombstone. No letters were legible but there was the stylised outline of a medieval woman. Maxine pushed her finger into the marks on the stone to try and tace the outline and make it clearer.

The church stood in the centre of the graveyard but the path which approached the porch where Maxine stood had been overgrown. She stepped outside to locate the whereabouts of Peredur. They were separated by a forest of headstones and tall grass. She called to him and he waved and she looked relieved. With some difficulty she made her way towards him, and concerned for her, he came to meet her. She was a little out of breath and took his arm gratefully. He put his lips against hers. But once she was reassured she wanted to speak again.

'It's a bit weird isn't it?' she said.

'How do you mean?'

'That church is weird for a start. All damp and mouldy. And there are bats in there. Like vampires.'

'All buildings get damp and mouldy if they're not used,' Peredur said.

'I suppose they do, don't they? Isn't it amazing the simple things we never think about. I never think about anyway. You know, sometimes I get really scared at the thought of my own ignorance. After all my years of being educated. And if I'm ignorant, what chance have all the rest got?'

He was enchanted by the frankness and apparent naivety of the way she spoke. She was like a child throwing a handful of stones at a chosen target in the hope that a few of them would strike home. She started pulling at the heads of the long grass again and this time scattered the seed over the flat surfaces of the slate sepulchres.

'What's the fish for? Do they worship fish or something?'

'What fish?'

'On the slab in the porch. There's the shape of a fish. You can't mistake it.'

'Well I know what that is,' Peredur said. 'Must be very old. The Greek word for fish was ixous and the letters

49

of the word made up the initials of 'Jesus Christ the son of God.' ἰχθυς I'm not sure that it wasn't some kind of slogan against the Arian heresy . . .'

He frowned with the effort of trying to remember.

'Aren't you just a mine of useless information. Look at all these. They're all in Welsh. I suppose it is Welsh is it? Can you read it?'

She bent forward to look at an inscription that had been blotched by circles of pale lichen.

'There are nine people buried there,' he said. 'The parents, with six children who died under the age of fourteen, and one that lived to be sixty-two.'

'Ugh.'

Maxine shivered.

'What a place. Why are we here anyway?'

'It's peaceful,' Peredur said.

'Who wants peace?'

Her question was spontaneous and immediate.

'The Egyptians used to call their graveyards the Place of Truth,' he said.

'That was something I just had to know.'

She looked around her, discontented now with her surroundings.

'Have you finished yet? You must have read them all by now. What are you looking for?'

'My father's grave. He's buried here somewhere.'

'Your father?'

Maxine screwed up her nose and put out her tongue.

'Now he tells me.'

'You said you wanted to see where I came from.'

'Okay. But does it have to be archaeology?'

She made a brief play of being annoyed. Peredur continued his patient search. She followed him at a few yards distance.

'My goodness,' she said. 'It's a funny man that can't find his own father's grave.'

He straightened his back and turned to stare at her without speaking. He pushed his hands deep into the pockets of his tweed jacket.

'No offence. I only wish it was my old man's we were looking for. I'd take great pleasure in dancing on it I can tell you. And I'm not joking.'

He smiled forgivingly as though he were learning to give a wider tolerance to the things she said as their knowledge of each other slowly increased. It was a gradual process about which he was resolved to be infinitely patient.

'I was thinking of Thomas Bridle Hackett when I was in the church,' she said. 'It just came to me. Something he said about the war. When he was in the army. Something he did. There was a light burning on an altar. In the Balkans somewhere I think it was. Or a village in Greece. This light was supposed never to go out. So he just went up and blew it out. That's my old man for you. A bloody barbarian from Birmingham.'

The sound of her own words dispelled her mood of despondence and she ended up laughing.

'He died when I was twelve,' Peredur said.

He wanted to talk again about his own father.

'You lucky thing,' Maxine said.

'What do you mean?'

'That would have been just right for Thomas Bridle Hackett,' Maxine said. 'Then I would have missed him for my adolescence. Anything and everything that's wrong with me is entirely his fault.'

They were moving again, Peredur continuing his search and Maxine helping him in a sporadic sort of way.

'What was his name then?'

'John Cilydd More. He was a poet. Cilydd was his bardic name.'

'That's it you see! That's where you get it from. That dreamy poet look. Very romantic. Was he a lady-Cilydd?'

She clapped her hands with pleasure at her own joke but Peredur showed no inclination to be amused.

'It's a "C" not a "K".'

'He must have given you all those funny names. Peredur! Gwydion! Bedwyr!'

She exaggerated her efforts to pronounce each name and made the flourishing gesture of a boxing referee in a ring introducing celebrated contestants.

'Stop looking hurt,' she said. 'It just goads me to worse excesses.'

'I'm not hurt. I'm just observing you.'

'Well you're not liking what you're looking at.'

'Yes I am,' he said stubbornly.

'Well you've got a funny way of showing it.'

He offered to embrace her, sticking out his arms awkwardly. She pointed at the next row of headstones.

'Come on,' she said. 'Keep looking. We're here now so we may as well try to find it.'

They continued their search. Maxine made an effort to be serious and demonstrated this by looking at the inscriptions with greater care.

'Didn't you come to his funeral?'

'No. I didn't. I was ill in bed at the time. With asthma.'

She looked at him with unconcealed alarm.

'Do you get asthma then?'

'Not any more.'

'Thank God for that. Are you like him?'

Peredur straightened up to give the question thoughtful consideration.

'I feel as if I'm growing to be like him. That's what interests me so much I think. All this business of environment and heredity. My brother says I make certain gestures in exactly the same way as he used

52

to. A whole pattern of gestures. I poke the air with my head like this when I get excited. He says my father did that. And I have a sniff he says and a way of clearing my throat when I'm nervous. And I walk exactly the same as he did. Now he was fairly tall and I'm short but my strides are his. As if I'd inherited the strides of a tall man. And I'm deeply suspicious by nature, as he was. And it seems I like the food he liked. I'm not absolutely sure of it but I think it's the basic reason why my mother dislikes me.'

'Does she?'

'She never says it in so many words. But I know my physical presence gets on her nerves in about twenty minutes flat. There's no need to look sorry for me. I don't blame her. No more than I can help. I try to be objective about it. It's quite interesting to be your own guinea-pig in your own lab if you know what I mean. Is there a soul in the sperm or just an attitude to life?'

'Perry!'

Maxine threw up her arms in a gesture of delight.

'I'm going to call you Perry! You've just made a joke! And you're laughing like a cocktail-shaker. Come here and I'll give you a kiss.'

Peredur obeyed her. He took her in his arms and squeezed her until she cried out. She struggled violently to free herself.

'Don't do that,' she said. 'I can't breathe.'

'I'm sorry.'

Peredur's arms hung loosely at his sides.

'I want to be excused anyway.'

Maxine spoke primly.

'You keep your mind on one thing at the time. I'm going up there into the trees. You keep looking down here and don't give up until you find it.'

9

'My father,' Peredur said. 'His first wife died in child-birth. His sister was burnt to death. His father was lost at sea. He saw his friends killed in the trenches. I remember thinking even when I was still a small boy you couldn't blame him for being on the gloomy side.'

They stood among the blocks of marble, granite and slate in the monumental mason's yard and Maxine felt the cold surface of a marble headstone with the palms of her hands. She was exercising patient restraint. Peredur was so absorbed in the contemplation of his father's life he did not seem to notice. The monumental mason's yard was in two halves on either side of the main road leading into the seaside town from the east. One half was alongside the imposing entrance to the municipal cemetery and it consisted mainly of a lean-to slate roof, kept in good repair and a length of working area decently concealed from the road by a thick cypress hedge. It seemed more of a storage area and the true workshop was around where they both now stood. Inside the hut a man had begun singing. Maxine's face lit with a new interest.

'Listen,' she said.

It was a quavering ageing high tenor voice. Beyond the hut there was the sound of measured blows and a chisel striking stone.

'I suppose I'm like him,' Peredur said. 'Gloomy and self-absorbed.'

Maxine paid little attention. A plump little man had emerged from the hut. He was wearing a dusty cloth cap and had a pencil stuck under it above his right ear. He still sang lightly as he walked towards them.

He tilted his red round face upwards, looking quick witted and knowing.

'Good afternoon,' he said.

His dentures gleamed in the sun as he drew back his lips. In spite of his jaunty manner he was old.

'Lovely day, isn't it?' he said. 'That's why I'm singing. Whenever the sun shines I sing and that's all there is to it. What can I do for you?'

'Mr Bailey-Roberts?'

'That's right.'

'The Vicar of Llanfair-yng-Nghorwg suggested I should call and see you. My name is More. Peredur More. I'm looking for my father's grave. I couldn't find it in the churchyard and he said you would be sure to know.'

'Did he?'

The monumental mason looked pleased. He inserted his hand between his loose overall and his trousers in order to press his palm against his hip.

'Well he's right you know. If anybody knows I know. And who else would want to? Forgive and Forget, isn't it? But it's my line of business and I like to be tidy and Tidiness is next to Godliness. Yes indeed. I could tell you about some places and Llanfair-yng-Nghorwg is one of them. It's all higgledy-piggledy and I'll tell you why. Nobody has taken an interest. It's all very well to talk about ancient churches and country church-yards and romantic settings, but that place has been shockingly neglected. Curates you see, obliging people. Of course he can be buried in Llanfair and all that sort of thing and before you know where you are they're digging up goodness knows what. I wouldn't like to tell you what I've seen Sam Spicer burning in the boiler of the heating apparatus. Talk about a crematorium . . . Aye well. We'll not 'persuit' it as old P.C. George used to say. Now then. What was your father's name?'

'John Cilydd More.'

The monumental mason grasped Peredur's forearm in a grip of melodramatic surprise.

'Not Cilydd?'

'That's right.'

'*Duw! Duw!*'

The monumental mason burst into unexpected melody. He sang softly giving special precision to his diction.

> *The hawk . . . the hawk . . . descends . . . descends . . .*
> *With burning . . . burning eyes*
> *And where he strikes*
> *The singing dies . . . the singing dies.'*

'That's Cilydd. And I'll tell you something more. You may not believe it. But I won on that one in the tenor solo at Ruthin in 1927. And of course you know what the Hawk represents don't you?'

His appreciation of the lyric gave way to graphic surprise that Peredur was the son of the poet. This in turn was succeeded by a deep frown.

'I never knew that Cilydd was buried in Llanfair-yng-Nghorwg.'

He held up his hand and then allowed it to sink slowly as a sign that he had regretfully abandoned a possible hypothesis.

'I suppose that only goes to show that we don't know everything. You wouldn't think that needed proving, would you? But I suppose it does you see. Otherwise it wouldn't keep on happening.'

He was looking at Maxine who was giving him one of her charming smiles. He seemed to be hoping for a more formal introduction.

'This is Miss Hackett,' Peredur said.

'How do you do?'

He studied her with great approval as they shook hands and was inspired to express himself further.

'No relation to Matthew Hackett the organist?'

'Oh no. We're an unmusical lot,' Maxine said.

His mind returned to the problem in hand. He scratched his cheek and then looked at his hand and showed it to each of the young people in turn.

'The price of craftsmanship,' he said. 'Hard and horny. Yes indeed. What about this grave eh? It's a mystery to me you know. I don't remember us ever making a headstone with his name on it. When did he pass on?'

'Nineteen fifty two,' Peredur said.

'Well there you are then. I did all the inscriptions in those days. And I would have remembered cutting out *Cilydd*. After all, he was a poet, wasn't he? National winner I'm sure he was. And I'm a bit artistic myself. So I wouldn't forget that, would I? Come inside a minute. Come on.'

He led the way to the hut and then stood aside and urged Maxine to enter first.

'I call it the office,' he said, 'but I do most of my clerking at home of an evening you know. I take the books out on the kitchen table and I get to work while the old lady sits watching television. Can't see anything in that myself. Funny isn't it? Behind the times you see. I mean, I look at it from time to time but I can't let myself go if you know what I mean. What I like is a good concert you know. Where you can let yourself go.'

Short as he was his arms were long enough to reach inside a cupboard above the tall counting house desk where he kept a ledger the size of a family bible. In the cupboard was a pile of rolled up plans in elastic bands. He tapped the bottom one with his finger twice and the second time the whole lot rolled out down the sloping surface of the desk and on to the floor. He waved his hands over them.

'That's where they belong. Plans for every graveyard in this part of the world. Maps of the other world I call them.'

He kneeled down with his hands on his thighs and studied them before picking out the one he wanted.

'Llanfair-yng-Nghorwg,' he said. 'Untidy place. Not many go there now you know. I don't encourage it. If people ask my advice that is. No upkeep. I think they'd close the place if they could you know. Now just look at this. It's full of blanks you'd think but those blanks are full. Chock a block. That's the trouble.'

He rose to his feet and sighed with the effort.

'I take an interest, you see. It's not that I'm morbid it's just that I'm tidy. And it's good for business if you want to put it at a lower level. Let's get the registers.'

He stood on a chair to reach down a ledger from a higher shelf. He put on a pair of spectacles and licked the tip of his index finger before turning over the pages.

'It's my own system, you see. Very unscientific but I understand it. And that's all that matters.'

He paused, his finger on his tongue for a thoughtful moment.

'Except when I'm gone of course. But then "*records and mountains roll away and crumble in the stream of time*" . . . was that Cilydd? I don't remember.'

He turned to look at Peredur.

'What was Cilydd, tell me? Baptist or Congregationalist?'

Peredur was a little embarrassed.

'I'm not sure,' he said.

'Well, that's how it is.'

The monumental mason was full of philosophical patience.

'Nobody's religious nowadays. Not the same as they used to be. I sing in the choir you know. In the Parish church although I was brought up a Methodist. It gives me a lot of pleasure. People don't know what they're missing. Not the way I look at it. It's consciousness you see. It's all a question of consciousness. Like a great

58

big beautiful ball of insubstantial beauty. And you live inside that. Like Abraham in his tent. That's the secret. In my opinion.'

He examined his registers more closely, turning over the pages in a silence broken only from time to time by his deep sighs. He shook his head sadly.

'I'm forced to only one conclusion,' he said. 'I may be wrong of course. There are other monumental masons. But not in this part covering Llanfair-yng-Nghorwg. If your father is buried there Mr More, nobody has both-erd to put a stone on his grave.'

He closed the ledger with a dramatic slam.

Maxine opened her mouth and then restrained her-self from speaking.

'There's no legal obligation of course. It's nothing more than a custom. But in my opinion, friend, for what it's worth your father's remains are lying out there without a single cross to show respect or mark the spot.'

He began to gather up the plans from the floor.

'Of course I know I've got a vested interest as they call it. But it doesn't seem right somehow. And him a poet apart from anything else. A National Winner! Not the way I look at it.'

10

Maxine swung the croquet stick between her legs. Peredur was kneeling on the edge of the lawn di-viding his attention between the girl playing croquet and the underside of stones that he was turning over. The weather was sultry and he had some shade from the laurel bushes behind him. Through a gap in the bushes there was a glimpse of cattle in the park sheltering from the heat under the leafy branches of a great oak tree.

'Well, what do I do now,' she said. 'Go on. Tell me!'

'One of two things. Knock my ball out of the way or get your ball straight through the hoop or knock my ball out of the way and get yours through the hoop.'

'That's three things,' Maxine said.

Her tongue was out as she took aim.

'Now watch me.'

With some excitement she swung her mallet. More by luck than by design her ball hit Peredur's and came to rest in front of the iron hoop.

'Is that good?' she said. 'Is that good?'

She was anxious for approval.

'Very good.'

Peredur bent further to examine the underside of a stone.

'What are you looking for?' Maxine said. 'Buried treasure or something?'

'Cocoons.'

He did not lift his head.

'Full of spider's eggs. Fascinating things, spiders.'

'Are they really?'

She looked sceptical.

'Come on, it's your turn. It's a lovely game this. I love it. Makes me feel all lady-like and Victorian, and to think I had to bully you into bringing me here.'

Peredur looked uncomfortable.

'It's such a set up,' he said. 'I didn't think you'd like it.'

'Out of my class. Is that what you mean? I'm not good enough for Brangor Hall?'

'No of course not. Anyway. I don't like it myself. I never come here unless I have to.'

Maxine smiled to show that she accepted the explanation and they continued playing with pleasure and intense rivalry until Maxine looked back in the direction of the Hall.

'Who in God's name is that?' she said.

A fat woman dressed like a little girl was shambling towards them across the tennis court. The net was down and she tried to skip over it. She was wearing a frilly muslin frock, with a bow at the back to match the bow in her straight hair, and new white plimsoles on her feet. She stopped to admire the pumps from time to time, coming closer with the timidity of an animal tamed by hunger approaching a human habitation.

'Milly Huskie,' Peredur said. 'I told you about Milly. She probably wants to play.'

'I don't want to play with her,' Maxine said under her breath. 'Quite honestly she gives me the creeps.'

Milly came up to the starting peg. A sly smile on her smooth shining face showed that she anticipated pleasure, but her mongoloid eyes were swollen as though recently she had been crying. She put her hands behind her back and began to swing from side to side like a little girl.

'Do you want to play, Milly?' Peredur said.

He pitched up his voice to speak with exaggerated amiability. Milly shook her head shyly.

'Just like to watch?'

Milly lowered her head and closed her left eye.

'I am watching aren't I?'

She was enjoying the interruption

'Come on,' Maxine said. 'It's your turn.'

Peredur went to his ball and took aim. He paused and looked up.

'I can never remember the rules,' he said. 'I think I've got to strike back now and just get to a position where I can get it through next time with a bit of luck.'

Milly was watching him taking aim. As he was about to strike she spoke.

61

'Your mother wants you,' she said.

She looked pleased with the way she had delivered the message and with the effect it had.

'She's on the West Terrace.'

She leaned sideways to point in the direction they had to take. Peredur did not look pleased.

'What's it about,' he said. 'Do you know?'

'She's got the keys out.'

Milly spoke shrewdly as though she knew the full significance of the information she had just obligingly shared. She looked at Maxine to include her in the impending scheme of things. Peredur took aim with his mallet and drove his ball against Maxine's sending it outside the area marked out for croquet.

'Hey!'

Maxine protested loudly.

'What are you doing!'

'Croquet.' Peredur said. 'At least I think it is. Come on. I've got to take you on the Tour of Inspection.'

They walked past a clear pond where two swans drifted on the water with their wings slightly open. Maxine stopped to admire them and then her gaze lifted to take in a view of the Hall.

'To think you live in a bloody castle,' she said, 'and you weren't going to let on.'

'It's nothing to do with me. My mother just happened to marry the owner.'

'Sacrificed herself for the sake of her children!'

He could not judge the extent of the sarcasm.

'It's nothing like that,' he said.

'Took it all in the name of love? And where is he now, poor creature "The late Lord B. Suffocated by affection. R.I.P."'

Peredur looked hurt so she put her hand on his arms very apologetically.

'You shouldn't take too much notice of me,' she said. 'I just blabber anything that comes into my head. To

62

prove I'm not just a pretty face. My mother used to say that it proved I was a fool. Look at those windows!'

She made a childlike effort to change the subject.

'They make that part look like a church.'

'It is. That's the family chapel.'

'Cor,' Maxine said. 'I'm no end impressed you know.'

'Exactly.'

'What do you mean, exactly? There are times when you look unbearably knowing, Mr More. If I may speak frankly.'

Peredur smiled rather unsteadily. Her aggressive irony was so unfamiliar to him he always appeared nervous of misinterpreting it.

'No. What I meant was the building was designed to impress the neighbours. All the other gentry. Visible evidence that the Barons of Brangor and the family of Rice-Pughe were bigger and better and more important than any other family within the Field of Force. Or at least this corner of it.

'Ah!'

Maxine mimed gestures of devoted discipleship. She clasped her hands together to show her pleasure at hearing again familiar and loved concepts and phrases from the seminar room. Peredur refused to join in the joke.

'You said you wanted to learn,' he said stubbornly.

'Oh I do. I do. I do.'

Maxine abruptly gave up her game.

'But only things I don't know already.'

He caught her arm and drew her back into the concealment offered by a well-shaped lilac bush. She looked pretty, pert and rebellious.

'Mind my feet,' she said. 'There's muck on the ground.'

'Maxine.'

His voice was constricted with emotion and he watched her closely to make an instant recording of her response. Her face was in repose and her smile enough to allow him to hope she was not annoyed or displeased by his action. He cleared his throat and made a conscious effort to control the sound he was making as well as the sense.

'Let's make an effort to understand each other, shall we?'

'What do you think I'm doing?'

'I know, I know. You've been marvellous. You've helped me. And I'm grateful. That's why I want you to let me help you as well. That's what makes a constructive relationship. These terms sound awful when I say them, but I'm so bad on the personal level I have to use them. That's why I'm asking for your help really. Need me a little, for my sake.'

Either to bring him comfort, or for the sake of peace, she touched him on the face, passing her fingertips over the marks on his cheek. The sympathetic smile vanished from her face when she looked beyond Peredur's shoulder to see Milly Huskie only a few yards away staring at them in their ineffective concealment, her open mouth watering with curiosity. Peredur turned around and lifted a spray of lilac in order to give Milly a frown of unimpeded disapproval. But she was not at all put off. She moved her head from side to side and spoke to Peredur.

'Where's Gwydion?' she said.

It was a question that had clearly been on her mind for some time.

'Will he be coming?'

She bent her head suddenly to stare at the whiteness of her pumps. Peredur relented a little. He spoke in a tone that was an attempt at gentle understanding.

'I don't think so, Milly,' he said. 'He's in London I expect. You may see him on television.'

'Now?'

She spoke eagerly, ready to walk away and find a

set and sit in front of it until such time as Gwydion would appear. Peredur shook his head regretfully and Milly moved away, her hands clasped behind her back, moody, and openly disappointed.

'She dotes on my brother Gwydion,' Peredur said. 'She always has done. It's so pathetic.'

'Creepy,' Maxine said. 'That's what I'd call it. Now come on or your mother will be cross with you. Come on. Don't be so sensitive. I'm only teasing you. You've got to make allowances for me. I'm out of my depth you know. My tiny mind can't cope. Where am I? I say to myself. What century for God's sake? And I've no idea. So I get all trembly and aggressive. Can I hold your hand?'

Peredur looked at her longingly as he took her hand. Milly followed them at a distance as they crossed the lawn. As soon as they were in sight of the terrace Maxine pulled her hand free. The west terrace was raised two feet above the level of the lawn and the group already assembled there sat like an audience watching the harbingers of some approaching pageant for which they had been waiting for sometime. The immediate impression they gave was of being elderly. In their country house setting they could have been survivors from an earlier age somehow overlooked by the tide of social change. The centre piece was an elaborate deckchair of antiquated design and faded colours in which sat an aged white-haired cleric with his panama hat lying alongside the chair on the warm paving stones of the terrace. His clerical collar encircled his scraggy neck without touching it. A silver watch chain was secured in the worn button hole of the lapel of his alpaca jacket and his grey flannel trousers were limp around his thin legs which stretched out in awkward length since he lay a little sideways in the chair. The trousers ended above highly polished black boots which seemed sunk into the stone. His shrivelled lips were stretched in a euphoric smile.

Behind the chair a strong-looking woman stood like a personal body guard shadowing a royal personage, pleased to occupy her position but content also to be unobtrusive. Her jet-black hair was gathered into a disciplined bun on the nape but ringlets were allowed to escape and form a decorative fringe around her long sallow features. Her open-necked silk blouse was her only concession to the heat. She wore a severely cut brown tweed suit which had the vague appearance of a uniform.

Next to the cleric, in an early Regency chair taken out from a drawing room, sat a woman in her sixties who clasped her hands together in a way that was meant to conceal their arthritic deformities. Her face was glazed with suffering and yet her tight skin was drawn in by her small mouth into a puckered smile. Her limp hair, which was dyed a courageous black, was showing white at the roots. She was obliged to turn her whole body when transferring her attention from the clergyman to the only vigorous and moving figure on the terrace, a bright-eyed woman with plump bare freckled forearms and a way of pacing up and down that suggested a love of action and taking the initiative. Her manner was youthful and there were still traces of beauty in her strong face which had become heavier and more masculine with advancing years. Her grey hair still had traces of its original fairness and was arranged in what appeared to be natural waves. She could have been a popular school mistress in front of a class of adoring children made to bloom by the continuing rays of approval that shone from their attentive eyes. Her hands were still conspicuously beautiful and she wore rings that drew attention to them. At the moment they held a bunch of keys on a steel ring and she held them up and rattled them, laughing as she did so, so that

Peredur and Maxine could see them as they walked up the brief flight of stone steps from the lawn.

'Come along,' she said. 'I'm going to give you a conducted tour before tea.'

She took a few steps in the direction of the open doors and then came back smiling gaily.

'What am I about?' she said. 'So much seems to be happening today. I'm getting quite confused. We're having trouble with caravans aren't we, Irene? At any rate you are. Real trouble. Now this is Maxine. Miss Maxine Hackett, Irene, from Peredur's university. A very clever girl as you can clearly see. Maxine this is the Countess Lapescu. And you mustn't blame her for her title any more that you must blame me for mine. We're both of us good socialists, aren't we, Irene?'

The Countess looked rigidly patient.

'Isn't it nice to have young people around?'

Peredur's mother lifted her hand and spread out her fingers.

'I was just going to say that,' the countess said.

The clergyman had raised his hand a little too, wanting to be noticed.

'What is it, dear?'

Peredur's mother smiled at him with loving care.

'Oh my goodness. I'm so sorry. You haven't met Maxine. I'm such a scatter-brain today. Well here she is.'

'Sorry I can't get up,' the clergyman said. 'Not all that easily anyway. A man is as old as his arteries!'

His voice had a bell-like clarity and sharpness, unimpaired by his physical infirmity. He held out a cold limp hand and Maxine took it.

'This is my bother-in-law, Maxine, and my dear friend. He prefers not to be known as the last Lord Brangor and who can blame him? Let me tell you here and now he was and remains a great champion of women's rights. Isn't that so, Hubert?'

67

'If you say so, my dear.'

'You might well have read his book – *The Power of Love* by Hubert Pughe.'

'No,' Maxine said. 'I'm afraid I haven't.'

'I remember reading it when I was young,' Peredur's mother said. 'It seemed such a daring book in those days. I was thrilled with it. I never dreamt I would become the author's sister-in-law I must say. I must find you a copy. It's been translated into fourteen languages.'

'Nineteen,' the clergyman said.

He spoke promptly and brightly as though he had made the correction before.

'A great champion of women's rights and loving equality in modern marriage.'

She held the keys in both hands and looked at the seated man with great affection.

'I differed from Russell,' he said.

He smiled at Maxine appreciating both her beauty and his own undimmed eloquence.

'A different approach. I took what you might call the Celtic Christian point of view and developed it. The Celts you know, the British Celts that is – I wouldn't care to speak for the Irish and Scots – they always had a profound idealistic respect for women. Did you know that?'

'No, I didn't,' Maxine said.

'The Pedestal Tendency. That's what I called it. Very marked.'

'You must read some of Hubert's books,' Peredur's mother said. 'I'm sure he'd love to know what you thought of them. I think they need to be read again, Hubert, by a really brilliant, modern, young mind. I really do.'

Hubert took her hand and squeezed it appreciatively. The woman behind his chair spoke unexpectedly.

'Milly!' she said. 'Get up from there at once!'

68

Her voice was adenoidal and the accent in some sort of Liverpool origin. Maxine looked at her with quick interest. She had encountered an accent as impenetrable as the one she herself cultivated for her more aggressive moods.

'What was that, May? What did you say?'

Peredur's mother spoke with a breezy freshness and lady-like clarity.

'I was just telling my sister to get up off the damp ground.'

May Huskie made a scooping movement with her head as if she were quite prepared to lift her sister Milly up at the end of a long shovel, were she not so committed to her position behind the clergyman's deckchair.

'She gets cold easily,' May Huskie said. 'You know that. Will you get up Milly, that's a good girl!'

Milly was lying on the grassy bank beneath the terrace, watching her stalwart sister with careful admiration through a seasonal gap in the herbaceous border.

'Yes indeed,' Lady Brangor said, 'get up Milly dear, do. We don't want you catching one of your big snuffles.'

Milly was respectfully obedient and she was rewarded with a nod and a smile. Lady Brangor took Maxine's arm and led her into the house.

'She's very delicate,' she said in a soft voice. 'Very delicate. And her sisters are quite quite devoted to her. May and Rose. It's very touching.

Maxine looked around for Peredur.

'It's all right, my dear,' his mother said. 'He won't let you out of his sight. And quite right too. Now then, where shall we start?'

They stood in a sitting-room panelled in light oak with three doors left open because of the warm weather.

'I know! the Presiding Deity!'

Maxine looked at Peredur who shrugged his shoulders.

'I've hung her in the Hall.'

Lady Brangor laughed as though the phrase were a joke.

'You wouldn't believe it but when I came here first she was down in the cellar. So you could say I rescued her.'

The entrance hall was pillared and not well lit. At the foot of the great Jacobean staircase she drew their attention to the portrait of a woman in Tudor costume; she was robust looking with a bulging forehead and fair hair under a black velvet cap. In her right hand, like an orb of sovereignty, she held a human skull. The initial C.P. and *aetatis suae 31* were painted in the top right hand corner.

'I had it cleaned,' Lady Brangor said. 'Goodness knows how many coats of varnish came off. And there she is just as she was at the age of thirty-one and the founder of the family fortune. She was married four times. Now her father was an illegitimate son of King Henry VII. And she was directly descended on her mother's side from the royal house of Gwynedd. Now isn't that interesting?'

Maxine nodded politely.

'I never know why,' Peredur's mother said. 'But it is. And I may add it is nothing at all to do with me. It's all Hubert really. My brother-in-law, bless him. He's the end product. The last of the line. Lying out there in a deckchair. So that's history for you.'

She turned suddenly, aware of a discreet presence standing by a pillar.

'What is it, Salter?'

The man wore the solemn clothes of a butler. The dark suit had been pressed so often that there were brown singe marks on the striped trousers. He was grey faced and managed to appear resentfully impoverished in spite of his surroundings.

'I beg your pardon, your ladyship. You are wanted on the telephone.'

'I didn't hear the telephone.'

He seemed to lack the mental energy needed to disguise his indifference.

'Who is it?'

'The County Council, ma'am. The surveyor's office.'

'Aha!'

Lady Brangor raised a finger to gain Maxine's attention.

'Caravans,' she said. 'Let battle commence!'

The butler had more to say.

'Excuse me, your Ladyship,' he said. 'May I take it that you would like tea served on the West Terrace?'

'In about half an hour, Salter. Thank you.'

She held out the keys to Peredur.

'Take Maxine to see the Japanese Room. If she hates it as she may well do, that's the key of the Blue Drawing-Room and that's the key of the roof door if you want to go out on "the battlements". I'll join you as soon as I can.'

11

'It's a bit much isn't it,' Maxine said.

They sat facing each other with self-conscious amusement on a pair of short sofas placed on either side of a fireplace framed in white marble. The sofas were

71

upholstered in blue shot silk and the curved woodwork was painted white with gilt edges. The area between them was the only part of the large room where a person could move freely without being in danger of knocking over something valuable. The room was crowded with stands, display cabinets, shelves, whatnots and small tables all loaded with tea-sets, vases, figurines and ornaments of all shapes and sizes. In the centre of the room, under an electric light enclosed in a hexagonal shade of brass set with painted oriental glass panels that looked heavy enough to pull down the moulded centre of the ceiling, there stood the main collection set out on open shelves; ivory and alabaster figures of ploughmen with yoked oxen, warriors and noblemen, muscular slaves in loincloths carrying a lady in a covered chair, broad rumped horses, mythological figures, elephants and gods. In each corner of the room tapering whatnots stood like emaciated Christmas trees loaded with decorated rice bowls and tea-sets that looked too fragile ever to be used.

'It's all very well,' Maxine said. 'But what did they want to get lumbered with this lot for?'

'It's supposed to be valuable,' Peredur said.

He looked at the keys he was cradling in his two hands.

'Okay. I take your point,' she said. 'But why so much of the damned stuff?'

'Apparently there was a younger son, in the middle of the nineteenth century, who had plans for the conquest of Japan.'

Peredur gave the information in all seriousness but Maxine burst out laughing and drew up her knees to make herself more at home on her sofa.

'Crikey,' she said. 'What a family.'

'He went mad.'

Peredur smiled as he meted out poetic justice.

'Quite right too.'

She studied him with narrowed eyes.

'Now I'm beginning to understand you.'

Peredur sat up indignantly.

'What do you mean? All this is nothing at all to do with me. My mother happened to marry the late Lord B. I want no part of it.'

'You shouldn't make it too obvious,' Maxine said. 'Where did they meet?'

'In Estoril. Portugal. They were both staying in the same hotel. And this Countess Lapescu.'

Maxine snapped her fingers.

'That's the way to do it,' she said. 'Book your hols with Bluebird Tours and land yourself right in the middle of a celestial junk-shop.'

Peredur stood up.

'Is there anything else you'd like to see,' he said. 'There's a collection of Dresden China in the Blue Drawing Room.'

Maxine had comments to make and she wanted to make them brightly.

'Talk about the *Herrenvolk*,' she said. 'Here they were all the time. Ready to conquer anywhere or anybody. And that's what the Law was for. To protect these palaces of property. Welsh or English. Scots or Irish. All the same. A great feudal network of fat families all sitting on their great big golden eggs like bloody-minded broody hens. Fantastic.'

'It's all over,' Peredur said. 'Just a museum now. That's all.'

'Is it hell?'

Maxine was quite excited.

'One lot have faded out, too decadent to survive, but the system hasn't changed, mate. Not one little bit. The workers have just been fobbed off with a car, a telly and a fridge and the National Health. It's the same rotten system. I'll tell you what I'd do with the Past if I could, I'd pull the chain on it!'

73

Peredur smiled bleakly.

'I would! If there's one thing I can't stand it's the Past.'

'Do you mean that seriously?'

'If only we could wipe out the Past by one magic stroke, then we might, we just might have a chance of rebuilding the world into some decent shape. I'd start off in schools. I would impose a proper scientific curriculum that would be taught everywhere in the same way and the same words from China to Peru.'

'You wouldn't really.'

'Yes I would. By satellite.'

Peredur was inclined to tease her.

'You'd rent that,' he said. 'From the Americans.'

Maxine stood up and looked dark and threatening.

'*Their* days are numbered,' she said. 'They'll crack up from within.'

She stopped abruptly to listen to a noise outside.

'What's going on out there?'

In the corridor there were whispers and the sound of scuffling feet. Peredur stepped carefully towards the door and looked outside.

'Oh, it's you, Mister Peredur . . .'

Maxine followed quickly to identify the speaker with a quavering voice. There were two women in the corridor. In front, a queer old woman in black with an aggressive stance. Her long face thrust forward almost directly from her stooping shoulders was crowned with wispy white hair that seemed too scanty to be worth gathering up under a fine hair net. Her scalp gleamed in contrast to her pallid sagging features and her red rimmed eyes were restless with unquenchable suspicion. Behind her stood a taller woman in early middle age, plainly related to May Huskie: from an identical mould, but more feminine and less confident. She surveyed the scene with the nervous curiosity of a hen strayed into the house.

'I'm sorry to disturb you, Mister Peredur, but Rose said she heard voices coming from the Japanese Room . . . I see you've got the keys.'

'My mother gave them to me,' Peredur said.

'Of course she did.'

The old woman wore a black belt on which keys were accustomed to hang. She looked as though she had spent a long lifetime guarding treasures in obscure country houses.

'There you are, Rose,' she said to her companion. 'I told you it was probably her ladyship showing the guests around . . .'

'Yes, well, how was I to know?' Rose said.

Her gargling tones were like her sister May's, but fractionally softer and more intelligible. The two women seemed prepared to blame each other for the intrusion and yet the mistake in itself was not enough to account for their excited state.

'Is anything the matter?' Peredur said.

The old woman limped a few steps nearer. She spoke in a hoarse whisper, pushing the words out of a mouth enlarged by false teeth, and gasping from time to time with indignation and the difficulty of getting her breath. Peredur was her mistress's son. He was also a man she trusted, in whom she was prepared to confide.

'It's that Ruby Salter,' she said. 'She's been drinking. Her Ladyship said she couldn't have her wandering about the house in a drunken state. Especially with guests. And the doors open and all that sort of thing. We thought she was up here. She could break things. The trouble is, you see, Salter can't control her.'

'I see.'

Peredur was obliged to appear sympathetic. These were women showing complete devotion to their duties and to the safety and well-being of the house and the family. His sympathy encouraged the old woman to

75

speak at greater length. He was a member of the family she did not see so often and his responsible and serious demeanour entitled him to a more detailed explanation. There was a lilt of mild but steady complaint in her voice.

'It's all very well,' she said, 'but in a house of this size, you see, you can't be everywhere at once, keeping an eye on everything! When I was housekeeper at Cranforth Royal I was in charge of forty indoor servants. I know things were different then but this house isn't all that much smaller. In the old days I would have had at least twenty-five indoor servants to make it function properly and to do things in the way that they should be done. It's not easy you know, Mister Peredur.'

'I'm sure it isn't, Mrs Clayton,' Peredur said.

'And Salter is *quite* useless. He can't even control his own wife. Rose here is a great help. I don't know how I would manage without her to tell you the truth. And Mrs Williams is a good worker, isn't she, Rose? That's Mrs Williams from the village. Married to a dreadful good-for-nothing. And there's Florrie Barr from the lodge when she condescends to turn up. You never saw such a one for excuses. Her father is very thick with the Salters.'

'Anyway you manage,' Peredur said.

Mrs Clayton drew back conscious of having let her tongue run away with her. She was filled with a fluttering concern to re-establish her image as a woman who was efficient and unobtrusive and not only knew her place but maintained it with a religious discipline and an unimpeachable loyalty to her employer.

'I am very sorry we disturbed you, sir,' she said.

'That's all right, Mrs Clayton,' Peredur said.

She limped back a few paces but still hovered at the end of the corridor to make sure that he closed the door to the Japanese room and locked it properly. Only then did she give a respectful nod and lead the way back to another wing of the house, Rose Huskie reluctantly following behind her. Maxine was amused by the old woman's behaviour.

'Who's she?' she said. 'Dracula's grandmother?'

Peredur sighed and rattled the bunch of keys in front of his face.

'There's a war on,' he said.

'There's always something weird about people who have spent their whole lives as domestic servants. I had a great-aunt a bit like that one. Old bitch she was too.'

Peredur led the way to the Blue Drawing-Room. Here the Dresden china was housed in two matching display cabinets standing facing each other from opposing walls. Maxine looked at the pieces with some distaste, shaking her head. Peredur shut the door. Many pictures hung on the walls in ornate gilt frames.

'There are some decent landscapes in here,' he said.

He spoke almost apologetically.

'And that's an eighteenth-century French Pedestal Clock. Very rare.'

Maxine refused to be impressed. She sat down in a chair upholstered in blue velvet.

'Tell me about this war,' she said. 'People are more interesting than things.'

She nodded approvingly at the sound of her own wisdom.

'It's between my mother's retinue and the Old Guard,' Peredur said. 'When she married she brought Connie Clayton with her and the Huskies and they infiltrated into positions of power. Especially when Harry died. Her third husband. The late Lord B.'

'Palace politics,' Maxine said.

'That's right. I don't pretend to know the ins and outs. I don't really want to know. The whole thing nauseates me too much. But in six years or so my mama's faithful have taken over and the Old Guard are really only hanging on by their eyebrows. That's why Salter looks so down in the mouth. I don't know whether a battle between the housekeeper and the butler is traditional in places like this but that's what has happened here. You see them scudding about the place all day like rival fish in a tank. Unable to kill each other but dying to strike. You'd better look out for it. You never know when you'll come across them glowering at each other down lengths of corridor.'

Maxine gave a comic shudder.

'Ooh,' she said. 'It sounds quite exciting.'

'I think it's only old Hubert that stops my mama from sending the Salters and the Barrs and the remnants of their party packing. I don't know the details of the set up but I fancy he has some say in the estate still as well as the title.'

'But they are big pals,' Maxine said. 'Or aren't they?'

'Oh he loves her.'

Peredur spoke bitterly.

'Everybody loves Amy. Wonderful Amy. They are soulmates bound by elective affinities and God knows what mystical rot. The conflict of interest only comes out in their followers and underlings. They are above such mundane, petty, squabbles.'

Maxine looked thoughtful.

'There's a lot to your mother,' she said.

'Yes. There is, isn't there?'

'She knows how to get her own way.'

There was admiration in Maxine's voice.

'Always has done.'

'And all these Huskies . . .?'

'Her Praetorian Guard.'

'And what about you?'

She looked at Peredur anxious to assign to him an intelligible role in this new setting.

'What have you got so much against her?'

'Have I?'

'Of course you have.'

78

Her manner was abrupt and demanding, insisting that he should speak frankly no matter how much the effort cost him. He raised his shoulders and tilted his head down so that it appeared he was studying a complex pattern in the costly carpet under their feet.

'I always feel as though I were an inconvenience to her. Ever since I can remember. She's got this power to make me feel that I should be for ever apologizing for my existence.'

'But she's so nice to you. And she talks about "my boys" as though they were three fabulous knights in shining armour.'

Maxine giggled naughtily.

'She thinks you're a genius,' she said.

Peredur struggled not to be diverted from his train of thought, keeping his gaze on the carpet.

'But for me she would have become a Member of Parliament, I was always a stumbling block. As if she came within an ace of marrying a millionaire until he found me there hiding behind her skirts.'

Maxine laughed aloud at a picture he picked out with a deeply serious intention. He raised his head quickly. He looked defenceless.

'What's so funny?' he said.

She was enjoying attacking him.

'You take yourself so seriously. I'm not being catty now or anything like that, but just try and look at it objectively. You dramatize yourself. From morning till night. You can't help it. Just try and compare your childhood with mine. I could tell you things that would make your hair stand on end. I could. Really I could. And what have you got to complain about? Your home is a damn great castle. You've got a cushy academic job. Plenty of money. I mean your old bird may have her faults, but who hasn't for God's sake? She may be a bit gushing but she's definitely civilized and she does her

79

best to try and be "with it", poor old thing. So where's the grudge?'

Peredur said nothing.

'Just because she hasn't slapped a great big tombstone over your old man's grave and him a bit of a poet and all. I've been watching you for the last few days, Perry boy, and you've been letting it grow and grow in that little obsessive nut of yours. I'm not stupid you know.'

'I know,' Peredur said.

He seemed glad to acknowledged this fact freely.

'A molehill into a mountain,' she said. 'Literally.'

Her eyes shone with delight at the way in which she had been inspired to sum up Peredur's situation.

'I'm right, aren't I?' she said. 'So why don't you admit it?'

Peredur stood by a polished table and pushed his thin fingers into the surface. He seemed unwilling to dispute, unable to cope with her special way of hammering her argument home.

'How do you know what kind of a man he was anyway? Just because he was a bit of a poet doesn't mean he was an angel. He may have been a proper bastard. Your national winner could be a pig or a horse. How do you know?'

He sat down again and pressed both his hands down between his knees.

'He's gone, hasn't he?' Maxine said. 'There isn't much you can do for him any more. But she's here. In the Land of the Living. That's the difference.'

He gazed at her as though her words had set off a series of reverberations in his mind that he could barely control. Outside they heard a lady-like voice calling. It was his mother looking for them.

'Here she is,' Maxine said. 'On the word. Give her a shout or she'll climb up to the battlements. She's so energetic.'

Lady Brangor tapped the door tactfully before she came in. She was a little flushed with physical effort but her eyes were wide and youthful looking and full of a kind of innocence that hardly belonged properly to a woman of her age.

'Phew!' she said, girlishly. 'Bureaucrats! I used to think our Welsh ones weren't so bad, but now I'm not so sure. Poor Irene. I don't know whether I'm doing her harm or good, but I hope it's better than doing nothing. But she needs protecting. She can't really fight for herself.'

'What's the matter?'

Maxine pushed her head forward a little and fluttered her eyelashes. This was part of her manner when she wished to indicate she was being extremely polite.

'A caravan site,' Lady Brangor said. 'Right behind Irene's cottage and ruining the poor woman's view among other things. I don't want you to think I am automatically against caravans. I once had an interest in a site myself when Peredur's father was alive. Years and years ago. But there are caravan sites and caravan sites. And I believe in this part of the world we've reached saturation point. Anyway it's quite clear to me that petitions are a complete waste of time. And poor Irene is really a cripple so she can't do it properly. It's a political and legal matter. I've got that across anyway. I'm going to get a jolly good counsel and he's going to prove once and for all that a caravan site on Dulas Point is against the public interest!'

She looked determined and already triumphant. She gave Maxine a dazzling smile and then spoke with characteristic frankness.

'What do you think of it?'

She gave a brief flourish to indicate as much of the house as Maxine had been able to see during her absence on the telephone. Maxine was tactful.

'It's a bit overwhelming,' she said.

'You are quite right.' Lady Brangor said.

She looked at her youngest son who had withdrawn into a moody silence.

'What a sensible answer.'

She looked again at Peredur.

'Isn't it nice to have somebody who is sensible as well as beautiful? They don't always go together.'

Against his will Peredur was obliged to smile his agreement.

'What do you think I should do with it?'

Lady Brangor made herself comfortable in her armchair shifting about a bulky blue cushion until it fitted where she wanted it.

'I may as well pick your brains while you're here,' she said pleasantly. 'I daren't ask Peredur. He'd just tell me to put a match to the lot. Is that what you would do?'

'Oh no I wouldn't. Indeed I wouldn't.'

'Well that's a relief anyway.'

Lady Brangor smiled at Maxine very winningly and Maxine responded until the dimples appeared beyond the corners of her mouth.

'Can I talk freely?'

Lady Brangor made the demand modestly.

'Can you spare me a few moments?'

Maxine was eager to listen.

'Let me start by making my own position quite clear. You mustn't think I have any romantic attachment to this place. I haven't at all.'

She glanced at Peredur issuing a brief invitation for him to challenge the veracity of her statement.

'But I have a dream,' she said. 'I've had it several times since Harry died. I dream I'm asleep in a deep, old-fashioned, leather study chair. The leather is old and shiny and a bit chilly to touch. I wake up to find this huge model of a building in my lap. I can't move without toppling it and my hands are too small and too cold to do anything about dismantling it because it's so huge. Sometimes I wake up calling for help but it never comes. It's not a nice dream at all.'

Peredur cleared his throat and stirred uneasily in his chair. Lady Brangor looked at him with patient fondness.

'He's so fastidious,' she said. 'But it's not a dream really. It's a situation. I find myself in effect responsible for this huge place. Now all my life I've never been one to shirk a responsibility. But don't worry, I'm not going to bore you with the story of my life. Let's just say I am an optimist. In spite of everything. I still believe that life is an opportunity to build a better world. I really do.'

'So do I,' Maxine said.

They were both warm with enthusiasm.

'Now there must be an opportunity here,' Lady Brangor said. 'And that's the way I see it. I wouldn't want to offend or upset Hubert in any way, because this is his home after all and he wouldn't want to see it changed during his lifetime. Bless him, if he could get them he'd go out into the highways and by-ways tomorrow and hire twenty or thirty servants to run the place exactly as it was run in his grandfather's time. It's rather sweet really. Such a revolutionary in so many things but so far as his home is concerned Brangor must remain as feudal as possible. Harry was exactly the same. Ancestor worship I used to call it. But that's all by the way. What is to happen in the future? I've given it a lot of thought.

She paused and sighed very deeply.'

'Hubert has been a lifelong champion of women's rights. Now what I had in mind was a kind of centre of cultural and social effort towards the advancement of woman's place in the world. And just call it simply the Hubert Pughe Centre. Now what do you think of that?'

'It sounds very exciting,' Maxine said.

She spoke thoughtfully, as if her imagination as well as her critical faculties had been stimulated and that ideas and suggestions were already stirring in her mind.

'I'm so glad it appeals to you,' Lady Brangor said. 'I really am.'

She looked at Peredur to try and judge his reaction.

'I've talked about it to Hubert. In very general terms. And I can say that he is in agreement. But it all needs enormous thought and preparation. There will need to be a Trust. Hubert has agreed to that. He doesn't have a large personal fortune but what he has he will leave to the Trust. That's more or less settled.'

Maxine was respectfully silent. Peredur rose to his feet and went to look at a dim landscape painting in the corner of the room.

'I don't know what plans you two may have for the future,' Lady Brangor said. 'And I certainly won't pry. I've always been a very independent creature myself and I've always tried to respect my sons' independence . . . not that I'd ever dare interfere to tell you the honest truth! But I want you to know my plans in outline anyway. And now I'm going to make a proposal to you.'

She leaned towards Maxine as if she would have liked to pat her knee had it been in reach.

'You've got your post-graduate diploma I know,' she said. 'Now what are you doing to do next?'

'I've applied for a job in television,' Maxine said. 'As a research assistant.'

'She was deeply fascinated by everything', Lady Brangor said. Peredur rubbed his forehead as though he were developing migraine.

'Now then,' Lady Brangor said. 'How would you like to work here? You could become the first organizing secretary to the Centre. You could have a flat on the third floor. As many rooms as you like. And together we could do all the preparatory work and organize it all on a truly ambitious scale. What do you think of that?'

'It sounds marvellous,' Maxine said.

'Hubert likes you,' Lady Brangor said. 'And of course you would have enormous freedom. You would be in on the ground floor so to speak. Just imagine the cottages for example as homes for women artists who need peace and quiet to get on with their creative work. Whoever thinks of providing the time and the space for a woman with children who wants to get on with her sculpting or her pottery or her composing or what have you? Can you think of a more peaceful and inspiring place for someone who wants to do research on some social problem, from anywhere in the world? Don't you think it's an exciting concept?'

'Oh I do, I do.' Maxine said.

She was pleased and anxious to please, but also a little overwhelmed.

'Yes. Well, you think it over.'

Lady Brangor rose to her feet, radiating confidence.

'We don't want to rush into things. We'll do this properly. By careful degrees.'

She looked at Peredur. He had no opposition to provide.

'And it would have all sorts of delightful side effects for me,' she said. 'I don't know whether Peredur has told you how much I want him to come and live nearer home?'

Peredur shook his head.

'Come and see me when you've thought it over. I'd like to show you my little dream house up on the hill. You haven't seen it, have you?'

'No,' Maxine said.

'Designed for me by Bedwyr. My eldest son. I'm sure I've told you already what a brilliant architect he is? Haven't I?'

Maxine smiled and shook her head.

'Oh dear,' Lady Brangor said. 'I am slipping. Well you can see can't you, that's all I am really. Just a doting mother.'

12

'Perry! Perry!'

Maxine stood by the bedroom door dwarfed by a giant wardrobe built against the wall with a narrow mirror that seemed to vanish into the high ceiling. Peredur's bedroom was in darkness and the shape of her body in her thin nightdress was reflected with a ghostly dimness in the long mirror.

'Perry, are you awake?'

Across the room a rushing wind disturbed the long curtains that were only half closed across the open windows. They were made of stiff material and they made a noise as though a company of people were advancing into the large room. Maxine shivered.

'Can't you hear me?' she said.

She sounded too afraid to be really angry.

'I'm not coming any nearer I can tell you. I think the whole place is alive. You can hear the walls groaning . . . is that you? Where are you going?'

She caught a glimpse of his thin naked form flitting across the room. A door in the furthest shadows opened and closed. From the distance there came a roll of thunder over the hills. The wind dropped and outside the open window the loose ivy covering the crenellations of the narrow terrace made a sinister patter of its own as it was played upon by the first heavy drops of rain. She put her hands against the long mirror of the wardrobe and then pressed her cheek against the cold surface.

'Perry, Perry. Come out, please come out. Don't frighten me. I'm frightened enough already.'

She paused to give him a chance to say something. No sound came from beyond the heavy door.

'Peredur. Don't leave me. I've had a dream. A bad dream. And I can hear noises.'

She listened intently and heard the water flushing in what was obviously a bathroom behind the door. Peredur emerged, clearing his throat apologetically.

'Have you got a weak bladder or something?'

She spoke as though she wanted to hit him. He came close to her without speaking.

'And don't stand behind me,' she said. 'You're like a bloody ghost about the place. Now where have you gone? Do I have to bring my own candle?'

He had opened a cupboard and she could hear the tinkle of glasses. He stood behind her again, controlling his breathing with an effort.

'Drink this,' he said.

He put a liqueur glass into her hand.

'What is it? Hemlock?'

'You like it,' he said. 'You said you like it.'

She sipped it. She was eager to talk.

'I don't like thunder,' she said. 'It frightens me. And I heard noises?'

Peredur was ready to comfort her.

'I heard a woman shouting in the yard. She sounded drunk.'

'That must have been Ruby. Salter's wife. She gets drunk sometimes. She goes under the housekeeper's window and shouts abuse until Salter comes along and drags her away. I think he beats her.'

He sounded grimly pleased with his explanation.

'What a place,' Maxine said. 'It was a nightmare really. There was a procession passing down the corridor. The old clergyman was sitting in a wheelchair and that awful Milly was pushing it. And behind her came her big sister carrying one of those samurai swords. She held it up in the air, holding it with both her hands ready to cut off my head.'

Peredur inexpertly tried to murmur his sympathy.

'And the old man had a basket on his lap with the lid open. And that was meant for my head.'

He touched her, offering comfort and she turned to place a hand on his bare chest. It kept him at a distance and yet encouraged him to come closer.

'It's a strange set-up,' she said.

'I told you it was.'

'You don't want me to come here do you? To this Centre thing of your mother's?'

He moved away from her. He spoke so softly she had to strain her ears to hear what he was saying.

'They're playing into her hands,' he said. 'They're so stupid.'

'Who?'

'The Salters. They used to run the whole show. Old Lord B. was never here and they had a free hand. So that when they came back, the new Lady B. and the old Lord B., Salter never grasped the elementary fact that my mother had taken him over. He made the elementary mistake of complaining to his lordship when my mother turned the laundry into a studio for herself and that old countess you saw on the terrace – she was a potter until her hands were crippled. And Ruby Salter clashed with Clayton over the cooking. And lost because Clayton was so much better at the job . . . You don't really want to come here? Surely not?'

'I feel better now,' Maxine said. 'Can't you put a light on. Just a soft light. I want to see where I am.'

He switched on a light under a blue shade and stood beside it.

'You are so white,' Maxine said. 'You're like a girl. You've got a waist like a girl.'

'Let me look at you,' he said. 'Please.'

Maxine moved boldly into the room. She studied the large bed with interest and then looked at her bare feet on the chinese carpet.

'I could get used to it,' she said. 'It's just because I'm not used to it. That's why I was scared. I could learn to like it.'

'Please.'

His voice was full of pleading. She was revived and encouraged by the effect she was having on him.

'We look so small in here,' she said. 'Like a pair of white dwarfs. Tell me a story.'

'Maxine . . . let me see you . . . please.'

Impulsively she climed on to the bed and drew her nightdress over her head. She raised up her arms.

'I'm not afraid of being naked if that's what you think.'

Suddenly he moved across the room so that he could kneel at the bedside and reach her feet with his lips. He was trembling with a cold that seemed to come from inside himself.

'You are beautiful,' he said. 'You are beautiful.'

His hands reached up her legs to her thighs.

'You must keep still,' she said. 'Keep your hands still.'

He obeyed for as long as he could. Abruptly she allowed her knees to bend and she collapsed laughing into the centre of the large bed. Unable to restrain himself a moment longer he lay on her and tried to cover her with kisses. At first she laughed as though they were children playing a game, but his ardour and persistence became more than she could endure.

'Stop,' she said. 'Stop. Stop.'

She dug her nails into his back and he gasped with pain. Sulkily she hid herself under the white sheet and moved away from his placating touch. She was trembling and uneasy.

'I love you.'

Peredur whispered awkwardly.

'That's what you say.'

Her head found the pillow and she stared fixedly at the distant ceiling.

'I love everything about you. It's not just your beauty. I mean everything.'

'That's because you want something. It's easy to say things like that if you want something.'

'Believe me, please, Maxine. Believe me.'

His whispering was desperate and isolated in the large ornate room.

'I want to prove it,' he said. 'That's all I ask. Let me prove it. Show that you need me a little.'

'You're not gentle enough,' she said. 'You've got to be gentle with me. Very gentle. You've got to understand me. I can't tell you what I suffered when I was a child. I told you my father was a monster. I meant it. I meant every word of it.'

'What did he do?'

'Don't ask me. You are with me, aren't you? If you only knew the effort I make. I want to give myself to you. I want you to have me. I've told you that before. But you must be patient and gentle. I know there's something wrong with me. But it's not my fault is it?'

'No, of course it isn't.'

'You can criticize me as much as you like once you teach me to love you. But you haven't done that yet. You're not gentle enough. You're all words and ideas. You have to have more feeling. More sensitive feeling. That would bring me closer to you.'

'Please,' he said. 'Please.'

'I can't tell you what it feels like. I feel as if I'm losing my hold on the world. Just falling into space and I get so tensed up and frightened, Perry. I can't move. I'm absolutely rigid. Can't you feel how tense I am now? And this place makes it worse somehow. More oppressive, more frightening. No. Don't, please. Keep your hand still. Talk to me, please. Just talk to me.'

Gently but determinedly he fixed his lips over the lobe of her ear and played the tip of his tongue against it. She remained still, anaesthetized, and he was encouraged to pass his hands fondly down her back. She turned away slightly, giving way at last to some measure of excitement. He scratched her back gently and she murmured her pleasure. Then quite suddenly there was thunderclap overhead which made her jump and tremble with fright.

'Oh my God,' she said. 'I should never have come here. Never.'

'Maxine . . . my darling . . .'

He tried to take her completely in his arms but she pushed him away.

'There's nothing to be frightened of,' he said. 'I'm with you and I love you. I would die for you.'

'That's what you say.'

'I mean it. I really mean it. I want to help you, Maxine. I want to think what you think. I want to feel what you feel. That's what our bodies are for. I don't want to talk; I want to fill you with these feelings that are overwhelming me. I want to worship you with my body and you must let me do it so that a real communication can flow between us. I'll be gentle. I promise you. I will be gentle.'

He stroked her trembling body with tender care and whispered his praises of her beauty. She listened with a trance-like fascination to what he was saying and watched with wide eyes the attention he was paying her body with his lips. Outside there was an outburst of torrential rain and she moved her head on the pillow to listen even as he was carefully kissing her waist. He worked patiently to win her acquiescence and he gained some small reward when her breathing became faster and she began to mutter words he could not understand, like a patient in a fever. But when at last he gained sexual possession she was overcome with a rigidity more intense than when she had first lain alongside him in the bed with the sheet between them. He struggled to maintain his self-discipline as he whispered a stream of reassurances and desperate pleas. But nothing could calm her or persuade her. No matter how

91

gentle his thrusting her response made it clear that in her mind she was converting his love-making into an attack or the threat of an attack against some inviolate centre of her personality. Ultimately his patience gave way. As if it were some last resort when every other treatment had failed he gave a free rein to his male instinct and tried to master her. He cried with joy when she appeared to submit but when he had reached his climax and was ready to caress her with endless thanks, she pulled her body away from his and went to crouch at the bottom of the bed, covering herself with the loose sheet and exposing his panting body glistening with sweat. She glared at his body with open hatred.

'What's the matter. Darling. Please tell me.'

At first she would not speak. Her silence and her stare frightened him. He tried to come closer to her, moving on his knees. She shrank away from him.

'What's the matter?'

He repeated the question over and over again. She spoke at last in a whisper he could not hear.

'Tell me, Maxine. I love you. Please tell me. I don't understand.'

'You've destroyed me,' she said. 'You've destroyed me.'

13

'Well my God,' Maxine said. 'What a dump! What a tip!'

Peredur sat in the passenger seat, his arms folded as he looked gloomily through the windscreen at the isolated row of tall houses standing at a right angle to the promenade and the sea front.

'It's gone down in the world,' Peredur said.

Maxine held the steering wheel with both hands and pulled herself up assertively.

'Shall I tell you what it's like?' she said. 'It's like the front of a great prison. A great big quadrilateral prison. But they ran out of money and never built the other three sides.'

Peredur looked about him unhappily.

'It all looked so different when I was a kid,' he said.

The weather was cooler and a stiff wind was blowing up sand from the sloping beach.

'I've noticed this,' Maxine said. 'With these small Welsh towns. They are like little sores on the landscape.'

She turned back to look down the wide cob that led back across to the centre of the little town. It served as a barrier between the marshy land and the large square harbour. The tide was out and the glistening mud banks were in full view. In the railway yard on the north side of the harbour a small steam engine puffed up a cloud of smoke and gave a lonely blast on its whistle.

'I think you are being a bit hard,' Peredur said. 'It was a good place to grow up in.'

'I'm not saying Walsall is a beauty spot,' Maxine said. 'But at least we've got something to show for it. At least the Midlands is the workshop of England. All you've got here is a little self-pitying tip.'

She looked at him sternly as if it were his personal responsibility. She shifted the gear lever and the car crawled alongside the pavement. They both stretched their necks to survey the grey terrace. Two slate steps led down from each solid doorway directly on to the pavement which was on a level with the top half of a basement window protected by an iron grill.

'I keep on expecting to see the man in an Iron Mask,' Maxine said. 'Perhaps he's still in there locked up somewhere. You never know. Your old man . . .'

'Stop here,' Peredur said.

She glanced in the mirror and applied the brake. The road was so wide it appeared free of traffic. In fact there were occasional cars making the journey to the beach the long way round, perhaps in the hope of finding some extensive area of sand unspoilt by the presence of other people. These were not to be discouraged by the overcast sky.

'Look at the walls,' Maxine said. 'It was a prison designed to incarcerate complete families. And look at the windows. They're like blind eyes. They've got no tears left for the torments of family life inside.'

'Don't overdo it,' Peredur said.

She was quick to take offence.

'What do you mean?' she said.

Peredur had his hand on the door handle.

'We mustn't colour the world with the misery we happen to store inside us.'

'Misery?'

Maxine took the word as an insult.

'Who said I was miserable? I am basically a very happy person. That's all I want is to be happy. It's not my fault is it?'

She looked at him with intense reproach.

'Wait here,' he said. 'I'll just see if she's in.'

'You're a fine one to talk. You are the original misery guts. You like being miserable. You enjoy it. You want to nurse your grievances for the rest of your life. What the hell are we doing now except chasing your grievances?'

She had more to say but he left her to cross the wide avenue and she sat brooding at the wheel of the white sports car. She turned her head to watch him knock at a door painted dark green. He stood facing the door waiting for it to open. It seemed easier for him to face the painted door than turn while he waited and face her critical glare. It was opened eventually by a harassed looking woman wiping her hands on her apron. There was a brief conversation between them. He moved back with an awkward stiffness as she emerged on the pavement to make gestures that implied she was pointing the way to another address or even another town. Peredur had some difficulty in withdrawing. The woman's curiosity had been roused. She watched him with continuing interest as he returned to the white car. He fitted himself neatly into the passenger seat.

'It's absolutely absurd to call me miserable,' Maxine said, 'I had more friends than anybody else at Redbatch because I was always the life and soul of the party – and you know it. It's just that you want to drag me down to your level and be miserable like you. That's all it is.'

'She's dead,' Peredur said. 'And her sister doesn't live there anymore.'

'This car you are sitting in was lent to me by someone because he liked me. Just because we were good friends he lent me his car.'

Peredur listened obediently.

'That's real friendship. I wouldn't have some so many friends if I was miserable all the time.'

'It's me,' Peredur said at last. 'I suppose I'm feeling guilty because I might have made you unhappy.'

'Well that's different.'

95

He leaned towards the wheel and pointed at a house two doors down from the house where he had made a call.

'That was our house,' he said.

Maxine appeared a little more cheerful.

'We'll put a plaque on it,' she said.

'We called these two sisters Aunty Flo and Aunty Menna. That was their house. Where I called. They played a big part in our lives when we were small. They had a nephew called Clem. I keep on expecting to see him coming out of that door with a football under his arm. He was mad about football. Clem was Bedwyr's friend. About ten years older than me. I used to look up to them like legendary heroes. Clem and Bedwyr. Kings among men. The two sisters were always bickering. Jealous of each other really over possession of their nephew, the young hero.'

'I've never seen a family yet that didn't bicker,' Maxine said.

He gave her a quick look of understanding and sympathy.

'I always assumed they were devoted to each other,' he said. 'That was enough of a paradox to make it possible to live with. I used to think of it as a sort of loving teasing. I can remember watching them without embarrassment and telling myself, it's all in fun. They don't really mean it.'

'You must have been a bit of a prig,' she said. 'Even when you were a small boy.'

'He's teaching somewhere in north London. Clem. And Aunty Menna is dead.'

'Well that's that then,' Maxine said. 'Aunty Menna and Queen Anne.'

'It was once a field of force. We attended the same chapel. The two sisters were very keen on amateur dramatics. They had a great respect for my father because he had written a one-act comedy in his youth about an old sea captain and his two unmarried daughters and they had won a prize somewhere playing the daughters. And now she's moved. Aunty Flo has moved. Gone away.'

'Do you think we could?'

'Such a closely knit society. A field of force. And now it's been de-magnetized. Now we only connect with people we choose to connect with. Or try to connect with. Perhaps it is a loss.'

'Well that's up to us,' Maxine said. 'Can we move?'

'I wonder if you'd mind,' Peredur said. 'I'd like to see her. She's moved to a small seaside place not far from here. About seven miles. Would you mind?'

'I suppose not. You'd better know the way . . .'

They drove along in silence. Peredur crouching low in his seat still a little nervous of Maxine's erratic driving. She was inclined to accelerate wildly whenever they came to a length of road that appeared reasonably straight and then to apply her brakes with savage suddenness as they approached the inevitable corner. It spite of the wind and the overcast sky, the hood was down. When they wanted to speak they were obliged to shout.

'I needn't ask what you think,' Peredur said.

'About what?'

'Where I come from. That's what you said you wanted to see.' She smiled.

'You've told me already. A tip. A dump.'

He closed his eyes with weary resignation as the sports car roared towards yet another twist in the road. When he opened them he seemed astonished to see a golf course on their right, between the road and the sea and a house in the middle that looked as though it might have been a rectory once, painted a gay pink and given some decorative protection from the prevailing wind by a clump of attractive pine trees.

'Well look at that!' he said.

97

'What's the matter?'

'This is all new,' he said. 'There used to be nothing over there, only gorse and rough grazing and a Rectory completely hidden in the trees.'

'Not to worry,' Maxine said. 'It's not new or old to me. It just is.'

She had completely recovered from the bout of irritation outside the terrace.

'How much is she worth?'

The wind snatched at the words as they emerged from her mouth and scattered them into the air stream. Peredur failed to catch them all. He stretched his mouth, pulling a face to show incomprehension.

'Your mother. How much is she worth do you think?'

He frowned, unable to find an answer.

'It doesn't matter,' she said. 'I was only wondering.'

'It must be quite a bit,' he said. 'I've no idea really.'

'I suppose you think I was indelicate to ask?'

'No. It isn't that. I couldn't really work it out. She's been married three times.'

'That's the way to do it,' Maxine said. 'If all else fails . . . I'll marry a millionaire!'

'I want no part of it.'

Peredur sat up to make sure that they were following the right route. He looked around for a familiar landmark.

'I only want clean money. Money I've earned by my own work. Nothing else.'

His expression was stern and adamant. He was enunciating a principle. She looked at him with awe and a certain alarm.

'The secret is to keep your needs as few as possible.'

'What secret?'

'If you want to lead the kind of life I lead. You have to discipline yourself to survive on the minimum.'

'What a funny idea,' Maxine said. 'Tell me why.'

'The pursuit of Truth doesn't pay.'

'I'm sure that's true.'

Maxine emphasized the word "true" by bending her head prettily as she said it, but Peredur did not seem to notice.

'Sometimes I think I can see the Future clearly,' he said.

'Gosh, if only you could . . .'

'You've only got to ask yourself certain questions,' he said. 'It becomes very clear that in most practical circumstances in life a devotion to Truth is a major disability. Now . . .'

'I can't hear!'

Maxine shouted loudly to prevent him elaborating his theory any further. He looked a little hurt and folded his arms and sank down in his seat. He had wanted to speak with a serious purpose and she had responded by being deliberately facetious.

'Here we are,' Maxine said. 'Is this it?'

She gave a comical splutter as she mispronounced the name on the old signpost. He nodded without smiling.

'It's opposite the bakery,' he said. 'A pebble-dashed house with a verandah. That's what she said.'

The bakery was conspicuous. A low building with tall chimney and a single window blank with flour dust. The proprietor's name was spelt in brass on an iron frame over the door which was closed. Maxine was intrigued with a series of enamelled advertisements for mustard and cigarettes which were nailed to the upper half of a wide door at the side of the bakery. They dated from the 1930s or even earlier and yet were only marginally attacked by rust.

'I'd love one of those,' she said. 'I really would.'

'Will you come with me?'

Peredur was studying the house across the road with some misgivings. It stood by itself but all the woodwork needed painting. They crossed the road together and Peredur opened the small gate into the strip of front

99

garden. The soil was a dusty mixture with too much sand and the hedges and the flowers looked parched and stunted from lack of nourishment. The concrete path to the front door at the side of the house was cracked and broken. Weeds grew with solitary strength in the cracks. A heavy black knocker hung on the door. Peredur lifted it and let it drop with a dull thud. No one came. Maxine lifted the knocker and gave it a determined series of taps while they waited. Peredur looked at her with open admiration. She was wearing her white trousers and a loose fitting purple silk jersey, an image of self-possession, elegant and confident in spite of her short size.

The woman who opened the door was apprehensive. She used the door as a shield for her body and showed only her pale puffed face. Her eyes jerked nervously behind eyelids that were closed as a defence against the breeze from the sea and the raw daylight. Peredur smiled, very pleased to have found her at last, but apologetic for the intrusion. The woman was not prepared to smile.

'Miss Cowley-Jones,' he said. 'Aunty Flo.'

The names reassured her a little. Her lips curved into her plump cheeks ready to smile if the correct signals were continued.

'I am afraid I don't know you,' she said.

Her voice quavered delicately.

'I'm Bedwyr's brother,' he said. 'Bedwyr's brother. The little one. Peredur.'

She was delighted. Her hand stretched out towards him and self-reproach escaped like pent up steam from between her pursed lips.

'Well come in,' she said, 'come in. Both of you. This is such a surprise. You've grown. You're a man and a very clever man too, I hear.'

She ushered them both into the interior of the house, torn between the unexpected delight of having visitors and the distasteful task of having to apologize for the untidy state of the place. They moved slowly down the narrow passage. Maxine took a quick glance at herself in the tarnished mirror of the umbrella stand while Aunty Flo fumbled with the loose door knob of her drawing room door. She paused as she did so to chuckle with embarrassment.

'I was never any good in the house,' she said. 'You remember, Peredur? And to think you've come all the way to visit an old woman in her chimney corner. You don't mind me still calling you "Peredur"?'

The room smelt damp. With some effort and in spite of Peredur telling her it was unnecessary she switched on the single bar of an electric fire of antiquated design. The three-piece suite was protected by pink covers and lace curtains on the big bay window concealed the interior from the outside world.

'Sit where I can see you,' Aunty Flo said.

Herself she sat on the piano stool and plucked at the shrunken grey cardigan she was wearing over shoulders. Her fluffy slippers helped to conceal her swollen ankles. She gave Maxine a coy girlish smile when they were introduced. She patted the air between them with a plump hand and the gesture was meant to indicate her shy but sincere admiration for Maxine's youth and beauty.

'Yes, well, I can see you now,' she said, giving her attention to Peredur. 'I couldn't before you know. The light was hurting my eyes. You are the living image of your poor father.'

Peredur sat up.

'Am I really?'

She puckered her lips again and tapped the closed lid of the upright piano behind her.

'Well now,' she said, leaning forward and smiling, theatrically filled with friendly secrets. 'Remember this piano?'

She began to hum and then drum a fist rhythmically into the palm of her other hand.

'Ta, ta, taffi, taffi, ta . . . you wouldn't think I gave him music lessons would you? Music without tears!'

She shook with laughter and pleasant recollection and Maxine looked at the plaster cast of a sulky Beethoven on a pedestal in the corner of the room. She seemed to find its stillness an easier focus of contemplation while she resigned herself to the role of listener.

'Sweet memories,' Aunty Flo said. 'Those were good old days. They were happy times you know. I often think of them. When we all lived in the South of France, the terrace by the sea. I'm alone now you see. Everything is different.'

'I was so sorry to hear about Aunty Menna . . .' Peredur said awkwardly.

'Yes it was sad, wasn't it?'

She spoke about her sister with extreme objectivity to relieve him of his embarrassment, but then she fell silent, looking first at Maxine and than at Peredur, trying to assess their relationship, perhaps, or suddenly taken with an awareness of the loss of contact between his family and herself and an inability to account for their unexpected visit.

'Would you like a cup of tea?' she said.

They had begun to shake their heads before she finished speaking.

'It wouldn't take me a minute.'

'No thank you,' Peredur said.

He cleared his throat and added.

'How's Clem?'

Aunty Flo lifted her left hand and let it sink as a signal of resigned disapprobation.

'That one,' she said. 'I'm lucky if I see him once a year. Does Bedwyr keep in touch with him?'

Peredur was uncomfortable.

'I don't really know,' he said. 'I'm at Redbatch you see. It's such a long way away.'

'I sacrificed my life for that boy,' Aunty Flo said.

She pulled down her lips to show that she was sad but still philosophical.

'I could have married, you see, when I was young. I was asked. But I turned them down to bring up that boy. I kept them both really. Clem and my poor sister Menna. And this is my reward. Solitude.'

She lifted her lips with some effort trying to smile and be brave. She shivered a little with cold and adjusted the cardigan over her shoulders.

'Where is he?'

Peredur cleared his throat and held his head to one side, trying at short notice to develop some skill in the art of listening sympathetically to ageing people with a grievance.

'The same place. Ilford. A boy like that with all those brains teaching general subjects in the lower forms. And it's not even a grammar school. He's an M.A. you know, give him his due. He's been there all those years. His first job in fact. I think it was the year after your poor father died. And he's still there, like a fly in glue. And it's not as if he couldn't get back. He's had jobs offered him. There was one in Colwyn Bay about five years ago. Welsh History throughout the school. He fancied it too. But Sylvia wouldn't let him come. Sylvia's his wife. It would be too near his old aunts you see and she couldn't stand us. Especially me. Said we'd spoilt him when he was small and all that sort of thing. "You've damaged him for life," she said. Those were her exact words to me. Now I never spoilt him. But Menna did. Poor Menna couldn't refuse him anything and I just had to stand by watching helplessly. But it's not as though it made him bad or wicked or anything like that. But he is weak and he needs a lot of affection and a lot of mothering. He likes to be happy and carefree, you

103

see and he doesn't like responsibility so what happens is Sylvia wears the trousers.'

Peredur was making an effort to listen with intense sympathy and Aunty Flo leaned towards him as though to facilitate the spate of pent up words that had to be released.

'They came here, you know, the year poor Menna died. The summer I moved to this house. This isn't an easy place to run you see and it was even worse then. I had to boil all the hot water on the open fire and to tell you the honest truth there are still only two power plugs in the whole place. She didn't lift a finger to help me. And they've got this boy you see. Andrew. Their only child. And talk about history repeating itself! He's thoroughly spoilt. Much worse than poor Clem. I don't want to go on about it but I could give you endless examples. And I'm not a fool you see. I've seen it all happen before and she's far worse than poor Menna ever was. But she's English, you see, and you can't tell her anything. She knows all the answers. Born to rule. You know what they can be like. And not an atom of sympathy for our language and culture. She wouldn't allow Clem to use our own language in her presence. Intolerant you see as well as arrogant. And bringing up that little boy in her own image. Well, I'll give an example. You see that sideboard over there? I've always liked a little smoke you know on the q.t. I'm old fashioned, you see, and I don't want people to know so I hide them in that cupboard and come in here for a quiet smoke after supper and sometimes after lunch as well. There's no harm in it. Although, mind you, if my poor old father were still alive he'd hang me on the spot if he saw a cigarette in my mouth. I have to make do on my teacher's pension which isn't much so I don't reckon in using more than two cigarettes a day and I keep a very careful count. But obviously little Andrew had been watching my moves very closely and when I was out shopping he'd popped in here without being seen and pinched half of them. But his mother wouldn't hear of it. And Clem of course, as usual, he was hopeless. Anyway . . .'

Maxine jumped to her feet. She mumbled an excuse and found her way down the dark passage to the front door. After a brief struggle she succeeded in opening it and rushed out into the open air. Aunty Flo remained seated on the piano stool. Her mouth was open and she had a vast amount of evidence still to unfold before her sympathetic guest who was now on his feet and weaving slightly from side to side like a helpless defender still sketching out preventative measures after the ball had reached the back of the net.

'She's not too well,' he said. 'She gets migraine sometimes.'

Aunty Flo's mouth closed and she swallowed with some difficulty.

'I'll just see if she's all right. I shan't be a moment. Excuse me.'

Maxine had already reached the white sports car by the time he got outside. She had left the low wooden gate half open, dragging against the ground on its sagging hinges. She leaned against the car with her back to the house and Peredur was obliged to walk around the car to see her face. He came back and opened the car door and helped her to sit in the driver's seat.

'She's a monster,' Maxine said.

Peredur was embarrassed and placed his body between her indignant face and the view from the bay window of the house.

'That room gave me claustrophobia,' Maxine said.

'It was a bit much.'

Peredur agreed in a subdued voice.

'I could see rows of women just like her barring my way. They were all standing like witches and dragons in front of the palace doors in a fairy tale. And they had

105

no right to be there because they were all dead. She's a spectre from the past, isn't she, sent to haunt you?'

'You are so sensitive,' Peredur said.

It was admiration not criticism.

'Aren't you?' she said. 'Can't you feel it?'

'You'd better stay in the car for a bit,' he said.

'Can't we go?'

'I just can't leave her . . .'

'Well I can. I don't want to breathe the same air as the old horror. I don't want to belong to the same species.'

'She's not all that bad . . .'

'Oh yes she is. And worse. She's spent a lifetime poisoning the air around her.'

'Oh no,' Peredur said. 'She used to give me music lessons.'

He tried and failed to recapture an accurate vision of what that particular experience from the past had really been like so that she could understand. When he spoke all he said was:

'My mother never liked her.'

'How right she was.'

'I think they taught in the same school once . . .'

'Look,' Maxine said. 'I want to go. I'm sick of this game anyway. What sort of a holiday is it for me? I may as well have gone on a package tour of the sewers of Paris.'

She banged the steering wheel with the palm of her hand.

'I'm sorry,' Peredur said. 'I know I've been self-absorbed. But I can't just leave without some word of explanation. She must be looking out of the window now.'

'Let her look.'

'She's old and lonely.'

'Well that's not my fault,' Maxine said. 'I'll give you three minutes.'

She looked at her wrist watch.

'I shan't be long.'

'You'd better not be.'

Peredur hurried back to the house with his finger tips on his lips. He tapped the open door with a nervous knuckle and walked back to the drawing-room which was smelling now of a warm damp. Aunty Flo, having just reached the piano stool, had cradled her hands to demonstrate innocent inactivity and was waiting for a proper explanation.

'I'm sorry,' Peredur said. 'She's not too well. It's a form of claustrophobia.'

'She can't bear being in this house.'

Aunty Flo submitted her conclusion with grim determination and Peredur found it difficult to invent comforting phrases.

'She often gets it in strange places.'

'She's English of course.'

Aunty Flo sounded disapproving.

'That Sylvia's the same. They're as hard as nails. No regard at all for other people's feelings.'

Peredur tried to defend Maxine.

'Oh she's very sensitive,' he said.

'They always are. About their own feelings. No one else's.'

She lifted her handkerchief as if she were about to apply it to her eye. When it was half-way there, she shook her fist and then let her arm fall. Peredur suffered in silence, blushing, but unable to move or speak.

'People are awful,' Aunty Flo said. 'You can't really depend on anybody. That's what you find. When you're old and lonely.'

She looked at Peredur, her eyelids swollen and too heavy to lift.

'I know I'm not wanted,' she said. 'I'm not a fool, you know. I've had some education. The sooner they put me in the incinerator the better they will all like it. My Clem included.'

'Please don't say that . . .'

Peredur was very uncomfortable.

'Why shouldn't I say it?'

Her voice filled with reproach.

'Your mother didn't come to poor Menna's funeral.'

'She was abroad I expect.'

'She didn't even write. Bedwyr sent a note. He was always polite, give him his due. But she didn't bother to put pen to paper. And she must have known. We weren't any use to her anymore.'

'I'm sorry.'

'She made plenty of use of us when she lived in South Marine Terrace. Especially Menna. Menna was always dancing attendance on her.'

She sat on the piano stool brooding over the past. Peredur moved away clasping his hands behind his back.

'Aunty Flo,' he said. 'Can you tell me how my father died?'

His question seemed to revive her spirits. She turned her head so that Peredur should not see her inclination to smile. Her whole body trembled as if conscious of a new surge of power and she steadied it by digging her fists into the upholstery of the piano stool.

'If you are asking my opinion,' she said. 'I'd say they drove him to it.'

'Drove him to what?'

He spoke too sharply and she became subdued and cautious.

'You'd better ask your mother,' she said. 'Why come and ask me? She wouldn't like it if she found out you'd been here to ask me questions about your father, poor man.'

'I wish you'd tell me.'

He was detached and calm.

'We had a great respect for him, you know, Menna and I. Do you remember us acting in *The Kitchen*

108

Captain? That was a lovely play that was. He should have written more plays like that. They would have been very popular. Have you heard they're thinking of putting up some sort of memorial to him?'

'Who?'

Peredur's surprise pleased her.

'Well they are. I know that for a fact ... It's that young chap, you would remember him, he's about your age. He's got on the Council and he's full of ideas. John Artemus. You remember John Artemus? His mother kept the sweet shop opposite the station. He's full of the ideas and they say he's got a lot of influence with the Mayor and I'm surprised he hasn't written to your mother.'

There was a new slyness in her voice.

'I'm surprised you haven't heard about it. Why don't you let me make you a cup of tea and we could have a bit of a chat? It would be nice to go over the old times. I don't see many people and it's my own fault to tell you the truth. I was always one for my independence and now I'm paying the price. The price of my pride you could call it.'

She pushed her plump chins into her chest and enjoyed a prolonged chuckle, but she stopped abruptly when she heard the sports car across the road rev up noisily for a quick start. Peredur rushed to the window. Maxine was being held up by an unexpected procession of cars following a cattle lorry which they could not overtake because of the double white line.

'She's leaving,' he said.

He called out desperately.

'Maxine! She's leaving without me!'

In the gloom of the narrow passage he collided with the umbrella stand. He set it upright and then ran outside shouting. Maxine was determined to get away without him. She shot out in front of an oncoming car which hooted with such insistent anger that people emerged from their houses and peered over their hedges to see what was happening. Aunty Flo remained in the safety of her own doorway, intrigued by what was going on, but not willing to venture too far into a potentially dangerous situation. Peredur grasped the garden gate and shook it on its loose hinges. He was angry and bewildered and yet he did not move. He looked down the road as if he expected to see the white car return at any moment. He could have been trying to make himself believe it was just one of her unexpected jokes. When he turned at last Aunty Flo was still standing pale and nervous in the entrance to her lair.

'I've got a bus time-table,' she said, not wishing to appear unhelpful. 'But I'm afraid it's out of date.'

14

'Who is it up there? Who is it?'

Mrs Clayton the housekeeper stood trembling at the foot of the narrow staircase. She looked up at the broken cobwebs hanging low over the stone stairs and listened apprehensively to the thuds and bangs of furniture or heavy chests being moved in one of the three rooms above the old kitchen. There was no answer to her calling. Resolutely she looked around the long room for a weapon with which to defend herself. A cane brush seemed too light and ineffective and a baker's shovel standing near the wall over too long for her to manage. Near the ancient kitchen range there was a long steel poker. She picked it up and was able to wield it about with sufficient ease to restore her confidence. She limped back to the foot of the staircase with the poker in her right hand and her normal stoop transformed into a shape of aggression. She was a little daunted by the steep rake of the stairs and the nine inch height of each stone step. Angrily she struck the first stone with the steel poker until sparks flew.

'Listen!' she shouted. 'I'm armed! Come down at once.'
She waited to hear some reply.

'I've sent somebody for the policeman,' she said.

It was a warm afternoon and many doors and windows were open. But the Hall was so oppressively silent a dog could be heard panting with thirst in a corridor that led to the south front. A man's footsteps stamped confidently on the bare boards of the middle room above. Mrs Clayton looked around for some support. Her large eyes moved restlessly in her head and she held up the poker so that the man should see it the moment he appeared at the top of the steep staircase.

'What's the matter Mrs Clayton? It's only me.'

Peredur appeared above her with a bundle of books under his arm.

'Oh my goodness . . .'

Connie Clayton lowered the poker and limped back to the long table which had been scrubbed so often that the bleached surface was streaked with cracks and crevices. She leaned on the edge of the table and placed a hand under her breast to feel the beating of her heart.

'Oh you put the wind up me, Mister Peredur! You really did. I worry so much about all these doors being open. But at a time like this I don't want to upset your mother with this that and the other. You know what I mean. It's my duty to relieve her mind as I see it and not to add to her burdens.'

She watched him descend the steep stone stairs, very curious about the bundle under his arm: there were magazines and ledgers in addition to books. Some were mildewed. Mrs Clayton moved closer to Peredur to brush the dust and cobwebs from his coat with her open hand. He suffered her ministrations, looking down at her hand. the knuckles thick with rheumatism.

'My goodness,' she said, 'it's filthy up there. Those rooms need a turn out. but I can't find the time to be honest. The day is too short and there's too much to do. And those Salters you see are quite useless. Work-shy I'd call them.'

Peredur moved out of her reach and she looked at him with deep curiosity.

'I didn't know you were back, Mister Peredur. I thought they had failed to contact you. That's what I was given to understand.'

'They didn't look in the right place. I wasn't far away.'

Mrs Clayton gave such a deep sigh that she shook from head to foot and her black gown trembled around her mis-shaped ankles.

'It's been such a tragedy,' she said. We've been so upset.

She looked around the bare room for somewhere to sit. She moved towards a bench under the window like a ship with a prow cutting through heavy seas. Still cuddling the bundle of books and magazines, Peredur watched her, ready to stand and listen.

'Milly found him.'

Mrs Clayton looked boldly across the room as though she and Peredur shared an interest in the naked truth and a distaste for illusions and inventions.

'He was lying with his face in the nettles and his walking stick beside him. He had fallen flat on his face. He always liked to go for a walk by himself in the afternoons, through the woods towards the old castle. That was his favourite walk. But it was too much for him. He must have been dead before his face touched the ground. There wasn't a mark on him.'

Mrs Clayton's voice was touched with awe as though at that moment in the quiet afternoon she had heard the rustle of the wings of the angle of death. Peredur listened too, aware of a new stillness. The birds in the trees beyond the stables had suddenly stopped singing. The heaviness of midsummer covered the environment like a pall and the two figures in the antiquated kitchen shared a silence which grew into a formal token of respect for the dead man.

'I don't know that it does for a gentleman to be as good as he was,' Mrs Clayton said. 'He was always very put upon. I don't know what would have happened if we hadn't been here to look after him. Those Salters you know, Mister Peredur, they took advantage of him. And I'm sorry to say I suspect that they are dishonest as well.'

She did not seem aware that her words were rapidly destroying the brief unity that had existed between them. Peredur rearranged the bundle of books under his arm.

'I'll be taking these,' he said.

'Aren't you you going to see your mother?'

He did not know how to answer the question.

'Do you want to see my car?' he said. 'I bought it second hand in Pendraw. I gave John Artemus's brother two hundred pounds for it. It's an old Morris. It goes like a watch.'

Mrs Clayton looked at him reproachfully.

'You were in Pendraw,' she said. 'All the time she was asking for you.'

'She didn't ask in the right place,' Peredur said.

Mrs Clayton was shocked.

'It's not my place to speak, but I'm sure she needs you. His Lordship's death has been a terrible blow . . .'

Peredur shifted his bundle and signalled his intention to leave through the door that led into the old laundry.

'Mister Bedwyr is coming up for the funeral,' Mrs Clayton said. 'But Mister Gwydion isn't coming.'

'I'll just put these in the back of the car,' Peredur said.

'That's what I was saying to myself when you were coming down those steps. I was saying to myself, thank goodness Mister Peredur is here. Somebody you can rely on.'

He was touched by her faltering attempt to pay him a compliment.

'You see that Frank Huskie's here,' Mrs Clayton said. As large as life and twice as natural. Milly got out of hand and May sent for Frank. That was the excuse anyway. But I tell you what I think, Mister Peredur, they've seen a chance and they want to take it. I'll say no more than that.

Her resentment seemed to shrink her into a small black figure sitting alone on the bench set against a long bare wall. She could have been a pensioned warder still living in an empty prison. Peredur moved his head about in an effort to break the contact between them.

'I must go,' he said.

Mrs Clayton looked up with a horrified expression on her white face.

'You're not going without seeing your mother,' she said.

He lifted his shoulders and hurried towards the door. As he crossed the stable yard an excited voice called out after him. The first time it was a shout, the second time more ordered and subdued. May Huskie ran after him and caught him up before he reached his newly acquired car.

'I said it was you. I recognized your walk. I didn't know the car of course. but I recognized you. Your mother wants to see you.'

She blinked her eyelashes at him amiably, a slight smile on her face which seemed to anticipate the inherently comic or ridiculous element in any reply he would make. She looked pleased and filled with a new confidence like a police officer enjoying the first day on duty after a promotion. Peredur turned the chrome handle on the boot of his car. Inside there was cardboard box into which he placed the books and magazines he had been carrying. Miss

114

Huskie watched him with a detached interest, bending closer to take some note of the material he was preparing to carry away.

'She's in the Oak Room,' Miss Huskie said. It's been a shock to her you know. She's taking it rather badly. They were such friends after all. They understood each other.'

She was impressed by the wisdom and moderation of her own words. Peredur took a short cut between the azalea bushes and appeared without warning outside the window where his mother was sitting contemplating the view with a melancholy stillness. She could have been absorbing the consolations of the view. She made no sign of having seen him. Her hair was neatly arranged and in her high-backed chair, upholstered in pale blue she looked regal as well as thoughtful. Peredur hurried across her line of vision with his head bowed a little guiltily. With uncharacteristic forethought he scraped his shoes on the iron scraper alongside the open door. There was a large dog panting in the shadows looking for some new human master to whom he could attach himself in a household dominated by females. Peredur raised his arm until his elbow was across his face and hurried towards the L-shaped Oak Room.

Near the door Milly was sitting with her plump little hand held by her brother Frank Huskie. She had calmed down but still sniffed occasionally. She gave Peredur a look of sustained reproach as though in some way she held him responsible for the terrible experience she had suffered. Frank Huskie, like all his family, was infinitely patient with his sister. He was dividing his attention between Milly's emotional condition and the armchair by the window where Lady Brangor sat alone with her grief. When he saw Peredur, he winked at him familiarly and mimed his craving for a cigarette. Near the empty fireplace, the arthritic countess sat in an upright chair, nursing her hands and worrying about her friend who stared with

115

such trance-like intensity through the garden window. Amy, Lady Brangor, seemed intent on the cool behaviour of the two swans floating around the deep foliage of the bushes in the centre of their small lake. Miss Huskie appeared behind Peredur obliging him to move further into the room. She studied Milly's condition and spoke to Frank about it in a hoarse whisper which was also a token of respect for Lady Brangor's bereavement.

'She looks much better,' she said.

Frank agreed. Their accents and sounds matched. Both spoke in a jerky adenoidal fashion, their voices still marked by a deep similarity: the cadences of a family existing as a closely knit unit over a long period in alien surroundings.

'I think she'd like a ride now,' Miss Huskie said. 'Would you like a ride, Milly? Would you like Frank to take you for your favourite ride?'

They waited with patient eagerness for reaction. When she nodded, Frank rose to his feet. He was wearing a brown tweed suit of the same material as his sister's. His dark hair was oiled and brushed back with precise care. He wore a thin moustache that could have been intended to underline his good looks but in reality made him look less trustworthy than his sister. With gentle care he helped Milly to her feet. She clung to his arm and Miss Huskie watched them leave with tender regard.

'She thinks the world of Frank,' she said. 'She really does.'

She pushed Peredur's arm and led him down the room towards his mother. Peredur withdrew his arm from her reach but submitted to her directions as though it relieved him of an initiative that he had been reluctant to take.

'Well look who's here,' Miss Huskie said in her most cheerful voice. 'Look who's turned up.'

He seemed suspicious of his mother's uncharacteristic stillness. Her face was worn and aged and her eyes when she lifted her head to look at him were glaucous in the

116

heavy light from the window, and her flat forehead was furrowed with close horizontal lines. She turned her wrist on the arm of the chair and opened her hand inviting him to put his hand in hers. When he did so she gripped his hand tightly and the rings on her fingers pressed cold and hard into his skin.

'I knew you'd come.'

She drew strength from holding his hand. Her lips began to move in a way that made him uneasy and his body was tense with the effort of not pulling his hand away.

'We have to face these things,' she said, still drawing on their new intimacy. 'That's always been difficult for me. I never could face things.'

She looked in his face for some appreciation of her frank confession and he stood rigidly in his awkward position like a conscript soldier on parade for the first time.

'Take me to him.'

She stood on her feet with a determined display of self-discipline, still holding Peredur's hand tightly. The countess, sitting by the fireplace, was alarmed by her movement. With some effort she raised a restraining hand and her action caused her pain. She bent her head and shut her eyes. Lady Brangor stopped to ask Miss Huskie about his sister Milly.

'Is Milly better now?'

She was being consciously selfless. Miss Huskie nodded gratefully.

'Oh she's much better,' she said. 'Frank's with her. She loves being with Frank. He's taking her for a little ride around the park.'

Lady Brangor nodded approvingly. She stood still for a moment at the bottom of the wide staircase. Then she released Peredur's hand and with a firm step, her toes pointing slightly outwards like a dancer's, she mounted the stairs. From the open doorway of the oak room Miss Huskie watched her friend and patron with admiration, feeling in the pocket of her tweed jacket for a packet of cigarettes.

Peredur had no choice but to follow his mother. Each step she took became firmer in a pattern of resolution. She passed down a darkened corridor, her steps muffled by the patterned carpet running down the centre. She reached a bedroom door. Her hand was on the glass doorknob. She waited for Peredur to reach her side. She looked down at her own hand.

'We weren't able to shut his mouth.'

She gave him time to say something but he pressed his lips together. They went inside.

The pale blinds were drawn and the long narrow room was bathed in a milky light. The heavy floral pattern on the wallpaper had taken on the movements of green tendrils under water. The open coffin lay on the single bed which was draped in a purple cover. The white satin interior of the coffin glowed brightly in the subdued atmosphere. Lady Brangor lifted her hand to place it on her son's shoulder but he moved closer to the bed before she could touch him. The corpse lay in a white dressing-gown with the bright cord neatly tied and tasselled. It was made of a material to match the trimming of the three empty pockets. Although his eyes were closed and his dentures were in place the dead man's mouth was stretched wide open in a frozen cry of protest or surprise. Peredur forced himself to stand still and contemplate the corpse; his fists were clenched tight and small inside the sleeves of his jacket which appeared a size too large for him. His mother moved quietly to the window, holding back the blind with one hand to look at the world outside.

'We understood each other,' she said.

She was ready and anxious to talk to her son.

'He understood me better than any other man I've known.'

She waited to hear some expression of the sympathy she needed.

118

'This has really broken me. I knew he was old and ill. But he had such a gentle soul. It's awful to think I shall never talk to him again.'

Peredur became alarmed that his mother would break down and need comforting. He looked around desperately for an escape.

'Why have you put him in here?'

'This was the room he liked best,' Lady Brangor said. 'It used to be part of the nursery. Where he slept when he was a child. His grandmother changed the chapel into a music room and he never liked it he told me, even when he was a boy. He was always deeply religious. These last few years we got to know each other so well. We were so close. I wish you had known him better, Peredur.'

'Why didn't you marry him?'

He muttered the question with a bitter sharpness before he could stop himself. She walked past him and opened the door.

'I can answer that,' she said, 'I can answer anything you want to ask me.'

He stood in the corridor, his head hanging, a picture of regret after his brief outburst. His mother assumed a new dignity.

'Come to my bedroom,' she said. 'I want to talk to you.'

He followed her. In her bedroom too the blinds were drawn down but here the room was suffused with a pink haze. There was a smell of eau-de-cologne and although Lady Brangor never appeared heavily made up, her dressing-table was loaded with creams, powders, and expensive preparations. There was a pale pink canopy over her bed, chinese prints of birds on delicate branches on the walls, and everywhere efforts at decoration that Peredur obviously found distasteful.

'Please sit down.'

He sat in the chair nearest the door. His mother sat on the stool of her dressing table.

'It's not my fault if I survive. Sometimes that's harder than dying. For the last three days I've been feeling like an insect trapped in a bottle. That's the only way I can describe it. I felt it coming even before Hubert died. He could have helped me. I'm sure he could have helped me.'

Peredur sat looking at his hands prepared to listen as long as she was prepared to go on talking. She looked at him and saw challenge and silent criticism and nothing of what she wanted.

'We had no idea where you were,' she said. 'And where's Maxine? Has she gone? I thought she would have come to say goodbye before leaving so I just assumed you'd gone off somewhere for a trip in that white car of hers.'

'It wasn't hers,' Peredur said.

He sounded relieved to be able to contradict something.

'Where is she?'

'She's gone. She just left me.'

'Left you?'

She studied her son's face. He looked blackly miserable. She made a gesture of despair with her right hand.

'She seemed such a bright girl. I really thought you'd found someone to suit you. I know you like people to be intelligent.'

She reached out a hand towards Peredur. He refrained from looking up so as not to be caught seeing it.

'You mustn't seal yourself up,' she said. 'Because you've been hurt. I'm hurt in my own way. Bitterly hurt. But I'm not going to seal myself up. I'm alive still things I would like to achieve. I'm not old. Not really old. There are many things I can do. We must help each other.'

Peredur made no response.

'I know I've not been a wonderful mother. I know I've been selfish sometimes even though I never meant to be. There must be something wrong with me. I know that. I can't make my own sons like me. But I'm still willing to try. I really am. That's something surely. Hubert always said that was one of the things that made me so attractive.'

120

Peredur glared at her.

'I don't mean in many physical sense. There was nothing like that between us. Our relationship was really spiritual and that was what made it so precious.'

She made a fresh effort to reach him.

'I know you are a dedicated scholar Peredur and admire that so much. I can't tell you how much I admire it. Now look, why don't you come and live here? Not with me. I know I'd get on your nerves. I'd live in *Y Nyth* – up in the trees! But you could have all this place if you wanted it and turn it into a research centre. All of it. Hubert has left me more money. What do I want with money? You could have that as well.'

He began to shake his head.

'It's sociology now, isn't it? Quite right too. A research centre. These old country houses have got to be put to new uses. Hubert agreed with that. You could call it the Hubert Pughe Centre perhaps. He was a sociologist, wasn't he, in his own way? But that wouldn't matter. He was a wonderfully modest man. Put it to good use. That's what I mean, Peredur. It doesn't matter about me . . . What have I done that you should dislike me so much?'

He stopped shaking his head.

'I don't dislike you,' he said. 'It's just that I don't like being emotional.'

Lady Brangor decided to accept the excuse.

'You can't go through life being afraid of emotion,' she said.

'I'm sorry,' he said.

'You are not cruel.'

She stood up ready to leave.

'Sometimes I think Gwydion is cruel. He deliberately tries to hurt me. He wasn't very nice to Hubert either. He used to make fun of him every chance he got. He could be quite cruel. At least you sometimes try to do what I want.'

Peredur lowered his head.

'I want you to criticize me. There you are. That's an open invitation. I say the same to Bedwyr and he does it. But he does it very gently. And he's not my son at all really. Perhaps that makes it easier. I wish you'd say some of the things that are on your mind. It can't be good for you, all that brooding.'

'I couldn't have a research centre here,' Peredur said. 'I need an urban area.'

He swallowed as he tried to sketch out words that would be a more accurate and less grudging expression of his gratitude.

'Let's go down.'

Her sign was an admission that once again she had failed to get closer to her youngest son. But Peredur was unwilling to move. He had something he was determined to say.

'Why are you against my father having a Memorial?'

She was clearly puzzled at first, unable to grasp what exactly he was talking about.

'Memorial? Oh you mean that silly idea about Cilydd's Rock?'

She seemed very surprised that he should know about it.

'Why is it silly?'

'Very vulgar and ridiculous. I'm quite sure it's the last thing your father would have wanted. He was a very fastidious man.'

'Is that why he hasn't got a gravestone?'

Peredur stood up to face his mother, unable to conceal his hostility any longer.

'What are you talking about?'

'I couldn't find his grave. I don't know where he's buried.'

Peredur's voice was petulant and childish and he seemed aware of the fact but unable to control it.

He was moving about the bedroom consciously trying to simulate the actions of some distant childish
ritual. By the dressing-table he glared at the ar-
ray of bottles as though he could barely restrain
himself from reaching out his arm and sweeping
them all to the floor. Lady Brangor shook her head
sadly.

'You just want to hurt me,' she said. 'That's all.'

'I don't.'

Peredur thrust down his fist in a strenuous denial.

'I don't at all. I just want to know the truth. Tell me the
truth. That's all I'm asking.'

She sighed deeply.

'Oh I will. Whatever you want to know. After the
funeral.'

Her voice was quiet but completely authoritative.
She indicated that it was necessary for her to return
downstairs.

'We have to keep things going,' she said. 'However sad
the occasion.'

'Why can't tell me now?'

Peredur was dissatisfied.

'Can't you see why?'

Her superior calm infuriated him.

'You've not known this man ten years. And yet you are
arranging his funeral as if he were your husband, as if
you'd lived with him all your life, as if he were some
king or royalty. He was just the last of a pretty useless
line of petty squires who happen to have acquired a title
. . .'

'Peredur!'

Her voice was full of warning.

'Do you expect me to go about in sackcloth and ashes or
something?'

'You are being so childish.'

'That's all right for your miscellaneous band of hangers-
on, but if you think I'm going to take a leading part in such

123

a pantomime you are quite mistaken. I'm not one of the Huskies, you know.'

'Peredur . . .'

He marched out into the corridor flushed with an excitement that could easily have been mistaken for a flush of victory.

'Peredur! Where are you going?'

He stopped on the stairs to shout up at her.

'Anywhere! Out of this antiquated . . . phoney set-up!'

BOOK TWO

1

Bedwyr unbuttoned his shirt in order to scratch his chest. The door of his office was open and he looked at it resentfully as though the noise from the drawing office just down the corridor was distracting his train of thought. He took out a packet of peppermints from a drawer in his desk, popped one in his mouth and rolled it around on the pointed tip of his tongue. He swung about in his black leather chair, turning his back on the flat expanse of his neat desk so that it would not distract him from the problem upon which he wanted to concentrate. On the wall in the recess he was now facing hung a bold abstract oil-painting and on the walls to the left and the right were blown up photographs of some of the firm's prize-winning designs: two schools, a recreation centre, a mineral water factory, and an old people's home.

As if to help himself think he walked over to the window. Unappetizing fruit hung on the cherished peartree in the small area of green carefully preserved after the office expansion. The fibrous looking narrow pears seemed satisfactory objects for contemplation. Bedwyr began to pull at his black beard. He was losing his hair and the pallor of his brow made his large brooding brown eyes more conspicuous. Buttoning up his shirt he moved back to his desk and pressed a key on the office intercom system.

'Keith!'

He did not raise his voice.

'Yes Bedwyr.'

There was an immediate reply.

'Could you spare me a few minutes?'

'Now?'

The talk-back key clicked impatiently.

'If you would. It's rather important.'

Bedwyr turned to look at a scale model in balsa-wood that stretched over most of the working surface of the inside wall of his office. It was a redevelopment plan for the derelict end of an industrial valley town. He switched on a display light, appeared to take some mild satisfaction from what he saw, and abruptly switched the light off again. He moved quickly back to his chair, put the palms of his hands on the desk and surveyed the few papers that were in sight to satisfy himself perhaps that none were too confidential, and then closed the thick appointments book and pushed it to the left side of the desk.

The young man lingered by the door. He was carefully dressed, equally proud of his wavy fair hair and his smart suit, on the verge of being a dandy, but too uncertain of himself or of his origins to carry the role with the necessary degree of flamboyance. His lips were drawn in with nervous suspicion and at intervals his eyelids fluttered with a strange rapidity.

'Shut the door, Keith, will you? I can't hear myself think.'

Keith shut the door with obedient care. His fingers held on to the chrome door knob longer than seemed necessary and he did not move from the shadowed space between the working surface and the door.

'We've got to be frank about this,' Bedwyr said. 'Or we'll be wasting our time. Come and sit down for God's sake.'

There were three black leather chairs set against the wall and Keith sat in the chair nearest to the door. He clasped his elbows in his hands and waited for Bedwyr to speak.

'God knows,' Bedwyr said, giving a very deep sigh. 'I don't want to have to start going in for psycho-sessions or business brainwashing. But it's my unpleasant duty as the functioning senior partner of this firm to tell you that you have boobed pretty badly.'

Keith began to blush. Bedwyr watched him closely, maintaining a deliberate silence and searching the other man's face with such a steady gaze that a purple tide of resentment spread all over his narrow face and even his eyes seemed to change colour.

'You are saying that I'm not doing my job properly?'

Keith's voice was choking so much with wounded pride, he could not trust himself to utter more than a hastily contrived defensive question.

'You are perfectly entitled to lose your temper if you feel like it, Keith. And you can say whatever you like to me. I don't mind. But you will appreciate that I have a deep sense of responsibility to the practice and if I don't speak with complete and utter frankness, I'm not doing my job properly. So you don't expect me to go pussy-footing around out of respect for your feelings. Right?'

'You can say what you like.'

Keith spoke sulkily.

'You can be sure I shall. And I'll begin with an accusation. You left that woman alone in your office for at least four minutes. Possibly longer. She shouldn't have been there in the first place. But she buttered you up and you couldn't resist it. She played on your vanity and you let her in. That was bad enough.'

'What do you mean "bad"?'

'You knew she was a freelance journalist.'

'I suppose I did . . .'

'Either you did or you didn't. I'm saying you did. What is worrying me, Keith, is whether you also knew she was the girl-friend of a friend of the alderman who is one of the leading opponents of the scheme?'

'Of course I didn't know.'

Keith straightened his neck, righteously indignant on his own behalf.

'Well that happens to be true and we'll all have to pay for it.'

'How could I have known . . .?'

'How indeed.'

Bedwyr leaned forward.

'You can call it ignorance or innocence. I am now going to call it an unhappy combination of immaturity and personal vanity.'

'You just want to enjoy the chance of insulting me. You always enjoy insulting me . . .'

'Do I?'

'I don't see that all that much harm was done.'

'Don't you?'

Bedwyr embarked on one of his long silent stares. Keith became desperately anxious to justify himself.

'It's a good plan,' he said. 'It's original. Brand-new in this part of the world anyway. Sooner or later it had to be made public . . .'

'Ah!'

Bedwyr interrupted so suddenly Keith was startled into stammering.

'What do you mean "ah"?'

'You couldn't wait,' Bedwyr said. 'Was that it?'

Keith hurriedly tried to change course.

'She couldn't have had time to photograph it. Lewis came in.'

'I know he came in and I wish to God he had come in four minutes earlier. She was a smart girl. She memorized the elevations. And she drew some sketches on an envelope. And she shot down to the graphic department of the College of Art and got somebody there to knock her out a few drawings . . .'

'How do you know all this?'

'I'm thorough,' Bedwyr said. 'When I find things out, I find things out.'

'They couldn't have been accurate,' Keith said.

'Accurate be damned.'

Bedwyr was overcome by a surge of anger that he could not control.

'What you don't seem to realize my friend is that I had given my solemn word to the Mayor and the Town Clerk that these plans would not be made public or shown to anybody outside this office until I personally unsealed them in the presence of the Developments sub-committee. Now it's not just my word. It's the word of Morgan, More and Partners. I don't think you've realized yet just what you've done.'

'They were my designs,' Keith said. 'Most of them anyway.'

He sounded stubborn and unrepentant. Bedwyr breathed deeply to preserve his patience and when the telephone bell gave its brief buzz he reached out to pick up the receiver without taking his eyes off Keith's face.

'It's Mrs More on the line,' the switchboard operator said, 'I'm sorry to disturb you.'

'Put her through.'

Bedwyr automatically pulled his appointment book within reach, opened it and picked up a pencil.

'Darling,' his wife said. 'I'm sorry to disturb you. You couldn't come home early today could you?'

'Sian . . .'

He whispered her name like a soft warning.

'I know you're busy, but this brother of yours is driving me up the wall!'

Bedwyr smiled to cover any embarrassment that would be caused by the other man in the room overhearing Sian's loud despairing call.

'He's been under a bit of a strain . . .'

He spoke soothingly.

'So have I. He's been here for the best part of a week, sleeping in the guest-room like visiting royalty, sending back eggs to be boiled harder and paying absolutely no attention to me or the children!'

'I'll come home as early as I possibly can.'

The indignation in her youthful voice made him smile and the smile grew out of his stern mouth with an unexpected winning brilliance.

'I promise.'

She had more that she wanted to say.

'He had the nerve to complain to me this afternoon that he had been here nearly a week and still hadn't had a proper chance to talk to you. You know what "proper chance" means of course. A chance to get you all to himself. Away from your encumbrances . . .'

As she went on speaking his smile slowly faded.

'Sian,' he said sharply. 'I have someone with me. I'll ring you back.'

'You just come home early,' she said, 'that's all I ask.'

There was a reckless note in her voice and she plunged on with her complaints regardless of his displeasure. He sighed so that she would hear him.

'All right,' he said. 'All right. I'll be home early. I promise.'

He put down the phone with great care and pencilled a faint note in his appointments book before swivelling his chair once more in Keith's direction. Keith was relaxed now and smiling quietly, diverted by audible clues of family matters. Bedwyr made a solemn but silent recapitulation of the position and without speaking he gave the younger man to understand that he had allowed no detail of the case to escape during the telephone conversation.

'They were your designs.'

He spoke at last.

'Of course they were.'

Keith was more confident now than he had been earlier in the interview.

'And you were very proud of them?'

'I had no reason not to be. You know that.'

'And you were worried that I wouldn't take you along to the Developments sub-committee?'

'No I wasn't.'

Bedwyr was not convinced by the denial.

'You thought that you wouldn't get your proper share of the credit for your brilliant work. You didn't trust me to give you the full credit. So you let that bitch in there on purpose!'

Bedwyr did not raise his voice. He kept it very soft but with an edge of contempt that was beginning to make Keith look unhappy. He continued thoughtfully.

'She was sitting out there, in the waiting area, hoping for some kind of an interview. There she sat.'

'I'd only once seen her before in my life,' Keith said, snatching at a straw. 'I never asked her to come . . .'

'She's not a woman to wait for an invite. She didn't have an appointment. Nobody wanted to see her. I didn't. Lewis didn't. Warren didn't. We all knew her too damned well. And we all made use of the office rule. Interviews of any kind by appointment only with the approval of one or both of the senior partners. A good rule and a wise rule and you deliberately broke it.'

'It's not a rule in any legal sense . . .'

'We've had trouble with that woman before. And we left her waiting there on purpose while we tried to dream up something that would put her right off the scent.'

'How was I to know?'

'By asking. You've got to be fairly circumspect with a bird like that. You mustn't let her see you hate her guts and you mustn't just chuck her out or she'd have every excuse to start on one of her little vendettas. And we can't afford to have journalists, not even part-time journalists, conducting a vendetta against this firm at this crucial stage in its development. And that was why she was sitting there looking at back numbers of smart architectural magazines when you happened along with your nose peering over the glass partition. Ready to keep in touch. And I expect she gave you a girlish little wave, did she? And you probably waved back. A few minutes later with your eager little brain ticking away at twice its normal speed you pass that way again. Quite by chance. And this time you stop for a chat. Because your beating heart has told you that this could be a wonderful opportunity to get some personal publicity. And because you are already sweaty with suspicion that B.T. More of Morgan, More and Partners is all set to steal the honour and glory that rightfully belongs to you and you alone. I hope you don't find that I'm being too fanciful?'

'You are deliberately trying to put the whole thing in the worst possible light.'

'Well I'm glad you should say that. That's a start anyway in the right direction.'

'You are not trying to see my side of it. You're not trying to see my side of it at all.'

Bedwyr leaned back in his chair.

'Your side,' he said.

'I've had to struggle', Keith said. 'Every inch of the way I've had to struggle. You know that.'

'I know that. And I admire you for it. I've said so before. Now you tell me what that's got to do with it.'

Keith struggled for the right words to use in his own defence.

132

'There are people in this firm who don't pull their weight.'

Bedwyr was playing with his ivory paper-knife. With a little smile he turned it to point at himself and then raised his eyebrows interrogatively.

'No, of course not,' Keith said. 'You know who I mean. I mean people who take out a damn sight more than they put in.'

Keith looked defiant. He was on firmer ground.

'And this state of affairs made you invite that woman into your office?'

Bedwyr's style was smooth, slow, deliberate. By long practice he had made his voice pleasant to listen to, in order to deal with employees restive for quick promotion, with brash and ignorant councillors and with irritable clients. His manner had become considered to the point of being pompous in order to give an overall impression of rational responsibility and remorseless logic.

'I'm not saying that.'

'Then what are you saying?'

'I work hard,' Keith said. 'I work as hard as anybody in this office. I'm not much good at public relations because that's not been my responsibility.'

'You are a good designer,' Bedwyr said. 'And we appreciate that to the full. Unfortunately you know as well as I do that in a practice of this size good office management, admin, the handling of clients, committee work, public speaking, common sense and good judgement are just as important as the ability to design a good building.'

'I know that!'

Keith burst out in protest.

'You do? I'm glad to hear it.'

'I'm kept out of all that because I'm not classy enough. Because of my working-class origins.'

'If you believe that,' Bedwyr said. 'You'll believe

133

anything.'

'I can't find the capital to buy myself a full partnership.'

'That's taken care of,' Bedwyr said. 'And you know it. It's just going to take that little bit longer. But it's the little bit longer I suspect that you can't stand. Is that why you let that woman loose in your office?'

'I never let her loose in my office.'

'Didn't you? Then how did she find the plans so quickly? Did you just happen to leave the right drawer in your drawing cabinet open? How did she know where to look?'

Keith was defeated but still angry.

'What do you want me to do?' he said. 'Go on my knees or something.'

'That wouldn't be a bad idea,' Bedwyr said. 'By way of a start.'

The telephone buzzed quietly and Bedwyr picked it up.

'Mr Eslit for you,' the switchboard operator said.

'Warren?'

Bedwyr's voice was quiet and guarded. His partner sounded loud and confident.

'I saw Trevor this afternoon. He had Philips with him. He's definitely interested.'

'Look, Warren, I've got Keith with me. We're going over the Nant Development Scheme. Can I ring you back?'

'That piddling thing. I don't know why you bother. Could I come over this evening? This looks big, you know. Really big.'

'We've got my brother staying with me. Peredur.'

'The silent genius . . .'

Warren chuckled confidently, still under the influence of a good lunch.

'Okay. I'm not fussed. Just give me a buzz as soon as you can. This could be it, partner.'

Keith was adjusting the length of blue cuffs visible below the sleeves of his jacket. He looked rather satisfied with himself. Bedwyr watched him with a degree of objectivity as he replaced the receiver.

'Warren thinks the Nant Development Scheme is a piddling thing. I quote.'

Keith's chin went in and out.

'Well that's a matter of opinion,' he said.

'Warren is getting tired of architecture,' Bedwyr said. 'Did you know that?'

'No,' Keith said uneasily.

'And what you have done rather makes me sympathize with his point of view.'

'I don't see that.'

'Of course you don't. And that's what is worrying me. It's just as well for you to know this. We are being courted by one of the fastest growing Developers in this part of the country. We are being tempted with very big offers. I'm holding out – and you've got to keep this under your hat absolutely – because I still hope it will be possible to arrange this practice to give me a little bit more freedom to be what I started out to be – a man who designs good buildings. I can't do that if I haven't got people working with me that I can trust. Is that understood?'

Keith nodded, worried into some sort of submission.

'I was talking about possibilities and probabilities. Now I'm talking about facts. It's always the devil of a job establishing the facts. All I know is a certain woman came into this building, managed to worm her way into your office and went out with a load of information to use against us in certain quarters, including a newspaper office.'

Keith licked his lips nervously.

'A journalist who works there tipped me off. Let me tell you that I have wasted most of this working day going down to the offices of the newspaper and begging and pleading with the Managing Editor and the Editor not to publish that snooping woman's picture and story until the day after the Developments sub-committee meeting. I was obliged to promise them an exclusive release on the damned thing and that means bad feeling with the local papers that come out on that very same day . . . what the hell are you smiling about?'

Keith made a gesture with his long fingers that suggested that the whole trouble was rapidly dissolving into thin air.

'It looks as if it's going to be all right,' he said.

This seemed to annoy Bedwyr so much he almost tipped himself out of his chair and slapped his palm down on the desk to save himself.

'No it bloody well isn't,' he said. 'It's all wrong. This isn't the way to run a railway, it isn't the way to run an office and it isn't the way to run a practice and I'd like you to understand that. Now the question is, *do* you?'

His head was lowered and his aggressive gaze was fixed unblinkingly on Keith's face. He held this stare until Keith spoke and his lips were tightly shut while he waited.

'I'm sorry,' Keith said at last.

Bedwyr nodded approvingly in slow motion before he spoke.

'So am I,' he said. 'The one good result out of this little mess could be that you and I understand each other better.'

Keith stood up. The interview appeared to be at an end. He waited as if he were expecting Bedwyr to make some more elaborate demonstration of reconciliation. A handshake perhaps or some friendly remark at least, or a parting joke. But Bedwyr did nothing and said nothing. He seemed restrained by some integrity or scruple that would not allow him to display signs of friendliness or affection that he did not genuinely feel. And the clear implication was that Keith was still on probation with a series of further tests to pass before he was received into the senior partner's close confidence. He left the room with his narrow walk passing through the door without opening it wide and closing it behind him without saying another word.

2

Peredur sat in the corner of the long settee watching a children's programme on television, but lost in his own thoughts. The stare he gave the television set seemed hostile and critical because he was frowning a little. His strong white teeth protruded slightly and since his lips were parted this created the impression of a sneer. There was a copy of the *Manchester Guardian* scattered on the hearth rug near his feet. From time to time he examined his spatulated finger nails and glanced at his wrist watch. When his sister-in-law appeared on the further side of the glass door carrying a plump tired baby girl he stiffened in his seat against the impact of the intrusion. Sian was a strong handsome girl in her late twenties. A well-to-do mother determined to bring up her own children without being encumbered by au-pair girls. The other two stood behind her now, Nia, the restless little girl aged four, and her brother David who seemed a solemn small replica of his father, always conscious of his responsibilities and approaching his seventh birthday as though it were a time for taking priestly vows. Sian opened the door and they advanced into the room.

'I'm sorry to disturb you, Peredur, but the children want to watch television while I give Christina a bath,' Sian said.

She was clearly a young woman who attached importance to frankness and sincerity. She tried hard to stop herself staring reproachfully at the newspaper spread messily over the floor. The effect on Peredur was to immobilize him in the corner of the settee that he occupied. He seemed to shrink inside himself and his lips covered up his teeth as if to hide them from her. Sian's voice was a little boisterous. She spoke habitually in ringing tones and the way she spoke now suggested she had settled on a formula that allowed her to exercise complete authority in her own home while at the same time conforming to her own notions of hospitality and how it should be exercised towards a guest who was also a member of her husband's family.

'This isn't the one they usually watch,' Sian said. 'Do you mind if we turn?'

'Of course I don't,' Peredur said. 'You don't think I'm watching it do you?'

His nervousness made him hiss defensively, not unlike the noise a gander would make on a remote upland farm to repel a cheerful human intruder into his territory. Nia rolled on to the other end of the settee. She was inclined to suck her fingers and she turned to look at her uncle with a fine balance of amusement and apprehension. David sat correctly in a chair six feet away from the screen which was his customary position. Still holding the baby Christina, Sian swung down with an athletic ease to turn the knob at the side of the set to get another channel.

'It's such a rotten picture,' she said. 'I could draw the blinds I suppose. But it seems such an awful thing having them sitting in here in semi-darkness while the sun is still shining outside.'

Peredur cleared his throat with an odd double cough which was characteristic of him. He was about to make an effort to be conversational.

'I thought you said he was coming home early tonight.'

'Well, it is still early.'

Sian was quick to defend her husband. Peredur made yet another glance at his wrist-watch.

'Well I wouldn't call this early,' he said. 'It's nearly ten to six.'

'Well that is early for Bedwyr,' she said. 'Most evenings he isn't home until eight or nine. You've no idea how hard he works.'

Peredur showed his teeth. They slipped into view so easily it could hardly be counted as a smile and there was no means of telling whether it registered approval or contempt of his brother's hardworking habits.

'I shall have to go back to Redbatch tomorrow.'

Sian attended to the baby's vest which was hanging out above her woollen trousers. There was no point in what she was doing except to conceal the expression of satisfaction on her healthy face. She used no make-up and her long fair hair was swept up and held in place by combs revealing the clean line of her determined jaw and her small ear, pale in the controlled warmth of the interior of the modernized smallholding, and moulded close to her head with the fine convolutions of a delicate sea shell.

'There's no need for you to go,' Sian said. 'You can have your room as long as you like.'

She spoke with honesty and sincerity, but without warmth, and what she said must have suggested to him that having said it she would keep her word if only out of a sense of duty towards her husband's brother. She moved a few feet away from the set so that Christina could make out what was taking place on the screen.

139

For a while they all gave their attention to the coy behaviour and jerky movements of the soft toys on the screen. Nia became so deeply involved that she removed her fingers from her mouth and held them out gleaming with saliva towards her favourite, a woolly lamb, that gave out musical bleats. With the dexterity of a conjuror, Sian produced a paper handkerchief and gave the wet fingers a quick wipe without interrupting her daughter's viewing. She sank for a few moments rest on to the edge of a chair while Christina smiled contentedly at the pranks going on among the puppets.

Peredur had stopped watching the screen. He gave his attention to his sister-in-law and her children. He studied them with open interest as though he wished to memorize details of his visit to his brother's home. This was Bedwyr's family: his wife and his three children, and for a while he marvelled openly at their harmonious existence inside the elegant but comfortable domestic interior which was yet another reflection of his brother's personality. Sian moved her head and caught something of the mood of contemplation that possessed him. Now that she had been given a glimpse of the nature of his thoughts he was no longer inclined as he had been previously to conceal them. He glanced openly at his wrist-watch, aware that she was looking at him. The television programme absorbed the full attention of the children. He could say what was on his mind.

'Do you think he knows that he was baptized on his mother's coffin?'

Instinctively Sian clutched her baby closer to her breast. She looked upon Peredur as a creature who never ceased to bewilder her. David became instantly aware of his mother's unease. He turned his attention from the merry puppets on the screen to the more tangible presence of his uncle; a stranger wedging

himself against the end of the long settee, who made
no attempt to smile at children or invite affection from
anyone and yet could never be ignored.

'Bedwyr?'

Sian rose to her feet and murmured his name trying
to imply that she was not anxious to investigate such
a mystery too deeply in the hearing of the children,
particularly her sensitive eldest son who at that moment was so obviously listening. Peredur showed no
inclination to take notice of her unspoken signals.

'It's amazing the things you find out,' he said. 'Once
you start asking questions. Mostly irrelevant things.
Never the answers you are really looking for. But always interesting.'

She stood still. He had chosen to talk at an awkward
time, but at least he was talking.

'Do you think I should tell him?'

Peredur held his head back so that he could make a
special effort to read her face. He had asked a searching
question and he was now entitled to an answer.

'It could account for a lot, you know.'

He sounded as though he were taking her into his
professional confidence.

'What do you mean?'

She already resented the way he was presuming to
judge Bedwyr's character and assuming that she was
willing to take a seat alongside him on the judicial
bench.

'This anxiety he has, to be correct. To observe the
conventions. To do the right thing.'

'Well my goodness,' Sian said. 'What's wrong with
that?'

She shifted the baby to one side so that her question
could be more direct and challenging. His attitude,
displayed at that moment and in that very place, in
the heart of his brother's home, seemed objective to
the point of being hostile.

'I'm not saying there is anything wrong with it.'

He seemed mildly pleased at the effect his words were making on her.

'All I'm saying is that it might account for it.'

Sian took a lighter tone because David was listening intently and even Nia's attention had been stolen from the screen by the animated voices. Nia glanced back at the flicking light from time to time in case something should happen while she wasn't watching, and, lifting her wrist, thrust her fingers what appeared to be an alarming distant down her throat. Her lower eyelids were almost pulled down inside out by the pressure.

'It's a bit late in the day now to do anything about it,' Sian said. It all happened thirty-eight years ago.

'And obviously it explains why he attaches so much importance to all this.'

Peredur gave an abbreviated but imperial flourish of his pale hand to indicate the contents of the house, the children and the domestic felicity of a small farmhouse converted into a modern home and surrounded by an acre of garden not more than three minutes' walk from the centre of the Edwardian seaside town where they lived, within easy reach of Bedwyr's office in the city. The 'all this' made Sian bristle.

'You don't have to be baptized on your mother's coffin to enjoy being married,' she said. 'Now I must give Christina her bath.'

She hoisted Christina from her hip so that the child could put both its arms around her neck and she marched determinedly down the corridor to the downstairs bathroom which had been installed into what once had been a dairy. Here on the bath were the plastic ducks and the water toys the children played with the bath. All the equipment she needed was in nearby cupboards or on a neat trolley which was loaded with powders, salves, loofahs, safety pins, shampoos and scissors. She was a woman who took pleasure in the chores of motherhood and housekeeping, and carried them out with determined efficiency.

Christina was a placid baby. She put out her tongue and played contentedly in the warm bath water. Sian sat on a stool alongside the bath and examined the little girl's curly hair with minute care, wondering whether or not to embark on the task of washing it and disturbing Christina's pleasure and the peace and quiet of the house. Gently she soaped her daughter's dimpled knees. She was surprised to see Peredur standing in the open doorway but not displeased. He seemed to be studying his niece with profound interest. Hitherto it had not been his custom to show so much interest in the children.

'Aren't we strange creatures?' he said.

She restrained herself from making any facetious comment and shaped her lips into a kiss for her daughter who was looking up with an almost toothless ecstatic smile.

'As a species I mean,' he said. 'This prolonged immersion in the waters of love gives us the strength to grow. Where does all the destructiveness come from?'

He put his hands behind his back and leaned forward in a stiff attempt to be friendly.

'You're a Christian, aren't you?' he said.

'Yes. I am. Or at least I try to be.'

'Do you believe in Original Sin?'

'I don't know. I suppose I should. I've never really thought about it.'

'I have.'

Peredur made the statement very simply.

'The Early Fathers taught that Procreation was the work of the Devil.'

'Not all of them surely?'

'Quite literally in some cases. That meant that the end product, that is the baby . . .'

He pointed at the example in the bath.

143

'. . . was quite literally a little devil.'

'Surely not.'

'I'm not making it up,' Peredur said. 'I read it in Tertullian.'

He frowned for a moment.

'Or was it Cyprian? I don't quite remember. 'But I certainly read it.'

'I go by the New Testament,' Sian said. 'There's nothing like that in the New Testament.'

'I was thinking about Baptism really,' he said. 'The point is, in the early church baptism was a very elaborate sacrament to convert a screaming red devil into an obedient little white member of the Christian Church.'

Christina was slapping the surface of the water cheerfully and Peredur leaned forward and snapped his fingers at her in an unpractised attempt to show a benevolent interest in her. She blinked and found his action totally unaccountable.

'That's why baptism was always considered such an important sacrament. The question was, how far, or to what extent shall we say, did it mitigate the power of Original Sin? And most of the argument raged between a little and very little.'

'It's all a bit academic really, by today surely?'

Sian gave him a brief smile and began to reach out for a warm towel from the nearby radiator.

'Well I don't know,' Peredur said. 'Languages and concepts change of course but babies haven't changed all that much have they? Or the way you make them? In Ancient Greece a father baptized his own child as a public act of responsibility for the child and to show that he didn't want it exposed on some bare hillside.'

'Goodness,' Sian said. 'You have gone into it.'

Peredur nodded quite seriously.

'It must have been this thing about Bedwyr. Being baptized on his mother's coffin. Doesn't it impress you at all? It impressed me no end when I heard it.'

'I didn't want to discuss it in front of David,' Sian said. 'He's very sensitive.'

Peredur looked surprised as if David's being sensitive had not occurred to him before.

'Does he ever talk about her?'

'About his mother?'

'Does he?'

Sian shook her head.

'He thinks of your mother as his mother.'

'Ah, but she's not.'

The fact was incontrovertible and this in itself gave him profound pleasure.

'Doesn't he have a picture of her?'

'I think there is one somewhere. In a suitcase in the attic. A sepia-coloured thing. A very wistful-looking woman. I supposed that's something to do with the fashion in those days. The way they took pictures in the twenties.'

'I'd like to see it,' Peredur said.

'I can't look for it now,' Sian said a little impatiently. 'I've got to bath the other two, give them supper and get them to bed.'

Expertly she leaned down to pick up the wet baby. She suspended Christina in the air above the thick warm towel spread over her knees and the baby laughed gleefully and kicked her legs. Mother and child were delighted with each other and Peredur leaned forward to look at the baby more closely.

'Petals and pearls,' he said.

Sian did not understand. His tone was so neutral sometimes it could be mistaken for critical hostility and with her brother-in-law she tended to be on her guard.

'That's what she's made of,' Peredur said.

As soon as the compliment made itself plain, she gave Peredur a dazzling smile which brought out the dimples in her flushed cheeks. He stepped back, a little shame-faced, alarmed perhaps at being suspected of flattery.

Sian began to dry the baby at the same time singing a little and sometimes jigging her up and down on her knees. The scene caused Peredur a little embarrassment. He withdrew from the bathroom and stood in the corridor just outside.

With great muscular ease Sian reached out for a pink plastic pot and placed her daughter on it with a square confidence that assumed that she would perform with ritual ease, if only to please her patient and loving mother. Peredur watched all the processes with the objective attention of a scientist watching work in an unfamiliar laboratory.

'What's that?'

Sian had dug out a quantity of white cream from a large jar and was preparing to apply it liberally between the baby's buttocks and thighs.

'Zinc and castor-oil,' Sian said. 'The old-fashioned stuff. The cheapest and the best.'

Their conversation had moved to an easier and more familiar plane.

'As used on generations of baby's buttocks?'

The question sounded quaint and Sian laughed.

'I suppose so.'

'A sort of anointing,' Peredur said, with a certain learned hesitation. 'But on the bottom instead of the head.'

Sian laughed again. She had discovered a more amusing side to her solemn brother-in-law.

'I got lost in a department store yesterday,' Peredur said. 'I found myself in a place called Babyland. It frightened the life out of me. Everything for baby. Prams, baby powder, patent nappies. There was a huge tin of baby powder as big as a Chinese temple. And women jostling about in their best clothes and huge hair-do's and their children in harnesses and a sprinkling of dejected looking men. Everything for baby. I had a nightmare about it.'

146

'Poor women,' Sian said.

'Why poor women?'

'They're so gullible when they have babies.'

'In my nightmare they were all dressed in feathers and they were looting a warehouse filled to the rafters with dolls and prams on skis and blankets shaped like birds' nests.'

Sian was inserting Christina's limbs into a patent night garment, but she was watching Peredur with interest as though she were waiting her opportunity to ask him a more intimate question. The front-door bell rang, three brief notes.

'That's Bedwyr,' Sian said. 'Go and let him in will you. I expect he's forgotten his key.'

He opened the door and they stood facing each other, both ill at ease. Bedwyr was wearing a hat and Peredur looked at it like a man who has seen a house for the first time in a field that was part of the open country when he was a child. Then he looked at Bedwyr's beard as if it were something he was only just getting used to.

'I forgot my key,' Bedwyr said.

He waited for his half-brother to stand aside so that he could have free access into his own house. He was carrying a briefcase so stuffed with papers that it had to be left open. Peredur moved out of the way and he marched into the house glad to be home and anxious to make a demonstration of affection for his family.

His daughter Nia gave him a wild welcome. He picked her up and swung her about in the air in a way that made her laugh hysterically. The little boy looked up anxiously, and when he was sufficiently reassured shared his attention between the events in the room around him and the picture on the television screen. Bedwyr carried Nia off to the bath and the whole house was alive with excitement because Daddy had arrived home in time to take part in the preparations for bed. Peredur lingered about in the entrance hall and caught as much as he could of the whirlwind of action that appeared to be taking place. Bedwyr rushed about in all directions, at first engaged in a comic exaggeration of helpfulness to amuse the children: but this eventually developed into a more authoritative role and he became the general who rode all over the battlefield exhorting his troops to speedier action by a sequence of ineffective interferences.

'Look, for goodness' sake go and look after Peredur,' Sian said laughing. 'He's standing there in the hall like a man come to read the meter.'

'Are you sure you can manage?'

Bedwyr was all concern.

'I should hope so,' she said. 'I manage every other night, don't I?'

There was a fierceness about the way she spoke that clearly added to her beauty in his eyes. Her hair was dark now with the steam of the bathroom and strenuous physical effort but her blue eyes were bright and enlarged, her cheeks were flushed and she was a picture of youthful fitness and healthy motherhood that he was able to stare at with open admiration.

In the living room he switched off the television set and glanced generously at Peredur as though he had rid him of an annoyance by one turn of his wrist. He moved over to the Welsh dresser against the far wall and opened the cupboard where he kept his drinks.

'What will you have?' he said.

'Anything.'

Peredur showed little interest.

'Sherry, gin, whisky? You name it.'

He left Peredur to go to the kitchen and returned with a glass jug filled with ice cubes. Peredur took a dry sherry and he made himself a large gin and tonic. He sat back in his armchair with a deep sigh, kicking off his shoes and putting his feet up on the low but solid occasional table. He loosened his tie and unbuttoned his collar at the neck. He seemed to be in two minds whether or not to talk about the day's problems and difficulties. They sat in silence, each prepared to communicate with the other, but neither sufficiently able to take the other for granted to make an easy start. There could have been a barrier of old disagreements between them or old criticisms that still rankled: or the mere difference in age could have seemed hard to surmount. Peredur became the first to speak. He was not concerned with casual conversation. He had something he wanted to say.

'I'm going back to Redbatch tomorrow.'

Hurriedly Bedwyr tried to look disappointed.

'There's no need for you to go,' he said. 'I've told you. Your room is your room for as long as you like. We haven't seen enough of each other, have we? That's the trouble. It's been absolute hell in the office. I've got a battle going on two fronts. I get so fed up with it sometimes.'

'I've got work to do,' Peredur said. 'I shall have to go back.'

Bedwyr held his glass out in Peredur direction.

'I've been meaning to ask you,' he said. 'Why did you give up philosophy?'

Peredur considered the question frowning hard in a way that made Bedwyr smile.

'You needn't go into it in too great detail,' he said. 'An interim answer will do.'

Peredur did not appear to notice the teasing.

'It's a subject that's committed suicide,' he said.

'How? By disappearing up its own arse?'

Peredur was not inclined to take the matter so lightly. 'The field of inquiry has become so narrow. In British philosophy anyway. A kind of scholastic epistemology. Anyway I had nothing to contribute. It just took

149

me five or six years to discover I wasn't a philosopher.'

'And now you're a sociologist?'

'Of sorts.'

This wasn't the subject that Peredur wanted to pursue. He fixed his gaze on Bedwyr's face and asked the question which was on his mind.

'Am I like my father?'

Bedwyr returned his stare.

'Physically you mean?'

'In any way.'

Bedwyr needed another drink. He looked inside his glass and then struggled out of his comfortable position to get across to the tray on the dresser.

'I suppose you must be. You don't remember him all that well?'

'I do and I don't,' Peredur said. 'And I find that peculiar. I have odd little childhood recollections and then a whole set of preconceived ideas. And notions other people have pressed on my consciousness. Like those letters we used to print on strips of metal. That machine in the railway station. A penny for twenty-four letters. It's still there you know.'

'The station? That would be a miracle in itself. Another drink?'

'And the machine. I wish I'd spent more time there. It was a strange experience. Removing the surface of myth and finding little fragments of truth underneath.'

'Sociology?'

'Not really.'

Bedwyr returned to his chair. He gulped down a mouthful of gin and tonic and the ice tinkled in his glass.

'What's the point?' he said. 'Research?'

'What do you think of his poetry?'

'Cilydd . . . *Yr hen Gilydd* . . .'

Bedwyr spoke his father's bardic name like some old affectionate joke.

'A bit old-fashioned, wasn't he?' he said. 'Even in his own day. Strict metres and all that. I wouldn't know quite frankly. I've got no sense of what you might call verbal aesthetics. None. I'd almost go as far as to say I didn't have any aesthetic sense at all. Many of my colleagues would agree with me.'

Peredur was not to be diverted from the subject of his father.

'He wasn't bad,' he said. 'He wasn't bad at all. He was trying to say something but with his mouth and his brain filled with out-worn conventions. You know what I mean? This apparent obsession with birds. Hawks. Pigeons. Geese. Starlings. Curlews. They weren't just birds. They were people. He was trying to say something about people. Things he couldn't say out-right and directly because he was a member of what was still a very closely knit community.'

Peredur grew more excited.

'And what I feel is, somewhere in the marrow of my bones I feel it, he wrote things we've never seen. Really good things hidden away somewhere . . . I try to think of him sometimes as I can remember him standing on top of a flight of stairs and looking down at me. He seems fantastically tall and his face is long and narrow and he's wearing that hard collar. The absolute image of a small town lawyer. Remote and forbidding. I was always afraid of him. He was so distant. And inside him was all that poetry. Didn't he make any impression on you at all?'

'What do you mean?'

'Well you never talk about him. He's like a forbidden subject. Amy never mentions him. I suppose that's understandable. He was only the first of three husbands and they didn't get on. I know that. But he was your father.'

151

'Life goes on,' Bedwyr said.

Peredur wriggled about with uncharacteristic restlessness in his end of the long settee.

'We are what she made us,' he said. 'That's obvious enough. She was the power in control. You are ten years older than I am and you must be more aware of it than I am. She's not your mother. And he was your father. But you accept her view of the story. I've always wanted to ask you why. You are the one that's closest to her. I don't get on with her. Gwydion just teases and provokes her. But you are always good to her. She relies on you.'

'She had a tough time,' Bedwyr said. 'And she managed to bring us all up with great success.'

'That's her version.'

'It's true.'

Bedwyr sounded annoyed. But Peredur was determined to press on with his inquiry.

'Do you know he committed suicide?'

Peredur had raised his voice in his excitement and Bedwyr jumped to his feet to close the glass panelled door. The voices of the children eating their supper in the kitchen were cut off.

'Don't raise your voice,' Bedwyr said. 'I don't want Sian to hear.'

'So it's true.'

Peredur was more relieved than triumphant.

'And she got it all put down as accidental death. I knew it. I knew it. For all these years she's imposed her version of events on the world in general including me. I suppose I must have been very willing to believe it. He just walked over the edge of a cliff into eternity. You can see now what I'm after. I want to know why.'

'It's not absolutely certain,' Bedwyr said.

He went to fix himself a third drink.

'It could have been accidental death. In any case, don't talk about it when Sian comes in.'

'Why not?'

'I don't want her to worry about it. It could upset her.'

'The Truth?'

Peredur was unsympathetic.

'She doesn't strike me as the kind of woman who would want to live in a world of Make-believe.'

'It's not that,' Bedwyr said impatiently.

'We were talking before you arrived,' Peredur said. 'She struck me as one of those rare women who are really interested in Facts and the Truth.'

Bedwyr looked concerned by the extent of the naivety his brother was revealing so frankly.

'She worries about David,' he said. 'He's such a quiet little boy. He'll go for hours on end without saying anything and I know that worries her. If I started telling her that my father was a melancholic who committed suicide that would just worry her even more.'

He stood behind his chair and picked up the telephone from the side-table and held it in the air.

'Why don't you give her a ring?' he said.

'Who?'

'Amy.'

Peredur was not willing to be taken by surprise.

'What on earth for?'

'Just be nice to her. She's a lonely woman. She thought the world of old Hubert and now he's gone. She's got nobody to talk to. Give her a tinkle. What else are telephones for?'

Peredur was totally unwilling.

'She's got those women,' he said. 'She could talk to them.'

'She's up in that place by herself. Every night. Completely alone. She can't talk to them. They're just camp-followers and she knows it. You are her son. What's wrong with giving her a little tinkle? What would it cost you?'

The authority of convinced righteousness had crept into Bedwyr's voice. Peredur became more stubborn.

'It's a phoney set-up,' he said.

'All right,' Bedwyr said. 'Call it phoney. But she's trying to do something. She doesn't give up. You've got to admire her. She's got guts and she keeps on going.'

'I find it completely repulsive.'

'Well, be a little less self-centred and overcome your fastidiousness for the sake of a little simple human kindness. You've got this holier-than-thou attitude about every damned thing. It's very annoying.'

Peredur looked hurt.

'I'll be gone tomorrow,' he said.

'Oh for God's sake take advice for once instead of umbrage. Make allowances for the poor old trout. She's a bit eccentric and self-absorbed but who isn't when it comes to the push? And she doesn't do anyone any harm.'

Peredur looked at his half-brother from the corner of his eyes.

'I think she may very well have driven him to it.'

'That's absurd.'

Bedwyr spoke hotly, driving off something he did not wish to hear. He took his hand away from the telephone.

'I've got evidence,' Peredur said. 'It isn't much to go by and yet it is most certainly evidence.'

'That business about the Memorial? That's not evidence at all. I don't agree with her, but I think her objections were perfectly understandable.'

Peredur was shaking his head when Sian opened the door. She had tidied herself up a little and was looking a little weary, but satisfied and beautiful. They stopped talking as soon as she appeared.

'What's the matter with you two?'

She smiled and Bedwyr moved towards her.

'Come and sit down, darling,' he said. 'And I'll make you a lovely drink.'

'Oh dear.'

Sian flopped into a chair and gave an exaggerated sigh.

'A drink!' she said. 'What a lovely idea.'

They went on to talk about Bedwyr's day in the office.

3

Christina stood on the back seat of the car. She was just big enough to lie on the padded surface in order to stare at the road that seemed to behave like a long ribbon being paid out behind them and by some magic means always neatly stretched and in place between the high kerb stones. Sian sat sideways so that she could look in the direction the car was taking and at the same time support the baby with the palm of her hand. Nia was also in the back. She had a sticky hand on her mother's knee and a red sweet protruding from her pouting lips. The weather was unsettled. There was a stiff breeze from the west and at the moment the sun was bright on the windows making the interior of the large car very warm. Nia was wearing a green bonnet and coat. Her cheeks were red and she looked roguishly happy pushing the red sweet out of her mouth with the tip of her tongue and sucking it back in again. In the front passenger seat David sat inside his safety belt, silent and intense, pushing his straight fair hair out of his eyes, and trying to do everything in the same way as his father. He noted now that Bedwyr was driving the car in a relaxed fashion inside the speed limit, with his right elbow on the plump arm-rest, taking the weight of his body and the sole of his right shoe touching the side of the accelerator ready to apply gentle power. David arranged his own body in the same manner and kept a close check on the instrument panel, watching the mileage clock and the red fluid in the speedometer that fluctuated delicately in response to the movement of the car. Driving up a steep hill on the outskirts of the conurbation they were brought to a halt by temporary traffic lights. The road was being widened and a substantial concrete retaining wall had been built to prevent any land slide. There was a raw depth of red soil in view and the exposed roots of the nearest trees in the wood that covered the slope. Bedwyr wound down the door window to examine the work that went on with close interest. The children scrambled to the left side of the car ready to marvel at whatever he would choose to point out.

'This is where the action is,' he said.

There was irony in his voice and Sian leaned forward to listen to him more closely. She was a busy young mother in a fur cap and a sheepskin coat, a little too warm, perhaps, but enjoying her unaccustomed inactivity, deeply contented to be surrounded by her whole family.

'What do you mean, darling?'

She was receptive to anything her husband wanted to teach, free now to listen and to learn.

'This is the real building,' he said. 'Motorways. Roads. The governing factor that controls our lives and the way we build our cities.'

'Yes I see,' Sian said. 'Of course.'

Her attention was taken by the car immediately in front, a Simca whose maroon colour was almost completely obscured by a coat of dried mud. It was driven by a cheerful young man with heavily brilliantined curly hair and he was leaning out of the open window to make jeering shouts at the two stone masons who were building a facing wall in trimmed local stone to cover the sloping strength of the concrete. Among the bulldozers, lorries and earthmoving machinery, they looked minute and human, practising their ancient craft. The older stone mason was a short man and the ladder he was using was not high enough for him to reach the top of the new wall without stretching uncomfortably.

'My goodness,' Sian said, nodding at the Simca. 'That car needs a wash.'

She spoke as though she herself wanted to take on the job. The lights only had to stay on red long enough and she would jump out and get it done on the spot. She stretched her mouth a little so that dimples appeared in both cheeks.

'Jack him up, Dai!'

The young man in the Simca shouted. His cry was drowned by the aggressive roar of a bulldozer working on the other side of the road. Alongside him sat his wife, with a basket on her knees and a diaphanous scarf over her freshly built blond hair-do. She put a restraining hand on the sleeve of his best suit but he shook it off.

'Dai!'

He stretched his neck and shouted louder than ever and this time both the stone-masons heard him. He grinned at them cheekily and made jerky signals with his fingers to suggest they should stand on each other's shoulders. Bedwyr smiled as he watched them and David checked his father's reaction before giving the scene the same kind of benevolent attention. The stone masons seemed to know the driver of the Simca and to take his teasing in good part. The older mason went through the exaggerated motions of picking out a stone big enough to hurl at the driver of the Simca. This was followed by an even more elaborate mime to suggest that the young man should get out and come and give them a hand. All three men seemed delighted with their own comedy. Even the young wife in the headscarf was induced to smile. The stone masons put down their tools and prepared to advance over the heap of trimmed stones to engage the driver in the Simca either in hand to hand combat or in conversation. They made mock threatening gestures and David glanced anxiously at his father's face to see if he still approved. The lights changed and the line of traffic lurched forward. The stone-masons waved reluctantly at the playmate being borne away from them.

'Brickie taking a day off,' Bedwyr said.

'What's a brickie?' David said.

'A bricklayer. Making quite a lot of money I expect. Enough to buy a second-hand Simca. Working overtime. No time to clean it. He can't be more than twenty-four. There he is. All set up. Good fat pay-packet and a brand-new wife to spend it.'

'Bedwyr!'

Sian sounded mildly shocked.

'What's up.'

'You are such old cynic. You don't even know that they're married. He looks rather a cheerful boy. And how do you know he's a bricklayer?'

'It's time he learnt to drive properly.'

The young man was trying to light a cigarette and his car swerved erratically on the road. His wife made a small protest but he exhaled smoke savagely in her direction in a way that suggested he was telling her to shut up.

158

'Oh my goodness,' Sian said. 'What a nasty thing to do.'

'Affluent workers,' Bedwyr said. 'The other side of the coin.'

David was confused and puzzled by the connection between what they were saying and what was happening in the car in front.

'He shouldn't smoke, should he?'

He looked at his father first and then turned to look at his mother.

'It's bad for him, isn't it? Very bad for him.'

He was anxious for confirmation and his father nodded soothingly, glancing into the driving mirror to exchange understanding glances with his wife. Nia slapped her mother's knee to gain her attention. She held up her fingers and wriggled them.

'What do you want darling?'

Nia wriggled her fingers again. Bedwyr glanced in the mirror to keep a critical eye on the proceedings. David turned around in his seat and looked at his sister with open disapproval.

'What is it, sweetie?'

Sian sounded infinitely warm and patient and David looked at his sister as if to say that he hoped she realized how lucky she was. Had he been in charge, her treatment would have been a good deal sterner. From the travelling bag at her feet, Sian extracted a wet flannel. She turned to wipe Christina's lips with it. The baby screwed up her face and shut her eyes tight pressing he head into the flannel but opening her eyes wide as soon as she sensed the ordeal was over and smiling broadly when she heard her mother tell her she was a good girl. Nia let out a squawk followed by a wail.

'Excuse me,' Sian said. 'I didn't hear.'

'My fingers . . .'

'What about your pretty fingers?'

'Want you to wipe them with that . . .'

159

Sian nodded encouragingly to show that there was more of the speech yet to be spoken.

'. . . Please . . .'

'There's a good girl!'

She clasped her daughter's fingers in the flannel and wiped each finger in turn, chanting a nursery rhyme as she did it, until a smile broke over Nia's face.

'*and this little piggy cried wee-wee-wee all the way home!*'

On the last line she wiggled Nia's little finger about until the little girl burst out laughing and cried out for the rhyme and the action to be repeated. After a third repeat, David intervened.

'She's getting over excited,' he said.

Sian gave him a reassuring smile.

'What about a song then? What shall we sing? Let's ask Daddy, shall we? What shall we sing, Daddy?'

Bedwyr made tuning up noises through his nose which amused all the children. Christina turned around and sank down to sit comfortably in her mother's lap ready to be amused. He had a light tenor voice with a tendency to croon which seemed so uncharacteristic that Sian, even as she sang herself, frequently had to lower her head to conceal her giggles. At first David was reluctant to join in but when his father nodded in his direction and winked in a cool encouraging fashion, he forgot his inhibitions and was particularly loud on the chorus which consisted of a succession of *ha-ha-ha's* to rhyme with Bala at the end of the first line. While they were still singing, Bedwyr turned right into a narrow road with high banks on either side. There were sharp corners and the tyres of the car swept close to the ditch.

'Darling,' Sian said anxiously. 'Where are we going?'

'There's a site just a couple of miles up here. Since we are going this way . . . I just want to have a look at it.'

'But this is your day off!'

She tried not to sound cross.

'It's your first day off for weeks . . .'

'Won't take a jiffy.'

'We want to get to the seashore for our picnic, while it's still nice and warm. Don't we, Nia?'

Nia straightened up and looked important. She nodded, very pleased at being consulted.

'There may be conker trees. Near the site. Keep a look out for them, David.'

When it emerged from the afforestation belt, the road climbed upwards more steeply. There were many sharp corners at which Bedwyr asked David to press the horn on his driving wheel to warn anyone using the road of their approach. Sian lay back in her seat, resigned to the diversion, palefaced and unnaturally still, as though too much movement would bring on car sickness. She closed her eyes to make the journey pass more quickly and then was obliged to open them again to keep an eye on the children. But Nia and Christina had both climbed on the seat and were perfectly happy to stare down through the rear window watching the land fall away and catching the first glimpse of the chimneys of a steel-works emerging faintly out of the long yellow dunes on the distant seashore.

'I hope you know where you are going,' Sian said in a faint voice.

Without answering, Bedwyr slowed down until he was able to bring the car to a standstill on a hard roadside surface intended for a heap of grit for spreading on the road in winter. Immediately in front of them the road was carried over a mountain stream by an ancient stone bridge. In full view it ascended in a narrow line over the windswept moorland to cross over the rounded summit of the mountain. In the small ravine below the bridge willows and alders grew and were still in full green leaf. As they emerged from the car, the children were enchanted with everything they saw, particularly mountain ponies in the rough

161

grazing beyond the rusty fence. Nia wanted to catch one of them. She jumped up and down excitedly as two of the ponies approached in the hope of scraps of food.

Bedwyr extracted an expensive Japanese camera from the glove compartment. He removed the black leather case and began to finger the circular collars on the lens barrel and to peer more closely at the markings. He opened the glove compartment again and took out a light-meter. He studied the instrument and frowned hard, trying to recall the details of the correct method of taking readings. As he did so his white teeth dug into the upper roots of his beard.

Tentatively the ponies extended their necks over the wire fence. They were beginning to grow thicker coats. Nia gave a sudden scream of delight that made them back away in fear. With an empty hand and glancing at Bedwyr to see what he was doing, Sian tried to coax them back. Delighted with her new freedom, Christina walked on to the firm dry surface of the road and began to walk back the way they had come, her little legs kept wide apart by the nappy pack she was wearing under her woollen trousers. David had made for the bridge and was hanging over to stare into the stream that had shrunk to the centre of the rocky torrent-bed because of the unusually dry weather.

'Bedwyr!' Sian said. 'Get Christina!'

Bedwyr was hanging the strap of his camera around his neck.

'David!'

He called his son who responded immediately.

'Go and get Christina.'

The boy dropped off the bridge and galloped down the road concentrating earnestly on his mission. He soon caught up with his little sister and with the right amount of firm tenderness persuaded her to turn back. On their return the boy took her hand and Bedwyr was able to kneel down and take their photograph as they came towards him. Then he altered the stops and took a quick snap of Sian and Nia trying to lure the nervous ponies back within reach of their hands. His knowledge of photography had returned and he had stopped frowning.

'Let's cross,' he said. 'Come on darling. It will be safer when we get off the road. Then we can let them all run loose.'

Over the road a sagging wooden gate barred the way ineffectively to a farm lane green with disuse. The ground was soft and in wet weather must have been easily churned into a muddy quagmire but now made a carpet of delicately green grass growing between the stones and the ridges. There were trees on either side of the lane, mostly moss-covered oaks of stunted size growing out of fallen walls. David raced on ahead, anxious to explore a new territory. Christina trotted after him very pleased to be walking on her own again. Sian was occupied with persuading Nia to leave the ponies while Bedwyr with his camera hanging from his neck was looking about him with a professional eye. There were photographs he needed for his survey. If members of his family appeared in them, they would be useful figures in a landscape, small familiar objects that would help to keep a sense of scale when estimating dimensions and distances.

Once round the corner the lane descended to a long hollow where ruined farm buildings could be seen through a ragged belt of young conifers. David came running back to his father, breathless, with a disappointing report.

'There are no conker trees,' he said.

They walked forward together and Christina turned around to watch them approach.

'Yes. That's true.'

Bedwyr examined the view with a keen eye.

'You can see what's happened. There were trees all round this place. To protect the homestead from the high winds. And then the place was sold you see and the trees were cut for a quick profit. Below the house, David, you can see all the tree stumps.'

Bedwyr began to take more photographs.

'Look at the roof!'

David sounded deeply shocked.

'It's full of holes!'

'It will all have to come down.'

Bedwyr muttered as he held the viewfinder of the camera to his eye.

'Go and see what Christina's up to David, there's a good chap.'

'Can I explore?'

'Of course you can. But be careful. And keep an eye on her as well, there's a good chap.'

Eager to explore the outbuildings David plunged forward with his arms stretched behind him like the wings of a paper dart until he remembered his responsibility and straightened up and slowed down to a ponderous strut that could have been a caricature of the stride of a television police inspector. Sian came up to Bedwyr's side, picking her way carefully over the soft soil. She had Nia by the hand. The little girl was sucking another sweet and holding herself back so that her mother's arm was fully stretched drawing her reluctant weight forward.

'What's it all going to be?' Sian said.

Nia needed more patient attention than her other two children, but she looked intently at Bedwyr while the little girl continued to pull at her arm. She wanted to demonstrate an intelligent interest in his work.

'A crematorium.'

The information took her completely by surprise.

'It's an interesting study. An important piece of social engineering. You can't imagine how much research it needed. I know more about crematoria than anybody since Auschwitz.'

'Darling.'

Sian was disturbed. He breathed deeply and set the viewfinder of the camera to his eye to make a more detailed pictorial record of the immediate landscape.

'Essential to the balance of the industrial landscape,' he said. 'That's what I like about our practice down here. Organic variety. Factories. Drinking Clubs. Housing sites. Community Centres. Schools. Old People's Homes. And now a Crematorium. We've got a good chance with a steel works extension, and a university theatre. Then I'll have seen it all. Chimney to chimney. And when the great call comes I'll be quite happy to go up here in a puff of smoke. We'll make a proper job of it.'

'I don't like them.'

Nia pulled Sian's arm first in one direction and then the other. There was nowhere she particularly wanted to go. She just enjoyed pulling at her mother's arm.

'That's because you are the product of a rural culture. I know you were born in a small town, but the furnishing of your mind is rural. You've got open fields in your mind and plenty of room for chapels and churchyards. This is the cheapest and the most efficient method of disposing of the dead. Absolutely essential on an overcrowded island. An overcrowded world. We have to face these things.'

'I'm quite prepared to face them.'

Sian sounded annoyed. She had many things that she wished to say and her inability to know where to begin made her look youthful to the point of being child-like. Her lips pushed forwards and her eyes shone and the complexion of her face seemed softer and more pink and white than ever in the clear mountain air and the sunlight. Bedwyr was moved to put his arm lovingly around her waist but she shrugged him away. Then Nia

165

stopped pulling at her arm. She was looking up at them both making an unconcealed assessment of her parents' emotional relationship at that moment. Bedwyr's manner became tender and he bent his head in a special effort to be more understanding and sympathetic.

'You are probably right anyway,' he said. 'Emotionally every generation lives in the Past, or longs for the Past. Sometimes they call it the Future, but in fact it's only the Past idealized.'

Sian frowned. His reflections were breaking across her own line of thought. Nia at last let go of her hand and began to wander off towards the farm outbuildings where she could hear David's voice giving his little sister simple instructions.

'I don't know what you are trying to say,' Sian said.

'Neither do I.'

Bedwyr became suddenly gloomy with a sense of his own inadequacy.

'I noticed that on more than one occasion last week. Talking to Peredur. It's not just that he's a trained academic and that I'm basically inarticulate. I don't really know what I think about anything. Except you.'

He looked at her lovingly.

'I'm only happy when I'm getting something done. That's why I'm such a glutton for work. It gives me something to think about. Crematoria or smelting plants or any damn thing. I love doing them. When I stop to think, as the saying goes, thinking in the abstract, it just depresses me. Perhaps because I'm no good at it. Especially thinking about people. And what else is there except people? One generation after another. Punctuation marks in a clear sky. One puff of smoke after another. And then the whole damn thing starts again. Burning and Breeding.'

'No,' Sian said. 'That's not true at all.'

She was distressed and he immediately wanted to comfort her. He took her face between his hands and did not seem to see that she was struggling to say something.

'It's all right,' he said. 'I may sound pessimistic but I'm a very happy man. Really I am. Thanks to you.'

'It's not that.'

She freed her face from his caressing hands.

'What is it then?'

As she groped for the words she needed there was a piercing scream from the barn. Christina had fallen over. They both rushed to pick her up.

4

The small children played on the sands with complete safety. The smooth beach was a graceful curve that swept westwards in the face of the advancing sea until it ended at the base of abrupt dark rocks which seemed to support a low promontory at the end of which a white lighthouse had been constructed. The beach was inaccessible, separated from the rudimentary car park under the maritime pines by a mile of steeply undulating dunes. Now it was after the holiday season and the children were in sole possession of the whole area. From a defensive position in the last line of dunes, Sian and Bedwyr kept an eye on their offspring, particularly Christina who ran about naked from the waist down deeply intent on the group behaviour of the oyster catchers wading in the shallows on the margin of the sea. She clapped her hands from time to time in an effort to make them take to the air. Even at a distance David was behaving visibly in a fatherly fashion. He had persuaded Nia to play with him in order to relieve his mother and give her a rest and he was rolling a great white ball towards her and training her to play a simple game that needed more regular and patterned responses than she was accustomed to making. They were all happy and fully occupied and with a deep sigh of contentment Sian rolled over on her back and exposed her face calmly to the warm rays of the sun. There was a brisk wind blowing from the sea but in the sandy hollow where she lay the air was hot and still. Her head was pillowed on her sheepskin coat. Not far away were the remnants of their picnic and a heap of children's overcoats and a bag with a soap and wet flannel and Christina's day nappies. Bedwyr made a half-hearted attempt at tidying up. He was wearing a dark suit which appeared incongruous in a seaside setting and he came to sit alongside Sian, hugging his knees, his waistcoat unbuttoned, unable to relax. Sian spread the palms of her hands over the sand which was hot to touch. She became aware of her husband's silence and opened her eyes to look at him.

'You don't like sand,' she said.

He smiled, not displeased that she remembered something he had told her about his childhood.

'You don't mind giving us your time?'

'Don't be silly.'

'You don't mind wasting time sitting on a sand dune when you could be in the office, making great decisions?'

She lifted her head and shaded her eyes with her hand to take a more searching look at Bedwyr's face. Her frankness was loving but remorseless.

'You are asking for trouble.'

He made a mock threat.

'No I'm not. I'm asking for the truth. I don't usually have time to think about it.'

'That *is* asking for trouble.'

'We live in such a pattern of busyness. We never stop. You are building away in your great practice and I'm slaving away in my routine. It's like one of those indoor plants that spend all their strength in growing and never have time to pause and burst into flower.'

Bedwyr slid down the slope and took off his jacket. He rested on his elbow so that he could stare admiringly at Sian's face. Her eyelids were lowered but she lifted them enough to reassure herself that he was near.

'What were you thinking about up there?'

He ran the tip of his finger along the bridge of her nose.

'Curiosity,' he said. 'Terrible thing.'

'It's not curiosity,' she said. 'It's more like hunger. I need to know what is going on in your mind. You are so remote sometimes. It makes me feel lonely.'

He brought himself closer, ready to embrace her.

'Talk,' she said. 'What were you thinking about?'

'Nothing exciting. I was thinking about my young brother. He will end up a crank. Not "end up". He is a crank.'

'What do you mean by "crank"?'

'I never got that far,' Bedwyr said.

He gave some thought to preparing a definition for her.

'Obsessed with a small fragment of fact at the expense of total reality.'

'What do you mean by "total reality"?'

Bedwyr groaned.

'My God,' he said. 'It's time you were back at the sink. All this sea air is turning you into an intellectual.'

'I liked him better this time than ever before.'

169

She made the announcement quietly, but it came to him no less of a surprise.

'Did you really? I thought he drove you up the wall.'

'Well he did ... It's just that I came to understand him a little better. He's such an idealist. He's quite like you in a way.'

Bedwyr made a noise of protest.

'Somebody has hurt him,' she said. 'Some girl I shouldn't wonder.'

'He's just obsessed with my father,' Bedwyr said. 'It's unhealthy.'

'I wouldn't say that. I would call it very natural.'

'He's not a boy any more,' Bedwyr said. 'He's a grown man and he's got to live in the world as it is. He's an arrested adolescent. He wants to use everything connected with my father to strike at his mother. This thing about a Memorial. And all that business about collected poems ... it's all part of the process, girding up his loins to do battle with his mother ... and if that isn't a Freudian phrase ... You don't really think I'm like him?'

She smiled at his concern.

'He's such a funny little chap.'

'How do you mean, funny?'

'He used to lie on the drawing-room floor in the middle of the afternoon with his eyes wide open. I found him there twice. He wasn't a bit embarrassed. He said it helped him to think.'

'Well I'm glad you found him more tolerable. To be quite honest I found he made me more uneasy than ever. He's building up trouble.'

'How?'

'This Memorial business. Somehow or other he's stirred up the Pendraw Borough Council. They want to put up a Memorial to the old man.'

'I should have thought that would be nice.'

'As a tourist attraction? Like Lloyd George's grave?'

'Well why not? Poets are just as important as politicians.'

'It's not that. He was such a minor poet. And it's bound to be something excruciatingly vulgar.'

'Not if you do it.'

He gave her a look of suspicion, but her eyes were closed and she did not see it.

'No fear.'

'No fear what?'

'I don't want to be pig in the middle. I've got enough troubles of my own. I don't want to be caught in one of their dog fights. If she doesn't want it, she won't have it. And the more she doesn't want it, the more determined he'll be to get it . . . oh dear.'

He exaggerated the groan to show he was able to look at the problem with humorous objectivity, but Sian gave him all her sympathy.

'Come down here,' she said. 'Let me comfort you. And don't worry about it now. It's such a marvellous day.'

When he was close to her she sighed deeply.

'This is perfect,' she said. 'Absolutely perfect. I'm lying on that cloud. Floating between the sun and the sea. It's lovely.'

He put his hand on her knee and slid it up her skirt.

'Keep still,' she said, 'there's a good boy. I'll fall off my cloud . . .'

He gave up and they lay silent next to each other until he started again more determinedly.

'Oh God,' he said, 'these stupid tights . . .'

She pushed his hand away and sat up briefly to satisfy herself that the children weren't anywhere around watching.

'Forget them for a moment, my love.'

Bedwyr's voice became intense and romantic.

'I worship you. I really do. I adore you. Let me touch you, darling. Please let me touch you.'

His lips were very close to hers as she whispered and she turned away her head covering her mouth with her hand.

'What's the matter?'

He was immediately sensitive.

'Nothing. It's just your beard. You were blowing into it as you were speaking. It was tickling me.'

Bedwyr leaned back and stared at the blue sky. He felt for her hand and squeezed it between his fingers. It was small and soft and comforting as it gave his hand a returning squeeze.

'I've been meaning to ask you for ages. Shall I shave it off?'

He spoke casually enough, but it was obviously a question that he took seriously.

'I don't know.'

Their hands were still clasped tightly together.

'Does it make me look older?'

'No I don't think so.'

'More repulsive?'

'Don't be silly.'

'If it tickles you . . .'

'That just happened.'

'Which do you prefer?'

'I don't mind.'

'But surely . . . you must have a preference.'

'Honestly I don't mind. If you like it, I like it.'

'Oh my God.'

Bedwyr rolled over in mock anger and agony. He sat up and began to throw handfuls of sand into the marram grass. Then he leaned back on his elbow to study his wife's face again like a page of a sacred book that defied understanding no matter how many times he read it.

'You're too young to understand,' he said.

'To understand what?'

'How much I love you.'

'Of course I know.'

Sian smiled modestly.

'I have a sensual heaven that springs from you and that's where I live. Everywhere else I just exist. I love all of you in the most annoying way and all you do is lie there driving me mad.'

Sian began to laugh. She took the finger that was tracing the outline of her eyebrows in both hands and touched it against her lips. Bedwyr was made instantly active. He embraced her with excited urgency and his hands passed up and down her body.

'Come on,' he said. 'Come on. Now. Please. Darling. Here.'

Sian resisted.

'No,' she said. 'No. Bedwyr. Please no. I can't take them off here. The children. The children . . .'

'They're alright. Leave all that to me. You just relax and let me worship you. Let me touch you . . . In my own way . . .'

'No, please Bedwyr. Please don't!'

Her voice rose to a near shout.

'It's wrong. That's wrong. Bedwyr. Don't.'

He pulled himself away from her, angry and disappointed.

'Wrong. What's it got to do with wrong, for God's sake?'

'Don't be cross.'

Sian was instantly apologetic.

'Well what do you expect me to be? Anybody would think I was some red-eared goat with no technique. Can't you see you're undermining my confidence in myself?'

'No. I'm not. Really.'

'I'm just a house of cards. I want you so much more than you want me. You can blow me down whenever you fancy.'

'I don't want to.'

173

'You hardly ever want me anyway. You don't know what it's like.'

'Don't say that, Bedwyr. Please. That's not true. I love you.'

'Whatever that means.'

'It means I love you.'

'I hate pretending. I like to be honest.'

'I know you do. That's what I love so much about you.'

'What?'

He looked as if he was making a special effort to listen to examine every word she spoke in order to fully understand. Sian sat up eager to grasp an opportunity to speak and say all she had to say while he was giving her such close attention.

'It's what I cling to more than anything.'

'What is?'

He sounded mystified.

'Your righteous integrity.'

'Oh my God . . .'

He groaned aloud in a way that made Sian abandon her resolution to expound her thoughts and feeling in elaborate detail.

'Your integrity.'

'My what?'

'Your goodness.'

'Charming.'

'I wish I could say what I mean.'

Sian searched around her mind for words like a woman dressing in a desperate hurry, opening and shutting drawers.

'It's what I need most in the world that you give me. Trust. Fidelity. Honesty.'

'You make me sound like the bloody District Bank.'

'It's not what I mean at all. What I'm saying. I'm listening to the words just like you are and it's not what I mean at all.'

'What do you mean then?'

'The things you've done . . . The way you helped my father. It was the most wonderful thing I ever saw anybody do.'

'You'll tell me next that was why you married me.'

'And the way you let David come to chapel. Even though you don't approve . . .'

'What?'

He made large eyes of incredulity but she struggled on to add to the list of his virtues.

'And the way you help people. That demanding old step-mother. You are so good and you don't really know it. That's best of all.'

'Shut up,' he said, 'or I'll strangle you.'

'You're making fun of me. You always make fun of me when I want to talk seriously.'

'There's only one way of talking seriously.'

Patiently she allowed him to bend her back so that her head was once more pillowed on the sheepskin coat. Her long hair began to fall out of the combs which held it up. It was newly washed and Bedwyr pushed his fingers through it, drawing it out so that the sunlight picked out a reddish tint in the fair hair. She closed her eyes and made an effort to keep still as though there was something dangerous in his overwhelming desire for her.

She was pale and still and beautiful and he embraced her as though they were completely alone in the landscape of dunes. The cries and laughter of the children in the distance were sounds on the very edge of the afternoon, like the pleasant clamour of the oyster catchers on the fringe of the tide. Above their heads the herring gulls glided closer, drawn by scraps of food dropped by the children near the picnic basket. The man and the woman lying together were turned inward on themselves caught in a communion. The shadow of a gull's wide wings fell across the woman's upturned face. She

175

seemed to be willing herself to become absorbed in her response to his love making. The birds came closer and one gave a sudden isolated scream that made Sian open her eyes and shudder from head to foot.

'What's the matter?' Bedwyr said. 'What's the matter?'

'Nothing,' she said. 'Nothing. That seagull crying. That's all. It seemed so desolate.'

'If you desired me as much as I desire you. Then we could talk.'

'I do.' Sian said. 'You know I do.'

'I always have the feeling you resist it a little.'

'Oh no. That's not true . . .'

'As if it was something dangerous you didn't want to play with.'

'No . . .'

'What is it then?'

Sian put her two hands on his cheeks.

'I want you to make love to me. I'm not going to try and put it all into words. You do it beautifully.'

'But . . .'

'I know how lucky I am.'

'But . . .'

'Love isn't sexual love alone.'

Bedwyr pulled his face away.

'Good news week,' he said.

'You satisfy me perfectly. It's not that. You've given me . . . oh, I can't say what I mean.'

'Say anything. Then I'll try and work it out.'

Sian put her hands inside his trousers. She was suddenly shy as she touched his taut skin and she buried her face in his chest and mumbled a sequence of words he could not follow.

'What?'

'Your great goodness . . .'

The words came with isolated clarity as she moved her head back.

'That's a new name for it.'

176

His voice was gentle. She was not discouraged.

'Your goodness,' she said. 'That's what I love most of all.'

She looked at him hopefully but he did not smile. She pressed her face against his chest and put her hands about his waist to squeeze him tightly as though he needed comforting.

5

Sian was anxious that they should not be late leaving the beach. This seemed to make Bedwyr uncharacteristically indolent. He lay back in the oblique sunlight with his hands behind his head and he was unwilling to look at his wrist watch when Sian asked him the time.

'Why can't we live like drop-outs,' he said. 'Just for one day. Forget about time and being on time. Forget about clocks and watches. You told me to!'

'It's the children,' Sian said.

'Well what about the children? Do they govern our lives or do we govern theirs?'

'They like routine,' Sian said.

'Ah, but do they? Are you sure it isn't you? It's all a reflection of mum's psyche. She belongs to the "service is perfect freedom" brigade. That's the way she likes to operate. Why not take a day off from virtue? Be a devil for just one day.'

Sian was on her knees tidying up the picnic basket.

'Would you like some more tea? It's pretty foul by now in actual fact.'

Bedwyr bent his head up a little with his hands so that he could look at his wife.

'I never thought I'd live to see the day when I would partake of the mentality of tyrants.'

'What do you mean?'

'You're kneeling there like an early Christian martyr. Butter wouldn't melt in your lovely mouth. You deserve to be raped on the spot.'

'Well I have been, haven't I?'

They laughed together.

'I ought to throw you to the lions,' Bedwyr said. 'Or dream up some really perverse torture.'

'The lions are coming . . .'

Christina was climbing determinedly up the sandy slope. Bedwyr leaned over the edge of their hollow and reached down a helping hand. The little girl looked up, her round face filled with pleasure at her new achievement. He picked her up and gave her a warm hug.

'My God,' he said. 'Her buttocks are like blocks of ice.'

'Well there you are,' Sian said.

She took Christina on her knee and gave her some milk to drink and a cake which the little girl crumbled between her fingers.

'It's all very well talking about drop-outs and envying gipsies and hippies. But when it comes to the push you are ten times more bourgeois than I am. You can't stand untidiness in any shape or form. And that's why I try to keep everything tidy. So there you are!'

Their attitude to each other was good-humoured and loving. Even before Sian asked him to do so, he went down to the water's edge to collect Nia. She was entranced with one particular rock pool and the coloured stones and shells that nestled under the shallow water. Bedwyr detached the more colourful specimens so that she could take them home with her. He tried to name as many colours as he could, asking her to repeat the words after him: but she was absorbed by a great feathery underwater moss which was clinging in a snakelike spiral around her little finger which was beginning to turn blue with the cold. David came running up. He was quite ready to leave and anxious for orders. Bedwyr sent him to help his mother. He gave Nia more gentle attention until he realized that she had no intention of moving. He snatched her up quite suddenly and swung her body through the air trying to land her on his shoulders so that he could carry her off at a dramatic gallop. But she wriggled about and kicked her legs with reckless abandon. Her screams spread out all over the deserted beach and caused wading birds near by to scamper away. Bedwyr tried to tickle and tease her back into a good humour but this only served to make her scream louder and throw away the shells he had collected for her. The discordant sound almost blotted out the liquid calling of the disturbed birds. Bedwyr was obliged to hold her tightly as he carried her struggling back to the dunes.

Sian calmed her down by giving her something to eat and at last they were able to move off. David had gone ahead. Sian pointed him out to Nia as she explained patiently how far they had to walk and how long the journey home would take. He was standing dramatically on the highest point of the dunes pointing out the direction they should take to where the car was parked under the maritime pines. He was carrying the picnic basket. It was bulky for him and he swung it from one hand to the other as he waited for them to notice his signs.

'He really is so responsible,' Sian said.

She was helping Nia to mount up on her father's shoulders. After her bout of crying her nose was running. Sian produced a paper handkerchief as though by magic from the pocket of her sheepskin coat and deftly wiped her daughter's nose.

179

'Takes after his ma,' Bedwyr said.

'His pa, you mean. He admires you so much. He senses your attitude to everything even when he can't possibly understand.'

'Nonsense,' Bedwyr said.

But he could not conceal how pleased he was to hear it.

They disputed amiably as they began to move along. Bedwyr began to amuse Nia by behaving like a horse, then like a camel and then like an elephant rocking his burden about in a way that gave her great pleasure. Christina stopped walking and demanded to be put on her father's shoulders, pointing upwards at the great height to which she desired to be lifted. There was more crying and confusion while they changed places, until Bedwyr persuaded Nia to act as his driver. He found a long withered stalk bleached in the sun and wind and put it in Nia's hands telling her to use it as a whip and beat him about the legs whenever he slowed down. The stalk broke after the first blow. Sian was obliged to find a new stick. She dragged Nia along, her other arm trying to hold on to the rest of their luggage. The journey was difficult. Three times Bedwyr had to stop while Nia and Christina took it in turns to ride on his shoulders. He began to gallop to cover more distance and this worked well until the speed of his movement against the cold breeze made Christina's eyes water. His first reaction was to move faster until he realized that this caused more stinging salt tears to flow. She was put down.

He took advantage of the rest to look at his wrist watch.

'Maybe I ought to call in the office on the way home?'

He spoke very quietly but Sian heard him.

'Bedwyr,' she said. 'Don't you dare.'

'Um?'

He raised his eyebrows in an attitude of vague paternal interest.

'This is a day off,' she said. 'So don't you dare leave me stuck with these kids in the back of the car.'

'I wouldn't be a tick.'

'They are dead tired. You can see for yourself. It's a long way for children.'

Christina began to whimper and Nia clamoured to be lifted on her father's back. He was slow complying with her wishes and in no time both the little girls were wailing stridently.

'Family life,' he said. 'Oh my God. Who in their right senses would have any?'

David had reached the car. He busied himself with opening the boot with the bunch of keys with which his father had entrusted him. He managed to put away the picnic basket in its accustomed place. When he had done all he could do he shaded his eyes with his right hand and watched his family approach like pilgrims along the last ridge of the dunes silhouetted against a sun that was now low in the western sky. He ran to meet them ready to relieve them of some of the loads they were carrying.

6

'I'm sorry Sian couldn't come,' Bedwyr said. 'She's taken David to chapel.'

His host nodded understandingly. He was a tall good-looking man with prematurely grey hair. He moved about with great confidence, seemingly delighted with a small social occasion on a Sunday morning.

'You know your way around,' he said. 'You ought to. You built it.'

He leaned back to laugh appreciatively at the way he put it. Bedwyr glanced about critically at details in the entrance hall of the ground floor flat.

'No complaints?'

He smiled and adjusted his shirt cuffs.

'None at all!'

His host spoke with a congratulatory flourish.

'Except one . . .'

He raised his finger as it came to mind. Bedwyr was instantly serious.

'You won't mind me mentioning it?'

'Of course not.'

Bedwyr ventured a little smile.

'It's all trial and error anyway.'

'The ventilator fan. It's very noisy.'

Bedwyr immediately began to consider the problem. He shifted his weight from one foot to the other as though he were mentally changing gear.

'I'm afraid I'm sensitive to noise. I know I shouldn't be in this day and age. But I am. And so is Doris.'

'I'll take a look at it . . .'

'Oh not now for heaven's sale. And it's a minor detail.'

'Details are important,' Bedwyr said.

'You know of course that Doris and I are delighted and privileged . . .'

He nodded solemnly in spite of Bedwyr's depreciatory smile.

'. . . to have a ground-floor flat with garden,' he said. 'In the centre piece of the most interesting residential complex – is that the right term?'

'A bit ambitious,' Bedwyr said.

His manner was steadfastly modest and his mind was on

the ventilator.

'. . . in South East Wales,' his host said enthusiastically. 'I'm quite sure of it. A wonderful blending of the old and the new, and a great place to live in.'

'I'm very glad to hear it.'

Playfully Bedwyr pushed his hand against the wall and lifted his eyes in mock trepidation.

'I'm always afraid these things will fall down,' he said.

The prize-winning block of flats stood on the site once occupied by a large mansion built by a shipping magnate at the end of the nineteenth century. The sturdy stables and outhouses were still standing, skilfully converted into mews flats. And the larger trees had also been preserved. But the forbidding brick walls and lachrymose evergreen hedges had been swept away and all the large houses in the neighbourhood which still remained and had been converted into flats and maisonettes were linked together by an open landscape of lawns and trees and flowering shrubs. Neat walls of varying heights supported by well chosen screens of small trees and shrubs concealed service roads and the concrete working areas in front of the new garages.

On the terrace outside the living room of the ground-floor flat, a portly man with a compact face, narrow eyes and a pink flush high on both cheeks, with an expression of comic whimsicality, was pointing out the virtues of the neighbourhood and the architecture to three people who were newcomers to the area and clearly related as husband, wife and son. The group of four were neatly framed by the narrow window of the entrance hall and Bedwyr was able to observe them with open interest.

'There he is,' Bedwyr's host said, a note of marked fondness in his voice. 'Talking about it all as if he owned the lot. What a P.R.O. eh?'

Bedwyr looked dutifully grateful and continued to study the family group on the terrace.

The husband's face was screwed up ready to make some humorous but inoffensive comment. The wife looked faintly bored and the son stood like a lay figure a few feet behind his father, unable to move in a confined space and obliged to be a motionless replica of what his father must have looked like a quarter of a century ago. He held a crooked smile at the exact angle displayed by his father and gave the same impression of calculating amiability. The portly man was making handsome gestures to accompany his elegant phrases. Bedwyr's host took the opportunity to speak about him in hushed tones, touching on a question of sympathy and understanding and with accelerating speed as they moved into the flat.

'We have him to lunch every Sunday. Poor old boy. He's still not adjusted you know to being a widower. And he adores the company of children. The girls call him "J.M." None of the Sir Joseph business. He likes that. Come and meet the Gobroths. J.M.'s trapped them on the terrace. The new Principal and his wife and son. You haven't met them before have you? I thought you ought to meet them. It's the one thing I enjoy. Bringing what my uncle Jonas used to call "men of calibre" together.'

He leaned back and shook his shoulders as he smiled at the delightful expressions his old uncle used to use. They went outside through a glass door built at right angles to the living room which faced the terrace.

'Here he is,' the host said, lifting his right arm as if it were a trumpet on which he would blow a fanfare. 'The man who designed it all, my friend Bedwyr More!'

'Oh I wouldn't say that . . .'

Bedwyr murmured modestly.

'. . . I was just one of the team.'

'Ah yes.'

Sir Joseph Macsen Morgan lifted a finger, very ready

both to conduct a chorus of praise, and to add a rich bass solo himself.

'But the master-mind! It's always been my experience that no great enterprise can succeed without a master-mind behind it.'

He lowered his voice and glanced around his small audience to demand their full attention.

'You've heard my definition of a camel, I dare say? A horse designed by a committee.'

Everyone laughed obligingly and Sir Joseph passed his left hand over his well groomed white hair as he indulged himself in a prolonged chuckle.

'Now then,' he said, checking himself with a disciplined regard for social correctness. 'I know you are the host, Phil, but you won't mind me introducing our architect friend to Mrs Gobroth and Principal Gobroth? And not forgetting Mr Kenneth Gobroth.'

While hands were being shaken and agreeable noises were being made, Sir J.M. presided over the ceremony with a stately smiling silence registering each prolonged remark in turn as though the smile in itself were a stamp of official recognition. He had more to say and when the introductions had subsided he gestured again in the direction of the landscaped neighbourhood.

'Such a delightful name,' he said. 'Trevecka Close. Absolutely right and yet it fell quite by chance. I was telling the Principal just before you came how beautifully appropriate the name is. We have to educate these foreigners you see.'

The Gobroths did not altogether enjoy being called foreigners but they smiled politely all the same.

'I don't want to give a Sunday morning lecture,' he said. 'But I am so taken with the philosophical appropriateness of it all. You see there's absolutely nothing new about it, in a certain sense.'

He paused dramatically, ready to answer any questions they might involuntarily ask out of their dazzled bewilderment: or to continue, encouraged by their deepening interest, to elaborate on his vision.

'It's not new to me you see. To me it is a renewal. Trevecka Close has most of the happier characteristics of the old South Wales village in the valley. Do you know what I mean? And I find it quite marked. Quite by chance there is a solid core of Welsh-speaking families and that gives the whole place an atmosphere. Right away. Everybody knows everybody. *Cymry*, you see. Comrades. And they all smile easily. When the sun comes out, and I admit we've got no control over that, have we Bedwyr? – there's always a feeling of excitement in the air. And it's classless you see. The old desire for friendliness is there, deep down and not so deep down, under the layer of sophistication. Affluence has not made any impression at all on our ancient egalitarian inclinations.'

The Principal wanted to say something but J.M. held up his hand to ask him to wait because he had more thoughts clamouring to be expressed.

'D'you know, I notice it all the time. Little things. Outside that swanky new inter-denominational church. The men linger on to talk about the match and to give their womenfolk time to get home first and get the Sunday dinner ready. And they give each other lifts home in the cars the women have left behind. Just the same as it used to be in Pentre when I was a boy. But not a car in sight then, of course. The same ethos at work. And look at me coming here for Sunday lunch with Phil and Doris. I had an old uncle in Pentre who did exactly the same with *his* good neighbours. And I haven't begun to tell you about the significance of the word "Trevecka."'

He paused to smile expansively. The Principal took his opportunity to speak. There was a querulous trembling note in his voice but his crooked smile stayed on his face as he spoke.

'Neighbourliness isn't an exclusively Welsh characteristic, Sir Joseph,' he said. 'It's pretty marked anywhere among industrial communities.'

J.M. nodded his agreement, but he had an anecdote in mind and he was determined to share it.

'I'll give you a classic example,' he said. 'And a recent example at that. It happened to a second cousin of mine so there's *consanguin-in-ity* to boot!! Due to subsidence, the wall of his lean-to back kitchen collapsed when he was on a day shift and his injured wife was rushed off to hospital. Do you know, before he got back that evening four of his mates had rebuilt the lean-to *and* had put in a new window frame as well *and* another had a car outside ready to rush him off to visit his wife in hospital. Everything was taken care of!'

'That's wonderful,' Phil said, quick to support Sir J.M.

He felt obliged to show appreciation. Bedwyr too had nodded, but the Gobroths all looked as if they were turning the story over in their minds, testing it for inconsistencies which they could bring into the open when they were next alone together.

'Let me give you something more to drink.'

Phil took the Principal's glass and J.M. took Bedwyr by the elbow and led him back into the house.

'Among your many other accomplishments, Bedwyr, you are an excellent listener,' he said. 'I might tell you I never cease singing your praise from morning till night. Do you think it does you any good?'

He chuckled delightedly at the sound of his own frankness and Bedwyr kept his left arm unnaturally still so that it could remain at the disposal of the elderly man's heavy grip without registering any sign of unwillingness to the capture. He led Bedwyr away from the rest of the company in a way that made it obvious that he wanted to engage in confidential conversation. Should the general interest be aroused,

187

he would enjoy the quiet conference even more, perhaps raising his rich voice from time to time to keep his continuing presence in the forefront of the gathering's consciousness.

'I wanted a word with you,' he said. 'You know I was telling Phil the other day. Awfully nice fellow, Phil, isn't he? I have a vision of this kind of community being a pattern of Welsh life for the future. I really have, and I'm glad to have survived to see it. Perhaps all our labours were not entirely in vain after all? Cellular patterns. A bundle of localities. A loose cellular structure you see that can cope with a surprising variety of forms. I'm convinced this is the answer. This will be the salvation of everything that is best in Welsh life. It will save us from being swamped in the tidal wave of mid-Atlantic mass communications. Don't you agree?'

He jerked Bedwyr by the elbow as though he hoped this would have the physical effect of making his head go up and down. Bedwyr seemed to be hesitating, so he went on to produce more argument and give it additional weight by injecting his deep voice with even richer tone.

'In Welsh terms, the conurbation is Babylon and Sodom and Gomorrah rolled into one. And yet it is now the natural habitat of western man. How are we to translate the Welsh way of life into the sprawling conurbations of the next fifty years? This is your problem, you know, whether you like it or not. This is what architecture is all about. Buildings for people and people for buildings. Don't you agree?'

'I suppose I should.'

'Suppose!'

J.M. repeated the word with a calculated resonance that made most of the people at the other end of the long living room look in his direction.

'So what about the Age of Leisure in Trevecka Close? Will you think about it?'

188

He smiled at Bedwyr knowingly. He was about to ask a small favour with complete frankness because it was nothing in the scale of the services and favours and support that he still had at his command.

'Give it any fancy name you like,' J.M. said. 'But what does it amount to in the end? The natural nucleus of the neighbourhood. A place for collective activity and individual expression. And what does that remind you of?'

'Ah-ha,' Bedwyr said, good-humouredly.

'The chapel as I still remember it from my young days! Let's call it a Centre. A nice compact building. Now Bedwyr, will you think about it for us? We haven't got any funds as yet, but give us something in its setting that we can use as a rallying point for public support. Will you?'

J.M.'s voice had become wooingly soft. He could have been talking to a woman. Bedwyr remained silent long enough to give J.M. the full enjoyment of his own powers of persuasion.

'Of course,' he said. 'I'd be glad to.'

J.M. slapped him on the back and let him back in triumph.

'There you are,' he said, addressing Phil, the host, and Principal Gobroth, who had also moved a little apart from the company. 'He'll do it for us. I told you he would. And I can't think of anybody better. And I mean that.'

He stared sternly at Principal Gobroth to make clear that he wanted him to be deeply impressed by the recommendation he was making.

'If he has any fault at all, and I'm talking professionally now, as a public servant who has taken a lifelong interest in architecture – with a small "a" and a capital "A" – if he has a fault it is what I would call "perfectionism." A bit unwilling to compromise.'

'Oh I don't know about that,' Bedwyr said.

He spoke seriously. He was anxious to demonstrate that while he was unremittingly affable he was at the same time very much his own man.

'You'd better see the sketches first,' he said. 'You might very well not like them.'

'Of course we will,' J.M. said.

He became loudly jocular.

'He thinks because I'm getting on a bit, I'm a fuddy-duddy. Well I'm not you know. Am I, Phil?'

'Not by any means,' Phil said, waving his glass and rattling the loose change in his trouser pocket. Rattling his change seemed to be something of a habit. It could have represented high-spirits, a determination to present a manly front, or a nervous uncertainty. He was preparing a phrase that would flatter J.M. and impress the new Principal and while he waited for the words to take shape he smiled and rattled the change in his pocket.

'Who's that?'

The Principal pointed at the window, seemingly relieved to have found a diversion. At the same time Doris, Phil's wife, who was talking to Mrs Gobroth and a close friend of hers who lived nearby, gave a frightened squeal and pressed her hand hard into her pale cheek. It was noticeable that she was a little older than her husband.

'Oh my God,' he said. 'Who's that?'

Outside on the narrow terrace stood a well-built man who looked massive and menacing because his head was crowned with a black crash-helmet and his eyes concealed with bulky dust goggles. He was covered from the back of his head to the ankles by a coat of Rumanian sheepskins stitched crudely together, wellworn and stained with oil. When they noticed him, he grinned cheerfully and moved forward to press his hands in large leather gauntlets against the glass. Then he pointed playfully at Bedwyr.

190

'Good Lord,' Bedwyr said. 'It's my brother Gwydion. Where on earth has he sprung from?'

'Your brother?'

J.M.'s loud voice passed the message on.

'Not the one in "show-business"?'

His curiosity was infectious and Bedwyr became a little flustered by the close attention everyone in the room was giving to his reactions. He looked for somewhere to put down his glass and went outside. They were pleased to see each other and Gwydion particularly was in no way put off by the small groups of spectators in the living room on the other side of the glass.

'Dr Livingstone, I presume,' he said.

He quickly embraced his half-brother.

'That thing smells,' Bedwyr said, referring to the sheepskin coat.

'I know,' Gwydion said. 'It's foul, isn't it? I wear it to keep the women off.'

He had the ability to make his brother laugh easily. He removed the crash-helmet and immediately drew Bedwyr's attention to his retreating hair-line. He turned the baldness which threatened both of them into an hilarious family joke. He had a round face with lips that were conspicuously like a Cupid's bow. His eyes were like Bedwyr's, dark and glowing, but his eyelashes were longer and more feminine, like Peredur's. Somehow they matched the dimple hole in his chin. Although his head was rather large and inclined to be asymmetrical his confidence in his appearance and his general attractiveness was marked and yet did not seem unduly immodest.

'How did you know I was here?'

'The good woman looking after the two little ones . . .'

'Mrs Peace.'

'That's right. What a blessed name! She said that Sian had taken David to chapel and that you had gone

191

to the ground-floor flat at Trevecka Close. Number
Two. So there we are. I've found you. No problem at
all.'

Phil, the host, appeared on the terrace and invited
Gwydion in for a drink. He hesitated, looking at
Bedwyr.

'I've got someone in the car,' he said.

Phil stood still, with an arm extended, leaving the
decision to Gwydion who said,

'Well just a quick one.'

He stepped carefully to avoid the tub of red geraniums that narrowed the approach to the glass-panelled
door. Phil introduced him to his wife.

'I'm sure I've seen you before,' Doris said. She was
quite worried by the weakness of her powers of recall.

'And this is Mrs Gobroth,' Phil said. 'And her son
Kenneth.' Gwydion held on to her hand.

'You look much too young to have a grown-up son,'
he said.

He made the compliment without any effort and
with every appearance of sincerity, like a man accustomed to speak frankly whatever the consequences.
Mrs Gobroth was visibly pleased. For the first time
since her arrival she began to look as if she were enjoying herself.

'On the other hand he can't be your brother because
he looks too like his father.'

He dealt with the problem as if it were a scientific
matter, which made his attitude even more charming.

'I know,' Doris said. 'I've seen you on television.'

Gwydion nodded. He had brought an excitement
into the gathering which it was his business to fos-
ter.

'That programme they used to have on social and
religious questions ... What was it called? Oh no ...
what was it called?'

'"Used to have",' Gwydion said. 'But now as you can

see from my get-up, reduced to playing Ivan the Awful at the Pier Pavilion, Weston-super-Mare.'

He managed to be gay and nostalgic at the same time. Doris looked a little afraid of him.

'No it wasn't that. Oh what was it?'

'Alas, now receded into the mists of history. They "just - don't - have-good-programmes-anymore". All sunk into a grey mediocrity.'

'Yes, but what was it called?'

J.M. wanted to be introduced. Gwydion held his crash-helmet under one arm and this drastically shortened the extent of his handshake. But he behaved as if he were a knight being presented to a royal figure presiding over a tournament.

'Gwydion?' he said. 'That's a good name.'

'My father was deep in the Mabinogion at the time and I suppose he hoped I'd be good for one or two miracles.'

J.M. kept his mouth open for a moment before beginning to shake with appreciative laughter. Phil was watching him with care in order to gauge something of the intruder's importance from the degree of elder statesman-like response Sir Joseph Macsen Morgan would be prepared to show.

'Yes, well now, tell me,' J.M. said. 'Who was your father?'

'That's a good question. A good old Welsh approach!'

Gwydion was so amiable they all accepted what he was saying in the friendliest manner possible.

'I'm glad to say he was a poet. Otherwise it would be unforgivable, wouldn't it?'

When the laughter subsided, J.M. turned to Bedwyr and addressed him sternly.

'You are brothers,' he said.

'Half-brothers to be exact,' Bedwyr said.

'Yes, but the same father.'

'I hope so.'

Gwydion spoke lightly but J.M. was not to be diverted.

'You never told me your father was a poet,' he said. 'I always understood he was a solicitor.'

Gwydion was still cheerfully talkative.

'The contradiction is apparent, not real,' he said. 'It came out as you can see in all sorts of ways. He had a bardic name. Cilydd.'

'Not Cilydd!'

J.M. took a dramatic step backwards. Gwydion was a little slow to observe that J.M. was being serious.

'The same,' he said.

'Yes,' J.M. said, intent now on displaying an air of solemnity. 'But you must realize he was a fine poet?'

The hawk descends
With burning eyes
And where he strikes
The singing dies.

J.M. recited with a resonant intonation that drew everybody's attention. He pitched up his voice at the end of each line. Phil murmured with admiration.

'That's pretty good, you know,' J.M. said. 'He started off brilliantly. Won the chair when he was very young. A master of the strict metres. And then seemed to fade out into a long silence. D'you know what I mean? He could be witty too. I remember one to a second-hand car . . .'

He screwed up his small eyes.

'. . . Let me see, how did it go?'

He cleared his throat and began reciting again with so much evident enjoyment that those in the direct line of his gaze were obliged to smile and nod their support and approval.

Lumber on wheels, shaking
A shattered chassis quaking
A moving ruin baking
Cakes of rust in a hearse-dustbin!

Doris was frowning as though she had forgotten something again, but when she caught Phil's brief frown she laughed more loudly than anyone else.

'He was a prophet,' Gwydion said. 'I've got that very car in the road there now! I've been baking cakes of rust every inch of the way from Sheffield. I've got the star of my show in it too. Bedwyr, my old and valued elder brother, I just can't leave her there any longer.'

'I'm frightfully sorry,' Phil said. 'I should have asked, shouldn't I?' 'Bring her in, do.'

'And to think that you are both the sons of Cilydd. Well, well, well.'

J.M. was sonorously amazed. Bedwyr smiled.

'Everybody is somebody's son,' he said.

J.M. lifted a limp hand in mock-horror.

'What a Philistine, not to say Anglo-Saxon, attitude. Pedigree is all, even among the workers like myself. A part of life's mystery. Like lifting your eyes up unto the hills, you know?' Between the sea and the sky, visions are vouchsafed to you because you are your father's son as much as for any other reason.

'Not me I'm afraid.' Bedwyr said.

J.M. turned a crooked finger at Gwydion in a way that seemed to turn it into a link between the two brothers.

'Look here,' he said. 'You are not the same as him, are you? That would be too awful for an old man like me on a Sunday morning.'

He looked reproachfully at Bedwyr.

'I thought you told me he was a philosopher?'

He glanced back to Gwydion.

'You've got to forgive me,' he said. 'I'm insatiably curious. A sign of my village upbringing. Everybody in Cwmbach suffers from it.'

'That's my other brother,' Bedwyr said. 'Peredur. There are three of us.'

'Peredur!'

J.M. rolled the name over his tongue.

'Then what do you do?'

He spoke to Gwydion who was not at all put off by the directness of the question.

'I started as a philosopher of sorts,' Gwydion said. 'But I gave it up for the candy-floss of this world. The gossamer and filigree of show business! I was in television and I've just lost a small fortune on a Musical. So that makes me an unsuccessful impresario. That's what I've put on my passport anyway.'

Gwydion made the admission of failure sound like an understated account of acts of valour which would certainly in due course bring him a decoration. Bedwyr looked worried but the rest of the company, in one way or another, was deeply impressed: particularly by the phrase 'lost a small fortune'. Kenneth Gobroth moved from his father's side. He smiled winningly at Gwydion, tilting his head in the opposite direction to compensate for the crookedness of his smile.

'I would rather like to work in television,' he said. 'I'm doing my finals next summer in P.P.E. How does one get in?'

He moved his head out like a tilted receptacle into which the reply could be dropped with the minimum of inconvenience.

'You keep on kicking the door until it falls in,' Gwydion said.

Mrs Gobroth had come closer to overhear any advice that her son could be getting from the visiting celebrity. The Principal was looking pleased, as though the occasion was turning out to be far more fruitful than he had ever expected possible.

'You must give me a ring,' Gwydion said. 'The next time you come to London. My brother will have my number.'

Kenneth Gobroth thanked him a little breathlessly and his mother's lips moved too, rehearsing wordless thanks.

'Now I really must go. It's been a great pleasure to meet you all.' J.M. took him by the hand in a firm grip and shook it slowly.

'Cilydd's son,' he said. 'The blood of Cilydd!'

He took his time to register his full approval and with a graceful and easy courtesy Gwydion kept still until the little ceremony was over.

Outside, as they followed a path between expanses of well-kept lawn, Gwydion began to ask questions.

'Who was the old windbag?'

'Don't be deceived,' Bedwyr said. 'He's nobody's fool. He's one of the most influential men in Wales.'

'Well there you are,' Gwydion said. 'That's something I don't know about. But I can see you do: "Bedwyr the shrewd old bird". No wonder I'm such a fantastic failure. Not only do I not know the right things, I don't know the right people either.'

'Where's this car of yours?'

'Damn.'

Gwydion was cross with himself.

'You can see how inefficient I am. We've come down the wrong side. I've got no sense of direction.'

Bedwyr smiled forgivingly and they walked back towards the block of flats.

'I'd no idea the old man wrote such second-rate rubbish. That awful ditty about a second-hand car . . .'

'I don't think that was Cilydd,' Bedwyr said.

He made the dry statement in a way that made Gwydion stop to shake with laughter and slap him on the back.

'You're marvellous,' he said. 'Same as ever.'

'What's marvellous about that?'

Bedwyr was smiling but appeared genuinely puzzled.

'Not to correct the old windbag of course. The influential windbag. Never correct an influential windbag in public over trivial errors of fact. Rule number two and a half.'

Bedwyr looked serious.

'I'm not criticizing,' Gwydion said. 'I'm just admiring you. I've got to learn sometime, damn it all. I can't be an outsider for ever.'

'Cool down a bit,' Bedwyr said. 'They're still watching us.'

'Are they, by God! Well we're worth looking at. Shall I do them a quick strip? Maybe I've got some of my summer tan left . . . now this is the way. I remember now. I've a genius for finding short-cuts, haven't I, and then losing them again. Remember?'

They were two of a kind, glad to recognize in each other affinities that seemed to guarantee mutual support and to make the world around them less hostile and daunting. Together they had the capacity to generate a protective climate that they could both inhabit with comfort. And they were easy and agreeable together as only old friends or boys brought up together can be, ready at any moment to exchange vivid glimpses of the past, and cherished memories.

'Ah there it is,' Gwydion said. 'You wouldn't think it was possible to lose an old tank like that, would you?'

The car was a large but battered Jaguar and the rear bumper was stained black above the exhaust pipe by burning oil. It had a sunshine roof which was jammed permanently three inches from the closed position, leaving a narrow slit through which the wind and the weather penetrated to the interior of the car. Low in the passenger seat a black girl in a short fur coat and wig tinted with copper highlights sat glowering angrily. She ignored Bedwyr and had large white eyes only for Gwydion.

'Where have you been?' she said.

'Here she is,' Gwydion said cheerfully, 'the greatest girl in the world. Martha Appletown, star of stage and screen and about to sing before the crowned heads of

Europe! This is my brother Bedwyr. He may well give us a meal and a bed.'

She barely acknowledged the introduction.

'Leaving me here to freeze my ass in this stinking car,' she said. 'What do you think I am?'

'The greatest,' Gwydion said. 'And I'm going to look after you. So don't you worry about the single, smallest, littlest thing.'

7

'I don't see why I have to like her just because she's black.'

Sian sat on the bathroom chair watching the water run down her legs and sinking into the cork mat under her feet. She had been under the shower and her hair was still covered with a plastic cap with a frilly fringe. There was a mournful expression on her face which the cap transformed into something comically woe-begotten. Bedwyr, who had already put on clean underwear, stood in the adjoining bedroom doorway, amused by what he saw. In contrast to his wife he looked elated and happy.

'She thinks of absolutely nothing but herself. I didn't want to go shopping. I just went to keep her happy. It was the same thing all afternoon, "Wouldn't that look just wonderful on me" . . . she could have sung a song about it.'

Bedwyr moved away to his bedside table to find his wrist watch. As he put it on he glanced at it in the lamplight to see the time.

He called out to Sian.

'You'd better hurry darling or we'll be late.'

'I'm not coming.'

Her voice was quiet and sulky and he did not appear to hear it.

'Shall I get you a nice big towel?'

The airing cupboard was on the landing, near the bedroom in which Nia and the baby Christina was sleeping. Nia slept in the top bunk. The bottom berth was vacant for the time being, since Christina slept in a cot still and David had long ago objected to sleeping in the same room as his sister. The room was warm and smelt of talcum powder and sleeping babies. Nia had thrown off all her clothes and was breathing heavily through her mouth, her nostrils blocked with a dried film of mucus. Bedwyr smiled at wildness tamed by sleep and rearranged the clothes over her thin extended body. As he did so, without waking up she ploughed her face along her pillow in some form of drowsy protest. Bedwyr hurried back to the bathroom as though he were eager to describe his daughter's behaviour in detail before it vanished from his memory. He held open the large towel invitingly but Sian did not move from the chair. Anxious to help, Bedwyr knelt down and took her left leg on his and began to dry it.

'She makes me feel a prude,' Sian said. 'She makes me feel catty too. I don't like that.'

'She's had a hard life.'

'Oh I know all that. Her grandmother was a prostitute in New York and she was born when her mother was fifteen. I've heard all that.'

'So you mustn't be hard on her.'

'That's why I'm not coming.'

Bedwyr looked up in surprise.

'Not coming where?'

200

'I told you. Tonight. I don't want to come. I'm not coming.'

'But it's all arranged,' Bedwyr said.

'Exactly. And who arranged it?'

'He thinks of it as a treat. I like that about Gwydion. He always wants to make other people happy. He loves generating excitement. And just because he wants to, more often than not he succeeds. He's what you could call a life-enhancer. Warren thinks he's terrific.'

'Warren would,' Sian said.

She snatched the large towel from Bedwyr's hands and began to dry herself with great energy and vigour. Bedwyr shook his head with comic despair and held out his hands to show that they were empty and that he had been deprived of the opportunity of fondling her. When she had finished drying herself she took a tin of talcum powder from the bathroom cupboard behind the long mirror and applied the powder liberally over her naked body.

'Anyway, you are coming,' Bedwyr said.

'No I'm not. You can make any excuse you like but I'm not going to spend a whole evening jammed in some badly lit cellar listening to those two showing off.'

'He thinks you like Greek food. You used to you know. And the singing. He's arranged the whole thing especially for you. He said so. I was quite touched.'

'I'm sure you were.'

Sian had lifted her foot to balance it against the edge of the bath. She was applying a lotion to the sole of her foot to soften a callous.

'What do you mean?'

Her uncharacteristic behaviour made him uneasy. He stared at her hands as though they were working magic spells around her foot. She stopped and straightened her back in order to look directly at his face.

'Has he asked you for money?'

Bedwyr seemed reluctant to answer. He leaned forward to touch her smooth flank with the tips of his fingers. She shifted out of his reach.

'Has he?'

'Just a loan.'

Bedwyr spoke with authority, but she was not to be put off.

'How much?'

'Five hundred.'

Bedwyr flushed a little. It could have been himself who had been caught begging for a loan. Sian pressed her lips together. She took time to decide what best to say.

'He makes use of you.'

Bedwyr was ready with his defence.

'So what? I hope he does. What else are brothers for? He's in trouble and it's my duty to help him.'

'Trouble?'

'Debts. The show has folded. He'll have to sell his flat.'

'Well, he brought it on himself.'

She stood near the washbasin unscrewing the cap of another jar of lotion, this time for her hands. Bedwyr stared at her as though unable to account for the discrepancy between the beautiful proportions of her naked figure and the harsh attitude she was taking.

'I don't see why I should be obliged to defend him,' he said.

Sian dry-washed her hands and said nothing.

'I've enjoyed having them here. I didn't realize you were finding it such an extra burden. I don't suppose she does much to help?'

'Nothing.'

Bedwyr nodded understandingly.

'I think he finds Martha a bit of a burden too. But he feels responsible for her. She was all set for stardom and it didn't come off. He believes in her talent. He's prepared to have another go. I admire him for that. I admit his standards aren't my standards and I don't really pretend to understand his way of life or what he's doing, but he's generous and good-humoured and he always cheers me up. That's what I meant when I said I enjoyed having them here. What I meant was I enjoy having Gwydion with me and I'm prepared to put up with Martha in order to have him around.'

'He owes her money,' Sian said.

'I know that.'

Bedwyr pulled a face to show that he found all this talk about money distasteful.

'He hasn't paid her her salary for the last three weeks. That's fair enough. She'll get it in the end.'

'It's more than that,' Sian said. 'He borrowed money from her when he was setting the show up. That's why she won't let him out of her sight. She means to get it back.'

'Did she tell you?'

Bedwyr was disturbed.

'I put two and two together. It's quite obvious when you think about it.'

'Sian . . .'

He reached out to hold her, but she turned her greasy palms outwards and he let his hands fall. She walked past him into their bedroom and found a box of tissues on a dressing-table. She sat down to wipe her hands. Bedwyr followed her.

'I feel an obligation towards him, with all his faults. He's my brother.'

'Half-brother to be exact,' Sian said.

'You should understand this. You are a Christian. A practising Christian, and I respect you for it. I can't believe in it myself as you know but that's neither here nor there at the moment.'

'He's like his mother,' Sian said. 'The way he tries to buy his way into people's affection . . .'

203

'What do you mean?'

'He's been loading David with presents in the most nauseating way.'

'But he loves the boy,' Bedwyr said. 'He's never had any children of his own.'

'Just like Amy. She spoils David completely. Calls him her little cavalier and makes him quite impossible for weeks after he's been to Brangor.'

'But you won't let him go there if you can possibly help it.'

'Exactly. And now you know why.'

'But what's this got to do with Gwydion?'

'They are the same.'

Sian spoke forcefully to make up for any deficiencies in logic.

'How? They don't get on at all. You know that.'

'You don't understand them one bit.'

Sian shivered. Her dressing-gown was on the bed. It was white and voluminous. She put it on. Unexpectedly she sank to her knees and sat on the bedside rug.

'They make use of people. And they've got no scruples at all. They are terrible.'

'What do you mean "terrible"? Nobody is "terrible". It's a silly word to use.'

She was cross with herself for being emotional and not expressing herself in the objective and reasonable manner of which Bedwyr most approved.

'I know they can be pretty awful sometimes,' he said, 'but so can we all. As I see it, it's my business to help them when I can. It would be inhuman to be otherwise.'

'She wants to use you to get him back.'

In spite of herself Sian's eyes were filling with tears. Bedwyr sat on the stool with his back to the dressing-table mirror and she leaned against his knee.

'I know,' he said. 'I'm quite aware of that and I don't mind. After all he is her son and I'm not and she desperately needs to win back his affection. I'm quite prepared to help her. What's wrong with that?'

Sian took his hand in hers.

'I can't bear people making use of you,' she said. 'Taking advantage of your goodness.'

'But if I don't mind.'

Bedwyr stopped talking abruptly. There was someone outside the bedroom door, trying to move quietly. As soon as the soft tapping on the door started Sian jumped to her feet and got into bed. When Gwydion opened the door and poked in his head, grinning cheerfully, she was buttoning up the front of her dressing-gown and Bedwyr was holding in his stomach as he sat in full view in his vest and underpants.

'Can I come in? I'm trying to be quiet. Don't want to wake the kids etc.'

He seemed on the verge of giggling.

'I'm sorry to burst in on your marital privacy, folks, but I've not had a chance to speak to you alone all day. I want to apologize about Martha, who, I am glad to say, at this moment is in the bath.'

'That's okay,' Bedwyr said. 'You don't have to.'

'She's a bit rough,' Gwydion said. 'There's no getting away from it. I don't know what it is. Some unimaginable upbringing. She's a bloody savage really. Pardon my French. I have to be tight with her or she'll blow every cent she's got on the gee-gees. You never saw anything like it. It's an obsession. That's what I wanted to explain. She's got this weakness for gambling. It's like a disease and there's damn all I can do about it except sit on my wallet. So don't lend her any money whatever you do, or you'll never see it again this side of Jordan. We'll be off tomorrow.'

'So soon?'

Bedwyr looked genuinely disappointed. Sian said nothing.

'I've no right to drag my own personal mess into your lives. We've been here too long as it is.'

'Look . . .'

Bedwyr wanted to be helpful.

'I'll sort it all out. One way or another. So don't you worry. I just nipped in to get the record straight. I hope you don't mind.'

'Of course we don't,' Bedwyr said.

He looked at Sian to invite her to join in a warm understanding and sympathy for his brother's predicament but she kept her eyes averted. With some delicacy Gwydion changed the subject. The urgency had gone from his voice and his manner became pleasantly conversational.

'Fill me in about Warren,' he said. 'I'm so out of touch and I wouldn't want to put my foot in it. He's such a decent chap. What happened?'

'Divorce,' Bedwyr said.

Gwydion pulled a sympathetic face.

'She was no good.'

Bedwyr sounded implacable.

'He gave her everything, but it wasn't enough. I don't blame him. A chap can't function properly unless he feels his lines of retreat are safe. He was weak with her really. Indulged her, didn't he, Sian?'

He made a firm effort to draw Sian into the conversation and she conceded him a dutiful nod.

'A strange softness in Warren's character. He couldn't bring himself to swing the axe. Very curious really. I nearly had to push him into it. And yet in business he's far more ruthless than I am. That's another subject you'd better give a wide berth. We've got a tension on there at the moment. Disagreements over policy. And office management. Stick to show-business.'

The brothers laughed easily, full of confidence in each other.

'Leave it to me,' Gwydion said. 'I know just the formula. An evening to remember! Right ... well, up guards and at 'em! We'd better hurry or we'll be late.'

He smiled at Sian who was sitting up demurely in bed.

'I'm not coming,' she said.

Gwydion could not hide his disappointment. Bedwyr hastened to elaborate.

'She doesn't feel up to it,' he said. 'She's had a very tough day. No point in her coming if she doesn't feel up to it.'

'Of course not.'

Gwydion was deeply apologetic.

'I feel as though it's our fault. Martha sits around as if she'd been born in the Ritz. Treats everywhere like a hotel. It never ceases to amaze me ... What a woman! I'm very sorry. I really am.'

'Nonsense,' Bedwyr said. 'It's been a great pleasure ... how else can stick-in-the-muds like us find out how the glamour lot live?'

He advanced on his brother for a playful exchange of blows.

'Get moving,' he said. 'Go on. Out you go!'

'Fit isn't he?' Gwydion said, parrying the sketched-in punches. 'Good clean-living boy. There's a lot to be said for it.'

8

Sian lay on the settee with cushions supporting the small of her back and the furthest arm of the settee lowered so as not to interrupt her view of the television screen. She was dressed for bed, too drowsy to concentrate on the book which she had allowed to fall face downwards on the hearth rug. It was warm in the living-room and her white dressing-gown hung open. Beyond its opaque glass front the gas-fire showed a low fringe of comforting flame. There was a tray on the occasional table with biscuits and a blue mug containing the dregs of milky coffee. She was staring at the screen with a glazed sort of contempt, her mouth hanging open, when the front-door bell rang a brief chime. She sat up, instantly awake, all nerves and apprehension, as if this were a visit she had been dreading. She took a glimpse in the mirror at her own appearance. Her fair hair had been pinned up earlier in the evening but was now falling untidily about her ears. There was a sulky defiant expression on her face. She buttoned up her dressing-gown and pushed her bare feet into slippers trimmed with thick white fur.

In the narrow hall, she looked upstairs and listened to check whether the chiming bell had disturbed any of the children. When she was satisfied that they were all fast asleep she switched on the outside light. She could make out the vague figure of a man standing in the porch. She opened the door. Gwydion stood in the light smiling.

'I had to see you alone,' he said.

He sounded gay and ready to defend his behaviour with an easy eloquence.

'Why?'

Sian was hostile.

'It's so ridiculous,' he said. 'Being under the same roof and not able to speak freely. I want to talk to you. Aren't you going to let me in?'

'There's nothing to talk about,' Sian said.

'Well for God's sake of course there is. How do you think I feel? Have some consideration . . . Please.'

There was a begging note in his voice that seemed to persuade her. She stepped aside and he passed close to her, rubbing his hands. In the hall he put his finger to his lips to show he was aware of the dangers of waking the children. They went into the living-room and Sian closed the door. She switched off the television set and moved closer to the fire.

'Why wouldn't you come?'

His voice was a fresh vibrant sound in the closed room, a little chiding, but warm, friendly and eager. He had every confidence in the charm of his presence and his manner. Sian was not prepared to discuss her reasons for staying home.

'How did you manage to get away?'

'My Jaguar. My Jag.'

He felt his way delicately between jocularity and honesty.

'In the all-night place. The new silencer. I had to collect it. They're all very happy anyway. They won't miss me. Warren and that chap Philips are fascinated by Martha. She might even sing. *Cave canem.*'

She refused to be amused. She watched him carefully, openly suspicious of anything he said or did. He moved closer.

'You've no idea how beautiful you are,' he said.

She studiously ignored the compliment.

'What is it?' she said. 'What is it you want to say?'

He began to lift his hands and then let them fall.

'Well that's it,' he said. 'I feel better now I've said it. I never could bear pretending. You haunt me. That's why I came here.'

209

'Is it?'

'Martha means nothing to me.'

'Why tell me that?'

'She doesn't know what love means. She's not even interested in sex. She worships money. Lots and lots of it. That's her passion. And any form of gambling, but particularly horses. We're just stuck together now by grim necessity.'

Sian stood rigidly still, her head erect as though any movement would be a sign of weakness.

'I've slept with her. I'm no saint. But when I see her near you, in your house . . . God, you've no idea how miserable it makes me feel. Miserable and trapped. I wish I could be sane about this but there's something about your beauty that burns me up completely . . . I want to know . . .'

He came closer to her and reached out to touch first her arm and then her breast, soft and unprotected under her dressing-gown. She kept still and stared into his face as if she were bending her own will to pass through some obscure trial by ordeal.

'Sian,' he said. 'Don't you feel something still? I don't know what you think and I suppose not speaking and not knowing is choking me. It is so precious what we had, to me. The most precious thing in my life. I can't find words to describe it and it's in me still. I've got to tell you this.'

He brought his arm around her waist and tried to draw her body against his with gentle but insistent pressure.

'I must tell Bedwyr.'

She spoke quietly. He released her and she still managed not to move. He swung his arm about, inarticulate with sincerity.

'Sian,' he said. 'I wish you'd give me a chance . . . how do you think I feel? You are married to my brother. I love you. Can't you see I'm in a desperate position?'

He sat down on the settee, convinced by his own words of his plight. He was silent, overawed. She spoke again.

'Or do you want to tell him?'

He looked up at her, shocked by the heartlessness of her suggestion.

'God almighty, of course I don't.'

Sian at last allowed herself to move. She sat down in an armchair near the window.

'What is it you're proposing,' she said.

He turned to look at her.

'My God,' he said, 'you've become . . .'

He was lost for the right word and went on without ever finding it.

'It's being a mother of three, I suppose,' he said. 'And all this.'

He waved his hand to indicate the outward signs of domestic prosperity.

'You feel you owe him loyalty,' he said. 'I can understand that and I admire it. You have a fine nature. Of course you have.'

'Why did you come back?'

Sian's questions were quiet but persistent.

'I've told you. I wanted you to know how I felt. And I wanted to know how you felt.'

'Did you think I'd be in bed?'

'How was I to know where you'd be?'

'Did you think you'd make love to me? Upstairs in your brother's bed?'

Her voice was still firm and calm.

'Or down here perhaps. In front of the fire. Was that what you wanted?'

He jumped up and searched for words of protest.

'You're trying to degrade the whole thing,' he said. 'You're trying to hurt me and you're trying to hurt yourself.'

She shook her head.

'No. I'm trying to see you as you really are.'

211

'Me?'

Gwydion fingered his own chest.

'I was only a girl then,' Sian said. 'Very young for my age. Rather unhappy and very susceptible. You were so physically attractive and so expert and so sympathetic and so comforting. But I'm not young for my age any more. I'm a woman with three children. But you haven't grown up at all. I'm glad you came back.'

'Well there you are,' Gwydion said, as though they had at last reached a point of agreement. 'That's why I came.'

'I can say things to you now I couldn't say if Bedwyr was here.'

'That's it exactly!'

'You've been thinking I was jealous of Martha.'

'No I haven't.'

'You've been thinking that was the reason why I was so distant and restrained.'

'Well it would have been understandable,' Gwydion said. 'It was one of the things I hoped you would let me explain.'

'You've been thinking that all you needed was a few words with me alone and I would fall at your feet and worship you. Become your slave. And you'd be able to complete your conquest of yet another woman. And pop down here from time to time to see us. Be a magic uncle to David and a secret lover for his mother.'

'Sian! What's got into you? You don't want to understand . . .'

'Well, am I wrong?'

For the first time she smiled at him pleasantly. She wrapped her dressing-gown around her more tightly. The automatic central heating had switched itself off and the room had gone cooler. She glanced at the gas fire as though she were considering moving closer to it and turning it up. She remained patiently in her seat.

'If that's all you think of me . . .'

212

'What do you want me to think?'

He paced about in front of the settee, too annoyed to find the sequence of explanation that he needed.

'What's so wrong about it all? It wasn't wrong before. You said yourself at the time it was a stretching experience.'

Sian laughed suddenly, and then put a hand over her mouth when he frowned at her.

'I was helping you both. That was the way I looked at it. And it bore fruit. So why should it be wrong now? Tell me that. There are lots of societies in different parts of the world where it would be perfectly all right. It's not morality. It's just a question of custom. I told you all this before.'

'Yes you did, didn't you?'

'So what has changed?'

Sian shook her head sadly.

'No wonder the world is such a dangerous place,' she said. 'It's so full of men who refuse to grow up.'

Gwydion felt about in the pockets of his smart suit for a packet of cigarettes. His hands were trembling. He was angry and upset.

'You've become coarse,' he said at last.

'Coarse!'

The incongruity of the word made Sian laugh.

'In the spirit,' Gwydion said. 'You know what I mean.'

'Indeed I don't.'

'You were a fine girl with a spirit of your own. An independent spirit. You've been got at.'

'What do you mean?'

She was amused and this made him angrier.

'I'm not an absolute fool you know. You've reverted to type.'

'I have?'

'All this chapel business. Soft-headed sententious moralizing. Designed to defend and uphold all known domestic vested interests. Verbal cosi-wrap for the nesting season. It's the nest that really counts, isn't it?'

'What are you talking about?'

'You know damn well what I'm talking about. It's all rubbish and you know it's rubbish. You just choose to believe it because it suits what you've settled for. You are less than what you were. You are prepared to barter your own individuality and your own free spirit for a damn great fat fur-lined nest. So don't you lecture me about not growing up.'

Sian looked disappointed.

'There wasn't much point in your coming back after all,' she said.

'We had something wonderful,' Gwydion said. 'I really believe that. I haven't got the words to express it and if I did you wouldn't listen. It was a state of exultation ... an electric thing that transformed the world into our own private palace ... the kind of thing that moves mountains ... Doesn't it mean anything to you any more?'

'Nothing that you would understand,' she said.

'Oh my God. It's got to that stage.'

'I want to tell Bedwyr.'

'Tell him!'

Gwydion was horrified.

'Why shouldn't I?'

'It would kill him.'

'Do you think that?'

'Of course I do. He's a proud man. It would destroy his confidence in himself. I can't believe you would be so heartless.'

'You think so much of him?'

'Of course I do.'

'But you are quite prepared to go on deceiving him. You came here hoping to make love to his wife. A quick little flutter.'

'I don't look at it like that.'

'Well how do you look at it?'

214

He moved his head about as though the physical effort would stop the net closing around him.

'You hate me.'

He seemed so appalled by the fact that he could barely bring himself to utter the words.

'No indeed I don't,' Sian said. 'That's why I think it would be best to tell Bedwyr everything. Then we could start again . . .'

'Start again . . .'

He snarled out the words.

'What kind of a prison do you want me to live in? It would destroy absolutely everything there ever was between us. All the spontaneous trust . . .'

'Trust?'

'Yes. Trust!'

He spoke defiantly.

'It's not the way I want to live. I want to be a free man. I'm not going to be buried alive and you're not going to tell him.'

Suddenly a silence fell between them. It filled the room with a rapid dangerous expansion that threatened the well-ordered space like a tidal wave.

'How much money did he lend you?'

'So that's it!'

Gwydion pointed at her.

'You know exactly how much he lent me. Five hundred pounds.'

'For how long?'

'What do you mean "for how long"? That's not the way we deal with each other.'

'Have you ever lent him money?'

'Of course I have.'

'How much?'

'How much? The amounts don't count. You're talking like a damned book-keeper.'

'I don't mean to,' Sian said. 'But transactions are facts aren't they?'

'If that's the kind of fact you're interested in . . .'

'They stand out in people's lives like landmarks,' Sian said.

'Do they?'

He tried to speak with a fine contempt for such mundane considerations.

'It's when you get the truth out of people,' she said. 'When what they take to be their vital interests are at stake.'

'"Take to be" . . . what do you mean?'

'I won't tell him if you give him the money back.'

Gwydion moved quickly to the glass panelled door. He was in a hurry to leave. He frowned as he looked at Sian.

'I don't know you any more,' he said.

She moved towards him confidently.

'Perhaps you never knew me.'

'I keep thinking of you as you were. That day by the lake.'

'Illusions,' Sian said.

'Like the sunlight on the water.'

'Adolescent illusions.'

Her tone was friendly but the effect was patronizing.

'Don't tell him,' Gwydion said. 'Give me time. Give me a month or two. I've got some new plans. There's a chance of a film actually. In Sicily. Something I was involved in before. And Martha has some good offers for next month. In Malta and Istanbul. Don't tell him. Please give me time.'

'Three months,' Sian said. 'I'll give you three months.'

She held up three cool fingers. He stared at her soberly. All his gaiety had gone. He looked angry and resentful.

'You are just like the rest of them,' he said.

'What do you mean?'

'It's power you're after. The ultimate satisfaction. The only orgasm that really counts.'

Sian laughed as she shook her head. He was disappointed that she was in no way shaken by his attempt to speak savagely.

'What's so funny,' he said.

'I've noticed that. I've noticed it at the office. Whenever men lose or don't get their own way, which is the same thing I suppose, they always start discussing Power with a capital "P" as though it were a thing in itself. Oh dear.'

Suddenly she patted Gwydion on the arm in a motherly way.

'You'd better hurry back,' she said, 'or they'll be wondering where you are.'

BOOK THREE

1

Gwydion glanced at the dirt under his finger nails and then sank them into the skin of the orange he gripped in his other hand. He was unshaven and unwashed but he still looked youthful and his clothes were smart. A leather jacket, a thin white sweater, pink corduroy trousers and a pair of new suede boots which still seemed to give him pleasure since he raised first one leg and then the other to take a good look at them. His mouth crammed with juicy orange he stretched himself in the warming rays of the morning sun and lifted his arms to press them against the ruined Roman wall behind him. His good looks remained confident to the point of being theatrical: His mouth was wet with juice and the two peaks of the upper lip looked like the painted lips of a clown designed to tell jokes. The dimple in his chin was not hidden by the bristles of his growth of beard. He closed his eyes to warm his face in the sun and the long lashes gave him an appearance of childlike innocence. When he had swallowed the orange he opened his eyes to look for something to wipe his sticky fingers. He stood up and moved from the wall to pull out coarse grass from between fallen fragments of marble pillars. As he wiped his hands he studied the view, his large dark blue eyes apparently content and soothed by everything he saw.

Across the narrow valley near a cypress grove a young boy was chasing a small flock of sheep out of an orchard and the faint tinkle of the sheep bells could be heard in the still air. Higher up, on an isolated hill-top, from the tower above the brown walls of a monastery the rhythmic slamming of the hammer-tongue of the tolling bell reverberated authoritatively above all the other sounds.

On the horizon, cloud was dispelled by the powerful rays of the rising sun and the summit of a volcanic mountain came into view with the speed of a piece of spectacular theatrical magic. It pleased him so much he gave flourishes with his arms in that direction as though he were an authoritarian conductor of a symphony orchestra submitting all nature to the will of his baton.

'Listen to this, Molly!'

He was startled by the voice of a man speaking English in the amphitheatre below. He was not alone in the ruins. His first instinct seemed to be to hide. The voices were sounds that intruded into the early morning solitude he was enjoying. The blue sky and the spectacular changes the sunlight was making to the landscape were no longer his alone.

'Do listen. This is absolutely priceless. *"Below the amphitheatre a footpath leads to the sumptuous temples of Demeter and Persephone . . ."'*

'What's so funny about that?'

The woman sounded bored.

'I haven't got to it yet . . .'

Gwydion sat up suddenly. The note of irritation made the man's voice familiar to him. He rolled on the ground and struck his thigh in a sudden explosion of high spirits. He jumped to his feet as though he were ready to run shouting and laughing along the highest tier of the amphitheatre. Then he changed his tactics and crouched down again behind the ruined wall. The voices were coming closer.

'"*It was erected by Gelon in 480 with the proceeds of spoil taken from the Carthaginians . . .*"'

'So what? Do come to the point, Victor.'

The man's voice was loud and clear and all the words he read enunciated with a professional clarity and emphasis that was designed to bring out their full significance. The woman seemed to find nothing remarkable in the information: she sounded listless and preoccupied as if she was already regretting the early morning excursion.

'"*The custodian, Giovanni di Natale, who is seldom on the spot, should be inquired for at the tavern. He will awaken the echo in the grotto by firing a pistol (5 soldi). If accompanied by ladies however the traveller is advised to refrain from this experiment!*" I love this book! I really do.'

The echo of his laughter rolled around the amphitheatre and he was impressed with the sound.

'I say that sounds rather fine doesn't it? Shall I read it again?'

'I got it first time,' she said. 'Now why don't you tell me something useful. What's that hole under there?'

He made further tests of his voice, singing in a melodious tenor an imitation music-hall ditty.

'I'm Burbank with a Baedeker
Smoking a fat cigar . . . ah!

He sounded determined to be jolly. His voice was eager with the instinct to instruct and the woman his chosen pupil. He appeared on a narrow stone platform, at first in the deep shade and then making a deliberate move across the line of shadow into the bright sunlight. He stood with his feet apart and his hands on his hips with a camera swinging from a scrawny neck. He wore a loose shirt outside his trousers with laundry folds clearly visible as added marks of freshness. His skin was large-pored and his nose and cheeks red from acne rosaceay,

220

the nose slightly swollen from too sudden exposure to the sun. His fair crinkly hair was brushed close to his skull and he looked about through horn-rimmed spectacles as though determined not to lose any vital detail of the antiquities around him by lack of visible keenness and close attention. He kept his place in the old guide book by inserting a finger between the pages. His stockinged feet were clad in strong sandals and dust had already gathered over the well-polished surface.

Gwydion moved quietly to his right behind a remnant of thick masonry. His face lit with a playful and mischievous smile. Like a boy playing Cowboys and Indians he crept down the ruins and into the vaulted canal which passed under the stage on which the tourist named Victor was still standing. For a moment his progress was held up by the bright eyes of two stray cats. He glanced at his hands and then tried to move with greater caution to prevent his clothes getting completely covered with dirt and grime. He was able to creep quietly in his suede shoes until he reached an opening which gave a direct view of the orchestra and the semi-circle of seats that had been hewn out of the rock.

'Molly! Come here! Wouldn't it be wonderful to play Hamlet here before an audience of two thousand!'

'I'm not a frustrated actress, Victor.'

The woman kept out of the sun. She wore dark glasses shaped like a vampire mask. She was dressed in a trouser suit made of a yellow silk material and carried a matching bag on a shoulder strap. Her hair was dyed blonde and her stance resolutely youthful, but her age was probably nearing forty.

'And opera! This would be an absolutely superb setting. I can just see it. God, I would absolutely love to produce something spectacular here. Molly, can't you see it all?'

She refused to be infected with his enthusiasm.

'Only too clearly.'

'Molly! You are just being perverse. I don't know what has gotten into you.'

The Americanism was deliberate and consciously cosy.

'Victor Toiley!'

The sepulchral sound escaped through the opening out of the vaulted canal into the orchestra and filled the whole amphitheatre.

'My God.'

The uplifted shoulders of the man on the stage were frozen rigid with fright.

'What was that?'

The deep voice rolled out again.

'Sono il santo spirito di Giovanni di Natale, tornato per molestarsi!'

Molly began to laugh. The voice was a fair imitation of Vittorio da Sica in one of his more bombastic roles.

'It's somebody who's heard you reading. That's what you get for listening to the sound of your own voice.'

Victor was a little reassured, but still deeply apprehensive. He spoke in a whisper.

'Yes. But who on earth would know my name in this part of the world?'

'Il grande signor Toiley!'

'My God. It's somebody from the B.B.C. Where is he hiding? Come on Molly. We'd better get out of here.'

'Don't be ridiculous.'

The voice pursued its own joke with relentless energy. It rolled out in an even more sepulchral tone. Victor's irritation made Molly laugh. She refused to be disturbed by his fears: she was even prepared to join in the game. She cupped her hands around her lips and cried out.

'Come out! Come out! wherever you are.'

Gwydion crept forward along the canal under the stage and found a way to move unobserved to the vaulted area on the north side of the stage. He rubbed the palms of his hands against each other, and then brushed patches of dirt from his trousers. He breathed deeply to prevent himself giggling and then strolled forward to make his appearance in between two marble pillars as casual as possible.

'Good morning,' he said. 'What appears to be the trouble?'

'My God,' Victor said. 'Just look at this. Gwydion More. What in heaven's name are you doing here?'

'I was just passing.'

'And you were making that row I suppose. I didn't think it was all that funny you know.'

Victor was smiling frostily. His manner was schoolmasterly. He stood erect waiting for some reasonable explanation, a man among boys ready to be amiable or severe as the occasion warranted.

'You still haven't told me. What are you doing here?'

'The world is chock-a-block with people being where they shouldn't be,' Gwydion said. 'And it's getting worse.'

'But this is too ridiculous.'

Victor made a determined effort to regain his self-confidence. He turned to his companion who had come closer to observe Gwydion with some interest.

'I taught this boy,' Victor said, 'believe it or not. Maths and Divinity of all things. Can you imagine it?'

He widened his arms to suggest the great gulf that existed between the man of the world he was now and that conscientious schoolmaster of long ago.

'Quite easily,' the woman said.

She moved closer to Gwydion but took care to remain in the shade.

'I've seen you on the box, haven't I?' she said.

Gwydion smiled at her in his most charming manner.

'How nice of you to remember,' he said. 'You're an executive producer or something even more exalted, I hope?'

'Not a chance,' she said. 'I'm Molly Shilling and you mustn't make jokes about my name. I can see you *are* a joker.'

'I wouldn't dream of it,' Gwydion said. 'With a name like mine I could never afford to take such risks. Gwydion More.'

He bowed briefly. It could have been interpreted as an affectation, but it seemed to please Molly Shilling. Victor occupied his original position in the sunlight on the front of the stage but they were not looking at him. He pointed at Gwydion, his arm absolutely stiff.

'That boy was a first-class actor,' he said. 'The best Mark Antony we ever had. And he could sing. But his spelling was terrible and his Maths . . . oh dear.'

Molly Shilling ignored Victor. She was still studying Gwydion, her head slightly to one side as if to say she was in the process of making up her own mind about him.

'Gwydion,' she said. 'What that? Welsh?'

'Very much so.'

He made a mysterious flourish with his hands.

'It's the name of a magician in medieval legend. He was the first television producer.'

'Was he really?'

Molly was prettily intrigued by the idea.

'He was up to all sorts of tricks,' Gwydion said.

'That figures,' Victor said.

His tone had become briskly American and his attitude an open attempt to establish seniority and some kind of control over the unexpected situation.

'Now come on, More,' he said. 'The suspense is killing me. What are you doing here?'

Victor was doing his best to appear aggressive and worldly but the American twang in his voice only served to bring out his pedagogic past in sharper relief.

'I'm on the run,' Gwydion said.

'Are you really?'

224

Molly sounded pleased and excited.

'Well come on. Tell us. On the run from what?'

'Life,' Gwydion said, with the speed of a boy in class determined to answer without putting his hand up.

Victor groaned.

'Oh dear. The clown who wants to play Hamlet . . .'

Gwydion refused to be needled.

'Have you seen all you want to see?'

He spoke chiefly to Molly.

'Would you like a guide? Have you got transport?'

'I'm getting a little bored with ruins,' Molly said. 'I know I shouldn't say it, but I'm just a vulgar Philistine at heart. That's my trouble. Victor does his best to educate me but I just don't respond somehow do I, Victor?'

Victor stretched his arm out towards the amphitheatre.

'Look at it,' he said. 'Bathed in the true, the unique Greek light! How can you look at it without hearing the surge of a dramatic chorus? It's Greek you see. It's all Greek still. I find it very exciting.'

'I was bashing a typewriter in the city at the age of fifteen,' Molly said. 'That's as much as I know about the Past and I've spent most of my time since trying to forget it.'

She spoke soberly in an accent that had been ironed out by elocution lessons but the way Gwydion laughed was so friendly and infectious that she laughed herself and their laughing together gave her a new energy and vitality.

'You are not really on the run, are you?' she said.

Victor looked at Gwydion over the top of his spectacles and turned over a page of the old Baedeker he was carrying.

'Well I suppose I am in a way,' Gwydion said. 'And it's worse than that. I've been robbed as well.'

'Not by bandits?'

Victor smiled sarcastically and waved his guidebook.

'Baedeker warns against bandits. "*The banditti who have infested this pearl among provinces are not entirely exterminated!*"' . . .

'By one female singer. Black. My faithful companion and the star of my show that was. About one hundred and sixty pounds. Of course she might turn up again, but somehow I don't think she will.'

'You're joking,' Victor said. 'Another touch of fantasy.'

He could not conceal his disapproval.

'Oh no. It's a very sad story.'

Gwydion pulled a comic face.

'Would you like to hear it?'

'Of course I would.' Molly said. 'I'm dying with curiosity. That's *the* snag about being a woman.'

They were standing in a triangular formation on the ruined stage, Gwydion's position more precarious than the other two, his feet on a narrow fringe of even surface that slipped away into a hole filled with loose rubble. His movements were restricted but somehow he managed to turn the confined space into something approaching an imposing situation. With care he extracted an American passport from a pocket inside his leather jacket.

'There it is,' he said. 'Her passport. She gave it me as a security. "So long as you have this, honey-child, I cannot leave your handsome side!" She had this awful habit of talking in doggerel. I thought it was rather endearing at first. But now it seems a central part of the whole monstrous deception.'

He frowned and looked at Victor as if he were an acknowledged authority on American idiom.

'Isn't "honey-child" some kind of an insult?'

'What happened?' Victor said.

'She had another passport. She's one of those lucky people with two. One Swiss and one American. And off she went to Istanbul. She's singing there in a night-club.

226

She was even more on the run than I was. A trail of bad debts right across the world.'

Gwydion made a sweeping flourish with his right arm.

'What was her name?'

Victor looked very sceptical.

'Martha Appletown.'

'Sounds very unlikely,' Victor said.

Molly silenced him by wriggling her fingers.

'No. Wait a minute. I've heard of her . . .'

She gave Gwydion a look of real sympathy.

'You poor old thing,' she said. 'What are you going to do?

He moved along the even surface until he stood near Molly in the shade.

'Well,' Gwydion said, 'as I said before. I am at your service. Let me be your guide. I know the lingo as they say. I know the whole area like the palm of my hand – *coltivata, boscosa, deserta* – the lot. And I have the most splendid vehicle. A Daimler. I swapped it for my Jaguar. And you won't believe it, but I've driven it here all the way from Cardiff.'

'You haven't!'

Molly was intrigued and delighted.

'Indeed I have.'

'Well do let's go and see it!'

Gwydion lent her his hand to guide her down from the ruined stage and Victor followed them. By now he was prepared to be openly interested. He lost his place in the Baedeker and carried it like a monk with a missal. He was not as nimble as he would have liked to be because of his eyesight and he gave the uneven ground his closest attention. Gwydion led the way out the ruins to the road below. The black Daimler was parked on a gravelled lay-by that overlooked the long curving beach and the fishing village below them. Molly sat on the low wall to admire the view.

'We should have come up this way, Victor,' she said. 'You ought to have a modern map. This road hasn't long been built. See what you miss by being such an old antiquarian.'

'Well I *am* an oldy,' Victor said. 'Everybody knows that.'

'Would you like a drink?' Gwydion said. 'And a little something to eat? I've got the lot in my car. Everything except petrol. A little bread. A little salami. And wine of the country: Muscato Amarena. Please choose. I also have some very delicate fish paste.'

Molly rubbed her hands with pleasure and Victor confessed he was a little peckish. He didn't altogether approve of drinking wine so early in the day but the resourceful Gwydion produced a thermos full of hot coffee and Victor began to look more relaxed. He enjoyed eating. The mere act of chewing good food seemed to allay the suspicions that had so obviously beset him from the moment Gwydion appeared in the amphitheatre. He fingered his expensive camera and noticed again that the light with the sun still low in the east was perfect for his purpose. There were more photographs of a very specialized nature he wanted to take.

'It's for Melissa,' he said. 'Melissa's my daughter. She's doing an extended essay as they call it on "the theatre of the classic world" or some such title. I've simply got to get them. Details especially. Telling details.'

He hurried back to the ruins. He seemed to be conscious of being observed and made an effort to keep very erect and move in a military manner. His feet kicked up little clouds of dust. Gwydion sat next to Molly on the low wall, his arms crossed, openly critical of his former teacher and openly puzzled by the connection between him and Molly Shilling. Lighting a cigarette she read his thoughts.

'God forbid,' she said. 'Our relationship is purely business.'

Gwydion sat up, instantly polite and apologetic.

'I'm sorry,' he said. 'I didn't mean . . .'

'It's all right,' Molly Shilling said. 'I like being frank. I can afford to be. Now come on. Before teacher gets back. Tell me the full story.'

'About Martha?'

'What else?'

She watched him closely, trying to measure exactly how he felt, but the armour of his light-hearted manner seemed pretty impenetrable.

'It's very easily told,' Gwydion said. 'The plain fact is I am a failed impresario. I thought I was on to a very good thing. A Black Power Musical. Great script. Great music. You know. The usual thing. I don't blame anyone else except myself. It was a disaster. A complete disaster. I've learnt over ten thousand pounds worth of lesson. And the nasty truth is there are still quite a lot of bills outstanding. I can't really go back to the U.K. until a friend of mine has sold the losses. That will take a little time. So my idea was to take a long trip right down Europe over into Africa and then turn left and make for Asia. And this is as far as I've got.'

Gwydion slapped his thigh with the palms of his hands and grinned philosophically.

'And what about the girl?'

'Martha? Yes. Well. She was yet another miscalculation. I don't blame her. I don't suppose I treated her too well. And I was fair game wasn't I? A piece of the white world. The exploiter exploited. I don't know. I thought we had something real. She fascinated me. On the stage and off it. She could make the most marvellous sound and she looked like a black radiance on the stage – with or without a wig. She was ignorant, superstitious, cunning, very exciting to be with . . . I think that was part of the reason why the show went

229

wrong. I was so infatuated with her it clouded my judgement. It's more than possible. And all that time she was probably taking me for a nice long ride and avenging the accumulated wrongs of her ancestors. Even . . .'

Gwydion seemed to be embarking into more intimate details. But he pulled himself up.

'. . . My God,' he said. 'I'm getting obsessive. Anyway. This isn't a bad place to recuperate is it? And I feel ten years younger already. Believe it or not!'

He smiled in his most charming way at Molly and she offered him a cigarette which he accepted. They smoked for a while in silence.

'When did you find out?' Molly said.

'Find out what?'

Gwydion was guarded, as though it had occurred to him that he had already said too much.

'That she was . . . having you on.'

Molly was still firm and frank. He could take some comfort in her sympathetic interest.

'I don't know. How do we ever know? Whatever explanation I give myself sounds pretty unconvincing in the middle of the night.'

He laughed.

'I probably always knew. I'm a bit of a chiseller myself so I must have recognized a kindred spirit. Let's be objective as old Oiley used to say, bless him. Maybe she thought *I* was exploiting her. Who am I to judge?'

'Who's Oiley?' Molly said.

'Sorry. Victor Toiley. That's what the boys called him. Oiley Toiley. Aren't kids terrible?'

Molly was greatly amused. Her laughter was completely uninhibited and Gwydion chuckled away himself until he observed a cloud of dust approaching higher up the road.

'Hello,' he said. 'Take cover! Flock of rampant sheep approaching. Get in quick, there's a good girl.'

230

He opened the car door and hurried Molly into the passenger seat. He got in the back himself and leaned over to wind up all the windows.

'I'm sorry,' he said. 'There's a ghastly pong in here. I slept in it last night. But you look so pretty in your yellow suit I wouldn't want you covered in a cloud of dust.'

The noisy flock surged past the stationary car, their eyes glowing in the cloud of dust and their cloven feet tattooing the road with a sound that resembled subdued thunder. The tinkling of the bells around the ram's necks seemed a more precise expression of their thirst than the bleating. The shepherd's clothes were ragged and greasy but he raised his hat as he passed the car and Gwydion waved back.

'You like people,' Molly said.

She had turned in her seat to study him with a certain sober fondness that affirmed the quiet sympathy that she felt was growing up between them.

'I don't know about that.'

Gwydion moved the guitar that lay along the seat behind him and leaned back in a relaxed and easy fashion.

'I like you,' he said. 'I know that much.'

He smiled rather wistfully.

'Of course I've been alone for a few days. Nobody to talk to. And I'm very susceptible to female charm. And I'm probably spoiling everything now by being what our old maid used to call a "cheeky monkey".'

Molly remained agreeable, not at all put out.

'I suppose all men are cheeky monkeys,' she said. 'In one way or another.'

Gwydion closed his eyes and stifled a sudden yawn.

He poked his finger into the seat.

'It's not all that comfortable. Not really.'

'You mustn't grieve over her.' Molly said. 'Or worry about her either. I get the impression you are worrying about her. Of course I could be quite wrong.'

231

Gwydion pressed his lips together and shook his head sadly.

'I don't think it's her. It's the idea of failure. That's what really sticks in my guts. The irony of the thing. You know? I thought I was rescuing her from obscurity. I was going to build her up into a big star. All that sort of thing. And I was going to satisfy her emotional needs. I was quite ready to marry her. We spent hours and hours making the most fantastic plans. I gave her everything I'd got and quite obviously it wasn't nearly enough. I don't want to sound corny but we both sat side by side on the edge of a pool, worshipping her image.'

He had lowered his voice and in the stuffy interior of the car their conversation was taking the shape of the confessional. Under the hard sophisticated surface which had been so evident when Victor was present, Gwydion had been able to discover the warm sympathy of a natural aunt who loved to advise and listen to the troubles of her loving nephew.

'Oh dear,' Molly said. 'You poor thing.'

'And the big joke is, she will certainly make it. She's got the correct percentage of ruthlessness. She will get there quite easily, without the slightest bit of help from me.'

'Apart from the hundred and sixty pounds.'

Molly smiled and Gwydion sat up, determined to be cheerful.

'Look,' he said. 'Will you two hire me and my car for the rest of the morning? Or the rest of the day? What have you got planned? I'll fit in. You can pay me in petrol. This damn thing does about two kilometres to the gallon. I'd sell it if only I could find a victim to buy it. Look, I'll take you to see the grove of Saint Anastasia.'

'What's that?'

'You can't leave these parts without visiting the grove of Saint Anastasia! You just couldn't.'

Victor was outside. tapping the window of the car. He looked agreeable enough but his voice was peremptory.

'What are you two doing in there?' he said.

2

'I should imagine that the heat is absolutely unbearable in high summer,' Victor said. 'I don't like too much heat.'

He mopped his brow with a large blue silk handkerchief. They had left the car on the road below opposite a group of imposing farm buildings which appeared to be deserted. The path they followed wound its way up hill through a neglected olive grove. On the lower edge of the path wild asparagus grew between the stones. Gwydion led the way, stopping from time to time to help Molly where cactus grew and the path was difficult and to make sure that Victor was keeping up with the climb.

'How about a breather,' Victor said. 'Just a short one. I may be an Englishman but I'm not a mad dog. Don't you find this heat absolutely killing?'

Molly had taken off her yellow jacket and left it in the car. Determined to be cool she had unbuttoned her thin blouse so that her expensive white brassiere was visible. Victor still carried his camera around his neck. He refused to leave it in the car when Gwydion said he couldn't lock all the doors. He broke off a small branch of an overgrown olive tree and sat on the hard ground to fan his sweating face.

'How do you know about this path, anyway, "Gwiddy"?' he said.

'Why on earth do you call him Gwiddy?'

Molly looked about for somewhere comfortable to sit.

'Thank you very much,' Gwydion said. 'I never liked "Gwiddy". Sounds like a nickname for some kind of goose.'

'No comment,' Victor said in his tartest manner. 'How do you know this leads to the Tomb of whatever it is we are going to see?'

Gwydion found Molly a place to sit in the shade of a larger olive tree. After a rapid critical survey, Victor saw that her position was better than his own and moved up to join her. Politely Gwydion remained standing so that Victor could enjoy more room under the low roof of the boughs.

'If I told you how I first came here,' Gwydion said, 'I wouldn't expect you to believe a word of it.'

Victor squinted up at the figure of the younger man still standing in the sunlight.

'I came here with a Swiss camera team. About two years ago. I was told to be at the toll-gate of the Autostrada del Sol without fail at half-past ten on a Monday morning. This I may add was in early Feb. I got the message on the telephone. And those were my instructions.'

'Where were you,' Molly said. 'When you got the message?'

'In London. Hammersmith Grove actually. Doing absolutely nothing as it happened. So I upped and went.'

Victor frowned, irritated by the heat and still radiating a vague sense of disapproval.

'But I didn't you know,' Molly said. 'Who was asking for you and that sort of thing?'

'Well I had guessed,' Gwydion said. 'It was a Swiss company and the only Swiss film-maker I knew was this chap Fritz Sebald. I looked after him once in London for about four days and he was so pleased with the result he said he would find me something fascinating at the first opportunity. I didn't take him all that seriously. He was big boisterous sort of chap, mad about English women for some kinky reason and the worst snorer it has ever been my misfortune to share a bedroom with . . . Don't look at me so critically, Victor. You're putting me off my stride.'

'Well get on with it, man. It's too hot for me to concentrate on listening.'

'Well just lie back and fall asleep,' Molly said. 'You come and sit here, Gwydion, and tell me the story. I love stories. I really do.'

Victor looked about him on the ground and muttered about objecting to lying down on top of reptiles. Gwydion found this amusing and offered to keep absolutely quiet so that they could hear the snakes approaching. Victor went very pale.

'I'm not joking,' he said. 'I've got a thing about them. They paralyse me. I don't really like this country you know. The towns are so overcrowded. People everywhere. Like vermin. And then the countryside populated by goats and sheep and a special silence made of cotton wool. And I can always smell sulphur. The whole damned place is covered with owls and witches and howlings dogs.'

'Now be quiet, Victor,' Molly said. 'I want to hear Gwydion's story.'

'I'm not surprised he likes it so much,' Victor said. 'He's Welsh you know. Some kind of aboriginal warlock I shouldn't wonder.'

Gwydion leaned over so that Victor could see him smile and nod encouragement. Victor accepted this as if it were some form of payment and began to look more cheerful. He even smiled back briefly.

'Thank you. C.P.Tel3,' Gwydion said. 'For those few kind words.'

235

Victor sat up suddenly, forgetting all his physical discomforts, his hot face clouded with suspicion.

'Don't call me that,' he said. 'I'm on holiday. And how did you know anyway?'

Gwydion seemed pleased to have disturbed him.

'You forget I'm one of those fringe creatures that swim around the edges of your great corporation waiting for crumbs to nibble. It's our business to try and know what's going on inside.'

'I don't like those initials,' Victor said. 'I call it Civil Service parlance. I'm a creative broadcaster not a civil servant.'

'All right,' Molly said impatiently. 'We know all about that. I want my story.'

'Where was I?' Gwydion asked Molly.

'By the toll-house of the Autostrada.'

'Oh yes. Well they were there right on time. The Swiss camera team. Two smallish buses absolutely packed tight with personnel and equipment. And Fritz Sebald dressed like somebody going to explore the upper regions of the Amazon in the early twenties. And he was hugging himself with delight. He kept on winking and nodding all the way down the spine of Italy. Everyone else was absolutely worn out. As you know by now I'm not all that fussy about the way I travel but I found that little bus absolute hell. I shared a square inch of seat with a clapper-loader and a make-up girl because I was the last to board. Fritz kept on turning round to wink and raise his thumb until he fell asleep and treated us all to his well known snore which held its own very nicely with a very noisy engine. It seemed to go on and on for hours and hours and hours on end with only short stops at the most deserted places. I asked Fritz if we were being chased by the police or something. He was delighted by the idea. He has one of those big round solemn Swiss faces. His family made chocolate. And wild romantic eyes behind metal-rimmed glasses. And hair that seemed divided between going up or back or down, in three equal parts. He put his heavy hand on my shoulder and explained his plan. He was commissioned to do a series of four commercials on a certain Swiss man-made fabric – Dorflon. A new invention, guaranteed non-inflammable. But he was using this as a cover, as far as I could understand what he was saying, to make a documentary about the Festival of Santa Anastasia at the town of Monticello. And that was the reason for all the speed. He had the whole crew for ten days shoot-ing. He planned to get through the commercial stuff in four days and spend the rest of the time filming the festival and he hoped to persuade them to work for him privately for another three or four days. He had wallets on his belt next to his person stuffed with a variety of currencies. Bribes for All, he called it, in the name of Swiss Art.'

'What Festival?'

Victor lay with his weight on his elbow and his stubby fingers intertwined, the strap of his watch tight on his plump wrist. He studied Gwydion's face with the sober intensity of a form master waiting for an unreliable member of the class to reach his first lie.

'The Festival of Santa Anastasia. Just before Lent. A sort of local variation of the Carnival idea.'

'But where did you fit in?'

Molly stirred the still air with her index finger.

'You may well ask. He had me cast for a dual role. I was to record the English language commentary on the commercial and play the wicked Roman Governor. You never heard of such lunatic idea. He is a lunatic really, Fritz. Either he'll do something enormous one day or he'll end up in a lunatic asylum on top of a Swiss alp. Probably the latter.'

'I wish you'd be a little more consecutive and rational,' Victor said. 'What Roman Governor?'

'Gnaeus Domitius, the Praetor or whatever. Anastasia was a well-born local virgin. She became a Christian.'

'Good for her,' Molly said.

'Well it wasn't the best time to join up,' Gwydion said. 'In the middle of the third century. In the middle of a pogrom.'

'Now don't be frivolous,' Victor said. 'I'm a practising churchman. And persecution is the word. Not pogrom.'

'Well there was a secret meeting place up there. The Governor was out hunting early one morning and he came across this beautiful girl all dressed up with no-where to go kneeling in the middle of this olive grove. At her prayers.'

'Tell me more,' Molly said. 'I fear the worst.'

'Fritz had this bright idea of enacting the original legend and then cross-cutting that material with scenes from the February Festival.'

'Not bad. Not bad at all.'

Molly nodded her head judiciously. She seemed to know about such things and her attention was close and critical.

'Not bad at all except that we also had a commercial to do. You can't imagine the chaos. One morning we went above the snow line. This was in February remember. Not all that far from the crater. Talk about desolation. And cold. Everyone was coughing. Bronchitis all round. And a filthy smell of sulphur. A very nasty wind blowing from the east. He had about half a dozen shots set up. A couple of shots of the lava flow. And then these four girls in their non-inflammable dresses fleeing the wrath to come. Then Lisa Lotte dressed up as the Roman virgin fleeing from the wicked Roman Governor. Then a handful of locals holdings up the Veil of Santa Anastasia and averting the course of the lava stream.'

'I don't see the point,' Victor said.

'There was a sequence just above here. Anastasia praying in the olive grove. And the wicked governor coming across her. Very smooth at first but that gets him nowhere. Then he puts her in prison and threatens to torture her. But she doesn't give way. She escapes during an eruption of the volcano. He finds her taking shelter in a cave up above here. She won't have him of course. So he has her put to death. In the lava. And her footprints are miraculously preserved. Church is built. And a grotto. And a silver crown made and monstrance containing Anastasia's veil and other relics like the footprints in the lava.'

'Sounds like an epic of the silent silver screen,' Molly said.

'Just so. Exactly. That was the trouble. There simply wasn't time to do anything properly. Not even the simplest bits. The Festival itself for instance. Fritz had a second camera and he thought he'd use this one himself to pick out significant details and all that ... When the all-male procession brings out the Relics and marches very solemnly all round Monticello led by a very melancholy band, the women all disappear. Disappear completely. They got into hiding. You never saw anything so remarkable. The procession back inside the church and groups of men all around the place standing about with their hands in their pockets and looking very sheepish indeed. Even the dogs looked sheepish. And there was Fritz creeping about with his hand-held 16mm, completely absorbed in what he was doing. Then slowly the women began to emerge in twos and threes. They all had strange hoods over their heads which left one eyes visible and a hole for the mouth. And they were making the strangest noises, all directed against the men. A lot of it was in dialect which I didn't understand but the remarks seemed to be personal attacks and sallies of wit directed against

239

the male population, with particular reference to all their sexual failings.'

'What a wonderful idea,' Molly said. 'And of course they were all anonymous and they could say pretty much what they liked I suppose?'

'Fritz was hard at it. He had his eye glued to the view-finder and the tape-recorder hanging on a shoulder strap. He was determined to do the lot himself. Like a one-man band. He moved closer to a pair of women and they kept still as if they were enjoying the fun. But when he got near enough one of them pulled down his zip and the other went behind him and pulled down his trousers and underpants and gave him the most al-mighty thwack across his bare buttocks. And of course there was nothing he could do about it. He had his hands full. I turned up in the mini-bus with the other camera man otherwise I don't know what would have happened to him. Those women were in rather a nasty mood.'

They all laughed. Even Victor was amused, although for some time he had been showing signs of restless-ness.

'I can laugh now,' Gwydion said. 'But it wasn't funny at the time. He was defiling the temple. They could have castrated him.'

'Oh really . . .'

Victor was not prepared to accept such an extreme interpretation. Molly looked very thoughtful.

'You know it wasn't a bad idea,' she said. 'You ought to finish it.'

Gwydion agreed excitedly.

'Exactly,' he said. 'There was some really worthwhile stuff. It's there in the can. Or at least I hope it is. Fritz isn't keen to come back but I wouldn't mind finishing it. After all, these Festivals are dying out, aren't they? How about it, Victor? Would you be interested? Seriously? I could do with the work to tell you the truth.'

There was a sudden outburst of excited buzzing among the insects and flies above the ridge of the footpath.

'Look, we've got to move from here,' Victor said. 'These flies will eat me alive. Come on.'

3

The ruins of the amphitheatre were impenetrably black against the crimson sunset. From the terrace of the hotel where they had eaten after their strenuous excursion, they watched the night creeping across the sea and the darkness gathering with greater speed in the thick grey olive groves. Down in the village someone was playing an old barrel-organ.

'Listen to that!' Molly said. 'Isn't it delightful?'

Victor had finished his liqueur and he was smoking what he called his evening cigar.

'Thank God it isn't a jukebox,' he said.

'It's outside Time,' Molly said. 'It's such a place of dream and legend. Too beautiful to cope with. Dying of perfection. I'll wake up in the morning with just a picture postcard between my fingers, back in Streatham High Road.'

She fluttered her fingers and Gwydion compressed his lips so that his dimples came into sight.

'It's so relaxing,' Molly said. 'Do you know what I mean? "On such a night as this . . ." How does it go?'

'This sweet stuff is stronger than you'd think,' Victor said.

He lifted his empty glass and wobbled the stem between his finger and thumb. He glanced at his watch.

'I really must telephone my wife,' he said. 'I try to give her a ring every night wherever I am and whatever it costs.'

He looked defiantly at Gwydion and then at Molly.

'Marjorie!'

Gwydion uttered the name like a cry of triumph. Molly was ready to be amused but he kept a straight face.

'Such a nice person. Do give her my best regards.'

Victor frowned.

'I didn't know you'd met,' he said.

'Only briefly,' Gwydion said. 'In the old days at the B.B.C., but I liked her very much. She had a Welsh grandmother.'

'I'm still at the B.B.C.,' Victor said. 'What gave you the idea I wasn't?'

'Versatile men like you wouldn't want to be locked up there for ever . . . Surely?'

'The B.B.C. is not a prison,' Victor said primly. 'I'm going to telephone Margie.'

As he marched off towards the main building they both began to laugh. Molly put a warning finger to her lips.

'Touchy, isn't he?' Gwydion said.

He turned to stare at the dark interior of the hotel. A light went on further inside and he could hear Victor being loudly firm but polite with the manager of the hotel. Molly did not seem inclined to discuss her travelling companion. Gwydion breathed deeply and folded his arms, waiting for her to speak. She leaned forward to admire the view more intensely.

'I'm such a sloppy sentimental fool,' Molly said. 'But this place sends me. I could stay here for ever. I really could.'

'Why not?'

Gwydion entered into her mood with amiable ease.

'Come with me in my ancient motor! Pay for the petrol and we'll explore the interior.'

'You've given us a delightful day,' Molly said. 'You've looked after us so well.'

'Don't think I'm not serious,' Gwydion said. 'I am making you a definite proposal. A journey into the interior. Far, far away into those mysterious mountains. Across the long white plain and up among the harsh rocks, those marvellous little mountain roads, absolutely drenched with the scent of exotic flowers.'

A clock in the tower of a neighbouring village struck the hour with slow measured sounds that seemed to fly across the valley on heavy wings. Molly rose from her seat and walked towards the balcony at the end of the terrace. Phosphorescent lights had begun to appear on the surface of the sea and the first stars in the evening sky.

'There ought to be music,' Gwydion said. 'Shall I go down and get my guitar?'

Molly smiled, pressed her hands together, leaning over the balcony, reluctant to speak.

'It's been a lovely day,' she said at last. 'You've been very nice to us.'

'Would you like to go for a walk? Up through the vineyard. There's a little stone look-out. With a roof over the top. You can see the lava glowing in the darkness of the night. It's beautiful.'

She shook her head, firm but still regretful.

'I must go to bed soon,' she said. 'I'm quite worn out trying to keep up with a younger man. It's too much for me. And we have to be up at the crack of dawn.'

When she moved Gwydion took her hand.

'Why don't you stay. Let Oiley go wherever it is you have to go and you stay here with me. I'll look after you.'

She gave his hand a squeeze and then let it go.

243

'What's so important about it all anyway?' Gwydion said. 'That's how I feel these days. I just want to move on. Right across Africa or Asia. I'm not sure which. I've made such a mess of things I want to cut myself off from it all. Whatever "It" is. What is "It" Molly?'

'"It" is an office high above a noisy London street,' Molly said. '"It" is a telephone that never stops ringing.'

'Isn't it Success?' Gwydion said. 'Fame? Wealth? Power?'

'"It" is the Price you have to pay. What you can't live without. That's "It".'

They had drunk enough wine to delude themselves into believing that their conversation was sparkling and brilliant.

'"It" is what I am totally without,' Gwydion said. 'I have been stripped of "It", so "It" must be some kind of bark. All mine has been peeled off so I must keep on travelling until my skin gets nice and hard and thick again.'

'Yes, but not too thick . . .'

They were completely alone on the terrace. It did not seem as if Victor was coming back. Down below in the shade of a motionless palm a man with his jacket thrown over his shoulders had started to sing. He looked up at them and his face glimmered in the fading light. He lifted his arm towards them to show that he was singing for their benefit. It was a sad Sicilian love-song and he sang quietly, his voice humble and unobtrusive, ready to oblige. They listened together quietly. When he had finished he lifted his hat, bowed and walked on down the hill. Gwydion put his arm around Molly's waist and she rested her head on his shoulder.

'There goes a man after my own heart,' Gwydion said.

'That was wonderful. Simply wonderful.'

She lifted her head inviting him to kiss her. He was

244

most gentle and she sighed, deeply grateful for the comfort he was giving her.

'I've got to go,' she said, without moving.

'I know,' Gwydion said. 'I understand.'

They were silent together. They could have been absorbed in each contemplating the other's personality. They were motionless in a pose which suggested that each was prepared to play the role the other needed. Gwydion stood so firm and still the muscles of his body could have been demonstrating his capacity for restraint and the power of his self-control. Molly leaned against him in an attitude of complete relaxation: a woman used to making decisions and the strains of executive control, abandoning herself to unstinting affectionate, melting admiration.

'Are you really on the run?'

Her voice was little more than a whisper. He moved to brush his lips against hers.

'If you need any help,' she said, 'I'd like to help you.'

He led her towards the flight of steps that led to the garden at the side of the hotel. They sat down on a stone bench under a carob tree.

'What about the debts on your show? How much do they amount to?'

She tried to sound casual, but a practised business-like note had entered her voice.

'Money is such a bore,' Gwydion said. 'I could pay it off I suppose. It's not all that much. But I just didn't feel like doing it. My silly way of getting back at the world I suppose: if you don't want my show, you won't get my money!'

'That sounds more like Martha Appletown than you.'

'Oh I don't know. I'm pretty irresponsible. We must have had something in common.'

Gwydion chuckled to show how objective he had become.

'And there's my mother of course. I could get something out of her. If I can bring myself to ask.'

'You are awful,' Molly said in a playful voice. 'You have this technique of playing on woman's defenceless curiosity. What have you got against your poor mother?'

'She's not poor,' Gwydion said. 'It's just that I don't like her very much, that's all.'

'I don't think I like mine either,' Molly said. 'That's not so unusual. You don't have to feel guilty about it.'

'Oh I don't. Not one little bit. It's just that when I have to ask her for something like money it sticks in my gullet.'

'But if she's got plenty . . .?'

'Exactly. She's spent her whole life accumulating it. Married three times. She sent me away to school because I didn't like prospective husband number two. Having spoilt me as a small boy . . . I shouldn't bore you. It's very tedious. And it's all past and dead and done with anyway. What are you doing here, you and Victor?'

'Hum.'

Molly put her hands under her thighs and kicked her legs about in a girlish childlike way.

'It's all very hush-hush,' she said. 'I shouldn't really tell you a word about it. That's why Victor's been on tenterhooks all day. Scared quite rigid that you would charm some little bits of info out of poor little feather-brained Molly. And now you have done.'

'Have I?'

'Yes, you have. So before I tell you any more, I want you to promise that you will leave this place at the latest before ten o'clock tomorrow morning.'

'My goodness.'

Gwydion pretended to be shocked.

'If you don't I shan't tell you anything.'

He spread out his arms.

'Where shall I go?'

'That depends.'

'On what?'

Her voice became serious.

'On whether or not you want me to help you. Do you?'

Gwydion hesitated a fraction before he spoke. It was a commitment he was about to make. She spoke gently enough, but there was a quiet authority in her voice.

'Yes I do,' he said.

'Go to Rome,' she said. 'I shall be there next week. Wait for me there. Have you somewhere where you can stay?'

'Not really,' Gwydion said.

'I'll give you a letter,' Molly said. 'And a key. It's only one key of course. You'll need the other from Cecilia. She'll get it for you. She's an old friend. An Austrian. She has a flat in the same house. You'll have to be very discreet, Gwydion. For the next few days. Don't let anyone see you going in and out. Be as inconspicuous as possible. And get rid of that car. Do I sound very mysterious?'

'You do a bit.'

'Tomorrow morning a yacht will arrive just outside the harbour. It will be here for three or four days. A great deal will depend on what happens on the yacht. That's why poor Victor is so nervous. I'm not joking.'

'I know you're not,' Gwydion said. 'What's the name of the yacht?'

'Why do you ask? Are you making shrewd guesses?'

'Of course I am.'

Molly stood up and offered him her hand.

'Call it *Ulysses*,' she said. 'And trust me. Will you?'

Gwydion's face was pale in the fading light. He looked disappointed.

'You've got something,' Molly said. 'I'm convinced of that. A very real power. Maybe a very real talent. I want

to help you. But I'm older than you are and I want you
to trust me. I've probably told you too much already. It
isn't that I want to put you to a test . . . but I must know
I can trust you. It might be big, it might be nothing
and I've opened my big mouth far wider than I ever
intended. And it wasn't just the wine. Are you going
to take my hand?'

Gwydion took her hand. He stood up and drew her
into his arms. Once again it was his business to bring
her comfort by showing concern for her and affection,
by not demanding too much, by waiting upon her pleasure. She touched his cheek to show her gratitude.

'You leave at daybreak,' she said in her softest voice.
'I'll leave an envelope for you at the desk. Think of it
as part of your escape, darling.'

The branches of the carob tree began to rustle above
them: a breeze had begun to blow from the sea. They
heard Victor calling on the terrace.

'Molly! Molly! Where are you Molly, for goodness'
sake?'

Molly put her finger on Gwydion's lips and they giggled together like childhood conspirators.

4

It was already hot in the street. Outside every locked
gate and under every tree there were mounds of refuse.
At Gwydion's feet a horde of black flies were eating
the sticky remnants of an iced cake trodden into the
pavement. Cats prowled about, jumping on to the lids

of rubbish bins that were stuffed full to overflowing. Across the road two pampered black dogs were leaping about and barking wildly at the cats, unable to get at them because of the close-meshed wire fence that surrounded the rich man's garden in which they were confined. Far indoors, beyond the loggia, a woman's voice wailed complaining of a headache and the noise the dogs were making. A pale-faced serving woman in black emerged from the rear of the villa with a shallow basin of raw meat tit-bits to silence the dogs. She stared suspiciously at Gwydion so that he was obliged to move. He walked with a pretence of speed and urgency towards the Viale Aventino, acting the part of a busy man late for an appointment. But when he arrived at the thoroughfare he had exhausted the brief impetus that had brought him down the hill. Down the wide streets a hot wind blew a reddish dust and he turned his back on the wind to walk up into the shelter of the wooded slope. A narrow cobbled lane passed through the pleasant shade of the trees and the high garden walls and for some time he seemed content to wander. He arrived at the entrance court of a church with a long low portico and a bell tower built at an angle to the facade. On a bench set against the high retaining wall facing the church an elderly woman sat with a rectangular sketch book on her knees. She looked at peace with herself and she smiled from time to time as she worked. It was some time before she noticed that Gwydion was observing her with interest. This pleased her and they smiled at each other. She tilted her head upwards as she smiled. Her skin was mottled from age and long exposure to a southern climate. She spoke in a slow correct Italian with a marked Slavonic accent.

'Would you like me to draw your portrait, young man?'

Her voice and manner were cool and authoritative.

'Don't worry. I shan't charge you anything. Sit over there. And talk to me.'

She caught Gwydion glancing at his wrist watch.

'It won't take long. You can tell me about yourself.'

'Do you want the Truth?'

Gwydion smiled engagingly. Perhaps because they were both using a language not their own their communication promised to be easy and frank. He looked more cheerful than at any time since he left the flat. By chance he had hit upon an interesting way of passing the time in a forecourt that was as charming and as secluded as a garden terrace.

'Ah!'

The old lady lifted her pencil listening acutely to his accent.

'You are not Italian. Let me guess what you are? Dark hair. Light skin. Dark blue eyes. Very intriguing. Not very interested in old churches. More interested in people. Danish perhaps.'

Gwydion shook his head.

'Perhaps you are a Finnish boy?'

She worked as she spoke, producing wavy lines and smudges on her paper, a trembling form of life in a central European expressionist style that belonged to another era.

'Oh what a wicked smile you have,' she said. 'Just like a naughty boy. Have you ever seen that painting, which one is it . . . by Caravaggio . . . "The vocation of Saint Matthew"? There is a young man there with a big feather in his hat. He looks just like you. You must go and see it. It is in the church of San Luigi dei Francesi. Near the Piazza Navona. Will you go?'

She gave him a shrewd glance.

'If I get a chance,' Gwydion said. 'Yes I will.'

'When you are old, perhaps,' she said. 'Like me. That's how I spend my time you see. Trotting around churches getting to know them. This is one of my favourites. Because it is so undistinguished and friendly. And so near where I live. I haven't guessed what your nationality is, have I? I've been going too far north I suspect. But you're not German. And you're not Dutch or English. Now I wonder what you are?'

'Welsh,' Gwydion said.

'Now you've told me and the game is over. Welsh? That is part of Ireland I think. Or Scotland? I am never sure. In any case it is a long long long way away. Now what about this. Shall I give it to you?'

The old woman was pleased with her work. She stood up with some difficulty and on her feet she looked older. She could have been over eighty. She bent forward awkwardly full of friendliness and determined courage. She chuckled at her own infirmity as she held out the portrait she had drawn so that Gwydion could see it. Hovering above his head she had drawn a dashing sixteenth-century conical cap with a narrow rim and a sweeping feather.

'That is your crown,' she said. 'I always like to give my subjects a little coronation. That is better than telling your fortune.'

'Do you tell fortunes as well?'

'I think I could you know,' the old woman said. 'If I really wanted to. But this is enough I think. Do you want to see my sketch book?'

Gwydion showed a polite eagerness. It was filled with pencil drawings of Roman churches and human heads, often drawn from odd angles so that the detail of the head and the church were somehow associated.

'It keeps me quiet,' the old woman said. 'And that is the most important thing to do with old people, you know. Are you very wicked?'

She asked her question in a most innocent voice, looking up at Gwydion's smiling face from her bent position.

'Dear me,' Gwydion said. 'I hope not.'

251

'So do I!'

The old woman nodded solemnly.

'I shall keep your picture,' she said. 'I had thought of giving it to you. But you would only lose it. Now it is time for me to start my journey back to my daughter's house. It takes me twenty-five minutes. Then it will be time for lunch.'

She looked at the drawing again.

'I've made you look very wicked,' she said. 'I wonder why? And yet you were kind enough to stop and talk with an old woman. Why did you do that?'

She held her head to one side and considered him with a mild but frank disapproval, her mouth hanging open.

'I think perhaps you are being left behind in life. You are not achieving what you had the ambition to achieve and you don't like it. That makes you restless perhaps and discontented.'

She lifted a hand.

'Don't talk to me any more,' she said. 'If I waste any more time I'l! be late for my lunch.'

5

Gwydion was bored. It was late in the afternoon and his wandering had become tired and aimless. Sitting in a tram without bothering to check its destination he had gazed listlessly at the famous landmarks like a man in a news cinema watching a programme for the third time while he waits for his train. The tram

252

rumbled across the bridge into a region of the city which he had never visited before. He got off the tram at a point which seemed to promise new interest but in fact proved to be a busy shopping district full of supermarkets on main thoroughfares. He was obliged to walk some distance before he found the kind of narrow sidestreets that represented an older Rome and gave some shelter from the afternoon sun. He was thirsty and ready ro take some rest: to enter the first bar or trattoria with a sufficiently cavernous interior and the smell of something tempting to eat or drink. But nowhere attractive presented itself. This was an exclusively working-class area and after prolonged walking he gave up the search and entered the first bar that seemed from the outside reasonably quiet and deserted.

Once inside and his eyesight accustomed to the gloom he saw a group of men seated around a table in the far end of the room, playing cards. Suspended from the centre of the cracked ceiling a fan was revolving slowly in an anti-clockwise direction. The woman behind the bar had black hair and wrinkled gipsy features and her right arm was raised holding on to the handle of the espresso machine. In the dirty window behind her most of the flies were dead or asleep. A fat card player, with his hat tilted back so far that it seemed to defy the laws of gravity, slapped down a brightly decorated card and stared at it morosely through the smoke of his cheap cigar. Against the inside wall two men in overalls were working strenuously to repair a large glossy jukebox. Gwydion ordered a coffee and a glass of iced water. The woman set her machine in motion. From an inner room could be heard the click of billiard balls and the voices of youths. There was a bead curtain parted on the left and Gwydion took a seat near the entrance so that he could see the game going on inside. The billiard table was narrow and designed for a local variety of the

253

game. Against the wall inside stood a rickety glass cupboard displaying tarnished electro-plated silver prize cups. From her position behind the coffee machine the woman tried to keep an eye on the behaviour of the three youths in the billiard room. The smallest and noisiest appeared to be her son. He had the same gipsy look and his front teeth were broken. He was loud and aggressive and much given to showing off. His companions laughed encouragingly at all his jokes and antics. As Gwydion watched he balanced his cue in the air like a lance. Then he put it to his shoulders like a rifle and pretended to shoot both the other boys.

'Franco,' the woman said, in a harsh warning voice which nevertheless did not conceal her unrestrained affection for her son. 'I remind you once more. We need milk. Will you finish that game and go to the dairy?'

'Immediately, mother.'

The boy winked at his companions and continued playing. The other two were unfailingly impressed by his originality and daring. Beyond the billiard room yet another door had been left wide open and Gwydion could see an old man with a runny nose sitting in the shade of a dirty wall absorbed in the task of repairing the seat of a wicker chair. Franco placed his billiard cue between his legs and pointed it at the old man. He said something in dialect which clearly implied that the old man had something which was more in need of repair than a broken chair. The other two rolled about overcome with laughter and admiration of Franco's wit. The woman brought Gwydion his coffee and muttered some reproof into the billiard room before hurrying back to the shelter of her coffee machine. The old man heard nothing. He wiped his nose with the back of his hand and continued to mend the chair.

The noise of a quarrel broke out among the card players. It was sudden and intense and brought the three youths out of the billiard room to watch. Franco still carried his cue. All three passed Gwydion's table. Franco appeared eager to join in the row. The fat player was accused by two of the others of being headmaster of the South Rome Extramural College of Thieves. He pushed back his chair and made heated denials in a voice that sounded as though it had been shredded with broken glass. Franco moved around the table grinning and very ready to stir up more trouble. Gwydion watched with amused interest while the card players made an armistice among themselves and turned on the common enemy. Franco backed away, brandishing his cue as a weapon. He called on any two of the older men to attack him and take the consequences. He would pierce their loins for their pains. He would damage them for life.

'Franco!' his mother said, in her most shocked voice. 'What are you trying to do, eh? What are you trying to do with my business?'

The fat man waved a handful of cards towards Franco.

'Now mark what I'm saying,' he said. 'That boy will serve a prison term before he reaches his majority.'

The manner in which he spoke more than what he said made Gwydion laugh aloud. Franco, still busy dramatizing the situation called his two friends to stand behind him. They would take on all comers irrespective of age, colour, rank or race. The fat player waved a curse in his direction and then cast a nostalgic eye at the cards lying on the table. A paper boy passed outside in the street and Gwydion jumped to his feet to call after him. He moved to the door but Franco held the cue in a horizontal position to bar Gwydion's way. The mother by this time had become increasingly worried about her son's behaviour and her prayers and exhortations issued forth like the steam from her coffee machine.

'Excuse me,' Gwydion said, 'I want to buy a paper.'

'Franco, in the name of God, Franco my son, I beg you . . .'

The mother was intensely agitated. Franco seemed to be defying her more than the casual customer whose way he persisted in barring. Gwydion looked him in the eye. He remained calm and silent for a moment and then spoke quietly.

'Move your cue,' he said in precise English. 'Or I'll break it and break your bloody neck as well.'

The newspaper seller plunged into the situation at the door and then jumped back with an expression of sudden alarm. He stood in the narrow street with his papers under his arm, ready to run away but equally curious to see what would happen. Franco gave way.

'A paper for the Signore!'

He gave the order to the paler, weaker looking of his two companions and was instantly obeyed. The card players resumed their game with mumbles of discontent and echoing as much as they could bring to mind of their original quarrel. The woman behind the coffee machine had begun to a series of apologies to Gwydion and explanations of her son's uneducated behaviour. Franco told her to shut up. He snatched the newspaper from the hands of his henchman and bowed to Gwydion, begging him to accept the paper as a gift and as a token of cordial friendship and esteem. Gwydion accepted the gift and the youth was instantly delighted. He asked Gwydion to have another cup of coffee or perhaps a glass of Campari with ice and soda water? He handed his billiard cue to his friend and went behind the counter to interfere with his mother's arrangements there and to prepare his new friend's drink.

Gwydion sat down at the table to finish his coffee, drink the glass of iced water and read the paper. Franco's two friends returned to the billiard room.

The old man in the passage was still mending the chair, probably very deaf and certainly unaware of what was going on in the cafe. Gwydion opened the newspaper and on the illustrated page he saw a picture of a yatch. It was a blurred picture but the caption said it belonged to a celebrated millionaire who had loaned it to a film star and his wife for a select party of friends for a late holiday in Sicilian waters. Gwydion studied the text carefully and the picture. There was a sudden unexpected blast of music from the jukebox. The two men had got it to work at last and they were so delighted at their achievement that they left the volume full on, The card players, their concentration broken, turned in their chairs to make their protest. Gwydion rolled up the newspaper and left the cafe in a hurry, taking no notice of Franco who followed him to the door begging him to stay as the guest of the management and enjoy the drink that had been specially prepared for him.

6

As soon as he slammed the front door of the flat behind him, Gwydion began to take off his clothes. His shoes and socks first so that his bare feet were cooled by the marble floor. Because of all his walking there were painful blisters on his heels. He barged about the flat opening every door so that every breeze could be courted. He adjusted the shutters to the west so that narrower bars of sunlight cut across the living room, which was stifled with too much furniture. He tried to study the condition of his naked back in the reflection of one wall mirror into another. His skin burnt easily and there were patches ready to peel off from an exposure to the sun made earlier in the week.

He returned to the vestibule which was the coolest area of the apartment. On its solid marble plinth the bust of an ancient Roman seemed to cool the air that it displaced. Gwydion embraced the cold head briefly and then sat on an oak chest taking some of his weight on his hands like a swimmer who sits gingerly on the hardness of a rock just after emerging from the sea. He kicked his shirt and trousers across the floor in the direction of the bedroom. The double doors to the dining room were open. Here heavy chairs and a refectory table filled the limited space and suggested that they had come from a more spacious home. They were covered with a film of dust and there was even thicker dust on the arrangement of African drums on the wall above his head.

He moved to the bathroom and searched for something to smear on his blisters. It was a narrow room not provided with shutters and the white tiles were yellowing above a certain level from constant exposure to sunlight. The water supply was reduced to a trickle and there was not enough for Gwydion to wash let alone take a shower. He placed a pan under a dripping tap in order to collect water to boil on the kitchen stove. He picked up the newspaper in the vestibule and took it to the bedroom. There were two beds in the room but only one had been slept in. The white sheets lay where they had been thrown in untidy shapes on the shadowed floor. A wardrobe door hung open and inside could be seen an operatic looking Wehrmacht uniform covered with a torn polythene bag. Swords hung on the wall and upside down on the dressing table was a London policeman's helmet. There was nothing feminine about the room. Gwydion spread the newspaper on the floor and marched around it. He took down a sword and pressed the flat blade along his back as he kneeled down to stare at the picture of the yacht. Overcome with weariness or the desire to think he lay down on the unmade bed still clutching the sword. No sooner had he lain down than he wanted to see the paper again. He used the sword as a paper-sticker and dragged the paper along the floor until it was near enough to pick up. A further study of the picture did not appear to tell him what he wanted to know. He lifted the pages with the sword and tried to toss them in the still air so as to slice them about as they fell. But the sword edge was not sharp enough and he soon tired of the game.

He sat up and began to take an interest in the details of his surroundings. As though for the first time he walked around the flat, taking in its character. With clothes on, he could have been a police officer inspecting the scene of a baffling crime. The furniture was all so heavy it must have belonged to a much larger house. Somewhere in the Alps perhaps. There were paintings and photographs of romantic castles and many of the books in the living room were German and printed in Gothic script. In a long cupboard mixed with empty bottles of whisky and gin there was a curious collection of *objets trouvés*, broken Etruscan bowls and figurines, fossils, fragments of Roman marble.

The slow exercise in curiosity made Gwydion angry. He pulled at a locked drawer in an oak bureau. It refused to open. He kicked it ineffectively and then pulled out the drawer above it which was full of old photographs which told him nothing: the same anonymous women in 1930ish clothes, hair-do's and make-up, posing for the camera in an endless succession of alpine picnics; family groups on the steps of large houses and smaller groups on holiday caught outside the Doge's Palace or the Eiffel Tower. Behind the bureau there was a telephone which seemed even dustier than the rest of the furniture. He reached over to bring it out and a rectangle of dust from the bureau lid impressed itself on his bare chest. It did not look as though it were in working order. He picked up the receiver and discovered that he could speak to the exchange. The discovery changed his mood completely. He rubbed his hands together and jumped on the furniture.

Behind the bureau under a pile of old magazines he found a heavy directory and a dialling instruction booklet printed the previous year. He laid out the directory on the settee and amused himself by turning over the pages as though he were looking for someone whom he knew. When no name presented itself he examined the contents of another cupboard and found a further collection of old telephone directories, covering extensive areas of northern Italy. With some excitement he traced a number in Pisa and settled down in an armchair while dialling with the instrument on his knees. The number rang for some time before the receiver was raised and a trembling voice spoke at the other end. Gwydion spoke slowly in Italian.

'Is it possible to speak with Gabriella Severoni, please?'

It was a peasant woman at the other end, nervous and possibly a little deaf.

'Professor Severoni is in America.'

'I don't want to speak to the Professor. I want to speak to Gabriella. Is she there?'

'No indeed.'

The woman was reluctant to part with any information. He heard her sniff.

'Do you know where she is?'

There was a brief silence and the woman said in a sly tone.

'Who is that talking?'

'My name is More,' Gwydion said.

'What is that?'

Impatience made him frivolous.

'More,' he said, 'as in *morire*.'

'*Morire!*'

The name alarmed her. He was plainly a messenger with bad news.

'Can you tell me when she will be in.'

'You ask me something I cannot answer.'

The woman was anxious now to get off the phone.

'Is she away?'

'Of course she is away. She lives in Turin with her husband. Where else?'

'She is married?'

'Of course she is married.'

The woman was more confident now and also openly suspicious.

'Are you the housekeeper?'

'Why else should I be here? I must go now. I have something on the stove.'

She could be heard to sigh with relief as she put the phone down. Gwydion pulled a face and looked at the dirt on his hands and on his chest and thighs. He went to the bathroom to see how much water had accumulated under the dripping tap. It was still less than a quart. He wiped himself with a dry paper towel and returned to the bedroom to clear up the mess left by the shattered newspaper.

It was cooler now on this side of the flat but he appeared to find it even more depressing. He picked up a paperback novel on the chair by the bed and gave it some attention. But not for long. He let it fall on the floor and sank back to rest his head on the pillow and stare at the ceiling. Tilting his head to look at the wardrobe where the German uniform hung he seemed to notice for the first time a travelling case on top of the wardrobe. It was half hidden by a fringe of carved oak. It suddenly held his interest. He took a chair and brought it down. Like everything else it was covered

with dust. It was also locked. He wiped the case with
sheets of newspaper. Half-heartedly he attempted to
force the lock with his fingers. When it did not open
he threw the case on the other bed and continued clearing up the room. He deposited the crumbled papers in
the bin in kitchen which was already overflowing. In a
kitchen drawer he found a screwdriver. He held it in
his hand for some time as though deciding whether or
not to use it. Abruptly he returned to the bedroom and
forced open the lock of the travelling case.

It contained a headdress made for the most part
of glass beads, and a strangely lifeless pair of black
boots with high heels, made of soft leather. Under
these lay two photographs in elaborate brass frames.
The larger of the two was a collage of shots of a
woman in different nude poses, sometimes alone and
sometimes with a podgy man with black brilliantined
hair. The woman was Molly Shilling. They were not
recent photographs. Her hair was not blonde and it
was cut in an earlier fashion. The photographs had
been taken over a period of time and were of many
different sizes but they had been assembled consciously
to show the particular relationship between her and the
older man: a motherly mistress who pampered him and
submitted freely to all his sexual eccentricities. In the
second portrait, which seemed more professional, she
was boldly naked but wearing black boots with the
jacket of a Wehrmacht uniform over her shoulders
and a leather covered swagger stick in her hands. At
the bottom of the case was a stiff envelope of the kind
used to hold legal documents. In this were photographs
which seemed more recent, some taken at sea on the
decks of cabin cruisers or yachts, involving a pair of
small dogs as well as the fat man, who had grown
older, stiffer, fatter, more immobile, but still had the
shining black hair. Gwydion went through them with
speed and thoroughness. With some deliberation he

selected two photographs to keep and then put all the rest back, repacked the case and replaced it on top of the wardrobe.

Like a man whose mind was at last settled in a course of action he returned to the living room and rang up the Stazione Termini.

7

Three women sat in a row behind the long reception desk. Two commissionaires in dark blue uniforms with white gloves marched solemnly from one plate-glass entrance to another and a few people about to be favoured with interviews sat around on the pale leather seats, looking at magazines and studying the passing scene while taxis rolled up under the covered way and executives back from holidays bustled in, teasing each other about their flushed or sunburnt faces. Because it was raining hard outside, the foyer to the vast building became less intimidating and more of a shelter designed to house employees and the inquiring public in thoughtful comfort.

Inside the glass door Gwydion shook himself like a wet dog. His hair and his new beard were wet, but he was sufficiently elegant still to pass the commissionaire as, possibly, an eccentric actor disguised by his beard but still protected by a confident aura of being well-known. He was also a man privileged to be returning from a sunny climate. He approached the receptionist who was just putting down a white telephone.

'Can I help you?'

Her accent was disproportionately upper-class.

'I want to see Mr Toiley,' Gwydion said.

He leaned further across the counter to give a more comic performance.

'C.P. Tel 3,' he said and put a finger to his mouth.

The woman pushed her high chair back as if to keep out of his reach. She smiled a little frostily to show that in her job she was accustomed to coping with all sorts of queer people.

'Have you an appointment?'

She was firm and frigidly polite.

Gwydion could not resist continuing to tease her.

'Is that absolutely necessary,' he said. 'Among close friends?'

'I don't know about close friends,' the receptionist said pertly, 'but it's certainly necessary here. Do you have an appointment?'

'Indeed I have. May I say how deeply impressed I am by your ruthless efficiency?'

'What name is it, please sir?'

'I don't think people generally realize how much an organization like this owes to brave and resourceful employees like yourself guarding the front line.'

The receptionist's eyes enlarged as a signal of mounting indignation.

'What if every Tom, Dick and Harry from the street decided he would like to burst in and see the people who organize his evening's entertainment? Absolutely no work at all would ever get done. Do you see what I mean?'

'Indeed I do, Sir. Could I have your name?'

'For this reason alone it is necessary to install the Captains of our tender dreams well inside impregnable fortresses guarded by incorruptible women. More, my dear, Gwydion More.'

She was balancing the white receiver on her shoulder

like some white crustacean pet trained to absolute obedience and cleanliness and her hands were free to turn the large visitor's book in his direction. She listened closely to the voice of Victor Toiley's secretary, still intent on scrutinizing Gwydion's credentials.

'Would you mind spelling your first name, sir?'

Gwydion was prepared for the question.

'Nothing could be easier. G for Good, W for Women, Y for Yes and Youth, D for Dangerous, I for Insinuating, O for Organ and N for Naughty.'

The receptionist had decided on a policy of ignoring him. She rang a bell and a disabled, elderly page appeared to conduct Gwydion to the fifth floor of the building where the offices of the senior programme executives were chiefly located. Gwydion's exuberance was temporarily exhausted and he made the journey in silence. In the lift the disabled man compensated for the bronchial rasp of his breathing by smiling and making determinedly cheerful gestures when he pressed buttons or pointed the way. As they walked down a curving corridor Gwydion took a keen interest in his surroundings and even tried to read the names and titles printed on small cards slotted below the room numbers. The corridor was anonymous and impersonal but his manner became lively and possessive as though he were anxious to demonstrate even to himself that he was completely at home and full of confidence.

Victor Toiley was already standing in the connecting doorway to his own room when Gwydion entered the secretary's office. He was a more imposing figure in a dark business suit than he had been in the heat in his holiday clothes. A stiff white collar improved his complexion and drew attention to the dignified modelling of his carefully groomed head. He was clearly anxious that Gwydion should not dawdle about in the outside office making a memorable impression on secretaries. His manner was as schoolmasterly as ever. As he closed the door he could have been a housemaster about to interview a troublemaker in the lower school.

'I don't know why you insisted on coming here,' he said.

Gwydion was wandering around the large office. It was well furnished. There were armchairs and a settee and an occasional table as well as a large desk. There was a flourishing rubber plant in one corner and a sequence of four tasteful lithographs on the walls which were painted pearl grey. Gwydion pointed at a closed door in the wall opposite the door which he had entered.

'I bet that leads to C.P. Tel 2.'

Victor's head jerked up so that the light glistened on the lens of his spectacles. In spite of his authoritative manner he was nervous. On the corner of his desk there was a framed photograph of his wife and daughter in a swing in the ample garden of their Sutton home. A sheepdog lay at their feet with its obedient tongue hanging out.

'I was thinking on my way up about those classes you used to take once a week when I was in Form Six,' Gwydion said. 'What were they called? Civics or Ethics? I don't remember. You know they really were very impressive. It was a great loss to the school when you took that job in radio, it really was. Still the school's loss was the country's gain, so who am I to complain?'

Victor looked at his watch.

'I must keep an eye on the time,' he said. 'I've got an appointment in ten minutes.'

'I always remember one lesson you gave on the teachings of Karl Marx. It made a deep impression on me. You were a very good teacher you know. You really were. I wonder if you remember the lesson?'

Victor shook his head. In spite of himself he was taken back to those early days of his career and interested in what Gwydion had to say.

'Well that's it you see. I was at an impressionable age.

266

I can remember it. It was a defence of idealism really, very cunningly designed for growing boys.'

'Was it really?'

Victor sounded disbelieving.

'You were very heavy on Marx's economic determinism as I recall. You were not in favour of all men being motivated by their selfish economic interests and nothing more. You were very down on that.'

'Was I?'

Victor was making a visible effort to reach an imaginative understanding of the lesson he had given to a class of boys sixteen years before and had now so completely forgotten.

'I don't remember a thing about it.'

As always he sounded as though he derived a special satisfaction from being completely frank. His voice rang out with a concise clarity that tended to make even his simplest statements sound like quotations from an anthology of the world's best sayings. He appeared to be rapidly revising the situation and deciding that things were more in his favour than he had estimated at first. He stared sternly at Gwydion and determined to wait for him to speak.

'I wish I could. But I can't.'

'I hope you are not forming a poor opinion of me,' Gwydion said.

He sighed and sat down on the settee.

'It's so easy to be misunderstood. I travelled back from Rome with a dear old lady called Mrs Dwyer. The widow of a Police Commissioner. Very nice she was. A delightful companion. She approached me and asked for my help. With her luggage as a matter of fact. There was a mix up with trains and we were stuck for the best part of a day on Milan Station. Just a group of us. Poor stranded British travellers. There were two long haired students from Yorkshire. A boy and a girl. He was the one with a beard. She used to lift his hair from time to time and kiss his dirty neck. I was quite fascinated by them and they didn't seem to mind me watching.'

Victor looked openly at his wrist watch but Gwydion was not to be put off. He continued with his story in a most leisurely and confident manner.

'Her manner was a bit imperial, I suppose. Mrs Dwyer I mean. A life spent in governing lesser breeds without the law. But I liked her. We got on. She wanted to dash out and see *The Last Supper* and I agreed to go with her. She believed in making the best of things, she said. So we had that in common. But the two students were very disapproving. Proper little kill-joys. And do you know on the channel crossing . . . It was quite rough, Mrs D and I decided to make the best of it and we went into the first-class eating place to stuff ourselves with the best there was. When I went to the loo I found the whole place stinking with vomit and sea water and there was my hairy student friend gripping the wash-basin and very green about the gills. I tried to make some cheerful comforting remark, and do you know what he said to me?'

Gwydion paused to wait for Victor to settle all his attention on him.

'*You bloody Fascist lackey!* That's what he said. *You bloody Fascist lackey.* That's all. Just for being nice to a poor old lady and maybe getting a few free meals thrown in as well. It made a deep impression on me.'

'Did it?'

Victor's comment was impatient rather than sarcastic.

'Yes it did. You see my point?'

'No. I don't.'

'We are in exactly the same boat. So why not row me in?'

'I'm sorry.'

Victor spoke stiffly.

'I don't follow.'

'That article you wrote on Public Service Broadcasting in the *Guardian*. Last May I think it was. Stirring stuff. And now this meeting on the yacht off Monticello and the cloak and dagger forming of a new consortium and the kind of people you have to mix with in order to achieve quite possibly the very highest ideals of professional freedom and creativity and all that. Do you know what I mean?'

'I wish you'd say what you've got to say,' Victor said. 'I haven't much time for this kind of thing.'

'Molly is a wonderful person, isn't she?'

Victor pulled in his lips and made no comment.

'I wish you'd come and sit down over here,' Gwydion said. 'If this were an interview I would be having the feeling that I was talking myself out of the job. This distance . . .'

He made gestures to indicate the great space between them.

'. . . It doesn't help. It's all such a crude business, isn't it? I'm sure you must find it all very distasteful. Young men driven by such trivial aspirations . . . all these appetites for fame and success.'

He leaned forward to look meaningfully at the family photograph on Victor's desk.

'I wonder what Marjorie thinks about it all.'

'Now look here . . .'

Victor was pale and angry. He stood up, clearly eager to order Gwydion out of the building.

'I'm sorry,' Gwydion said. 'I really am. I went too far then. I apologize. I was genuinely curious. She has her church interests still I'm sure. I just wondered . . . but I had no right at all to think aloud like that. I do apologize. I really do. Please sit down. I just want to ask you one thing more and then I'll be on my way.'

Victor stayed on his feet.

'It's about Molly. I just wondered how much you knew about her and her relationship with you-know-who? But you must have guessed, I suppose.'

'It's none of my business.'

'Of course it isn't. On the other hand there are things in this business, aren't there, that you just have to know. This is my field after all. I know what I'm talking about. She was trained as a nurse. Did you know that?'

'Why should I?'

'Well, it is important you see. It must have been part of the reason why he came to be so dependent on her. Massage and all that. You could be in trouble there. Between you and me, it's a very kinky relationship. I know this for a fact. I've seen photographs. With my own eyes.'

Victor remained silent, but he was restless and uneasy.

'It's very strange really,' Gwydion said. 'I couldn't bring myself to describe them to you. Some ancient inhibitions no doubt. I suppose in my mythological Welsh mind you are still a divinity master and Marjorie is still a bishop's daughter. You are still trailing clouds of pure glory. A member of this divinely ordained corporation. By the way. Do they know you are going?'

Gwydion pointed his thumb at the door of the adjoining office.

'Does he know?'

'No,' Victor said. 'He doesn't. But I shall be telling him by the end of the week.'

'Of course you will.'

Gwydion smiled and nodded like a man anxious to be agreeable.

'If you don't mind me saying so,' he said, 'I always thought him a big-headed pusher.'

Victor pressed his lips together obstinately.

'I'm not one of those people who believe television is the special preserve of big-headed pushers. It's too exciting a medium for that. There's got to be a sense of responsibility as well as full scope for imagination and creativity. That's the goal we want to achieve. That's the end in view in my opinion and it justifies the means we adopt to get there. I really believe that.'

Victor's face went red.

'I'm not trying to send you up,' Gwydion said. 'I'm being absolutely serious. I really am. I don't know what you think of my abilities. It's difficult for you to be objective because you knew me as a boy. But I've got a lot to offer. A lot more than he has.'

Gwydion turned his thumb again in the direction of the adjoining door.

'All this "Youth at the helm" business cuts no ice with me. I respect maturity and wisdom. I really do. There is only one real reason why he's sprung so far ahead. It's because he's spring-loaded.'

Gwydion paused as though he half expected to hear Victor laughing in response to his quip. Victor was trying to hold his face in a mask of impassivity and only the twitch of the muscles at the top of his jaw betrayed the extent of his effort.

'Basically I'm very loyal,' Gwydion said. 'I wouldn't make use of older men and then go behind their backs and organize them into some harmless railway siding to twiddle their thumbs right up to pension time.'

Victor pounded the sides of his hands on his desk.

'What are you implying?'

'At the very least, dog should never eat dog.'

Gwydion jumped to his feet, full of gay confidence.

'Look,' he said. 'I'm having lunch with Molly tomorrow. All I am asking in reality is that you should not object to me as a suitable candidate for ordination or coordination!'

He stood in front of Victor's desk, smiling in his friendliest fashion.

'I know you can't accept this now, as of this moment. But you and I are natural allies. We need each other.

271

We really do. And nobody can ask for more than that, can they? Just think of what it will be like. A man of your integrity struggling to survive in a moral snake pit. At the very least you will need a right-hand man who will understand your principles and at the same time won't be afraid of going right into the very heart of the den of iniquity. Shall I give you a ring tomorrow? When I've had my long chat with Molly?'

Victor looked at the papers on his desk and nodded briefly. His shoulders bent as though they were taking the strain of a new weight for the first time.

8

The table was small. The room was crowded. Molly sat on the inside and Gwydion was forced close to her. He was so much at his ease that he stared into her eyes and fingered his necktie as though he was catching sight of a reassuring glimpse of his own person in a shop window. His clothes were smart and new and Molly too wore a new hat. Her gloves and her hand-bag leaned against the wall of the restaurant which was crowded with confident people eating and talking in a dim but comfortable gloom. The waiters were dressed informally but moved about their tables with the precision and polish of circus performers. The emphasis was on the excellence of the food and the faint smell of garlic bread lingered at the level of the table while a more exotic scent hovered in the air immediately around Molly's head. The noise of the restaurant brought them comfort and as they looked in each other's eyes and talked, they could have been singing. The expanse of stiff white tablecloth was lifted by their knees and a drop of spilt wine looked like a red sixpence ready to roll down into Gwydion's lap. Under cover of the white cloth they could have been holding hands.

'I'm sorry, darling. I really am.'

Molly's voice was a creamy purr. Her face was thrust forward and flattered by the holiday tan and the dim light.

'It was all so delicate. I just couldn't . . . I dared not . . . get in touch with you. I am taking the most fearful risk even now.'

Her eyes glanced with exaggerated awe around the restaurant. But no one appeared to be taking any notice of them.

'Binks is insanely jealous.'

Gwydion pressed his fist against his mouth to stop it twitching.

'It's a silly nickname I know,' Molly said. 'But I can't think of him as anything else . . .'

'I can,' Gwydion said quickly. 'Small arms . . .'

'Hush!'

Molly behaved as though she were frightened by his loud audacity.

'Will he have me shot or something?'

'Please,' Molly said. 'You must be careful. Seriously. You could spoil everything. And I really mean spoil.'

Abruptly she stopped speaking.

A swarthy waiter was pressing against the outside of their table and held up an order pad with his pencil poised. Gwydion leaned back as though he were drawing back a curtain to reveal as much as possible of the mature fascinating woman that his body was hiding from a world only waiting to admire her. The waiter recited mouthwatering items of sweet Mediterranean food but Molly exercised extreme restraint and asked for black coffee. She brought both her hands together under her chin and looked at Gwydion with an expression of childish innocence.

'I'm not ashamed of those photographs,' she said. 'I was his secretary and I still am in a sense. He has all my loyalty. I'm not one of your harlots with a heart of gold and an empty head. I've got brains and he knows it. I am not just a body but that's the way he shows his love. It does nobody any harm. It was just something between the two of us. Why didn't you trust me a little longer?'

'Oh I did,' Gwydion said. 'I did absolutely. But I was going out of my mind with boredom and loneliness in that bloody flat. I really was.'

'I thought you said you needed a place to hide . . .'

'I suppose I did in a metaphorical sense but not all that badly. It was like solitary confinement for a crime I had never committed. It was ridiculous. I was going out of my tiny mind. I'm a very convivial type. I don't like being alone.'

'I'm sorry darling. But you can see I was in an impossible position . . .'

'I began to think it was just a spot of holiday romance to pass the time . . .'

'But darling, I gave you the key . . .'

'Of a prison.'

The singing note had gone out of their voices, to be replaced by a low mutter of recrimination. The waiter brought the coffee. Gwydion offered Molly a cigarette and they decided to try again.

'I don't know what poor old Oiley has told you,' Gwydion said, 'but you must always allow for the fact that he hates my guts.'

'I was planning a place for you,' Molly said. 'I really was. Rome was out because Binks decided he wanted to go to Sardinia. He absolutely refused to go without me.'

274

'A royal whim,' Gwydion said.

'No indeed. Sound business, as always. When he moves he always moves for sound business reasons.'

Gwydion allowed himself to look a little sad.

'I couldn't upset him, darling. He is the absolute lynch-pin of the whole plan.'

She spoke as though the project was chiefly her own. He watched her hand reach for her handbag to take out a cigarette lighter; the hand seemed competent and even powerful, something to respect and cherish.

'I know,' Gwydion said. 'I know, I know, I know.'

Once more their hands touched under the tablecloth. He insinuated his fingers between hers. She gave him a tender smile.

'I must tell you about Oiley,' Gwydion said. 'You ought to know. He's on his way out anyway.'

'How do you know?'

Molly was curious. She turned her head so that the cigarette smoke she exhaled would not blow in Gwydion's face.

'I've got friends in there, my love. Simon calls me his number one ideas man. And it's the ideas people who are moving up . . . thank God. Oiley is really a hangover from an earlier age you know when the producers who were no good were pushed into programme planning or kicked upstairs. He's finished.'

'Darling,' Molly said. 'You sound quite vicious.'

'Sorry,' Gwydion said. 'I didn't mean to be . . . Yes I did. It narked me to think you were relying on him for an evaluation report on me. That really stung me.'

Molly patted the back of his hand.

'We need him all the same,' Molly said.

'Oh I can see that. Respectable front. Acceptable image. Stamp of high level expertise snatched from the rotting jaws of Aunty and all that. Son-in-law of a bishop . . . I never bear a grudge. That's one thing I like about myself. But he's got no ideas you know. He's

275

a squeezed orange. I doubt whether he's got a single pip left in him.'

Their heads had come closer together. They were animated and conspiratorial. Molly stubbed out her cigarette so that both her hands were free to hold his in her lap. She looked up from time to time and glanced about quickly to make sure that nobody in the crowded place was observing them too closely. Each seemed anxious to demonstrate complete trust in the other. Molly's attitude was wise and motherly and she spoke at speed as though there was little time to instruct him fully into the mysteries over which she was obliged for the time being to preside.

'It's becoming very clear what we need,' she said. 'T.V. know-how obviously. Admin and Production. The solid and the dazzling . . . S and D let's call it . . .'

'By God, yes,' Gwydion said.

He was nodding enthusiastically and keeping his voice down to show that he was willingly allowing himself to be swept forward on a tide of living admiration for her physical beauty and wisdom and mental powers.

'This has got to be married to big money. That's where poor old Binks is so vitally important. It's got to be big money. Really Big . . . let's call that B.M . . .'

They giggled together, clearly delighted with each other.

'Item three,' Molly said. 'A Chairman with a name of vast and unimpeachable respectability and prestige.'

'V.I.R.P.,' Gwydion said quickly, to show her how adept he was at improvising on her original joke.

She nodded approvingly.

'How about the Queen?' Gwydion said. 'Who could be more V or I or R or P than her glorious British Majesty?'

Molly patted the back of his hand again to calm him down. He stretched his hand across towards his empty wine glass and tilted it towards him to consider the purple dregs at the base. His face was slightly flushed. With some resolution he pushed the glass away and concentrated on giving Molly his whole attention, nodding encouragingly as she spoke.

'It's a very delicate business. You've no idea. And absolutely vital. I know at least one belted earl who has been wooed by eight different companies.'

'By God,' Gwydion said as though suddenly hit by an idea. 'My old ma's got a title. Wouldn't she do?'

'Your mother has?'

Molly was interested.

'What is it?'

'Lady Brangor. I was only joking.'

Molly looked at him with a new respect.

'Don't take too much notice,' she said. 'I'm a working girl brought up on the *Daily Mirror*. I'm always a little affected when I get near the sound of a title. Now item four, which seems to be growing in importance, I fear. It's what I've been calling W.L. – we really must stop this silly game – Wooing the Locals. We're not doing too well on this front at the moment.'

'I know, I know,' Gwydion said hurriedly.

'Know? How do you know?'

'Well, guessed. I tried to make this point to Oiley yesterday. I really have got local connections.'

Molly looked doubtful.

'I'm not sure how important this is . . . Binks thinks it's nothing.'

'Oh but surely it's important.'

For the first time Molly looked a little irritated.

'You can switch from one locality to another,' she said. 'It's a tactical question. It depends on the strength of the competition.'

Gwydion was respectful but urgent.

'Nevertheless in some parts it will be more important than others. And I tell you if it's Arthur's Kingdom

and all that they will be terrifically important. And
this is where I would be enormously valuable. Have
you ever heard of Sir Joseph Macsen Morgan? J.M. to
his friends.'

'Not more initials,' Molly said. 'No. I haven't.'

She glanced at her small gold wrist watch.

'You mustn't go yet,' Gwydion said. 'Have some more
coffee.'

Molly shook her head.

'No. It's bad for the heart. I really must go.'

He spoke urgently. A man with much to say in a short
time.

'He could have been the wire-puller in chief to the
Emperor of China and done it all standing on one
leg. We've simply got to get him. He's a great friend
of my brother's. Slobbers all over him every Sunday
morning.

'Who's your brother?'

'Bedwyr. He's an architect.'

The thought of Bedwyr made him pause and face
an obstacle he had temporarily allowed to vanish from
his mind. Molly took a second glance at her watch.
Gwydion noticed this at once.

'You're going cold on me.'

There was an embarrassed silence.

'Of course I'm not,' Molly said.

She looked at her handbag as though she were
contemplating picking it up and then moved her head
briefly to give Gwydion a tentative smile.

'Let's have the cards on the table,' he said. 'I want to
know what you really think.'

'I always planned a place for you,' she said. 'From
that first day. If there's one gift I've got it's recognizing
talent when I see it. I'm not creative myself. I only wish
I was. But I know you are. Why should you be bothered
with all the boring preliminaries . . . when it all could
come to nothing anyway . . .'

She moved her head to look at him with full face and the utmost sincerity.

'I have complete faith in you,' she said.

Gwydion pushed his cup and saucer away and placed his elbows on the table.

'I want to get in on the ground floor,' he said.

'But darling . . .'

Her voice was patient and understanding.

'What good will that do? You'll get what you want in the end.'

'I want a piece of the business.'

She smiled at him a little pityingly.

'What's that supposed to mean?' she said.

'A share of control. A seat on the board. That sort of thing. Don't laugh at me. I'm being serious. It's what I want.'

'You are making a mistake.'

Her voice was clear and firm. Gwydion was disturbed.

'How? How am I making a mistake?'

'You are an artist,' she said. 'You should confine yourself to the artistic and creative side. It doesn't work the other way.'

'Oh but it does.'

They were silent again. This time she picked up her handbag and gloves and pushed back her chair a fraction.

'You're worried about Binks?'

She stretched her jaw and nodded.

'Well just tell him I'm a brilliantly creative person full of ideas who wants to learn about power. And about money.'

'You're going the wrong way about it,' Molly said. 'Why don't you take my advice? He'd go mad if it was anything . . . You made a mistake going to Victor you know. A mistake.'

She was deeply serious but Gwydion patted his chest

279

confidently.

'I can't understand why you're not more enthusiastic,' he said. 'I'm the biggest asset you've got. And you just stumbled over me. It was like tripping over a gold brick in the dark.'

'He could have gone straight to Binks,' Molly said. 'Without contacting me at all. And that would have been the end.'

'I took a gamble.'

Gwydion was defiant, but cheerful.

'What would life be without the occasional gamble? It wouldn't be worth living.'

Molly looked tired and dispirited.

'It's all a gamble anyway,' she said. 'And I don't mind telling you sometimes I don't believe it's worth it.'

She could have been pleading with him not to be difficult.

'Molly I'm absolutely serious about this. It's what I've been waiting for all my life. Accident or no accident. You've got to let me in. A fully paid up member. You'll never regret it.'

'Fully paid up. . .'

She uttered the words slowly.

'That *would* be a way.'

Like a dog who hears a knife scraping a plate, he gave his instant attention.

'What way?'

'I'm trying to think of a way to present you to Binks. If you had money plus local connections plus your telly experience, in that order . . .'

'How much?'

Molly raised her eyebrows as she made an approximate calculation.

'I'm not trying to be awkward,' Gwydion said.

He spoke as though he were making a rapid series of concessions.

'I always trusted you. The real personal thing. I knew

it wasn't just a holiday dream. It was real, something to hold on to ... I admit I should never have gone near Victor. I wouldn't have done if I hadn't happened to know him so well from my schooldays. He's a weak man really, Molly, who makes a strong man noise ... How much do you think?'

'Well,' Molly said, 'not less than twenty-five thousand pounds.'

9

On a mattress in the middle of the floor of Peredur's bedroom Gwydion lay fast asleep. Like the rest of the flat the bedroom was spacious but very sparsely furnished. There was a spartan bed in the far corner, unmade, and against the other wall a large mahogany wardrobe with a door hanging open on one hinge. Gwydion's bare leg, well shaped and hairy, stuck out of the bedclothes at an awkward angle. However long the struggle with discomfort and bedclothes had lasted he was in a deep sleep now with the thumb of his right hand firmly wedged in his mouth, giving him the pouting babyish good looks of an angel in a humanistic fresco. His heavy closed eyelids and their long lashes reinforced the echo of a distant childhood. The naked arm seemed powerful but the pectoral muscle, although sunburnt and edged with black hair, was soft and easily pushed out by the bent arm.

Peredur opened the bedroom door quietly. He was wearing a limp black gown and under his left arm a heavy collection of books out of which hung white strips of torn paper to mark passages for reference. A new boil had broken out to trouble him on the back of his neck and he was sweating from the effort of hurrying back up the stairs. He left the door open and went to the living room where he dumped his load of books on the blistered walnut veneer of the heavy oval table. To recover from his exertions, he slumped on to the centrally placed sofa where he sat despondently, still wearing his gown, with both his arms hanging between his legs. He was completely still, making an effort to anaesthetize himself so that the pain from his neck should be reduced to a bearable dull ache and the complexities of his existence reduced to a minimum. Beyond the closed window the traffic on the arterial road maintained its muffled roar. Peredur closed his eyes as if to smother his dejection in darkness. When he opened them a seagull appeared as though by magic on the ledge outside his window. Peredur was caught up in the fascination of its appearance at such a close range, staring at the red marks on its yellow beak as though hurriedly deciphering a secret message. The bird tumbled its own weight into the wind and the smooth action of the wings opening and the webbed feet tucking into the fanned tail drew him to his feet, his mouth opening with admiration and his prominent upper teeth appearing in an involuntary smile. With a fresh surge of energy he marched noisily to the kitchen where he filled a cheap tin kettle at the tap and slammed it down on the old gas stove. He made tea and carried two mugs into the bedroom, giving the mattress a friendly kick to wake up his brother.

Gwydion pulled the bedclothes over his shoulder, reluctant to get up. Peredur bent his knees carefully and set the mug of tea on the floor as near as he could to his brother's nose. He straightened himself without disturbing his neck and stood waiting for his brother to perform in some amusing way, a smile of anticipation on his face. Gwydion opened one eye and then felt along the floor to put his fingers around the mug of tea.

'What's that bloody thing you're wearing?' he said.

As though to demonstrate to his brother how little he esteemed it Peredur shook the long M.A. gown off his shoulders and let it fall in a black heap around his feet. The shrug gave him a spasm of pain in the neck which made him screw up his face.

'Can't think why you live in such squalor. This place must be perishing cold in winter. It's bad enough now. How did the seminar go?'

'Nobody turned up.'

It cost Peredur an effort to say it and he blushed.

'The rude little bastards.'

'It was the first this term. There could have been a misunderstanding about the time.'

'You did all that preparation last night for nothing?'

'Not entirely,' Peredur said. 'A post-graduate student turned up.'

'How do you mean?'

Gwydion leaned on his elbow sipping tea and studying his younger brother critically.

'I gave him a reading list. That saves me seeing him at eleven o'clock.'

'What's his name?'

'Roebuck.'

'I've got very little time for students.'

Gwydion sat up and felt about in the pockets of his leather jacket for a packet of cigarettes.

'I was telling you last night,' he said. 'This is no job for a grown man. Universities are not what they were. And they never will be again. You want to get out, Peredur, before it's too late.'

Peredur looked happier. The company of his brother raised his spirits. He was restless with all the things he

283

longed to talk about. He gave Gwydion a vigorous nod that made him wince but he laughed at his discomfort and hurried back to the kitchen to prepare a cooked breakfast. Gwydion lay on the mattress enjoying his cigarette and cup of tea. He shouted out when he had finished.

'Be a hero and start running the bath for me, will you?'

The bathroom and the W.C. were two steps lower down at the back of the flat. While the hot water ran from the geyser on to a discoloured patch at the base of the bath, Gwydion stood naked in the W.C. urinating noisily and making loud cries of protest against the cold and the damp.

'Look at this wall! Covered in green mould! No proper foundations, see. Rising damp. Bedwyr would have forty fits if he saw it!'

He pulled the chain and jogged into the bathroom running on the spot like an athlete tuning up for training.

'If you go on living in a dump like this you'll end up crippled with arthritis or something awful . . . oh! oh! oh!'

With exaggerated cries he plunged into the hot bath. Peredur returned to the kitchen and concentrated on frying eggs and bacon and making toast and coffee. He worked fast at the stove and moved with jerky speed between one job and another, a man completely accustomed to looking after himself. Gwydion sang in his bath and splashed about recklessly.

'We don't appreciate water enough,' he said. 'Not even English water. I bet this is Welsh if the truth were known . . . Water is the most valuable raw material known to man . . . remember?'

Peredur made no attempt to stop and listen to the shouts and reminiscences coming from the bathroom. He just smiled contentedly and carried on working, until Gwydion yelled for a towel. In great haste, having turned down the gas, Peredur raced to the bedroom and dragged out a large stiffly laundered towel from the bottom drawer of the mahogany wardrobe. He took the towel to the bathroom where Gwydion was almost lost from sight in clouds of steam. When he pulled himself up he was pink all over.

'You're getting fat,' Peredur said.

Gwydion grasped a fold of flesh around his waist with both hands.

'I'm not,' he said. 'I'm not am I?'

'You're getting older,' Peredur said. 'It's only to be expected. How much do you weigh?'

'How the hell should I know? Don't put the towel there. The seat's wet.'

He soaped himself lavishly around the crutch and lifted a sponge heavy with water, drawing back his foreskin to squeeze water over himself several times. He splashed so much that Peredur had to retreat to the doorway to keep himself dry. He was still holding the towel and Gwydion held out his hand for it when he was ready to emerge.

'I'll have to take up squash again,' he said. 'But how the hell can I afford the time? . . . It's time we had a council of war. It's ridiculous you wasting your time in this godforsaken hole. It really is.'

He splashed more water on the floor as he came out of the bath. He became intent on a musical phrase and as he rubbed his wet hair with the towel he waved his other arm about conducting an invisible orchestra and he smiled when he saw that Peredur was amused.

'It's about time you had somebody around to cheer you up,' he said. 'What's tickling you anyway?'

'I was thinking about your flute,' Peredur said. 'Do you remember how you used to go up to your bedroom and play it for hours?'

'Did I?'

Gwydion looked surprised to hear about his own past, and ready to consider it objectively as though it were someone else's.

'I used to sit on the stairs and listen.'

'Did you?'

Gwydion continued to rub himself down with noisy vigour until he formed a conclusion.

'Antidote to adolescent melancholy no doubt,' he said.

When he was dry he padded back carefully to the bedroom. He was still critical of the flat and Peredur's solitary way of life, but Peredur seemed to enjoy listening to him. It was warm and friendly and acceptable and the bustle of his presence brought the whole place to life as he moved from one room to another, leaving a trail of untidiness wherever he went. The breakfast was ready. Peredur sat down at the small table in the kitchen, content to wait. Gwydion came in at last, a splendid figure, freshly shaved, in a white polo-necked sweater and tight jeans. He rubbed his hands together at the prospect of a good meal.

Peredur enjoyed watching his brother eat. In spite of the wolfish way he crammed his mouth, he radiated pleasure and Peredur could not but share something of it. He himself ate with precise care, cutting up his food into fastidiously small segments and chewing each mouthful many times.

'So you're not interested in television?' Gwydion said.

Peredur considered the statement carefully.

'Oh, I wouldn't go as far as to say that.'

'Well, that's something anyway.'

He took another mouthful of bacon and egg.

'I've come all this way to offer you a share in one of the new kingdoms of the earth, my boy. I hope you realize that.'

Peredur chuckled admiringly.

'You should learn to take me more seriously.'

He waved his knife at Peredur.

'I'm not just a pretty face. This is something very big and I want you in on it. The world needs your brains. You can't just go on burying yourself alive in a place like this. It just isn't healthy.'

'We must talk about it.'

Peredur looked amiably inclined to a long discussion later on during his brother's visit.

'I thought that was what we were doing.'

'Sorry.'

Peredur was deeply apologetic.

'What I meant was there are so many things I want to talk about with you. I'm in a bit of a mess to tell you the truth . . .'

'There you are!'

'What do you mean?'

'I thought you were. I've come in the nick of time, haven't I? Now come on. Admit it.'

Gwydion held out his mug for coffee and Peredur attended efficiently to his needs. As he did so Gwydion pointed to the boil on his neck.

'I'll fix that for you,' he said. 'Hot fomentations. I had a girl friend once who was a nurse. She showed me how to do it. You need looking after. Haven't you got a girl friend?'

Peredur smiled.

'With a face like mine?'

'Now don't start that nonsense again.'

Peredur sat down carefully.

'I know my problems will seem small and trivial to you . . .'

'Or that either!'

Gwydion held out a piece of toast with a glistening heap of marmalade. He glanced at the uneasy heap before he popped it into his mouth and sealed it in with a smile on his lips which Peredur responded to very willingly.

'I will not have you underrating yourself,' Gwydion said. 'You know my views. We are three formidable brothers. Our interests don't happen to converge, but my God if they did we would make the world shake!'

He banged the table.

'We could make the Three Musketeers look like the Three Stooges. All we have to do is learn to collaborate. I tell you brother there is such a reservoir of talent in the More brothers ... We need a motto "More makes more" or something like that ...'

Peredur pulled a face at the schoolboy pun.

'... We could do miracles. We really could.'

'I don't know about that.'

Peredur was inhibited by his brother's style of easy confidence and by his gestures, so uncomplicated and assertive in the confined space between the kitchen chair and the bare table. Gwydion sensed that he was becoming either too boyish or too boisterous and driving his brother back into his usual shell of reserve.

'What's this mess then?'

He spoke quietly, sobered and adult. Peredur was satisfied that Gwydion was ready to listen.

'It's time I got away from here.'

Gwydion spread out his arms.

'What have I been telling you?'

'I'm being put upon. In the Department.'

'Well there you are ...'

Peredur made a gesture of impatience and Gwydion responded by demonstrating a complete willingness to listen. He held up a milk bottle to the light as though it contained a rare fluid with which he was was unfamiliar and set it down again.

'There's a war on,' Peredur said. 'Between old Sable and the Professor. And I'm caught in the cross-fire. It all sounds ludicrous and incredibly childish when you put it into words but it's unbearably irritating to live through. It's a very unhappy department.'

Gwydion nodded understandingly but Peredur showed that he was still not in possession of the facts and that it was too soon for him to show so much understanding and sympathy.

'They've landed me with this character Roebuck. I've got to supervise his post-graduate work in spite of the fact that I don't consider he's good enough to do it. Do you see what I mean?'

'Sounds awful,' Gwydion said.

'It's quite intolerable. This Roebuck's got money, you see. Or rather his father has. And the Professor imagines that he's friendly with the old man. And he's got visions of putting himself right with the Vice-Chancellor by landing a Roebuck Foundation or some such thing. So I'm expected in reality not only to supervise young Roebuck's post-graduate work but also to feed him with some of my own ideas. That's what it amounts to. Do you understand?'

'Sounds absolutely immoral,' Gwydion said.

'Yes, but do you understand?'

Gwydion blinked and nodded hesitantly.

'It means in practice that I've got to live for the next two years with this objectionable bastard strapped to my back. He's lazy and arrogant. He's already changed his terms of reference twice in order to move in closer on my special territory. He's got no original ideas and he's quite determined that he has every right to help himself to mine.'

'How often do you see him?'

'Once a week this term.'

'That doesn't seem so bad.'

Gwydion quickly modified the comment when he saw his brother making signs of impatience again.

'But of course I can understand. It's a bit like industrial espionage isn't it?'

Peredur failed to see the relevance of the comparison.

'I said to him last week, "what have you got in mind Roebuck" and he said calmly, "That's just it. I thought you would be able to suggest something." He could have been asking a shop assistant to help him pick a new tie. "Haven't you got any ideas of your own?" I said. He just grinned like a jackass and said that all the best ideas had already been taken. And on top of that he had not had time to read the first book list I gave him, because he had wangled himself on to the Senate Committee for Staff-Student Relations as one of the student representatives and they had been holding a series of three hour long meetings . . .'

'My God,' Gwydion said.

But Peredur was too worked up to wait for his comment.

'He has been busy currying favour with the Professor. Last week he took the Professor and his family out for a tour of the Peak District if you please. Sable told me about that. But he's absolutely useless, Sable. He is so cynical about everything. It passes belief. He pins all his faith on a scholastic interpretation of the Rules and standing orders and Regulations. He knows them backwards. And he has great fantasies about tripping the Professor up over this or that at the next meeting of this or that – they live on committees – but he never does. And he'll never make a stand. He's got about as much moral courage as a toilet roll . . . do I sound obsessive?'

'You do a bit,' Gwydion said.

Peredur looked gloomy.

'That's how one gets,' he said.

'Shall I tell you what I think?'

Gwydion was anxious to speak.

'You are cut off from Life. That's what I think. You never have to worry about all the ordinary things that everyone else has to worry about so you invent things to worry about. They're not live issues because nothing

290

is ever really at stake. You are all so removed from the market-place, so far away from the risks of the arena, you're not part of anything at all. As a species I mean. Like a race of cloistered monks living on mattresses and eating peaches and cream all day with nothing to do that really matters. Now what you need . . .'

Peredur's face was red with the effort of keeping his indignation under control.

'I work very hard,' he said.

'I know you do.'

'It needs rigorous self-discipline to do what I do', Peredur said.

'I wasn't talking about you individually. I meant the set-up in general.'

'I want the Truth at whatever cost to myself,' Peredur said. 'There's nothing easy about that.'

'Okay. I agree with you. I wasn't talking about you personally.'

They moved to the living room and Gwydion stretched his legs on the sofa, enjoying a cigarette. The smoke he exhaled through his cheerful nostrils weaved patterns in the still air: twisting columns of smoke fed a blue wreath that hovered over his head like the ghost of a laurel crown. To his brother, standing in black silhouette in the bay window, he must have appeared exotic, oriental almost: above the white neck of his jersey his sunburnt face glowed with a handsome confidence. Peredur had more to say, more to complain about: but he was obviously nervous of giving his brother the wrong impression. It was easier to be silent when the alternative would have appeared a wallowing in self-pity. But the longer he remained silent the more difficult it was for him to break into the kind of things he wanted to say. His brother was watching him with a genuinely benevolent interest which was intended to encourage and not to inhibit.

'I'm going to get away,' Peredur said at last.

'Of course you are.'

Gwydion spoke soothingly.

'This place has served its purpose as far as I am concerned. It's not good anyway to stay put for more than four or five years. Not at my age. And even if I stayed here there's no hope of promotion.'

Gwydion became impatient with his brother's careful manner.

'Get out altogether!' he said. 'What's the point of shifting from one university to another? They're all the same. They're all bloody awful.'

Peredur smiled to show he appreciated the joke but Gwydion was serious.

'Get out into the world!' he said. 'What's the purpose of your life anyway? I can't imagine anything more awful than reaching middle age and then turning round and looking at your past and blaming yourself like nobody's business because you never had a go!'

'I do have a purpose.'

Peredur sounded stubborn.

'I know you have. We all have. But I mean something with real scope and sweep. Something ambitious, in the grand manner. Why don't you . . .'

'There's nothing more difficult than what I'm trying to do.'

Peredur interrupted sharply. He stood very still in the window bay and Gwydion looked at him with genuine curiosity.

'Well, what is it? Go on. Tell me. I've come all the way to this godforsaken town just to talk to you. What?'

Peredur cleared his throat and moved his tongue. He wanted to make an objective pronouncement in the coolest possible manner.

'I want to give my life a structure of moral imperatives.'

As soon as he heard his own words and saw Gwydion's expression he seemed to realize the statement had an effect quite different from what he intended. Gwydion did not laugh, but Peredur was obliged to move away as if his peace had been broken by a loud hoot of derision.

'What the hell does that mean?' Gwydion said.

He sounded genuinely puzzled. Peredur did not answer. He went into the kitchen, put on a kettle, cleared the breakfast table and prepared to wash the dishes. Gwydion followed him when he had finished his cigarette. He searched about for a dry tea-cloth but Peredur told him not to bother. There was a handy dish rack he had bought recently where he could put the plates and cups and cutlery out to dry.

'I am here to be helpful,' Gwydion said. 'Just because I'm no philosopher, it doesn't mean I can't be helpful on a purely mundane level.'

He exercised his gaiety and warmth of manner and in no time he had drawn Peredur back from his inward-looking isolation. For his part he grew and blossomed under the steady rays of his younger brother's unconcealed admiration.

'Look,' he said, 'what about this car? You said you wanted my advice.'

'I'm ashamed to show it to you.'

They began to laugh.

'Let's take it out and flog it,' Gwydion said. 'Now that's something I could do for you. Secondhand cars are my speciality. Would you like to exchange it or flog it outright?'

Peredur came near to beaming at the prospect of having his brother help him solve his car problem. More than once he remarked how wonderful it was to have someone with him he could trust. His exultation loosened his tongue and he became quite loquacious.

'I wouldn't like to become a car bore,' he said. 'Like Alan Thread from the French Department. He really is the limit. He pesters the life out of poor MacMasters who appears to have done a vehicle maintenance course at some time or other, because they both live in the same Hall of Residence. They were quite pally at first but MacMasters got so fed up in the end with repairing Alan Thread's car he stopped speaking to him.'

Gwydion's smile was almost fatherly. He was seeing his younger brother in a new light. The urge to anecdote came spurting out of him in jerks like water out of a tap almost choked with rust. Together they left the house and passed through the wilderness of back garden to an untidy row of garages made of corrugated iron.

'I can't think how you can live in such an appalling place,' Gwydion said.

He was sitting in the passenger seat of the Morris Minor, studying the controls and the interior of the vehicle with obvious disapproval.

'I've had nothing but trouble with it,' Peredur said. 'The trouble is I'm so ignorant about cars. I'm overwhelmed with awe and gratitude if it starts when I pull this thing.'

'"Pull" indeed,' Gwydion said. 'You'll be lucky to get fifty for it. How much did you give for it?'

'How much?'

Peredur blushed. The battery was new and powerful and the car shook as he tried to start it.

'Go on. Tell me. We all make mistakes.'

'Two hundred.'

'My God. You got taken. Where did you buy it?'

'In Pendraw.'

'What on earth made you go there to buy a car?'

Gwydion left his mouth open to show his amazement.

'I happened to be there.'

The car jerked as he reversed out, narrowly missing the garage door. He held on the wheel as he turned to put Gwydion a sudden question.

'Did you know our father committed suicide?'

Gwydion was holding on to the sides of his seat and laughing at Peredur's driving.

'Well there's no need for you to try and imitate him.'

He was amused by his own remark until he saw how stern Peredur's face had become.

'Sorry,' he said. 'I didn't mean to be frivolous. No. I didn't know.'

'Mother got it registered as accidental death. But I'm pretty sure it was suicide.'

'Trust old Amy. Close your eyes and say it isn't there. Not a bad policy in some ways . . . owch.'

Gwydion shut his eyes when the car shot out into the main road. He sighed deeply when he opened them, more to recover his composure than with any sense of regret for the past.

'I had a row with her,' Peredur said. 'When old Hubert died, I just couldn't stand the set-up. The Huskies all round her. Hangers-on everywhere . . . So I did some research.'

'It wouldn't surprise me in the least,' Gwydion said.

'What do you mean?'

'I thought you were about to say that she drove him to it.'

Peredur was deeply shocked. His hands shook on the driving wheel and he gripped it more tightly. Gwydion had opened up a vista of possibilities that he could not bear to look at. He screwed up his eyes until they were narrow slits and all his front teeth were prominently in view.

'You mustn't take these things too much to heart,' Gwydion said.

'She's a monster.'

Peredur drew in his lips and muttered the words as though he did not want to be overheard.

'Oh I don't know . . . think of her as a wolverine without cubs . . .'

Gwydion was calm and tolerant.

'I couldn't stand her interfering with my life so I give her a wide berth and she calls me a cruel boy because I don't come scampering back to earth every time she lets off one of her forest howls.'

He was so amused by his own invention that he threw back his head and gave a brief rendering of what he imagined a forest howl to be like. Peredur was reluctantly impressed by his brother's detachment.

'The trouble with you,' Gwydion said with mock severity, 'you've led too sheltered a life. You're up there by yourself in that awful flat brooding away for hours on end on ancient wrongs and God knows what else. I'll tell you what you need, P.C. More. You need London. You really do.'

Peredur pulled a face to represent distaste and disappointment.

'There's nowhere like London. I'm not talking about mixing with the famous or jostling with the great on the pavements or any of that sort of cock. And it's not just pitting your wits against the best in any field you care to mention. And it's not just the music in the air. If you are there on the spot, you are as near as you can get to where history is being made.'

Gwydion looked pleased with his lyrical outburst but Peredur shook his head as much as the boil on his neck would allow him to.

'And you call me romantic,' he said.

'Sheltered,' Gwydion said quickly. 'That was the word I used. And I meant it. You've got to be free to operate successfully and you've got to have a base in the capital city. It's as simple as that. Everything else is a pale provincial alternative and doomed to failure because it hasn't got the necessary power behind it. I'm a realist and I know what I'm talking about. You won't take me seriously, brother, but I tell you here and now and for the second

296

time I am on the brink of becoming a Telly Tycoon!'

Peredur smiled at him affectionately.

'You want to take a firm snip at the umbilical with a sharp pair of scissors,' Gwydion said. 'You don't want to let that old lady ride you. Old lady! What am I talking about. She's only in her early sixties. And "disgustingly healthy" to use her own phrase. She's got another twenty years to go on doing damage. You keep out of her reach boy, like I do. You come and join me. I'm absolutely serious about this. I want somebody with your brains. It's not just a question of brotherly love. It's ideas that really matter in the end. I'm bright enough to understand that. Take television and education for example. Surely to God we can do something spectacular there?'

Peredur nodded solemnly, but in tune with his own thoughts and not with what Gwydion was saying.

'They want to put up a Memorial,' Peredur said.

'"They"? What are you talking about?'

Gwydion sounded a little annoyed.

'In Pendraw. They want to put up a Memorial to Cilydd.'

'Do they?'

He seemed to decide to bide his time. He shifted sideways in his seat to give Peredur his complete attention.

'They want to put a statue on Cilydd's Rock and a sort of garden around it and make it a tourist attraction.'

'Not a bad idea,' Gwydion said. 'Perhaps the old place is waking up after all.'

He looked pleased.

'Good for them. You know what, we might make a film of the opening. A sort of small tribute. To show our interest in local culture. It could be useful.'

'She's against it,' Peredur said. 'She doesn't want it at all. And because she doesn't, I don't think Bedwyr does.'

Gwydion raised a warning hand and turned the palm outwards as if to ward off an invisible danger.

'In that case leave well alone . . . I don't want to tangle with the old lady and Bedwyr is heavily loaded with common sense. Leave well alone.'

'He hasn't even got a gravestone,' Peredur said.

His voice was soft with the sadness of his thoughts.

'We don't even know where he's buried.'

Gwydion decided to say nothing.

'She must have hated him. And yet we were born. You and I. That's what I don't understand. We are his blood. And hers.'

Peredur's voice dipped and rose digging into the situation to lay it bare and to demand some reaction from his older brother who sat beside him apparently undisturbed by this revelation of their terrible origins.

'In my view,' Gwydion said at last, 'it's an outmoded method.'

'I'm not joking.'

'Neither am I. I'm all for pleasure but not procreation . . . what's so marvellous about blood? It's no use bothering yourself silly about the relationship of a man and woman a generation ago. What the hell does it matter any more? All right, he hasn't got a marked grave. So what? Once you're dead, you're dead and that's all there is to it. So why make a fuss anyway? Let the dead bury the dead. You should be on the side of the living and there's a lot to live for. I keep on telling you and you don't take a blind bit of notice . . .'

'I want the Truth,' Peredur said. 'That's all.'

Gwydion pulled a face.

'You're not asking for much are you? Blimey. I never dreamt you were such a demanding little chap.'

Peredur would say no more.

'Where is this godforsaken automobile knacker's yard we are supposed to be visiting?'

'It's just beyond this new estate,' Peredur said. 'Between a rubbish dump and a canal feeder. The students use it a lot.'

Gwydion began to rub his hands.

'Well come along now,' he said. 'Let's get down to business. What kind of a car do you fancy?'

'Something a little bigger,' Peredur said. 'More suited for long journeys . . .'

'Aha!'

'. . . Well, it is a long way to Wales.'

'Nobody goes to Wales unless he has to,' Gwydion said.

Peredur ignored his brother's fresh attempt at humour as if to demonstrate quietly that it was not his practice to leap like a grasshopper from one topic to another.

'There was rather a nice Wolseley. It looked in very good condition . . .'

He pressed his foot repeatedly on the accelerator, but the engine spluttered faintly and then faded out.

'What's the matter?'

Peredur stared wide-eyed at his brother, expecting an instant diagnosis. The car drifted along down the slight decline in the road.

'How the devil should I know? Put your arm out and wave the traffic on . . . Oh my God, I shall have to push it. What a humiliation.'

The car stopped close to the grass verge.

'Will you look inside?' Peredur said. 'Shall I lift the bonnet?'

Gwydion raised his eyes to heaven in mock despair.

'I'm not a wizard,' he said. 'Now you keep a hold on the wheel and we'll push it as far as that bus lay-by down there.'

Laboriously Peredur got out and then wound down the window of the door so that his arm could reach through to the steering wheel. Anxious to appear competent in a crisis he forgot about the boil on his neck and he cried out with pain as he struck the boil against the frame of the door. He leaned inside the car to prevent himself fainting. Gwydion called out impatiently, telling him to release the handbrake. He managed to obey. The distance to the bus-stop lay-by seemed much further now that they were pushing the car. A white sports car slowed down so that the driver could lean across his passenger and make an offer to help.

'Mr More. Are you in difficulties?'

It was Roebuck driving. Peredur turned, leaning his back against the side of the Morris which was still moving, powerfully pushed from behind by Gwydion. Through eyelids almost closed he saw only Maxine Hackett in the passenger seat. She was wearing a hat and on the cramped rear seat a smart new suitcase had been set up on its side, just where his own suitcase had lain in early summer. Roebuck was openly amused by the situation. His thick lips when he smiled seemed to have an individual existence because he was wearing large spectacles which were tinted to protect his eyes. He continued to crawl alongside the disabled car and when they reached the lay-by at last he pulled up and got out to offer assistance.

'Can I help?'

His manner was curt and confident. Gwydion looked at him with interest. He seemed intrigued by the way in which Roebuck's fair hair was plastered so close down the sides of his narrow head.

'Well that's very good of you,' Gwydion said.

He sounded like a man who believed in responding cheerfully to people. Peredur moved along the side of the Morris car exhausted by the pain and effort of getting the car to the lay-by.

'This is Mr Roebuck,' he said with some effort. 'My post-graduate student.'

He turned to stare with unnatural intensity at the dusty hedgerow to conceal the distress in his face.

'Had a look at it then?'

Roebuck led the way to the engine. He lifted the bonnet and took an expert glance at the engine. Gwydion leaned over and played with the carburettor.

'I thought as much,' he said. 'We're out of petrol.'

He looked Peredur reproachfully.

'You realize the fuel gauge is permanently stuck at "Full".'

He and Roebuck enjoyed a brief laugh but Peredur turned away to hide his embarrassment.

'Look,' Roebuck said. 'I'll tell you what I'll do. I'll pop down to the Auto Palace and get some juice and bring it back to you here. Is that Okay?'

'Jolly nice of you,' Gwydion said.

He was wiping his hands with a paper handkerchief and bending his knees to catch a glimpse of Maxine, who had continued to sit with an interesting impassivity in the passenger seat of Roebuck's car.

'That's Maxine,' Roebuck said helpfully.

He looked around to make sure the information was passed on to Peredur.

'Maxine's down for the weekend. She works in television now.'

'Does she indeed?' Gwydion said. 'So do I, as a matter of fact. You should introduce us.'

Maxine was demure and distant. She smiled at Gwydion graciously enough but she looked away and remained silent while he talked boisterously. She remained small and still as if the beauty of her person were a secret that she preferred to keep to herself.

'Would you like to wait here while I go and get the petrol?'

Roebuck spoke to Maxine. His attitude was consciously ambiguous: he could see Peredur's white nervous face and yet his long arm was raised with

301

the fingers drooping in what was intended as a helpful gesture.

'No, of course not.'

Maxine muttered at him fiercely and then lifted her head to give Gwydion a brief compensating smile. When they had gone Gwydion realized that Peredur was upset.

'Of course,' he said. 'You were telling me about him. At breakfast. Poor little rich boy.'

Peredur walked away from the car and then turned to speak to Gwydion.

'I'm going,' he said.

'Going? Going where?'

'I don't want to be here when they come back.'

'Now come off it.'

Gwydion walked up to him and held his arm.

'It's that girl.'

Peredur looked down at Gwydion's hand on his arm.

'I've slept with her.'

Gwydion shook his arm.

'Well good for you,' he said. 'I'm delighted to hear it.'

'You don't understand.'

'Well how can I if you don't tell me anything.'

Gwydion persuaded him to sit in the car. Drops of rain had begun to fall and Peredur was discouraged from marching away. Inside the car he found difficulty in expressing himself and Gwydion coaxed him gently to say what he had on his mind.

'She wasn't going to move,' Peredur said. 'She wasn't going to budge.'

'How do you mean?'

'She'd written me off. Wiped me out. Couldn't you see it? I was something that had never been. Less than something dead on the side of the road.'

His voice was unsteady.

'Now tell me about it,' Gwydion said. 'Just tell me about it.'

'I took her to Wales,' Peredur said. 'It was in that car. She said it belonged to Roebuck's brother.'

'Well perhaps it does,' Gwydion said gently.

'It was all part of a scheme to humiliate me. He probably made her do it. They could have planned the whole thing together. I can just hear them talking and laughing about it.'

'Well, I don't know the lady,' Gwydion said. 'But she doesn't strike me as the type who would do anything unless she really wanted to.'

'Do you think so?'

Peredur was immediately eager to rid himself of his suspicions.

'You fell for her?' Gwydion said.

Peredur nodded, ashamed to make the admission.

'Well it was about time,' Gwydion said. 'The longer you leave it the worse it is. You've never been innoculated. You've been too harsh about yourself with women. All this crap about being ugly. For all you know they think you are the most beautiful thing moving on two legs. You should be glad it happened. She's a pretty girl too, and she doesn't look too tall, which is always a good thing for short-arsed lads like yourself. Although, mind you, I've seen some spectacular sparrows in my time. There was one little Portuguese I knew in Paris. He wouldn't look at a woman under six foot. Not enough to work on he used to say. He was a lad he was.'

Gwydion gave Peredur's shoulder a friendly jolt with the back of his hand and then apologized when he remembered the boil on his neck. Peredur was too miserable to feel the pain.

'Oh dear . . .'

Gwydion shook his head sadly.

'I'm not being too tactful, am I? You still fancy her.'

'I can't get her out of my mind.'

303

Peredur sank forward over the driving wheel.

'If only I knew why she came with me. It was her initiative. It really was. She used to watch me all the time. I was always conscious of being under scrutiny. It was her idea, going to Wales. She didn't really like me to touch her. Not really. I thought perhaps she found me fascinating because I was so repulsive. She did say I was like a spider once. When we were in Brangor. I was sitting in the corner of the Blue Drawing Room and she had been talking to Amy, I think. It was getting dark. "You look like a spider," she said. I suppose it was true. She used to enjoy saying things that hurt me. She wanted to know about me to get power over me. She wanted me to be her abject slave.'

'Quite a loathsome damsel,' Gwydion said. 'You are well rid of her.'

'I never thought that love would be an image of hell,' Peredur said.

'It's not love.'

Gwydion spoke categorically but Peredur was not to be consoled.

'When she left me,' he said. 'I thought my life was in ruins. I really thought that. I think I still do.'

'Well that's rubbish,' Gwydion said energetically. 'Absolute rubbish.'

'How can you say that? How could you know?'

'Because I'm a crude insensitive bastard,' Gwydion said. 'Now just listen. If you still wanted that little dolly, you could always have her.'

Gwydion tapped his nose and looked comic and worldly-wise.

'But my brotherly advice to you, is, to keep well away from her.'

'How?'

Peredur was anxious to know. He waited to be initiated into the seamy practices of some disreputable order.

'I could be wrong but I think I've seen the type before.'

'"Type"?'

Peredur hung on to the word as though his critical faculty might yet save him.

'People are individuals, not types,' he said.

'In my book,' Gwydion said, 'women are types. Especially this type. How could I ever operate with such glittering success if I started thinking about them as individuals?'

He laughed delightedly at his own joke and Peredur looked momentarily grateful for the efforts he was making to relieve something of the weight of his misery.

'Well you're not going to like what I'm going to say,' Gwydion said. 'But she looks and sounds to me like the kind of girl who would do anything for either money or ambition or, rather, both.'

'Money?'

The word seemed to mystify Peredur.

'She knew you were well off. Comparatively speaking.'

'Not at all.'

Peredur sprang to her defence.

'She had no idea.'

'As far as you know.'

'When she saw Brangor she couldn't get over her astonishment. It moved me. In a way.'

'Everything you say confirms my diagnosis,' Gwydion said. 'I can see you are ill and I've just seen what you're suffering from. The solution's all too simple.'

'Simple?'

It seemed the last word in any language that Peredur would use in relation to his problem.

'I repeat, simple. You're not going to like this
. . .'

'Go on,' Peredur said. 'Say whatever you like.'

'Offer her a job in television, or a better job.
Promotion. Say you can give her a chance in
front of the cameras, with an interpreter, or give
her something interesting to produce and she's
yours for life. Correction. Yours until someone
else comes along and offers her something better. Or until she decides she wanted something
else.'

'You're talking nonsense,' Peredur said. 'How could
I do that? You don't really understand at all.'

'Easily.'

Gwydion tapped his chest.

'Through me. Do I have to say again? I'm a telly
tycoon, or as near as damn it. Any time you
want to experiment . . . You could be cured by
a further brief course of innoculations . . . I'm not
joking.'

Peredur stared through the windscreen. The white
car had appeared in the distance.

'They're coming back,' he said. 'What shall I
do?'

'Just sit where you are and don't panic.'

'I don't want to see them.'

'There's no reason why you should. I'll deal with
them. I could eat a handful of this sort for breakfast.
You just watch.'

Gwydion got out, walked around the car and
leaned down to talk to Peredur through the open
window.

'Do you still want her?'

He made the offer with an air of extreme generosity.
Peredur shook his head.

'Pity,' Gwydion said. 'You could have seen my cruder
methods working. A ring-side seat.'

306

Peredur moved his head awkwardly to look up at his brother who was made angry by the sight of the unspoken misery in his eyes.

'You're too damn sensitive,' Gwydion said. 'You take after your old man. It's very annoying. It gives me toothache to look at you.'

He turned to lean his back against the stationary car and hid his brother from view. He folded his arms and watched Roebuck gaily manoeuvre his white sports car across the line of the oncoming traffic.

BOOK FOUR

1

With measured care, the solemn-faced boy steered his bicycle through the narrow door into the back garden of one of the gaunt row of tall terrace houses. The machine was well cared for and as the wheels turned the chrome gleamed and glittered on the polished rims. The boy frowned at the door as he closed it behind him. It needed painting. And it was absurdly higher than the garden wall which rose abruptly in a narrow arch of stone to contain it. The garden itself looked untidy in the late morning sun: cabbages run to seed were half hidden by the dead grass and the weeds; between the wooden shed, brown with creosote, and the stone wall that marked off the garden from the lane, there was a width of two feet deep in rubble and exposed sub-soil where nothing grew. Against the wall that ran from the back of the terrace down to the lane there was a ragged privet hedge, and where this hedge petered out there was just room for a struggling green fig tree to grow.

The boy kept a key to the shed in his trouser pocket. With the bike leaning against his body he unlocked the padlock, which he kept carefully greased with vaseline, opened the door and lifted his bike over the shallow threshold. The shed was his workshop. A carpenter's bench ran the length of the shade, with a great ponderous vice attached to it. Mounted on the wall, between the door and the window, was a tool-box which he had made himself. His name was stencilled neatly on the door of the box in capital letters: Bedwyr T. More. Underneath there was a notice in juvenile printing which said that the tools were his private property and were not to be used or removed without his express permission.

He leaned his bike carefully against its place under the window and extracted his football gear from the saddle bag. The boots were greased with dubbin. The blue shirt and white shorts were still laundered and unused. He gazed at them a little sadly. It was clear that he had not been called upon to play. He hung the boots up on a nail and wrapped the shirt and shorts in the clean towel. He considered locking the shed and decided against it, but closed the door. He walked up the garden path with his football outfit tucked underneath his arm. The boundary of each tall terrace house was marked by the stone walls that limited the width of the long, narrow back gardens. A lean-to glass conservatory stretched the width of the house and Bedwyr had to pass through it in order to enter the basement kitchen. He lifted the latch and pushed the door of the conservatory open. It was sagging on its hinges and dragged along the concrete floor. Inside the conservatory he saw his stepmother sitting on a narrow bench, a neat figure conspicuously well-groomed in the centre of a small wilderness. Strands of periwinkle and ivy hung down above her head and at her feet dried weeds stood like skeletons in large red pots. She could not have been comfortable sitting there in her smart two-piece suit. Her face was flushed and her body was covered in sweat. Bedwyr was unable to account for her presence in a part of the house where he would never normally see her. He moved nearer to her and pushed a disapproving finger against dry rot in the wooden frame hidden by a swollen coat of white paint.

'What's the matter?'

The sight of the concern in his large eyes seemed to make it possible for her to break out of the iron grip of her apprehension.

'Oh Bedwyr darling,' she said. 'I just can't bear the sound of his distress.'

Bedwyr went through the basement kitchen which was now only used as a place to do the washing and to store things like the lady's bicycle which was leaning against the old stove. He stood at the base of the awkward staircase which led up to street level of the narrow house, and listened for sounds of one sort or another, but could hear nothing. He moved cautiously up the uncarpeted stairway and poked his head around the corner until his eyes were on a level with the bar of daylight under the front door some twenty-five feet away. The whole corridor was covered with a Victorian pattern of red and yellow tiles which he seemed to study with objective calm as he listened again for any tell-tale noises. He stepped downstairs backwards and then made a brief examination of the front kitchen as far as the window which was on the level of the pavement. No one passed outside. There was a faint sound of the sea and children playing somewhere between the dunes and the promenade. He went back to his stepmother.

'I can't hear anything,' he said. 'Why don't you come for a ride?'

She closed her eyes, rigid still with anxiety.

'I didn't play,' Bedwyr said. 'It would be quite nice to have a ride.'

She shook her head without opening her eyes.

'You can't stay here.'

The lean-to conservatory met with his full disapproval. Normally she didn't like it either, but now it was an appropriate spot to nurse this particular affliction, and she was rooted to it as long as the pain had to last. Her fists were clenched and pushed together into her lap and her grey pleated skirt was conspicuously new and without blemish on the worm-eaten bench.

'Come outside then, mam.'

He made a gesture towards the garden seat on the outside of the lean-to. It offered an obviously fresher and cleaner place to sit. He could sit with her there and talk to her.

'Bedwyr sweet.'

Her voice was soft and persuasive and he responded instantly.

'You are such a good boy. So responsible.'

She opened her eyes wide and he seemed mesmerized by their blue innocence in the white light of the conservatory.

'Go up there and see what's happening.'

Bedwyr turned to stare apprehensively at the way to the basement stairs. It wasn't a task he would voluntarily undertake.

'He's only a little boy,' she said. 'He's only five.'

'Six.'

He made the correction automatically.

'I don't want them to hurt him, Bed. You go up there and see that they don't hurt him. I know your father means well but he can be so insensitive sometimes.'

He was reluctant to move. The effort to persuade him became an outlet for her pent up agitation.

'Bedwyr, my brave boy,' she said. 'I'd be so grateful if you'd do just this one little thing for me. I won't ask you to do anything for me again. I know I should be there myself and I would be, I'm sure, if your father wasn't there and that man Cupitt. And I don't trust him. He chats away about this and that and his mind is never really on his work as it should be because it's an operation really, just like any other operation. If

311

you went up there you could watch him and if anything
starts going really wrong you could come down and tell
me. I'm afraid your father won't say anything, you see.
He's like that. Cupitt is one of his cronies and says nice
things to him all the time about his poetry. You know
what he's like. People say he isn't properly qualified.
I've heard it more than once: but your father won't
hear a word against him. Oh! Listen! Did you hear
that?'

Her eyes were staring at him wild with anxiety.
Bedwyr drew himself to his full height. She was in
need of his care and protection. He had to go upstairs.
But he had one last question.

'Why didn't you take him to a proper dentist?'

'He wouldn't go,' Amy said. 'He just wouldn't. He
held on to the door post and wouldn't let go. You
know what he's like. I could do nothing with him. So
your father came down and said he'd get Mr Cupitt to
come here and do it in the house. I had my hat and coat
on, ready to go. I'd changed and everything.'

She spread her arms to show that she was dressed for
going out. Her smooth complexion was kept youthful
still with the help of very little make-up, and her strong
blonde hair was set in close waves around her head. A
squealing sound from upstairs brought both her hands
to her mouth. The beauty of her hands was emphasized
by the rings she wore on her fingers. Bedwyr looked at
them as though he were counting them to see that they
were all there. It was also possible that he was trying
to measure Amy's distress. The noise stopped. Some
of her fingers moved away from her face and she was
delicately poised between relief and greater despair.
There was a further brief yelp and without her saying
any more Bedwyr began to climb the stairs. He was not
eager to make the journey and he lifted his feet slowly
as though the earth had a greater force of gravity than
usual.

When he opened the door of the front parlour he saw his father awkwardly sprawled in a large armchair by the bay window. Part of the strange shape silhouetted against the bright light diffused by the net curtains was unmistakably his father. It was only when he moved closer that he saw the small boy perched cheerfully on his father's bony knee. Between the fastidiously extended finger and thumb of his father's left hand there was a large sticky sweet which the boy was allowed to lick whenever he felt like it. It could have been an ingenious device widely used by Mr Cupitt the dentist in dealing with small children. The little boy had a mass of black curly hair and even in his present situation looked confident about his own invincible attractiveness. There were tear stains on his cheeks and his red lips were pushed out babyishly each time it seemed to him he ought to protest about his position.

His father was dressed for the office in a dark suit with a stiff collar. The sharp edge was sticking uncomfortably now into the skin of his neck but he made no complaint. His round spectacles, although secured by tight metal springs around his thin flattened ears and a gold band pressing hard on to the bridge of his nose, stood out at an angle to the surface of his pale face and served to emphasize an expression of melancholy bewilderment. His hair was cropped back and sides and the top brushed back close to the skull as though to give his clients a reassuring image of sharpness and reliability. But the nature of his costume and the stamp of middle age could not entirely suppress an air of boyish innocence that chiefly showed itself in the way he stared at the world through his owlish spectacles. His lips were thin and yet slightly feminine. They parted easily, as though he were constantly a little surprised. His small son swayed about happily on his narrow knee with complete freedom, leaning over once again to take a lick of the sweet.

'Yes, well, there we are then,' Mr Cupitt the dentist was saying. 'Their's not to reason why. We'll have to try again sometime, won't we?'

Gwydion nodded contentedly. He seemed confident that they would have been well advised to listen to him much sooner. He smiled as if to show Mr Cupitt he bore no malice. Mr Cupitt was a small man with a brisk manner and a paunch like an inflated ball contained inside a well-buttoned waistcoat. He looked well scrubbed and his head smelt strongly of bay rum.

'It's all a question of nerves,' he said. 'I've always maintained that. He's a nervous type, isn't he? You're a nervous type, aren't you?'

Gwydion nodded in vigorous agreement.

'But we've all got to learn to be brave. In one way or another. Isn't that so, Cilydd?'

Mr Cupitt addressed Mr More by his bardic name. Mr More frowned deeply as he considered the question put to him. He cleared his throat with a double cough.

'Change of subject,' Cupitt said impatiently. 'Understand persons and you understand people, that's my approach.'

He leaned against the side table concealing the black box which contained the tools of his trade.

'I'm afraid he'll go through Russia like a knife through butter,' Cupitt said. 'And when he's finished there, he'll come over here. That's my view.'

Mr More looked uncomfortable.

'And with respect, where will your lot be then? All strung up on the nearest lamp-post. Poets and all.'

Gwydion had turned to look at his father's face. He could have been expecting words of wisdom. Bedwyr stood tense and expectant in the doorway.

'*I* don't hold it against you,' Mr Cupitt said. 'But you can't get away from it, many will. Has it affected your practice?'

Mr More became disgruntled.

'Can't we get on with it?' he said.

'Right.'

Mr Cupitt's manner became suddenly military and efficient.

'One more try then?'

Gwydion swung his head around and shook it so that all the curls on top tumbled about.

'You'll have to hold his arms and grip him in a firm vice you see . . .'

Mr Cupitt tried to speak to Mr More without moving his lips so that the little boy would not comprehend what he was being said.

'What can I do?'

Mr More sounded helpless. He struggled to sit up. His long body was still spread out with his elbows digging into the padded arms of his chair after his last unsuccessful attempt to pin down his son in a position that gave the dentist a reasonable chance to work. By now successive efforts were draining away his will to clasp the small boy in the relentless grip that was needed.

'Try and sit up for a start,' Mr Cupitt said.

He was losing his patience. He turned to Bedwyr and gave him a firm order.

'You come and hold his legs,' he said. 'We can't give up now or we'll never win the war. I tell you Cilydd, it will be worse next time. It's now or never. Give in and it will be nothing better than appeasement. You lie down there my boy and hang on to his legs.'

Gwydion had his tongue out ready for another lick of the large sweet between his father's fingers when Bedwyr took a firm grip on his ankles.

'Now then,' Mr Cupitt said. 'If we all pull together this won't hurt at all.'

As though from habit, like a tennis player who bounces a ball twice before he serves, he paused to glance at the flexing of the well-developed muscle at the base of his thumb. He caught Gwydion watching and gave him a friendly wink. He spoke in a tone of jocular friendliness.

'No needle this time,' he said. 'Just one little pull. I'll be going it with my finger and thumb. Muscle magic. No nasty pincers.'

Once more he flexed his muscle so that Gwydion could see it bulge under his thumb. He turned away to attempt a clumsy sleight of hand.

'Yes . . . well . . . now . . . on we go,' he said. 'Be a brave little soldier . . . hum?'

Bedwyr lifted his head and opened one eye to catch a low view of metal jaws opening inside the dentist's right hand. Out of consideration for his little brother's imminent sufferings he shut his eyes, but held on tightly to his ankles. The next sound, a sharp yelp, came from the dentist.

'The little devil's bitten me!' Mr Cupitt said. 'The little Devil! Just look at that! Just look.'

Indignantly he thrust his thumb under Mr More's sensitive nostrils. Bedwyr looked up and saw the marks of the irregular teeth quite clearly. Mr More mumbled an apology.

'He's a wolf,' Mr Cupitt said. 'A wolf!'

Bedwyr felt Gwydion's legs relaxing contentedly inside his conscientious grip.

'You'll have to find someone else!'

Mr Cupitt was packing his black box determinedly, still full of indignation.

'I admire your verse, Cilydd,' he said. 'Especially in the strict metres. And I'll even put up with certain sentiments that certain people would call anti-British. But I don't see why I should get bitten on the most valuable part of my working hand, just because you can't discipline your son. That boy, mark my words now, will give you nothing but trouble.'

Cilydd had no reply to give. Bedwyr looked up and saw Gwydion leaning with well-balanced stealth towards his father's outstretched hand which had moved further away. His tongue was out ready to lick the red sweet which had been selected to take his mind off the operation.

2

Mr More walked home from the office. His head was lowered so that the crown of his grey Homburg hat took the force of the wind blowing from the southwest. His hands were plunged deep into the pockets of his mackintosh and his long legs jerked a little with the effort he was making to cross the station square in the shortest possible time without running and without drawing attention to himself. He seemed to welcome the wind. Together with his broad-brimmed hat, it allowed him to look at the ground and avoid any encounter with townsfolk or even the obligation of calling out a cheerful greeting to a whole range of persons he preferred to ignore.

When he reached the cob his pace did not slacken. But he allowed himself to turn his cheek to the wind and to lift a pale hand to keep his hat in position. He squinted at the square expanse of harbour which was no longer in proper use. The tide was racing in over the mud flats driving the waders and the gulls closer together and he was tempted to linger by the wall and watch out for rarer birds to appear. He studied with obvious pleasure a mixed flock of waders which included dunlin, sanderling, sandpipers and grey plover until he noticed from the corner of his eye a woman with two children approaching from the town. To avoid the danger of being overtaken, he hurried on, crossing the wide road and taking a quick glance at the marshy ground where swans nested on the edge of the stagnant pools.

South Marine Terrace was still damp from roof to basement after the rain. It stretched in a long gloomy line from a patch of wartime allotments in the paddock next to the marsh almost as far as the relic of a burnt-out hotel on the sea front. The terrace stood out in extraordinary isolation. Opposite a mild undulation of dunes that protected the southern side of the harbour, the gaunt height of the terrace seemed rigid and forbidding. Even when the sun shone at its brightest and the tide was in and brightly painted fishing boats appeared in the harbour, the terrace managed to preserve its own rectangular gloom: facing north-east it manufactured its own shadows so that some part of the long facade of bay windows and solid front doors and shallow basement windows were always cut off from the sunlight.

Mr More hurried past the front doors of his neighbours with his head down and one hand on his hat. The houses in the terrace were named but not numbered: he passed *Sea View, Cartref, Moorings, Bodlondeb, Morfa, Glen* and *Afallon* before he reached his own front door. His house was called *Ardwyn*. Once in the hall, he took off his hat and coat and hung them in a cupboard under the stairs. Here also he hung up the jacket of his business suit and changed into an old velvet jacket. In the room opposite he could hear a sewing machine at work and the voices of two women. He hesitated as though he were considering knocking on the door, but eventually decided against it. He climbed up two flights of stairs to the security and shelter of his study.

From the bay window there was an uninterrupted view of the mountains which ran the entire length of the eastern horizon. They were surmounted now by vast clouds which broke off here and there to leave trails of cloud suffused with a green light hanging down those narrow valleys that faced the west and the open sea.

Two walls of the study were covered from floor to ceiling with bookshelves crammed with books in double rows. Other spaces were filled with smaller shelves. There were two desks. One near the window and alongside the door a higher desk at which if he chose he could work standing up. Above this hung a framed water colour of a lapwing posed alongside a rudimentary nest in a ploughed field. There were books on the floor – some still open where he had last been consulting them. On the desk by the window lay two folders, one black, one red, on top of each other. In the centre of the desk a more elaborate folder lay open ready for his eager inspection. It was made of white leather and decorated with an intricate art nouveau design stamped in gold. There were pouches inside marked *Lettres à répondre* and *Lettres répondues*. Here he kept the sheets of the poem on which he was clearly anxious to be working. Holding his arms out like two parallel shafts he turned away from the temptation offered by the large pair of German binoculars on his desk. It would have been easy and pleasant to stand by the window and study the birds in the dunes or on the mud flats being covered now by the incoming tide of the south side of the harbour. But there were lines to be put down, some kind of muse to be obeyed.

Pulling faces he sat down at his desk and allowed his hands to fuss over the surface before picking up a pencil. He scribbled down four lines which he could have been reciting to himself all the way home from the office. They were recorded quickly. He screwed up his eyes and bent his head until he touched the folder with his forehead. Lines were written down and then impatiently scrubbed out. He leaned over the side of the mahogany chair in which he sat and puffed heavily as if he had just been sprinting uphill.

When the front-door bell rang, he reacted in his chair as if he had been shot. He leaped up and then sank to the floor on his knees, shivering. Once on the floor he kept rigidly still, his shoulders hunched, straining his ears to identify the caller. He was like a man in hiding waiting for the sounds of his pursuers to get nearer. The bell rang a second time and he was stirred to frantic action. He began to close volumes and replace them in their proper places. He found scrap-paper to tear up into thin strips to insert in places that he wanted to mark. He put the folder away in the middle drawer of his desk and locked it with a small key. From another drawer he extracted a writing pad and he took a fountain pen out of his waistcoat pocket and arranged the desk to appear as though he had been interrupted writing something other than what was hidden in the folders. He leaned far forward over his desk with his right ear cocked to take in every sound that could be picked up from downstairs and he closed his eyes to intensify the effort.

Below, the front door opened and he heard his wife making noises of surprise and delight in her best English accent. The sound made him pull a face. He moved across the room with silent speed and opened the study door very quietly in order to catch any speech that would float up the two flights of stairs.

'I had absolutely no idea . . .' Amy was saying. 'Not the faintest . . .'

The visitor was laughing in a bluff and hearty manner. He sounded as if he were making compliments.

320

Mr More crept on to the landing and kneeling down thrust his best ear through the banisters. Now they were both chuckling merrily. From upstairs it sounded like a cheerful open conspiracy.

'Let's go in here,' Amy said. 'This is my own little room. I've been having some sewing done. Miss Cowley Jones. Aunty Menna the boys call her. Such an agreeable woman . . .'

The drawing room was too formal, too old fashioned, too much like a waiting room. The passage to the front door was too narrow and whoever opened the front door was obliged to withdraw four or five steps into the house in order to allow the caller unimpeded access to the drawing-room door on the left. In the drawing room now Peredur was probably playing with his toys, unable to go out because of the rain. Mr More moved away from the banisters and returned to his study.

His concentration had been broken. He moved to the window to look across at the harbour. The tide had now covered the mud flats and there was a disturbance between a number of seagulls and a swan over something brought in on the tide. Mr More looked at his binoculars as if he were weighing up whether or not it would be worth the effort to focus on the squabble. He returned to his desk and started to write in a small neat hand. But in no time he was crossing out what he had written. He was no longer at ease in his study. He paced up and down in the available space. He looked at his own image briefly in the mirror over the mantelpiece, found his pipe and began to clean it.

Amy tapped the study door lightly with her knuckles before she opened it. There was a freshly lit cigarette wedged between her fingers which immediately caught his attention. She was smart and relaxed in her afternoon clothes over which she wore an open blue smock which seemed to draw attention to the blue of her eyes. She smiled agreeably at her husband.

'John,' she said. 'Do come down. It's Colonel Ricks. I know he would like to see you.'

'I'm trying to work,' he said.

His tone was dismissive. The interruption and the lack of inspiration were equally irritating.

'I came home early in order to try and get some work done.'

'I'm sorry,' Amy said. 'But I didn't know he was going to call did I? It was a complete surprise.'

He could find no fault with her reasoning, but he continued to look dissatisfied.

'Is that Cowley-Jones woman still there?'

Amy smiled.

'She scampered away when she heard the bell go. You know how she is . . . Can't bear to be seen except in her best clothes. It is much too loud, isn't it? We ought to do something about it.'

'I can't stand the way she prattles.'

'John.'

Amy reproved him mildly.

'How can you be so callous? The poor old thing absolutely worships the ground you walk on.'

'People like that insinuate themselves,' he said. 'I never liked people who insinuate themselves. She's such a pointless busy-body.'

'You shouldn't be so hard on her, John. She thinks you are something marvellous.'

'Knowledge.'

He used the word with contempt.

'She has this superstitious reverence for knowledge. She'll ruin that boy Clem. Mark my words.'

'Well, are you coming down?'

'Why should I? He only wants something.'

Amy waved the hand that held a cigarette in the direction of his desk.

'You get so cranky when you can't write,' she said. 'He's just being sociable.'

Amy was clearly elated by the unexpected call and she held the cigarette as if it were part of a new experience, a fascinating white cylinder that was burning away slowly between her fingers.

'I think it's very nice of him to call. Especially when you hold such extreme views.'

'Extreme? I only wish they were extreme.'

'Now come on, John. Be civil. You'll enjoy it, I'm sure. You may as well come down instead of sitting up here making yourself miserable because you can't write. Now come on.'

She held out her hand.

'Extreme? My goodness me ... You can be quite sure there's something he's after.'

He touched her hand and then let it go. A brief signal of reluctant compliance.

As they came downstairs they discovered Colonel Ricks in the cloakroom at the end of the passage. His hand was deep in the pocket of his British Warm which was hanging there. He wore a ginger moustache and his pale blue eyes tended to swivel roguishly in his head.

'Tobacco,' he said, 'this damned tin. It's so big I can't get my hand out of my pocket. It's like the crow in the fable. All due to greed no doubt. Hello. How nice to see you.'

He stood to attention and waved respectfully towards Mr More as his host and the senior male present. They both wandered after Amy in to her sewing room. Amy persuaded them to sit in the two armchairs while she herself sat by the work table. But in no time Mr More was on his feet gazing absently at the view of the back garden through the window. The Colonel's mouth twitched with a rather nervous smile.

'Haven't seen you since the night of the school concert, have I?' he said. 'Got on your nerves a bit I dare say. Asking those damn fool questions about how to pronounce your boys' names. That's always been my trouble. I never had any tact.'

Mr More's head wavered up and down. It could have been agreement or an attempt to keep the flight of an erratic bird in sight through the window.

'I've probably blown your inspiration to smithereens,' the Colonel said. 'That's me all over. No tact. No consideration. What's it about then? Do you mind if I ask?'

Mr More considered the request before answering.

'Myrddin,' he said. 'Merlin, as you would call him.'

Colonel Ricks brightened up.

'Oh Merlin,' he said. 'The wizard chap? That should be rather splendid, shouldn't it?'

He looked at Amy to get her to agree with him. She smiled patiently and collected the repaired clothes on the table ready to put them away.

'Wizard?'

Mr More stuck out his jaw as he pronounced the word.

'He was a good deal more than a wizard, you know. He went mad in the woods.'

'Did he?'

The Colonel was polite and mildly enthusiastic.

'I didn't know that.'

He sat down so that he could get a full view of the Colonel's face.

'War drove him mad,' Mr More said. 'The sheer horror and brutality of war forced him as it were outside the human race. He lived in the woods with the trees and the animals for fifty years in a state of madness. And this was how he acquired the gift of prophecy.'

'Excuse me,' Colonel Ricks said. 'Correct me if I'm wrong. But that's not history is it?'

'It depends what you mean by history.'

324

Mr More glanced over Colonel Ricks's head once again as if some mildly interesting phenomenon was visible through the window.

'History?'

The Colonel was prepared to give the question some brief amused consideration.

'Facts surely. Who wins and loses and all that sort of thing.'

He gave Amy a broad smile as if to indicate that he appreciated that her husband was a very original fellow.

'Merlin was always on the losing side,' Mr More said.

'Was he?' the Colonel said politely. 'I didn't know that.'

'He told a woman his secret and she used it to bury him alive.'

'By Jove.'

Colonel Ricks was longing to be frivolous. But he managed to restrain himself.

'In the French and Italian versions he goes on talking from the grave,' Mr More said. 'Now that is very interesting. His body is corrupted in the usual way, but his consciousness still has a voice and the heroes search for his tomb in order to consult the oracle about their own behaviour, their courses of action, their decisions. So that the loser in the end turns out to be the only guide to the true winner.'

'I don't quite follow . . .'

Colonel Ricks had allowed his attention to wander.

'I'll make some tea, shall I?' Amy said.

She rose to the feet with rather self-conscious grace.

'We can have it in peace before the boys get home.'

'Ah yes, the boys.'

Colonel Ricks chuckled appreciatively.

'But look, I must tell you why I called. I'd like to put you both up for the Yacht Club.'

Amy looked pleased but Mr More resumed his examination of the view through the window.

'No objections I hope!'

Colonel Ricks threw back his head to laugh heartily and slapped the palms of his hands on his knees. His face glistened with visible good-will.

'I don't sail,' Mr More said. 'I don't have a boat.'

'Oh my goodness,' Colonel Ricks said. 'That doesn't matter. Any way, it's all a formality. You know, if you've no objections as they say, you're as good as in. I've more or less arranged it. Morris Burton and Major Roberts are in full support and one or two others. No shortages of seconders and all that. Three each I thought. That would look good.'

'You're being most kind,' Amy said. 'To have gone to so much trouble . . .'

'No trouble at all,' Colonel Ricks said. 'Nothing is too much trouble where friends are concerned. That's always been my motto.'

'Major Roberts?'

Mr More questioned the title.

'Well, Major in the Home Guard. But let's be fair. Poor old chap has the most awful trouble with his gout. I get so sorry for him. He really suffers. He calls me Colonel so I call him Major. We don't know the war is over.'

'It's a drinking club,' Mr More said, rather severely.

'John!'

Amy sounded shocked.

'What's the matter?'

'You are giving Colonel Ricks quite the wrong impression. He'll start thinking we have narrow views about drink.'

Colonel Ricks laughed obligingly.

'My goodness,' Amy said. 'As far as you are concerned, my dear, we know, don't we, that that is not at all the case.'

Mr More rose to his feet and walked towards the window.

'I shouldn't think they'd want me,' he said. 'Not the kind of people who go to the Yacht Club.'

'Oh my goodness,' Colonel Ricks said, 'I think you're wrong there. It's not the place it used to be you know. Not at all. It's very friendly. It has to be, I can tell you. Morris and I are on the committee.'

'You know I'm an extremist.'

Mr More turned to face Colonel Ricks, who screwed around in his chair to indicate his surprise.

'In what way?'

He was still ready to laugh if the opportunity presented itself.

'John,' Amy said. 'You are in such a mood. I can't think what's got into you.'

'I'm a home-ruler,' Mr More said. 'As bad as an Irishman any day. You wouldn't dream of having me.'

'Live and let live,' Colonel Ricks said.

'That's not all,' Mr More said.

'John,' Amy said.

She was adopting a warning tone.

'You musn't go too far. Colonel Ricks is our guest.'

He nodded solemnly, accepting her rebuke.

'You are quite right,' he said. 'But I don't want to join. You can of course. If you want to. I wouldn't dream of standing in your way, if that's the right expression. I wonder if you'd excuse me?'

Colonel Ricks was at a loss.

'I usually take my constitutional at this time of the day. I find that if I miss it I can't work at all in the evening. And I'm afraid that's rather important to me. There's no real reason why it should be. But it is.'

Awkwardly Colonel Ricks rose to his feet.

'Of course not,' he said. 'By the way . . . before you go . . . there was one other matter I wanted to bring up with you. I promised Morris I would. Could you give me a couple of minutes?'

Amy pressed her hands together and gave the pointed toes of her shoes a disapproving look. She murmured the word 'tea' again and left the room.

'It's business really, old boy,' Colonel Ricks said, 'when Amy had left the room. 'I hope you don't mind?'

'I prefer to deal with business in the office,' Mr More said.

'Of course you do. But this isn't strictly legal. It's just an idea. Purely formal. Just a notion. I don't know whether it will appeal to you. It's about *Ponciau*. Did I say it correctly?'

His shoulders shook with silent laughter at his inability to pronounce the word. Mr More showed that he failed to see the joke.

'What is it after all? Not much value as agricultural land. All that gorse and the old quarry and the rough grazing. But ideal for developing into holiday chalets. A marvellous site. Wonderful view. Right on the edge of the foreshore. Ideal.'

Mr More stirred uneasily.

'Now I'm not talking about caravans. I mean holiday chalets of the most superior kind. For the upper income bracket if you like. Something really ambitious. God knows I'm no snob, More, but I would shoot myself before I interfered in any way with the natural beauty of the place – I really would. Now I can say this with authority. There will be no shortage of capital. Does the idea appeal?'

'It was my mother's home,' Mr More said.

His voice was sepulchral.

'Good Lord! Was it really?'

Colonel Ricks struggled to show intense interest.

'She was born there,' Mr More said. 'I thought the world of my mother.'

Colonel Ricks looked as though he were peering into the mists of the past, trying to remember what his own mother looked like. He needed to maintain some kind of control over the situation.

'Obviously we don't share the same views,' he said. 'But there's nothing I admire more than a man who has principles and sticks to them.'

Mr More's long face slowly creased into a smile.

'Well, I've got plenty of those,' he said.

He laughed: a strange dry sound like the shuffle of an old man's feet in a dance. Colonel Ricks pressed home his advantage.

'I wouldn't agree that sentiment and business don't mix. As a soldier I couldn't agree. You can have good sentiment and good business. Preserve the best of the old and forge ahead with the new. We have to move. We can't stand still. But we can move with care and with respect. That's my view. I don't know whether you would agree with it?'

Mr More did not take up the unspoken invitation to make some comment.

'Suppose you drew a line,' Colonel Ricks said. 'Nothing like drawing a line! Separate the rough stuff on the foreshore from the farm and develop that. Something like twelve acres overlooking the sea and the view. Would you consider that? And let me add this, and I know you're like me, you don't really care about money.'

Colonel Ricks had his hands together and he pointed touching index fingers authoritatively at Mr More's head.

'Within reason, you could name your own price.'

Mr More lifted his head again to look through the window.

'After all,' the Colonel said. 'We all have to think of the future. God knows, I never thought I'd turn out to be some sort of a glorified estate agent. And of course you are very lucky. You have a fine spread of three sons to think of. It's a bit like laying down a cellar for them, isn't it?'

He sighed with deep regret.

'I envy you. I really do.'

Mr More rose to his feet. He was shaking his head.

'It was very nice of you to call,' he said. 'To see an old rebel like me. Make yourself comfortable. Amy will be along with tea any minute.'

He was halfway down the stairs to the basement when Amy discovered he was leaving. She rushed out of the tiny kitchen.

'John,' she said. 'Where are you going? You just can't walk out like that. Really. You can't.'

'I told you he was after something.'

Mr More was smiling grimly.

'*Ponciau*. He wanted *Ponciau*. There's your Rollo Ricks for you. You'll never see it, will you? They're not on the same side as us you know.'

'What do you mean?'

'If you listened to me a little more you'd understand. We're chapel people.'

'Chapel? What on earth do you mean? You haven't been near a chapel for goodness knows how many years.'

'Yes, but we're chapel people all the same.' Mr More said. 'My difficulties were and are philosophical. Yours appear to be social. Does that mean anything to you?'

'John,' Amy said. 'You are in one of your moods.'

'Hardy aboriginals. That's what we are. Natives. You musn't try so hard to forget that, Amy. Remember you're a native as well.'

He went on his way smiling grimly and left her speechless on the stairs.

330

3

Aunty Menna stood in the first-floor bay window of her house in the terrace. Her arms were folded under her exceptionally large breasts and she was tilted slightly forward in order to study the wide pavement and in particular a black Lanchester touring car parked opposite the front door of *Ardwyn*. She could tilt back with speed if at any time she felt that she herself was in danger of being observed.

'It's him,' she said.

'Well, it's not the doctor anyway,' Flo said. 'That makes a change.'

'What do you mean?'

Aunty Menna was instantly suspicious. Her sister was withholding information. Her sister lacked the spontaneous urge to share which was so marked in her own character.

'Dr Thomas is Cilydd's friend,' she said. 'He wouldn't call if Cilydd was away. Not unless there was serious illness.'

'Is that all you think doctors are for?'

'You're jealous.'

The words spilt over the edge of Aunty Menna's narrow lips. She shut them tight so as not to allow any more criticism to escape. But it was too late to prevent her sister Flo from catching the words. Flo was sitting in a low rocking chair smiling to herself as she studied the flames of the piled-up fire in the grate. Her sister had shown that she was roused and now she had an excuse to tease her.

'He's come to ask for your hand,' Flo said.

Her voice, which inclined to be sweet and tentative, began to quaver with the potential comedy she found in the idea.

'He's seen you on the stage, Menna, and he can't hold back any longer!'

Now she was openly amused by what she was saying and her voice gurgled in her throat. But more was happening outside to take Aunty Menna's attention.

'He's got Robert's five per cent with him.'

She became hot with surmise.

'Cilydd's out,' she said. 'I know that much. He's got a case in Chester. He left very early this morning. Five per cent doesn't waste his time. I bet you she's still trying to persuade him to sell *Ponciau*. But he won't you know. He won't you know. I'm sure he won't. Money isn't everything. That's his motto. There'll be trouble there. You mark my words.'

Flo rocked herself a little and smiled in anticipation of what she was going to say.

'What you need is a rifle,' Flo said. 'You could be shooting people all day long from up here and nobody would notice.'

'Don't talk like that.'

Menna pushed out her narrow lips until they were on the verge of folding over. She tightened her arms, which were still entwined under her breasts.

'Well, you ought to have something to do while you stand there,' Flo said, 'if it was only to pass the time.'

'Trying to say that I don't work . . .'

Menna was hurt but Flo smiled happily, somehow eased by the immediate effect her words were having on her sister.

'Don't be so touchy,' she said.

'And to think they let you teach little children,' Menna said.

She was clearly racking her brains to make a telling counter attack and making use of an old reproach in the meantime as a stop-gap.

'Aunty!'

A boy was shouting at the top of his voice in the basement kitchen. 'Clem's there,' Menna said.

She moved away from the window.

'You don't say.'

Flo patted her plump hand against her cheek and gave herself a little comfort by rocking her chair gently.

'Aunty Menna!!'

'Give him something to eat,' Flo said. 'He's a growing boy.'

Another impatient cry rang out from down below.

'He sounds hungry,' Flo said.

She could, for a moment, have been talking about a lion.

'Hungry.'

Aunty Menna seemed to resent the word.

'He shouldn't be so bossy. He walks about this house as if he owned it.'

'It's your fault,' Flo said. 'You spoil him.'

Aunty Menna pointed at herself, speechless with the injustice of the accusation.

'*You* say that *I* spoil him? That's a good one. That's a good one that is.'

'You'd better go and see that he wants.'

She spoke as though she would not answer for the consequences if her sister delayed her departure any longer. Aunty Menna moved to the door.

'Why doesn't he shout for you sometimes?' she said. 'It's always me. A fat lot you ever do for him, except make use of him.'

Her voice had dropped by the end of the sentences to a mutter which Flo barely heard.

'What was that? What did you say?'

She had frozen upright in her rocking chair, eager to receive the accusation. Satisfied that she had broken the smooth surface of her sister's complacency, Aunty Menna shut the door and made her way carefully downstairs.

'Aunty Menna!'

'What's the matter with the boy . . .'

She had to move sideways to see where she was putting her feet.

'The more I do for him the worse his manners get, and all she does is sit upstairs like the Queen of Sheba in her rocking chair. I've had more than enough of it, I can tell you. Anybody would think I was their hired slave or something . . .'

She was talking to herself as much as to anyone, so that when she reached the bottom of the basement stairs she was startled and embarrassed to see two other boys with Clem watching her careful descent. She pulled her cardigan around her bosom as though to protect herself from their crude masculine stares, although in fact the boys had turned to look at each other. They stood so still it was obvious that they were doing their best to save her any embarrassment.

They were handsome boys on the threshold of puberty. Bedwyr was dark and solemn and his friend Ken Lazarus was impressively fair, with a domed forehead under his golden curls, and standing still in the light of the window he had the innocent beauty of an angel of the school of Fra Angelico. Aunty Menna was unnerved by their presence. She stood silently waiting for an announcement until the silence took over and she surveyed the scene in a state of speechless panic. The fire had gone out, the grate was choking with a heap of ashes that should have been cleared away and the old-fashioned brown sink was filled with dirty dishes. And if they should turn and stare they would be seeing her bedraggled appearance and holding her responsible for all the signs of idleness and neglect. She compelled herself to smile as though the movement of her lips were a declaration of policy: she would show herself to be friendly and youthful and good-hearted and a fountain of affection that they could quickly learn to love and forgive.

'Boys,' she said.

Bedwyr and Ken turned to greet her. They were like page-boys, beautifully and neatly dressed and drilled to behave with perfect decorum.

'What you must think of this place with its feet in the air . . .'

Clem was marching about bending his back and his knees as though he were climbing a hill. He was taller than the other two and his voice had started to break. There were spots on his face. His hands and feet and ears looked many sizes too big for this thin body. He wore spectacles that kept slipping down the bridge of his nose.

'Now look, woman,' he said to his aunt. 'Don't fuss. These boys are starving but they're too polite to say it. How about a pot of tea for three and a bit of cake?'

'Where do you think this is?' Aunty Menna said. 'Bertorelli's?'

Her lips registered indignation first and then transformed into a smile faster than pulling a sock inside out.

'Listen to him,' she said. 'The way he talks to me. What am I going to do with him?'

She seemed to be genuinely seeking their advice, and they glanced at each other briefly, as solemnly as lawyers in consultation. Clem marched in giant strides across the kitchen and grasped his aunt by the shoulders and propelled her towards the table.

'You see the way he treats me?'

Her face suggested she was enjoying it but her arms stretched out appealing to Bedwyr and Ken.

'I've spoilt him, haven't I? And this is the result . . . I asked you to keep the fire going, you silly boy, and to clear the ashes away . . . and have you done it? Not likely. And what kind of a welcome is this to your friends, that's what I'd like to know . . .'

Clem waved his arms about with uninhibited irritation.

335

'Stop your blathering, woman and get us something to eat. We've got news for you.'

She was instantly interested.

'News? What news?'

'Anything . . . we can't wait for this devil's kettle to boil. It's nearly empty anyway.'

He banged the kettle recklessly against the hob.

'Listen, woman, we've got plans.'

He fought his way into the cluttered pantry.

'Come out of there, Clem Cowley-Jones!'

He took no notice of her order. There was a noise of bottles falling over and he emerged triumphantly with a bottle of Corona orangeade.

'Now, men,' Clem said. 'Sit down at the table and don't bother to say grace. It's not worth it.'

The centre of the kitchen floor was occupied by a dining table with its middle leaves removed so that its four legs were disproportionately thick for its limited length. Anxious as she was to hear the news, Aunty Menna felt obliged to give the fire a token poke. Clem blocked her way. There was a comic struggle which made her laugh and he forced her to sit down. Once down, she was clearly delighted to be relieved of any obligation to do housework and ready to listen to the boys and, as far as she was able, join in their fun. Clem grumbled about, found three glasses, lifted them to the light from the window to see if they were clean and, while Aunty Menna protested at the implied insult, he shared out the contents of the Corona bottle.

'Right,' he said, sitting down. 'Listen to this. We're going to Rhuddlan. Cheers.'

The boys were thirsty and they gulped down the sweet drink.

'Rhuddlan?' Aunty Menna said. 'What are you going to Rhuddlan for?'

'Let's be more exact,' Clem said. 'Four miles down the river.'

'River? What river?'

'Where's your geography, woman? Camp,' he said. 'That's what we are going to do.'

'Oh Duw, no.'

Aunty Menna showed every sign of incipient panic.

'Listen to her,' Clem said. 'What's the matter now?'

'Your Uncle Gwynfryn was drowned in that river.'

Clem croaked with laughter and banged the table with his hand but Aunty Menna was plunged into a tragic gloom.

'What river? You just asked me what river and now you say he was drowned in it.'

'Well, it was near there.'

'Well that was before the Flood,' Clem said. 'So do me a favour and forget it. The new age has dawned. Isn't that right chaps?'

'You can't go camping at this time of the year.'

'Not now, woman. Next month.'

Clem shook his head in mock despair. Aunty Menna felt obliged to demonstrate her warm approval of the company her Clem was keeping.

'Well, your Aunty Flo and I are very pleased that you have such nice friends. We really are.'

She looked at Bedwyr in search of sympathetic agreement.

'It's so easy for a young boy without a father to guide him to get into the wrong company and all sorts of trouble.'

Bedwyr obviously felt obliged to nod.

'His father's taking us,' Clem said, stabbing a bony finger at Bedwyr. 'So there you are. For once you've got nothing to worry about.'

He looked up to see his other aunt descending the basement stairs. She moved slowly as though to disguise the fact that she had been brought down by her curiosity. Aunty Menna turned to watch her and looked irritated by her sister's elegant approach. Her partner

337

in kitchen comedy always contrived to make the better entrance. The visitors now were sitting down and Flo had arrived late enough not to be confronted by any problems of hospitality.

'This boy,' she said, her voice tinged already with reproach. 'He's talking about going camping.'

'Camping?'

Flo used the word as if it were rather outlandish. But she spoke all the same with great calm, determined not to be ruffled in front of guests however young they might be.

'Isn't it a bit cold for camping?'

'Cilydd is taking them,' Aunty Menna said. 'I suppose it will be all right.'

'I've never heard of your father going camping before,' Aunty Flo said to Bedwyr in her smoothest tones.

'He's bought a new tent,' Bedwyr said. 'It's quite a good one.'

He looked solemn and judiciously approving of his father's purchase.

'It's a fine tent,' Clem said. 'Like a palace.'

'You haven't seen it.'

Aunty Menna put her challenge in quickly.

'On paper I have. The illustrations. Marvellous. And we'll have swimming and fishing. It's on a farm you see. That belongs to an old friend of Mr More's. Ken will bring his clarinet and Bedwyr his guitar. We'll have a bit of music around the camp-fire. It's all arranged.'

'Yes, well. I'm not sure that you can go.'

Aunty Flo spoke quietly and her sister looked just as surprised as the boys.

'Can't go?'

Clem was incredulous.

'What are you talking about?'

'You've got a weak chest,' Aunty Flo said. 'Suppose it rains. And it can be very cold at Whitsun. I'm not at all in favour of your going.'

338

Clem flung his arms about and began to grouse and groan. Ken laid his hand on his shoulder and he calmed down almost immediately.

'There's a very good barn at this farm, Miss Cowley-Jones,' he said. 'If it does rain, Clem will be perfectly dry.'

Aunty Flo looked at Ken as though he were a phenomenon she could not account for.

'Does your father say it's all right?'

'Oh yes.'

Ken's calm and lucid manner seemed almost supernatural in a kitchen so often filled with emotion and tumult.

'Well,' Aunty Menna said, anxious now for Clem to be allowed to go, 'if the Sergeant of the Police says it's all right we can't stop them, can we?'

She chuckled, hopeful that they would join in.

'We are talking about Clem,' Aunty Flo said sharply, 'and about Clem's health.'

Clem pushed back his chair.

'Come on boys,' he said. 'Let's leave them to it. All cows must be allowed to chew the cud.'

'Don't talk like that, Clem Cowley-Jones!'

Aunty Flo's rebuke flashed out with the speed of a reptile's tongue and he was obliged at once to mumble an apology. Ken and Bedwyr, well mannered as ever, thanked Aunty Menna for the refreshment and she looked at them with her mouth open as though in awe of their youth and beauty. They were so perfect she could not find the words to express her approval or her gratitude that they were so willingly prepared to take her headstrong and difficult nephew under their protection.

When the back door had closed behind them, Aunty Menna turned to her sister and demanded some explanations.

'What's wrong with them going?' she said. 'Sergeant

339

Lazarus says it's all right. And that means Mrs Lazarus says yes. The arch-Baptist. So if she says it's all right . . .'

'Oh shut up.'

Aunty Flo wanted to think.

'Don't you talk to me like that,' Aunty Menna said indignantly. Her sister took no notice.

'What's the matter?'

Aunty Menna changed her tone. She spoke in a humble voice, tormented by curiosity.

'Cilydd,' Aunty Flo said. 'A man of his age. Going camping.'

'He's not old.'

Aunty Menna was deeply puzzled.

'He's only in his forties. Why shouldn't he if he wanted to? There's no law against camping.'

'I didn't say there was.'

'You've got such a suspicious mind. I can't keep up with you. What's the matter?'

'Why should he go camping with a bunch of boys?'

'Bunch of boys?'

Aunty Menna was mystified. Flo took refuge in a declaration of general policy.

'We have to consider the welfare of that boy,' she said. 'That's our duty.'

And she would say no more.

4

Gwydion caught a glimpse of his father's second-best hat above the garden wall before it was hidden by the door and its stone frame. The hat was American in style, wide-brimmed, and there were unmistakable blotches on the sticky sweat band. Instantly he grasped his companion's solid shoulders and swung him round to face the direction they had come.

'Bob!' he said. 'Look!'

Bob shook himself free of Gwydion's grip, so that Gwydion fell away from him, still pointing with desperate urgency towards the allotment. Bob's hair was cut very short and it seemed to crown his sulky face with permanent resentment.

'What are you on about?'

He seemed fascinated by Gwydion and yet annoyed with his fascination. It was wrong that this younger companion should always be trying to snatch the initiative.

'Didn't you see it?'

'See what?'

'A blue rabbit!'

'Don't talk bloody rubbish.'

All the same he turned back the way they had come and scanned the lane as far as the allotments. Gwydion was moving back down the lane performing various antics to hold Bob's attention. His father had closed the garden door with deliberate care and was walking away now, with his hands deep in the pockets of an old mackintosh that reached almost to his ankles.

'There's no such things as a blue rabbit.'

Bob's voice was thick with anger and contempt but not conviction. Gwydion was making strange gestures

341

with his arms that Bob could not resist staring at, with a puzzled frown on his face.

'They'll lock you up one day,' he said. 'For telling lies.'

'There used to be a big one in old Huskie's garden,' Gwydion said. 'I saw him taking pictures of it. It escaped I expect. It came from a foreign country. He told me. And now it lives the life of a free rabbit, over there.'

'Don't tell bloody lies,' Bob said, with measured satisfaction. 'Old Huskie hasn't taken a single picture since before World War Two. And he never had a blue rabbit. And you never saw one.'

He pointed with triumph at Gwydion who was now bobbing up and down, and tempting his heavier friend to chase him. His father had stopped at the far end of the lane to stare with unaccountable concentration and his mouth wide open at the low end of the corrugated iron roof of a garage. His head was moving up and down as though he were sniffing at the rusty edge.

His figure radiated an embarrassing eccentricity and the longer he stood still the more deeply Gwydion was committed to his pantomime of assertions.

'I saw two,' he said.

'Two what?'

'Two blue rabbits.'

Bob growled out his objection. Down the lane Mr More had extracted a small notebook from the inside pocket of his jacket. He held it up level with his nose like a short-sighted man about to sing a hymn.

'You'll get smashed up one day.'

Bob spoke as though he himself could well be the person responsible.

'You'll be the first man to die from telling bloody woppers,' Bob said. 'Somebody'll ram them down your throat and you'll choke to death. Come on.'

342

'You can ask Frank Huskie,' Gwydion said. 'It's quite obvious what happened. When his old man died they escaped. There must have been two of them. I bet Frank could tell you what happened. And this one must be one of the children.'

'Which one?'

'The one I saw. Over there.'

Gwydion moved with exaggerated caution towards the overgrown edge of the allotments. He put his finger to his lips. Bob could not help himself following.

'It's in there.'

Gwydion moved back to him to whisper in his ear.

'Eating a Brussels sprout.'

'God, you're a . . .'

'Hush! come on. If you're quiet you'll see it. You watch now. Keep still. Just watch.'

Over Bob's bent back Gwydion kept a troubled eye on the figure of his father. Bob hooked his fingers into the chicken wire in front of his flat face, held his breath and watched intently in case an extraordinary phenomenon of nature would be made manifest in the weeds and the long grass. Mr More stopped staring into his notebook and put away his pencil. There was nothing to record. He took the path that led to the dunes. As soon as he was out of sight, Gwydion thumped Bob on the back and ran out of his reach, laughing and shouting.

'Ever been had!'

He raced up to the cob and made for the town. Bob could not run so fast. He followed, shaking his fists and cursing the increasing distance between them.

5

There was a tight settlement of boarding houses and hotels built in stone and yellow brick at the western extremity of the Promenade. Just beyond, the Promenade came to a sudden end. The last few yards had collapsed into a high tide of stones and pebbles like a monument to an ambitious plan which had run out of funds long before it could be completed: and the group of buildings had the same sad air of unfulfilment. The largest building was a hotel called 'Western Hydro'. It had not been painted since before the war, and now what paint was left was peeling away from every window frame. Its lachrymose facade stared at the open sea like a marooned and disappointed woman who had given up hope of catching sight of a sail.

Behind the hotel there was a labyrinth of gorse and Mr More's American hat could be seen bobbing up and down among the pale blooms. He was clearly a man bent on avoiding human contact and yet he was hurrying like one late for an appointment. The gorse merged into a wasteland where the wrong path could easily have led into a marsh or a complex of choked draining ditches. Mr More knew his way and never hesitated. He crossed a sandy lane which led to the White Club House of the Pendraw Golf Club, to find a gap in a wild hazel hedge. It led into a thick copse which he penetrated with complete ease, crouching forward at certain points to avoid having his hat knocked off by extended branches. He emerged to join a familiar path that led through the sand dunes to the open shore, well clear of every human habitation.

He slackened his pace a little when he reached the edge of the deserted foreshore. For more than two miles the beach curved smoothly towards a high blunt headland which thrust itself southward into the sea to overlook two modest islands. He trudged over the loose shingle to an exposed surface of firm sand. A brisk wind blew from the south-east and the long line of the white waves came in at an angle to the shore. Half a mile away to the west an isolated rock the height of a well-grown tree stood as solitary as a watch tower on the open shore. The surface of firm sand stretched like a narrow highway towards the rock. Mr More turned to look back at the group of buildings at the end of the promenade in the distance, as though he suspected suddenly that he was being followed. Three children had appeared from nowhere, accompanied by a lively young sheepdog. He watched them briefly, disturbed by their presence at first but then reassured by their muted self-sufficient cries and the barking of the excited dog. They were rushing to throw sticks and stones into the sea and were quite oblivious of his presence. He gave a tight smile, wiped the thin end of his nose in a handkerchief and hurried along the strip of sand towards the rock.

His way to the top of the rock was from the further side, a familiar climb, steep in parts, but easy. Once on top he moved to the edge, with a shoulder to the wind, a little out of breath from his exertions. The surface of the sea was alive with the glutinous restless light of the late afternoon and the entire expanse of water shivered with so much power that the two islands just in sight beyond the protection of the headland looked insecure in their moorings. A shaft of green light picked out a horizontal strata of exposed rock in the larger of the two islands and a black fissure briefly took on the appearance of the mouth of a magic cave.

Below the sheer edge of the rock the trunk of a tree had been scoured white by the waves and anchored in a depth of shingle. Caught in its stunted branches was the carcass of a dead sheep. The wool was dusted over with a film of salt and glittering fragments of shells. The shape of the animal was preserved perfectly except for a slit in the hide where segments of white rib were in view. The hole could have been made by the powerful beak of a bird of prey. The posture of the imprisoned carcass was strangely lifelike, as though the eyeless animal were still struggling to escape. Mr More lay down on the rock at full length to examine the sight more closely and to relate it to the overwhelming power of the sea. He remained perfectly still for a long time with his fist under his chin until he turned over to see Ken Lazarus standing above him. In his right hand he carried a tightly rolled cylinder of paper. Against the sky it looked like a black rod. Mr More shaded his eyes with his hands to study the handsome youth.

'You look like an angel,' Mr More said. 'And that is absolutely exact, not an exaggeration.'

Ken Lazarus was embarrassed. He lifted the hand that held the cylinder of paper in order to protect his eyes from the bright light off the sea.

'Don't move,' Mr More said. 'Please don't move. I want to tell you exactly what I was thinking. I think you will understand. I think you will. I saw that thing down there as the body of a man. My own possibly. Or perhaps the body of an old man with a long white beard soaked in sea water. The last man to speak our language and his mouth full of the music of the sea. At first I was quite excited because I thought it was an inspiration. The germ of a long poem. And in a way it was. But the poem was something being written by the sea. Not by me. It was a light on the water and if I wanted it I would have to walk out there and lose myself completely in it like a drop of rain falling in the ocean. I couldn't do that. And then I turned and saw you. And that's why I said you looked like an angel of life.'

Ken laughed a little self-consciously. He was wearing a white shirt open-necked with the collar outside his jacket, and a leather watch chain with a silver bar hung from the bottom hole in the lapel of his tweed jacket. Mr More watched every movement he made as though he were memorizing a record of his actions.

'Do you understand?'

'Well, I think I do.'

Ken's voice and manner were so modest they compensated for any disappointment Mr More might have felt in his lack of response. The breeze fluttered the young man's trousers against his strong athletic legs.

'I've brought the music,' he said.

His smile was naive and expectant. Mr More indicated that he should sit down alongside him on the rock. Ken unrolled the manuscript book that he had tightly held in his hand.

'I've set it for solo tenor and a cello,' Ken said. 'I couldn't set the other poem. I couldn't get the rhythm and I didn't know what the two last lines meant. I found them a complete puzzle.'

'I suppose they were vaguely sexual,' Mr More said. 'I always find it very difficult to write about sexual feelings except in the most indirect way. My Puritan upbringing. It's made me very strait-laced and priggish. Even when I know it doesn't matter, a kind of hand passes over my mouth. Do you find that?'

Ken was blushing hotly.

'I'm sorry,' Mr More said, sitting up. 'I didn't mean to pry. You must tell me when you think I am embarrassing. Let's look at the music.'

He stared for a moment at the score.

'It's very neat,' he said. 'You are very neat in everything you do, aren't you? I like that. It's part of your aura. But I'm not sure that it's really good for you.'

'It's the way I am,' Ken said.

'Of course it is. What a very good answer.'

Mr More looked at him as though he marvelled at his wisdom.

347

'Sing it for me. I can't really tell without hearing it.'

The youth sang softly in his pleasing voice and the wind carried the words inland towards the dunes.

Let us divide our days
With the diamond cutter's art
Untrembling hand
Untroubled heart
Accumulated love
Like water in a drought
Should carefully be stored
And parcelled out.

6

The front seat of the bus, to the left of the driver's cabin, gave an uninterrupted view of a road which twisted on ahead between wooded rocky slopes and a river meandering through water meadows towards its estuary. There was enough light left to make the surface of the river glow pink, but the wooded hillsides were disappearing quickly in a deepening twilight. Occupying the front seat Amy and May Huskie could see their own reflections on the polished surface of the window immediately in front of them. May's arms were stretched protectively over the Pembroke table which was wedged between the two women and the steel panel below the window. The table was ineffectively covered with brown paper which was already torn and escaping from its string. Amy sat on the inside and beyond her in the corner was a copper warming pan. By May Huskie's right shoe, a floppy-tongued brogue, there was a cardboard box full of porcelain oddments.

May was staring a little apprehensively at the side piece of the engine bonnet. It was loose and flapping on its heavy hinges. She looked up at the driver on his high perch as though she felt obliged to draw his attention to a potential danger, but he was shrunk inside his greatcoat, his glossy peaked cap tilted over his right ear, his hands in charge of the great steering wheel and an expression of irritated boredom on his lined face.

'I quite enjoyed it,' Amy said.

'I told you you would, didn't I?'

May's mock reproach was very protective.

'It does you good to get out. You mustn't let them all take you for granted.'

Amy smiled wistfully at her own reflection as though she had just heard a fragment of an old melody. May caught a glimpse of the smile. It encouraged her to go further.

'He doesn't appreciate you,' she said. 'I don't think he does.'

Amy sat in silence, staring at the twisting road threading through their still reflections. The interior lights of the bus were slowly becoming stronger than the waning light outside.

'Why doesn't he buy you a car? Think how useful a little car would be.'

May paused in case Amy should want to comment. But Amy was content to listen.

'Still stuck in that old house. A man in his position. He won't move I suppose, will he? You should be living in a large house by now. In my opinion. With a bit of grounds hidden by trees. Much better for the boys it would be.'

The reflection could have been that of two women sitting in a ghostly congregation listening to the monotonous but comforting delivery of a familiar litany.

'My poor old dad always used to say you were beautiful. Long before I knew you. He did you know.'

Amy's lips moved in mild protest, but the bus was making such a noise she could not be heard. May stared at the window and tried to read her lips. She was being allowed to continue.

'A "charmer". That's what he used to call you. I remember him saying to mother. "Nell," he said, "have you seen that fair-haired young woman living in the terrace? She's a charmer."'

Amy ventured to shake her head.

'Look at you now,' May said. 'You don't look a day over thirty. You don't, you know. He doesn't appreciate you, he doesn't really. And when I think of the men you could have at your beck and call just by raising your little finger.'

'May,' Amy said. 'What are you talking about? I've got three boys.'

'Well, that doesn't matter, does it? It's how you look that counts.'

May fluttered her eyelashes at Amy's reflection and rewarded her own daring with a little smile.

'Women have to put up with a lot, don't they? When I think of a woman with your looks and ability and the things you could do in this world, it strikes me that you're turning yourself into a living sacrifice on the altar of your family.'

Amy hardly needed to listen to hear what was being said. The bus seemed to grumble and roar and rattle in order to erase any words that May would utter unfit for her to hear. And the same noise gave May a special licence to grow more frank and fervid in her praise.

'If he had more pride in you, not just pride, but pride in *you* I mean, he would have more pride in his family and take more trouble to put you in a palace which is where you deserve and not still stuck in that old house with all those awful neighbours watching every single move you make and passing remarks and interfering in everything.'

'It's near the sea.'

Amy spoke quietly but May managed to hear.

'Yes, well, of course it is. Just because he likes it. Selfishness. That's what it amounts to. Dr Thomas says the same, doesn't he? There's too much work in that house for you.'

Amy made herself more comfortable in her seat. At least the bus was warm and it had taken over the responsibility of the homeward journey for them so that they could if they so desired completely relax. She allowed her eyes to close and when she opened them again May's lips were still working. She was in the mood to empty her mind of its contents and talk about her own family as if she were counting rapidly small change out of a blue bag of savings on the counter of a bank.

'We've got our faults like everybody else but there's one thing you can't say about us. We're not selfish. My grandfather was. I'll grant you that. He made use of my poor father. He left him with a load of trouble. And my mother use to say I'm the image of the old man. Isn't that awful? He just skidaddled over to Canada and left poor dad with a handful of trouble . . .'

May spoke in bursts, with brief pauses in between and the bursts became progressively more difficult to follow.

'. . . Basically they hold it against us because we're English and they always did. We can't help it after all, can we? And all my poor father was trying to do was to brighten up the place a little and I don't see how anyone could blame him for that . . . But they still resent it in Pendraw you know. They want the money without all the fuss and bother. My father used to say what they'd like would be for the

351

visitors to send the money by post and not turn up themselves. That's what they're like you know ... My mother said to me on her deathbed, "Look after Milly whatever else you do ... and keep Frank from the Fish Pond." I don't know whether she was right there. It would have been something for him, you see, but Rose said she wouldn't be seen dead there so I couldn't force her could I? and the long and the short of it was we lost the licence and in any case they didn't want us to have it ... And I had to get rid of the donkeys.'

May stopped speaking abruptly when she saw in the window reflection that Amy's eyes were closed. She pressed in her chin and looked around to see if anyone else on the bus had noticed she had been talking to herself. For a while she looked at her own image as something from which she was entitled to expect a little comfort and consolation. She closed her eyes. Briefly they both looked like women who had fallen asleep under the droning sermon of the engine: but May could not keep her eyes closed for long. She shifted about occasionally to check their position and to peer into the darkness for some landmark to reassure her. She was also concerned about guarding the slender legs of the Pembroke table. A jolt of the bus made Amy open her eyes.

'Oh,' she said. 'I nearly fell asleep.'

She suppressed a yawn and then smiled at May Huskie.

'It's been a lovely afternoon,' she said. 'I have enjoyed it.'

They both looked affectionately at the pieces they had bought in the sale. With some alarm May noted a spot of rain on the window.

'Look,' she said. 'It's beginning to rain. What are we going to do.'

Amy seemed unconcerned.

352

'I don't know how we'll get this lot across the cob. It's quite a job you know. It's not the wind so much. It's the rain. And this table is quite delicate in its own way . . .'

'Stop fussing, May,' Amy said. 'I've asked Soniatowski to meet the bus with his van.'

'Oh, have you?'

May Huskie was relieved and full of admiration for Mrs More's organizing ability.

'Of course you have, if you say so. You know what you ought to do Amy? You ought to be running a really big business.'

Amy began to laugh and touched the handle of the warming pan.

'Buying bits and pieces with my housekeeping money? The first steps in the direction of a fortune . . .'

'Well I think it could be,' May said obstinately. 'We could buy a lot more of it and store it in my father's old studio. And there's Soniatowski. He's got real skill as a cabinet maker. I tell you we could start a big firm . . . If you were a man, Amy, you could make a fortune twice over.'

There was a note of almost religious conviction in May Huskie's voice.

'Well I'm not, am I?'

Amy leaned back in her corner. The bus driver had changed down to take a steep hill and the engine roar made conversation impossible. Amy closed her eyes. The noise was giving her a headache. May Huskie leaned closer to speak in her ear.

'Why don't you call him Paul?'

Her voice trembled a little. She was staring at Amy's image in the window with intense devotion.

'Why on earth should I?'

'He'd do anything for you.'

'May!'

Amy sounded quite shocked.

353

'You've only got to lift your little finger,' May said. 'He'll do anything for you. He's got it worse than the doctor.'

She spoke as though the Pole was suffering from a secret disease known only to a select band of specialists among whom she herself was perhaps the most expert.

'You are silly sometimes,' Amy said.

'I can see what I can see. He's smitten. All over. He's an aristocrat you know.'

She seemed set on making the man sound as romantic as possible.

'Well, all I want him to do is to bring his van to meet this bus,' Amy said.

'I think it's marvellous the way he's taught himself cabinet making,' May said. 'Against all odds.'

'What do you mean?'

Amy was amused by the note of fervid admiration in May's voice.

'Well, he's a Count or something in Poland, you know. He's an aristocrat by birth.'

Amy burst out laughing.

'What are you laughing at?'

May sounded quite hurt.

'He's a carpenter,' Amy said. 'And none the worse for that. What are titles anyway? It's what a man's worth that counts. You ought to become a socialist like me, May, and then you would stop looking at the world through romantic rose-tinted spectacles. He knows how to work hard and that's all that commends him to me. I like people who work hard.'

'You're not a socialist?'

May was quite shocked by the sound of the word on her own lips.

'I'd never say that. Honestly I wouldn't. You don't look like one at all.'

'What do I look like?'

Amy had turned to smile directly at her companion.

'Like a lady of course,' May said.

The bus was about to stop and the noise of the engine suddenly subsided. May dropped her voice until it sounded like a whisper in church.

'Like a real, beautiful lady.'

The bus had arrived in the station square. There were few passengers. The Pole was already there. He was a large, loose-limbed man with a canine smile and eagerness to please. The little bus conductor watched him with suspicion. He would have liked to pass a sequence of bold remarks but he was inhibited by the presence of Amy who stood with dignified authority at the other end of the bus while May and the Pole manoeuvred the table over the seats. She did not make a bossy noise like May Huskie, but she looked more dangerous. When the Pole came back for the box of porcelain the conductor watched his movements with deep suspicion and stayed on board as though to check that the big foreigner did not remove anything extra. Amy gave the conductor two shillings for his trouble. She smiled and spoke to him soothingly so that all his misgivings quickly vanished. He took up a position on the open space between the bus and the van and asked repeatedly in a friendly voice if there was anything else he could do to help them.

7

'If you are on a raft in the middle of the ocean you
don't jump off just because you don't happen to like
the colour of the wood.'

Mr More was wedged a little uncomfortably in the
middle of the small oak settle in the back parlour of
the Mona Inn. Flames spurted high from the logs which
had been thrown on the fire but the room was still cold.
Dr Wilson Thomas stood in front of the fire with his
feet apart and his broad back kept much of the warmth
of the fire from spreading into the narrow room. With
something of the authority of a chairman he lifted his
pint tankard to point towards Mr More.

'There he is,' he said. 'Squeeze him a little harder and
goodness knows what precious drops of wisdom you'll
get out of him. Come on, Cilydd! Fulfil your bardic
function. Here we are, hungry sheep looking up and
waiting to be fed.'

Mr More looked down at the table and smiled
reluctantly. It was a small, elect assembly: but he was
not yet at his ease. Mr Cupitt the dentist sat nearest
the door. He lifted his nose and shifted his head about
anxious not to miss anything.

'What was that about a draft,' he said. 'I didn't quite
follow?'

There was general hilarity and even Mr More shook
his shoulders as an unaccustomed stirring of mirth fer-
mented inside him.

'All I am saying,' Mr More said, 'and I am saying very
little when I say it. It's all we've got. So let's hang on to
it.'

'Hear! Hear!'

An emaciated journalist with a mop of unruly grey
hair slammed the table with the palm of his hand. He

was visibly disappointed when Mr More made no sign to show he welcomed his support.

'But we must do more than that, man!'

Dr Thomas had grown suddenly aggressive. His moustache bristled and his face flushed. He had been drinking longer that the others.

'Not just cling on! Take over! And that's what Cilydd means too if he's prepared to follow his argument to its logical conclusion. Let me put it this way: if the Eisteddfod comes to Pendraw, it comes on our terms and lives up to our standards.'

'What do you mean by "we"?'

The man who asked the question was a teacher from the grammar school. He wore a bow tie and a colourful shirt. His manner was marked by a cautious gaiety.

'Who are "we" anyway when it comes to the push? Um?'

He had a habit of chuckling apologetically after saying something, which seemed designed to neutralize the effect of the statement in case anyone should suddenly decide to hold it against him.

'The Club, boy. What else do you think I'm talking about?'

Dr Thomas's accent was South Welsh. He spoke vigorously, like a man sent to stir up activity in a den of northern inertia.

'I don't care what you call it,' he said. 'You can call it *Tea and Toast* if you like. But if we don't cooperate, we won't stand a chance. The old guard will take over. The chapels, the town council, the cymrodorion, the mixed choir and before you know where you are you'll have a *penny Reading* for old ladies. Look at the list of subjects the year before last. Have you seen it? Cilydd! Have you seen it?'

'Yes, I've seen it.'

The appeal to Mr More was deliberate, and the company turned to him for an opinion, as the most distinguished man of letters present. It was his moment to make a significant statement but the aggressive stare of Dr Thomas was rather putting him off. He turned away slightly before he spoke.

'Every generation has to re-possess the Past,' he said. 'If it fails to do this, it is robbed of its proper food. Just as the animal body survives from the proper harvesting of the Past so the spiritual body lives on those parts of the past that poets make palatable. There are two processes involved. History, and that includes science; and Poetry, and that includes all the arts. These may appear hostile sometimes, but they must live together in organic harmony . . .'

'There you are!'

The doctor interrupted the discourse with a cry of triumph. Cilydd had much more to say but he was not going to thump the table for attention. If the assembly had taken enough intellectual nourishment to stir them to action, he would not burden them with further subtleties that might distract them and set them disputing concepts only partially understood.

'I told you you had to squeeze him hard before you'd get anything out of him! That man is a genius and I don't mind telling him so to his face. Well now then. What about it? Do we form a club? I suggest eighteen members, with a chairman, a secretary and a treasurer. Do I have to make a formal proposal?'

'I think you would make a first-class chairman, Wilson.'

The emaciated journalist let his jaw drop and his eyes moved about looking for signs of appreciation of his statesmanlike suggestion.

'And I can tell you this . . .'

He shifted up in his chair, moved to the daring verge of a prophetic warning.

'. . . if we don't act very soon, we'll be too late.'

'Well there you are,' Dr Thomas said, happy to ac-

cept corroborative evidence for his action programme
and content to relax a little now that it was clear that the
leading role was about to fall to his lot.

There was a knock at the door and the landlord's
sister, a prim looking woman in her sixties, put in her
head and looked around the company with a stern
eye.

'Mr More,' she said. 'Could you come here for a
moment please.'

The table had to be removed to allow Mr More to
get out. The corridor outside was cold and clean and
dimly lit. The landlord's sister's face was stiff with
disapproval.

'I thought you'd better know,' she said. 'I'm telling
you to your face. There's no sense in a boy of his age
hanging around the Conservative Club. And he's with
boys much too old for him.'

'What's the matter?'

Mr More spoke with professional precision.

'Johnny Melwas is in there. I just happened to be in
the back and he was on his way to the police, breathing
fire and slaughter. You'd better talk to him.'

The landlord's sister led Mr More into her kitchen.
Johnny Melwas was dressed in a chauffeur's cap and
an army greatcoat dyed black that was many sizes too
big for him. As soon as he saw Mr More he jumped to
his feet and began to march up and down kicking the
hem of the overcoat with his boots.

'The bastards!' he said. 'The little bastards.'

'Johnny,' the landlord's sister said. 'Sit down and
don't use language. Tell Mr More what happened.'

'I should have gone straight to the police,' he said.

His jagged teeth were covered with saliva and his eyes
were bloodshot.

'Saw Miss Hughes here and she got me in.'

'What's the matter?'

Mr More stood a little sideways as he tended to do

when faced with a threatening situation. But he did not take his eyes off Johnny Melwas and the light glittered on the flat lens of his spectacles with each slight movement of his head.

'They came in you see when I was asleep.'

'Where was this?'

'Where I always am,' Johnny said. 'Damn, you know it as well as I do. In my chair by the little window. I must have dozed off. It's late enough. But I stay there in case someone wants the taxi. I stay there till ten, don't I? Just to oblige. Just in case. I must have dozed off. And they slipped past me. On tip-toe because I didn't hear the little swine . . .'

'Robbery?'

Mr More interrupted.

'Of course it was.'

'Money?'

'Of course!'

'You'd better show me.'

Mr More had become sharp and efficient. It was as if all his worst suspicions about the world had been confirmed. With the single weapon of his wits he had to cut his way through a dark forest of unremitting hostility. Johnny did not hesitate to obey him. There was an edge to the lawyer's voice that threatened vague penalties. Kicking his coat all the way Johnny Melwas led the way up the narrow lane. It was wide enough for pedestrians only and it connected the rear of the Mona Inn to the wide yard behind the ironmonger's premises. There was still a light in the tiny cottage where Johnny lived alongside the row of three garages where the three licensed cars were kept. Johnny opened the door and by the time Mr More stood at his side he was pointing at the rocking chair by the window.

'They must have come in, you see, while I was sitting there,' he said. 'Think of the impudence!'

'Were you asleep?'

'Dozing. I was listening to that little wireless and the damn thing sent me off to sleep. They must have crept in, you see, and took the key from that nail over there. Can you see it?'

Mr More moved to look more closely at an old-fashioned key hanging on a nail on the distempered wall.

'The key is here,' he said.

'That's the devil of it,' Johnny said.

He was enraged by the recollection.

'They put it back. They took down the key, opened the door into the back of the shop and they got all the money in the bicycle cash box. And then the wicked little devils came in here, put the key back and calmly walked out.'

'And you were still asleep?'

'Well of course I was or I would have stopped them.'

'How do you know who they were then?'

'I know very well who they were. And I'm telling you to your face, Mr More, that boy of yours was one of them. Gwydion. He was one. And that's what happens when you let him hang around with English louts like that Frank Huskie and that other one, whatever his name is. Why doesn't he stick to boys of his own age?'

'You said you were asleep.'

'Dozing.'

'What do you mean by "dozing"?'

'I wasn't properly awake.'

'You couldn't move?'

'Not properly . . .'

'But you could open your eyes?'

'Half-open. The second time. Just after they'd put the key back.'

'Had you been drinking?'

'I wasn't drunk! I'm not drunk now am I? You can see for yourself.'

'I don't see how you could recognize them.'

361

'Oh but I did . . .'

'Then why didn't you stop them?'

'I told you. I was dozing.'

'Fast asleep.'

'No, dozing.'

'Then why didn't you stop them taking the key?'

'I didn't see them take it.'

'Then you were fast asleep. How many were there?'

'I'm not sure.'

'Three?'

'Could have been.'

'Or six?'

'I'm not sure. I woke up when they were leaving . . .'

'Woke up?'

'So you were asleep?'

'I said I was.'

'Fast asleep?'

Johnny Melwas snatched off his chauffeur's cap, threw it on the ground, and jumped on it, beside himself with anger. His bald head looked naked and defenceless.

'You're trying to mix me up,' he said. 'Because your boy was one of them. I'm not a fool you know.'

The solicitor was relentless.

'Go and stand in the archway,' Mr More said.

'Why?'

'Turn the collar of your coat up and put your cap on.'

'Why?'

'I want to see if I can recognize you through this window with this light in my eyes and this wireless on. It was on, wasn't it?'

'What?'

'The wireless. You had it on?'

'No . . . I don't know . . .'

'You said it was on. It sent you to sleep . . .'

'Dozing.'

'And this key . . .'

362

Mr More moved suddenly, switching his attention to the key on the wall.

'Is it the only key?'

Johnny Melwas scratched his head.

'As far as I know . . . The gaffer may have one in his house. I don't know.'

'It would be strange if he hadn't,' Mr More said in a softer tone.

'I suppose it would.'

'So the thief or thieves, if there were any, could have taken that key not this one?'

'What are you talking about?'

'What about the cashbox inside. Was that locked?'

'Locked?'

'Do you have a key to the cashbox?'

'No.'

'How much was in it?'

'About ten pounds.'

'How do you know?'

'Well, I counted it, didn't I? Don't I count it every night before locking up the bicycle shop. It's my job. Do you think I'm a fool or something?'

'So it's not locked?'

'What?'

'The cashbox.'

'No. Why should I bother? The door's locked anyway, isn't it?'

Mr More went silently from the kitchen and with the key opened the door into the bicycle repair shed situated behind the ironmonger's shop. Johnny Melwas hurried after him, suspicious now of his every move. On the bench there was a petty cashbox. The lid was open and there was still some small change on the black metal bottom of the box. Mr More looked at it for a long time without speaking. Johnny Melwas became anxious. Mr More looked at Johnny coldly.

'It wouldn't be difficult for a barrister to make out a case that you had taken the money yourself.'

His dry voice was void of any emotion. Johnny Melwas shifted back as though he were being attacked physically. He growled and swore and showed his discoloured teeth.

'Bloody liar,' he said.

He lifted his arm to point at Mr More.

'Your lad,' he said. 'That Gwydion. He did it. And that Huskie fellow. And Evans. The fat one. I'll have every one of them behind bars. Every damned one of them. So you watch it. And we all know about you, don't we?'

Mr More refused to be drawn.

'We all know what you're like . . . Butter wouldn't melt in your mouth.'

'You don't seem to have any proof,' Mr More said. 'Nothing that would stand up in a court of law. And the fuss of course could do you a lot of damage.'

'How?'

'People could say you were getting too old for your job. Too old to run a taxi service for one thing. Too old to drive and too old to be a watchman. Falling asleep on the job.'

'I wasn't asleep. I was dozing.'

'Even if you won the case with the best barrister in the land, you'd lose your job. For a few pounds lying about in an open box which any little child could have taken. It wouldn't be worth it.'

Johnny Melwas was sensitive about his age. He pulled his cap down more firmly over his eyes.

'I don't bear you any ill will,' Mr More said. 'I'll put the money back in the box myself. But I advise you not to go to the police.'

'You want to watch that boy,' Johnny said. 'He's in the wrong company.'

Mr More nodded, to show that he was prepared to concede that the rebuke was merited. This made it easier for Johnny to accept the restrictions the lawyer was weaving around him in the poor light of the bicycle shop. Point by point Mr More went over the incident until Johnny Melwas had begun to realize the vast legal case that could arise out of it and finally began to show the first signs of gratitude that Mr More had saved him from an experience of shattering unpleasantness that would more than likely ruin his life.

8

Mr More stood on the lowest step of the stairs, his wet hat in his hand. His head was bent back, his mouth was wide open and there were raindrops still on his spectacles. From higher up the house came the faint sound of a small boy crying. He satisfied himself about the nature of the sound and then walked briskly to the door of his wife's sewing room. Inside there was the sound of genteel merriment. He tapped the door briskly and opened it. A game of bridge was in progress. Amy was partnered by Soniatowski the Pole, and May Huskie played with Edna Thomas, the doctor's wife, a gay assertive woman with hair like hay lying in strange folds above her red face. She had a glass of whisky near her and she waved a card at Mr More when he appeared in the doorway. Like her husband she came from a South Wales valley and clearly felt an obligation to liven things up a bit wherever she went.

'Cilydd!'

She cried out in a familiar tone that instantly made him withdraw into his shell.

'Come and watch me make five diamonds! You never saw anything like it. Talk about diamonds being a girl's best friend.'

She gurgled at her own wit, pressing both her hands into the side of the card table while her bosom quaked above them. The Pole was also glad to be amused. His mouth opened so wide he had to lift the back of his large hand to stop the saliva dripping out. Mr More eyed his wife as sternly as he could.

'The little boy is crying,' he said.

Amy immediately resented the implied criticism.

'Surely he can't be? It's less than ten minutes since I was upstairs and he was fast asleep then.'

'He's probably having a nightmare,' Mr More said.

His voice was cold and serious.

'Well, why don't you go up and see?' Amy said. 'A boy needs a father just as much as a mother.'

The other bridge players were unnaturally still as they awaited the outcome of the encounter between husband and wife. With a slight smile on her broad face Edna Thomas could barely contain her curiosity. Miss Huskie kept pressing in her chin as though she had to restrain herself from intervening on behalf of her admired friend. The Pole totted up the scores, his great shoulders bent and his head almost touching the paper as he worked out the sums with his lips moving in his own language.

'I want to speak to you in private,' Mr More said. 'It's rather urgent.'

'Now?'

They glared at each other angrily. Mr More looked as if he were on the verge of tipping over the card table. Pale but self-possessed, Amy asked to be excused. She made it plain that she was acting in the interests of decorum and good order. When they were outside in the passage she turned on her husband.

'What do you think you're doing?' she said.

He ignored her and pointed to the stairs.

'A terrible thing has happened,' he said.

'What? What are you talking about?'

'See to the boy first. And then come up to my study.'

Amy hesitated on the stairs, puzzled by his masterful behaviour. The look on his face could have been triumph but his voice was harsh with foreboding.

He waited in his study for Amy to return from attending to Peredur. He switched on the reading lamp on his desk and bent the chrome-covered spine with his fist until the lamp almost touched a pad of paper on which he had been writing. He went over to the mantelpiece and picked up a pipe and sucked nervously at the stem until he heard Amy coming. She stood in the open doorway.

'What is it?'

She was on her guard, not prepared to come into the room or shut the door.

'What was the matter with Peredur?'

'I've no idea. A bad dream I expect.'

'Did he speak to you?'

'I just turned him over.'

'He's nearly six years old,' Mr More said. 'And he still wets the bed. And he cries in his sleep.'

'Why do you speak to me like that? Do you blame me? Is it my fault?'

Mr More made no answer to her questions.

'Come inside and close the door.'

'I've got guests downstairs' Amy said. 'You can't expect me just to leave them.'

She closed the door.

'Where's Gwydion?'

Mr More sat in his writing chair with his back to the desk. His attitude was stern and judicial.

'At the Huskies' I expect. I don't know.'

'At the Huskies'?'

His manner exasperated her.

'John,' she said. 'Don't repeat everything I say. What's the matter? Tell me and stop gloating.'

'Gloating?'

The word seemed to stick in Mr More's throat and force him to stand up to avoid choking. He pointed oddly at the floor in front of Amy's feet.

'How little you understand me,' he said. 'What's happened to us?'

She had regained some of her composure.

'It would be much easier if you told me straight-forwardly what was the matter.'

'Get him out!'

Mr More took hold of the edge of his desk unable to control the wave of emotion that was sweeping over him.

'Get that boy out and don't let him go back there. It's not too late to do something about it if we try.'

'I don't know what you've got against these poor Huskies,' Amy said. 'It's quite irrational. They seem to represent something in your mind quite monstrous. But in reality, what are they? Just a family struggling to live and struggling to hold together. Like any other family. And succeeding better than most against all the odds. But you've got this extraordinary habit of making everybody and everything fit the system of ideas in your head. It's no way to look at the world, John.'

Her voice was calm and reasonable and he looked at her with suspicious sideways admiration.

'You are an intelligent woman,' he said. 'And yet you've encouraged them. You've let that boy go there every hour of the day and night. And now you've brought disaster on our heads. You've turned your son into a thief, into a criminal.'

He stared at her as though he were expecting her to collapse into a helpless sobbing heap on the floor. Instead, all she did was frown a little and lick her lips.

'Let's have some facts for goodness sake,' she said. 'I can't bear this emotional cat and mouse game you so like playing. What has happened?'

'Get him.'

He whipped out the words. Amy stood her ground.

'You've got to tell me, John. I won't be bullied.'

He smiled sardonically at the idea of him bullying his wife.

'Gwydion was one of a little gang who stole money this evening from the cashbox in the bicycle shop behind the ironmonger's. Johnny Mclwas saw them. Frank Huskie was there – and Gwydion. And that fat boy Evans. There may have been more. This is the fine fruit of all your labours. You've destroyed that boy's roots.'

'Destroyed his roots? Taking him for nature rambles on Sunday afternoon instead of sending him to that suffocating Sunday School. You call that destroying his roots!'

'This is what we've made of him,' Mr More said. 'A small thief.'

He was deflated and depressed. Amy looked around for somewhere to sit. There was one other chair in the room, in the corner, furthest away from the desk.

'It could be just a prank,' Amy said.

'Robbing an old man! A prank!'

'A sleepy little town like this doesn't know how to cope with high-spirited boys.'

'Face it.'

He spoke savagely.

'Face what?'

'We've cut him off from his origins. We've let him stay away from chapel. We haven't sent him to Sunday School. And you've encouraged him to mix with the foreign elements. You've done your best to turn him into a little pseudo-Englishman and this is the splendid result.'

Amy looked at him in amazement.

'You're mad,' she said. 'You're unbalanced. What a way to talk. What a way to look at the problem.'

Mr More shook his arm in her direction.

'Oh, how you wish I were,' he said. 'That would excuse you completely, wouldn't it? That would let you off. Then nobody could accuse you of being disloyal . . .'

'You talk about chapel,' Amy said. 'You told me years ago you didn't believe a word of it! I can remember things, you know. You were picking primroses in the lane behind Madryn. You were so firm about it. I can see you now. You were kneeling down on one knee when you said it. "I don't believe a single word of it," you said, "Not one single word." It was such a relief to me. I felt really free for the first time in my life.'

Mr More looked appalled.

'That was long ago,' he said. 'Long ago.'

'Oh, I know you go to chapel now,' Amy said. 'But that's for the sake of the language, isn't it?'

'The language you won't speak,' he said.

'Don't exaggerate.'

'The language you want to die so that it isn't there in front of you every day as a constant reproach.'

'Chapel. Language. Language. Chapel. It just shows how muddled you are.'

'Muddled.'

He repeated the word quietly.

'And you're not muddled of course?'

'We can't sit here all night arguing,' she said. 'What are we going to do about Gwydion?'

'I'll tell you what we are going to do. Something that should please you. He will be sent away to school.'

'But this theft . . . ? This dreadful business?'

Concern for her son made her eager to cooperate and if necessary to compromise. She was ready to act with intelligent speed to protect him from any danger. She moved closer to her husband.

'I think I've settled it,' Mr More said. 'By a stroke of luck we've been saved from that. I put the money back and I persuaded Johnny Melwas not to go near the police. But that won't stop him talking. In a few days, some version or other of the story will be all round the place.'

Her relief was immediate. The prospect of public opinion appeared to worry her far less that it worried him.

'It will be used as a weapon against me,' Mr More said. 'You need have no fear about that.'

'I always wanted him to go to boarding school.'

Mr More's shoulders shook and he smiled to himself rather sourly.

'What do you find so amusing?'

'Doing the wrong thing for the right reason.'

'Is that supposed to be funny?'

'I don't know. It could be, you see. A pattern recurring.'

He relaxed a little in his chair and made vague gestures of drawing in the air.

'Do you think there is a pattern?'

Amy stood up and did not bother to answer his question. The crisis was over. A course of action had been decided upon. She was not inclined to sit and brood over the event in a dim corner of Cilydd's study.

'Oh, I've no doubt you will write a poem about it,' she said.

'I wish you would tell me why it is you can't stand my work.'

He was reluctant to let her go. It seemed an opportunity for him to speak with as much frankness as possible.

'When the yoke is on their necks the oxen are obliged to move in the same direction. They must want to speak to each other sometimes.'

371

'I must go down,' Amy said. 'I can't leave those people alone all this time.'

'If you could tell me honestly it would be some comfort. Is it because I insist on composing in a language that is dying. Is that what displeases you?'

Amy refused to answer.

'I seem to remember long ago you said something like that. But it's so long ago I can hardly remember. You wanted me to write in a world language. I'm sure that was what you said. And something about wasting my time. And something about a minority language being a pleasant refuge for the second rate. You've said a lot of things in your time, haven't you?'

'I'm thinking about Gwydion,' she said. 'It will do him so much good to go away to school.'

'I wish you'd tell me. Do you want it to die because you want me to die? Or is it the other way round?'

'I don't know what you are talking about.'

'I know I'm a great disappointment to you. I'm not really what you wanted. I appeared to be when you married me. I was a step up in the right direction. But I've never built the big practice you would have liked to see. I've never gone in for politics. No big house. No big car. I've wasted your valuable time scribbling second-class poetry in a second-classs language when I could have been working hard making a lot of money for you. Is that what you think?'

'I'm thinking about Gwydion,' Amy said.

'I have the impression sometimes that you wish I didn't exist. Is that a fact? I wish you'd tell me. You leave me alone in my smelly little ivory tower – you called it smelly do you remember? scratching away in sweat and agony, building things in words that are dying every day. The most ridiculous occupation known to man ... That's what you think isn't it? I could be going out into the world and carving out a bigger share of the world of the living and handing it over to you.

Piece by piece. A Cardiff office. A Liverpool office. A London office. It's not too late to start now you know. I could still do it. Tell me something Amy. If I did. If I did all that, would you think any better of me?'

'I'd better go downstairs,' Amy said. 'I'll ask May to go over and tell Gwydion to come home. It's nearly ten o'clock anyway. It's time he was in bed.'

'Did you hear me? I was asking you a question. I was making human noises. Here. Your husband in your house. Did you hear me?'

Amy looked at him coldly.

'Don't be so self-absorbed,' she said.

9

'There he goes!'

Aunty Menna stood at the side of her bedroom window. The room was only just big enough to contain the double bed with a feather mattress on which she slept. The imprint of her heavy form still lay moulded in the bulky mattress and the load of blankets were thrown over the metal rails at the foot of the bed. She was watching Mr More at the bottom of his back garden bending down to put bicycle clips on his trousers. There was a smile on her face as she took evident pleasure in observing the behaviour of her neighbours from such an ideal vantage point at the top of the tall house.

'You'd think he'd have a car, wouldn't you? Fancy saying he doesn't believe in them any more. You know what I think, Flo? I think he's developing into a miser. He's getting to look like a miser, isn't he?'

There were three rooms on the top floor of the house occupied by Aunty Menna, Aunty Flo and Clem. In a fourth space a water tank was housed. The echo of splashing water was getting on Aunty Flo's nerves. She was sitting on the edge of her bed writing a letter. The doors of each room were open. Aunty Menna crossed the small landing to take a look at her sister.

'What's the matter with you?' she said. 'I thought you were dead or something and I was talking to myself.'

Aunty Flo did not appreciate her sister's humour. Her shoulders were hunched resentfully over the writing pad on her knee.

'This is how we are,' she said. 'Bunched up in the attic for ten weeks of the year.'

'Now don't start complaining,' Aunty Menna said.

'It's all right for you. I'm next to that damned water tank.'

'Don't swear.'

Aunty Menna was amused by her sister's complaints.

'It drips all night. I never sleep properly up here. It's either too cold or too hot.'

'Be thankful you're not in Korea.'

'That's not funny. That's not funny at all,' Flo said.

Menna wandered up to the window of her sister's room. She ignored the view and looked down with unquenchable interest at the street below. Her lips moved but her mind was already keenly engaged in the arts of observation.

'Funny time to write letters.'

Her voice was just a murmur. Something to disturb her sister like the buzz of a wasp on the edge of her consciousness, too far away to swat, too near to ignore.

'It's the humiliation I can't stand.'

Flo spoke with dramatic bitterness.

374

'Having strangers occupying the best part of the house. Sleeping with my head in the water tank and my feet in the sink.'

Aunty Menna chuckled to herself. To her the visitors were a welcome diversion, a happy break in the dullness of her household routine, a lively incursion into the empty barracks which she guarded alone for so many hours in solitude and boredom while her sister and her nephew were out pursuing their enjoyable careers in the outside world.

'You should have married Cilydd when you had the chance,' Aunty Menna said. 'He would have bought you a bike and you could have gone on a tour of the village halls to recite his poetry – when you weren't starring in his plays of course.'

She stretched her mouth and squirted a slow hiss of amusement through her false teeth which persisted long enough to make her sister close her writing pad and bang it angrily on her bedside table.

'You've got no pride,' Aunty Flo said. 'Look at you. The way you let yourself go.'

Menna was impervious to criticism from her sister. She had seen something in the road down below which amused her greatly.

'Come here,' she said. 'Look at this one. Just look at him.'

'Haven't you got anything better to do?'

Her sister's annoyance seemed to add to Menna's pleasure in what she was watching.

'He's doing it quite deliberately. Oh my goodness, if his uncle comes out and catches him he'll half kill him. What a thing to do. What a notion.'

Flo was drawn against her own judgement to the window. She brought the writing pad with her as though to demonstrate that she had no intention of participating fully in her sister's idle pastime. Below a new Austin was parked outside their front door. A small boy, aged about nine or ten, was coolly wiping the soles of his shoes on the door panels of the car. He was a fat boy and his pink flesh glowed inside this gay holiday clothes. He was annoyed because the car was locked and he could not get in it. The wiping of his feet on the door was an act of revenge.

'Just look at him,' Menna said. 'Did you ever see anything so cocky.'

'Dreadful child,' Flo said. 'Thoroughly spoilt.'

Every so often the boy looked around, a little smile on his face, seeking applause or encouragement. His plumpness was still a condition of peculiar beauty and not an embarrassment, and like a cherished pet he seemed to expect loving nourishment from the air around him. Aunty Menna enjoyed looking at him. She loosened her folded arms in case she should need to raise a hand and give the boy a little wave. But it did not occur to him to glance higher than the first-floor windows.

'There's something lovely about a fat boy, isn't there?' Aunty Menna said.

'That's only because you're fat yourself.'

'Hark who's talking.'

They could have been nudging each other, just to make sure they were in contact at the most convenient level.

'Did you see him after breakfast?' Menna said.

'I don't spend all day "specking" through the window.'

'You should have seen him. He's got a toy parachute. Have you seen it?'

'Why should I want to see it?'

'Well he took his little sister's doll and threw it out of the window. The parachute opened beautifully and it floated down to the ground. You must have heard her crying.'

'Heard her,' Flo said. 'To think people like that can occupy our home. Where's the dignity of it?'

376

'Where are the rates?' Aunty Menna said. 'Perhaps you'd like to pay them and then we could stop having them.'

'It's your house. It's in your name!'

Flo clutched eagerly at an old argument. It would be more profitable than fruitless fencing over the antics of a fat boy. Menna was not to be drawn.

'Look at him,' Menna said. 'He's going to climb on the bonnet! Oh, he's a little devil isn't he?'

Flo watched, interested now, in spite of herself.

'Raymond his name is,' Menna said. 'I've always liked the name Raymond. His father's away a lot. That's what his granny told me.'

She shook her head nostalgically.

'You can have a lot of fun with them when they're small,' she said. 'But, by gum, you pay for it later.'

'Look!'

Flo, always more resourceful once her interest was roused, raised the sash window with steady care in order to be able to hear what was being said down on the pavement. The boy's uncle had emerged from the house carrying an open newspaper. A gust of wind fanned it about and added to his anger.

'You little bleeder,' he said. 'You bloody little bleeder!'

'Listen to that,' Aunty Menna said, 'enjoying her sense of shock.'

'To think that sort are occupying our house . . .'

'Just look at that!'

The man caught the fat boy by the shoulder and swung him around. The face that lifted up still looked half-expecting some sign of ultimate loving approval.

'You evil little bleeder,' the man said. 'Look what you've done!! Just look what you've done!'

He pushed the boy away violently and sent him sprawling over the pavement. The boy's first reaction was complete bewilderment. He stared at his uncle's distorted face as if he were looking at hatred for the first time in his life. A woman's voice floated down from the first floor window.

'Our Ned! Now you leave him alone. He's only a little boy.'

Raymond's little red lips had opened as he stared at his uncle with horrified fascination.

'Little boy? Is that what you call him. A bloody little bleeder more like. That's what I'd call him.'

The words were more than Raymond could bear to hear. He screwed up his eyes tight and howled.

'Now look what you've gone and done.'

The woman's voice floated out above the irate uncle's head.

'Done! Look what he's done! Just look! Look at my new car. I spent an hour before breakfast cleaning it and polishing it. Bleeding little porker. Fine bloody holiday this has turned out to be . . .'

'There's no need to stand outside there swearing . . .'

Flo was keeping a close eye on Raymond. The boy had opened one eye to make a quick check on the way the argument was going.

'He isn't hurt,' she said. 'He isn't hurt at all really.'

Menna was more sympathetic. She mumbled and cooed her concern. The angry man disappeared back into the house. A woman came out with both her arms extended. She helped the boy to his feet and they moved crab like back into the house.

'What a performance,' Flo said. 'In front of my own home. To think we have to put up with it.'

She pressed the window down as quietly as she could to its previous position. Menna was moving out to the landing, anxious not to lose touch with any further developments.

'Where are you going?'

There was accusation already in the question.

378

'Make my bed.'

Menna spoke sharply in her own defence. Such business as bed-making was accepted as legitimate priority by both sides.

'Well go and do it then.'

With a sudden flurry of resentful energy, Menna bore down upon her bed, grabbed the mattress, pulled it forward and then, flinging it over like a lioness with the flopping carcass of a dead beast, leaned forward to thump it all over with her fists and her forearms. She chose to work noisily as if the sound she made were a musical measure of the extent of her effort. Flo watched for a while and then closed her door as though she were averting her eyes from such a painfully plebeian sight. As soon as she had finished making the bed Menna gravitated again to her position at the rear window.

Beyond the huts and garages she saw a large pre-war car driving slowly down the sandy road from the promenade. It drew up outside the long white shack which still carried the faded sign *Huskie's Photographic Studios*. The wooden building had a verandah which ran the full length of the display windows. The windows were curtained across like a house in mourning, with grey material. The large car was being driven by Soniatowski, the Pole, and alongside him sat Mrs Amy More. Aunty Menna was drawn even closer to the window. She hissed out her sister's name in a loud whisper.

'Flo! Flo! Look at this then.'

'What's the matter with you?'

Flo emerged from her cramped quarters protesting at being disturbed a second time.

'You don't want to miss this,' Menna said. 'And it's cheaper than the pictures. Look over there.'

'Where?'

'Outside Huskie's old shack.'

The large car was loaded with cardboard boxes of various sizes. They were carried by the Pole with great care around to the rear entrance of the shack.

'Well, you know what they're doing,' Flo said. 'I don't know why you waste your time watching.'

'You're watching too.'

Menna was deeply absorbed.

'She's too much of a snob to have anything to do with a fellow like that,' Flo said. 'You know that as well as I do.'

'He's a Count after all.'

'A Count? What sort of a Count?'

'Polish, I suppose.'

'One two three, more like.'

'Well, they're pretty thick I can tell you.'

Menna spoke knowingly and her sister was annoyed that she should make such a pretence of omniscience.

'Of course you're in and out there,' Flo said. 'Bowing and scraping. You would know a lot more than anybody else. If it's worth knowing. Which I doubt.'

'She's glad of my help,' Aunty Menna said. 'She doesn't like the needle. She says I'm an expert seamstress.'

'Shows how much she knows.'

'You're very jealous.'

'What about for goodness sake. She says a few nice words to you and you drop on your knees and worship her.'

'There you are. Jealous.'

'Jealous? Me? Jealous?'

Once more their voices sank to nudging murmurs while they watched with the intensity of spectators overlooking a tennis match from the highest row in the stand. When Amy and the Pole remained inside, Aunty Menna shuffled quietly out of her bedroom, moving with quiet grace in the confined space in order to avoid touching her sister.

'Where are you off to now, Sherlock?'

Flo was relaxing a little. She showed that she was ready to laugh an immediately Menna set aside any animosity and pointed downstairs like a naughty child about to depart on a daring adventure.

'Well, I don't think you should,' Flo said. 'But there we are. It's no use me saying anything.'

Menna moved carefully down the narrow staircase. On the second floor she made excuses with a duster to loiter about so that she could overhear any sounds coming from the middle of the house. Everything was strangely silent. She proceeded downstairs with greater ease. She stopped suddenly when she became aware that she was being followed. She turned to see Raymond with his arms outstretched to give him a grip on both bannister rails. He had recovered from his burst of weeping and the stains had been wiped away lovingly from his plump cheeks. But he looked moody and anxious to restore his own self-confidence. He swung a loose right foot and it looked as if it could have been the sketch of a kick at Aunty Menna's back. There was no knowing how long he had been shadowing her. Aunty Menna smiled at him rather coquettishly.

'Hello, Raymond,' she said. 'Do you want to pass?'

'It's all right.'

His voice was hoarse after his emotional disturbance. She gave him a wink to show that she was secretly on his side.

'Would you like a butty?'

To emphasize her friendliness even further she tried to use what she took to be his native accent. Raymond's tongue pointed out between his small lips. He pressed his head down until a double chin appeared. She beckoned him to follow her down to the basement. He followed her very willingly. While she bustled about in and out of her larder, he kicked his heel against

381

the exposed end of the bottom stairtread. She declared she was hunting about for a pot of damson jam she had made herself. When she spread it on the thick bread and butter she made a great to do about removing the stones on to a saucer.

'I'll suck them myself in a minute,' she said. 'Isn't that an awful habit? Would you like a drink of pop.'

Raymond nodded. He looked about with interest. He had not been down in the basement before. Aunty Menna noticed this at once.

'Don't look at the mess whatever you do,' she said. 'I'm not houseproud you see. I suppose some people think I should be. But I'm not. I believe it's much more important to be kind to people. Especially little boys. I've always been very fond of little boys.'

Raymond became absorbed in eating and drinking. Aunty Menna moved quietly to the back door and opened it. She ventured out into the garden looking doubtfully at her bedroom slippers. She touched her hair and adjusted her dress and hummed loudly to reassure herself that she had a perfect right to take a little stroll in her own back garden if she felt like it. She put her feet carefully on the ruins of an overgrown rock-garden and stood up, craning her neck to catch a view of Huskie's Photographic Studio through a gap in the row of garages and huts. There was nothing of interest for her to see. She moved about staring critically at empty flower beds in case there were people watching in any of the numerous windows of the long tall terrace. Raymond emerged from the house, his mouth very full, curious about Aunty Menna's wayward movements and not unaware that there was something beyond the garages that had taken her interest. She put a friendly hand on his shoulder and guided him back into the kitchen. He looked up at her expectantly, hoping for more to eat.

'You like jokes, don't you?'

Aunty Menna screwed up her nose to make him laugh and he simpered obediently.

'Would you like to do something for me? A little joke. Just between ourselves. Will you do it? I'll give you a big butty when you come back. You know that white shack. Over there. No. You can't see it. You're too small, bless your little heart. You know the one I mean?'

'Huskie's?'

'That's it! You are a clever little boy, aren't you?'

Raymond nodded. He seemed familiar with the compliment.

'Do you think you could pop behind there and take a look inside?'

'Easy.'

'Yes, but without anybody seeing you. Real Cowboys and Indians. Take a good look and then come back here and tell me what you see.'

She put a warning finger to her lips.

'A big secret,' she said. 'Just between you and me. Secret mission.'

She watched him swagger importantly down the garden path. At the gate he turned around and gave her an exhibition mime of elaborate unconcern. He whistled windily, put his hands in his pockets, crossed his legs, polished his nails. Aunty Menna showed how amused she was and then waved him on urgently, signifying there was no time to lose.

Raymond ran between the huts and the garages and then paused at a vantage point to study his objective, biting his lower lips and breathing heavily, already dramatizing his mission. The white paint on the wooden facade was peeling away in long cracks. With the sand in front of it it would not have been difficult for Raymond to imagine he was approaching a saloon in a ghost town in a Western. Raymond decided to behave like a fearless casual visitor crossing

383

the road to look at the contents of the large windows. There were still small notices in the window but the ink had faded on them and they were illegible. On a display shelf there stood a framed photographed of a pre-war Town Council. This too had faded. Raymond pressed his nose against the glass. Through a crack in the thin grey curtain material he caught a glimpse of a man in his shirt sleeves bent over a desk, scraping away the old leather top before laying another one in its place. He was being closely watched by Mrs More who was hot from moving pieces of furniture about in the warm shack. As Raymond watched, she unbuttoned the top of her blouse and wiped away the sweat from under her arms with a coloured handkerchief. Raymond withdrew, looked up and down the sandy road and then made his way cautiously to the rear entrance of the building. The door was half opened and he was easily able to look inside. He watched the repair work going on, until Mrs More looked around for some fresh occupation for herself. Near the door there was a stock of pieces of antique furniture in need of attention. As she moved towards them Raymond withdrew speedily. Once back in the the sandy lane he looked at the large black car and appeared to be wondering whether or not his mission was complete. A small boy with unruly black curls and legs that were too thin to hold up his stockings appeared from behind a garage. The boys stood looking at each other. They had played together before and were considering whether to play together again. The little boy bent up his knees and pulled up his stockings. He seemed disinclined to speak first.

'Looking for your mum?'

Peredur lifted his shoulders. He didn't wish to appear impolite but he had no technique for concealing his feelings. He shifted his weight from one foot to the other.

'Can you play footy?'

Peredur made a grimace of indifference. Raymond was heavy, given to foul charges and never willing to lose.

'You get your ball then,' Raymond said. 'Go on. I'll be Villa, you'll be City.'

'It's gone soft,' Peredur said.

He was embarrassed as he said it. Raymond didn't look as though he believed it.

'Can you play flatters,' Raymond said.

'What's flatters?'

'You just go round looking for tyres and let them down. Two points for a bike, five for a motorbike, six for a van, seven for a four-door car and twelve for a lorry. That's all it is. It's easy.'

'There isn't such a game.'

'Well there is isn't there? I've just told you.'

'It's illegal.'

'Who says so?'

'My dad. He's a lawyer.'

'Is he heck.'

'Yes he is.'

'Well he ought to look after himself better.'

'What d'you mean?'

'Your Mum's in there.'

Raymond hoisted his thumb over his shoulder in the direction of Huskie's Photographic Studio.

'She's in there doing dicky-dicky with ever-so-nice-ski that long-faced foreigner feller.'

Peredur began to tremble and grow pale. Raymond was greatly impressed by the effect his clever words were having on the other boy. He lifted his arm and pointed at the shack.

'On top of a desk,' he said. 'I was just looking.'

Peredur opened his mouth and showed his teeth. The sound of strange snarl rattled in his throat. Before Raymond's arm came down a small bony fist had crashed into his soft nose. There were more blows before he moved away and opened his mouth to speak. When his mouth opened Peredur's knuckles split his plump lower lip and he began to bleed. He ran away towards the promenade clutching his hands to his mouth. Peredur ran after him, but he collapsed at the end of the sandy lane as if he had been tripped up by his own anger. Raymond moved his fingers from his mouth and when he saw the amount of blood on them he began to scream.

10

'Amy, you look marvellous! You look like a queen. You look more beautiful than ever. I mean that. I really do!'

Edna Thomas entered the private ward with her plump arms extended and her crocodile-skin handbag swinging from her wrist like a censer. Amy was sitting up in bed. Pale but composed, and prepared to see visitors. She smiled graciously at the doctor's wife.

'This is an excellent place,' she said. 'I'm so grateful to Wilson.'

'What else is a doctor good for?'

Edna laughed comfortably. She stood between Amy and the bright light pouring in from the rose garden. It had been raining, but now the sun was out and a pair of goldfinches accustomed to being fed by patients were perched boldly among the roses which were beginning to break into bud. They bent the slender branches so that raindrops spilt off the tilted leaves and then took to strutting importantly on the terrace allowing the feathers of their wings to drag along the floor like trailed coats. Amy shaded her eyes to see her visitor more clearly. She saw Edna's face flushed from a good lunch.

'It's an awful admission for a doctor's wife to make, but I can't bear illness. It catches my breath just here.'

Edna touched the expanse of skin between her modesty vest and her powdered throat.

'In people I like, I mean. It's as if I can't bear to suffer with those I see suffering.'

'Oh, I'm not suffering,' Amy said.

'Of course you're not. Not now. When Wilson told me it wasn't malignant I just jumped on my feet and cheered. Can you imagine it? Miss Williams thought I'd gone right out of my mind. Wilson said I was like a fool at a football match. Of course he admires you even more than I do. I get quite jealous. Look, I've brought you some perfume. It's nothing much. Just a little something . . .'

She extracted a small package from her handbag and settled it down carefully on its base on the bedside locker. With a loving smile she leaned over to give Amy a kiss on her pale cheek.

'Bless you, my love,' she said. 'God knows, I'm glad it's all over. I couldn't sleep you know, worrying about you. And Wilson was worried too, so that made me worse. You know what it's like? I wondered if he'd told me everything. I told him this morning, now you keep her in there, Wilson Thomas, and don't you let her out until she's had a proper rest. A proper convalescence.'

'I must go home tomorrow,' Amy said.

'Tomorrow!'

Edna was shocked and totally disapproving.

'Aren't they looking after you properly?'

'Oh yes. Everyone has been very kind.'

'I should think so too.'

Edna looked around as if she carried some authority in the nursing home. It was situated on the brow of a wooded hillside overlooking a wide estuary. Immediately below was a slate quarry, the terminus of a narrow gauge railway, and the streets that led down to a busy little market town.

'Treat it as a holiday,' Edna said. 'Let them come and see you here. The whole lot of them. Let them appreciate you a bit. You should you know. I can tell you, if it had been me, I'd have had them all here dancing attendance day and night.'

She laughed comfortably at her own notion and dragged a stool to the side of the bed.

'I didn't want the boys to know,' Amy said.

Edna snuggled close to the bedside and tapped the back of Amy's hand.

'Silly girl,' she said affectionately.

'I was frightened when I came in here,' Amy said.

'Of course you were. Who wouldn't be?'

'I felt as if I'd been caught,' Amy said. 'I saw myself like a young girl who was always rushing off, hoping to find something new and marvellous around every corner, and in the end just finding this.'

'A sort of nightmare was it?'

Edna was doing her best to be understanding.

'Oh no. The truth. I've had plenty of time to think since I've been in here.'

'Yes but you mustn't brood,' Edna said. 'That's not good for you.'

'I've never been good at thinking. That's been part of the trouble with John and me. He thinks too much and I think too little. He expects too little and I expect too much.'

'Oh you can go on like that for ever.'

Edna spoke with a fond impatience.

'I've always expected too much,' Amy said. 'That's been one of my great faults. I can't think why.'

'Don't you start blaming yourself,' Edna said. 'You know what I think. You've had an awful lot to put up with.'

'It's something to do with what's inside you. The world is only a reflection of what's inside you. That's what I think.'

'I don't quite follow, to be honest with you.'

Amy looked surprised at the admission her visitor had made. She tried again to speak in terms that Edna Thomas could more readily understand.

'When you're in a place like this your mind keeps on going back,' she said. 'You keep on going over things, trying to make some sense out of them. And that's the conclusion I came to. All my life I've been searching for the unattainable.'

Amy laughed and shook her head.

'What's the joke dear?'

Edna raised her eyebrows and opened her mouth, ready and willing to join in.

'To think I've had to wait until my fortieth year to find that out.'

Their conversation seemed to be getting too abstract for Edna's taste.

'You're not blaming yourself, are you?'

She sounded quite indignant. She sketched an oratorical gesture with her plump arms. She was longing to make a case for the defence and she was clearly warmed by their intimacy. She thrust her elbows deep into the side of the shallow mattress and was poised for an exchange of the closest confidences.

'I haven't made enough of an effort to understand him,' Amy said. 'I do feel guilty about that.'

'You shouldn't,' Edna said. 'You really shouldn't.'

'I've been going over things and I've tried hard to find out where we went wrong.'

'Well look at the way he's handled money, for example. . .'

Edna paused with her mouth open, seeking permission to carry the discussion further in that particular direction.

'He stood over there,' Amy said. 'The night of the op. There were just the two of us in here. Waiting. And we had absolutely nothing to say to each other. It was like a cliff-edge at the end of the world. He couldn't open his mouth. And I couldn't open mine. I was looking at him. Standing there in the twilight. Standing still and, as far as I was concerned then, turned into stone. A standing stone. I suppose I'd been drugged by then. When he moved it gave me a fright. He came towards the bed and I was ready to scream. Then he took a piece of paper out of his pocket and put it in my hand. I stared at it. It was a poem. I couldn't take it in at all. It was about a bird in a dark forest. Always about birds. I can remember thinking that. Always about birds and never about me. There were three lines in every verse and that's all I can remember. Every time I started to read the lines began to wave and dissolve in the air. I suppose the drug was beginning to take effect. I wanted to say something but I couldn't. He got tired of waiting I suppose. He came up and plucked the paper out of my hand, then the nurse came in.'

'You poor thing,' Edna said.

She took Amy's hand and squeezed it affectionately.

'How you must have suffered. All alone.'

'No. I didn't suffer. I just went numb. I'm glad it happened.'

'Glad?'

'It's taught me not to be so afraid. So I have learnt something after all. It's fear that makes us avoid things all the time. We shouldn't be so afraid.'

Edna made another effort to bring Amy into a more concrete frame of mind.

'To think over all these years,' she said, 'with the cost of living always rising apart from anything else, he's only once increased your housekeeping money. Only once!'

Amy looked at her friend as though she were listening to echoes of old controversies that had been made trivial by the passage of time, involving anyone except herself as she was at that moment exalted by fresh resolutions.

'I'm going to make an effort,' she said. 'From now on. Now that I've come through. Not just for the sake of the boys. Not just for his sake either. But for my own sake. Do you understand what I mean?'

'Amy,' Edna said.

She sounded intense and sincere.

'Amy. Is this wise?'

Amy's eyes widened to their fullest and most innocent extent.

'I don't mind being frank,' she said. 'I don't mind anything any more. I've been facing death. Not in reality as it has turned out, but, in my own mind and that is more real. I've been right up to the gates of death. Right up to the gates.'

Her smile and the things she was saying made Edna uneasy.

'You've had a very trying experience,' she said. 'It's very important that you have a long real rest and nothing to worry about.'

'I'm not worrying. I think I may well have experienced the most profound happiness of my life.'

'Happiness?'

'I know it will be a terrible effort. You can't just take the last sixteen or seventeen years and rub them out as if they had never been. That would be ridiculous. I've got to do two things really. Face the absolute truth. Nothing more or less. And that is terribly hard. And then put myself in John's place. And that's even harder.

But I'm going to try. I've made my mind up Edna. I'm going to try.'

'Well, I don't know . . .'

Edna did not conceal her dismay.

'What about the business of that boy? Ken Lazarus. You've got to think of yourself, you know.'

'Well what is that in the end? When all is said and done? The boy had lost his father. He had these musical gifts. John believed in him. And he wanted to give him his chance. He wanted to pay for his musical education. It's something which appealed to him as a poet. I can understand that. Why should I have any objection?'

Amy was stimulated by her own talk. She sat up in bed and her eyes shone with an anticipation of pleasure.

'Well, you know what I think,' Edna said.

'It would be wonderful really if we hadn't been so wrong for each other after all. It's no use wishing you are something other than what you are. You see, you have to accept that. I'm not trying to be somebody else. I was born Amy Parry and I'm still Amy Parry. I was an impulsive girl. I hated teaching in that school so much and I hated that headmaster even more. He gave me nightmares. He used to try and keep me after school and he was always pawing me. I would have done anything almost to escape from that smelly classroom. But it wasn't just that. I knew John was a poet. And he had principles. There was something so honourable about him. So what I've got to do, Edna, you see, is to trace back through the criss-cross of everything and pick up the right thread, very gently and very carefully, and draw it through the pattern of the years right up to the present day without breaking it. Do you see what I mean?'

Edna shook her head regretfully. She jumped when there was a sharp tap on the garden window. Outside stood a chubby-faced man with neat white hair in a green tartan dressing gown. He had tapped the window with the gold ring on his little finger. His skin seemed as soft as a woman's and even in his dressing gown there was something expensive about his appearance. He had a soft chuckle which Edna found immediately enticing.

'Princess,' he said to Amy. 'Pardon the intrusion. But will you be getting up this afternoon?'

Amy laughed at his excessively courteous manner.

'Ben,' she said. 'Stop being so silly and come in and meet Dr Thomas's wife. Edna my dear, this is Ben Marron. A fellow victim. He's terribly kind but you do have to watch out for his jokes.'

Edna was very pleased to meet the man who stepped in from the garden. He brought with him a promise of entertainment and an atmosphere of bustling charm and prosperity in which she could flourish. He was clearly a man of wealth determined to enjoy his convalescence in the Nursing Home.

'Watch out?' Mr Marron said. 'The one thing you have to watch out for here is Matron. Isn't that so, Princess?'

They enjoyed the joke as publicly as two people meeting at a party who half expect to be photographed for the social page of a magazine.

'A nursing home is a little world of its own,' Amy said to Edna. 'Quite enclosed. The victims tend to get together, you see. Fellow sufferers and all that.'

'Fellow prisoners you mean.'

Mr Marron settled down in the corner and crossed his legs elegantly. He wore slippers made from uncoloured leather and lined in white fur. His hands in the pockets of his dressing gown looked curiously idle.

'I'm not allowed to touch a drop am I, Princess, and the Matron watches me like a hawk.'

'And we all wonder why!'

393

He enjoyed the teasing. Edna moved her head first one way and then another, anxious to be put in the picture as quickly as possible. She looked astonished and even a little put out at discovering that patients in the Nursing Home could be enjoying themselves so much.

'She is jealous,' Amy said to Edna. 'We didn't realize it at first, did we?'

Mr Marron threw up his hands in self-protecting despair and then settled down to flicking his lower lip with his index finger while Amy went on talking. His easy manner made Edna smile happily. He had a way of treating people as if they were his friends of long standing from whom he had nothing to hide and to whom he would divulge even the most confidential information. He seemed an important man, and yet with absolutely nothing to hide.

'Ben has been giving me lessons on stocks and shares, haven't you Ben?'

'Indeed I have.'

He opened his hands towards them and it became an instant symbol of largesse.

'I'm allowed up for two hours in the afternoon,' Amy said. 'I don't know how it cropped up, but Ben found out how much I wanted to learn about the Stock Exchange. So we were sitting in the summer house, side by side on the bench. . . .'

'Don't laugh,' Mr Marron said. 'It was a first-class lesson. I'm taking you to the City as soon as we get out of here . . . "When we leave this bloody college" . . .'

In a light baritone he sang a line of college song with a totally inoffensive emphasis on the word bloody which gave Edna a sudden laughing fit that she had difficulty in controlling. He watched her, mildly amused by her reaction, pleased with having acquired an unexpected recruit to his appreciative audience.

'We were sitting there,' he said. 'Minding our own business . . .'

'The Princess here was making excellent progress . . .'

'When who should come upon us in our seclusion but the Matron herself!'

Army and Mr Marron chuckled together at the recollection. Amy held out a hand to indicate she felt it was her turn to speak.

'I never went to a boarding school,' she said. 'But I felt as if we'd been caught out of bounds or something. Didn't you, Ben?'

'Oh worse,' Mr Marron said. 'Much worse.'

'Ah well . . .'

Amy touched her hair modestly with her fingers.

'Here I was,' Mr Marron said. 'With the Nursing Home's most glamorous patient, sitting in the summer house. She didn't like it.'

Amy leaned over to touch Edna's shoulder ready with more detailed information.

'It's a joke you see among our gang . . . Oh dear, now I'll have to explain who the gang is . . .'

'I told you,' Mr Marron said. 'It's like a prisoner-of-war camp.'

'The Matron has taken a fancy to Ben. . .'

Mr Marron made a mock salute.

'Frau Obergruppenfuhrer!' he said.

Edna was allowing herself to be gradually but gratefully convulsed by the comedy that the two patients were outlining for her benefit.

'She is an old maid, you see,' Amy said. 'And Ben is an eligible widower . . .'

'Well, I wouldn't say that,' Mr Marron said, protesting gently. 'I have the most fearful temper! and a wide range of bad habits.'

'Oh dear,' Amy said. 'You shouldn't make me laugh so much. You really shouldn't. I've got a pain in my side . . .'

She turned to Edna to give her yet another explanation.

'We sit, you see, when we have tea together in such a way so that we can invent new bad habits for Ben and discuss them in the Matron's hearing . . . aren't we dreadful?'

She seemed suddenly smitten with conscience about their game.

'Oh, I don't know,' Mr Marron said.

He sounded wise and worldly.

'We've got to be light-hearted about these things. It's no use us all sitting around with long faces.'

He lengthened his own smooth and chubby features into a mask of despair and Edna gave a sudden nervous shout of laughter just as she saw her husband's face appear beyond the panes of glass in the upper half of the ward door.

The doctor looked distraught. In the bottle-green light his mouth opened and shut under the close clipped moustache like the mouth of a drowning man and the pupils of his eyes jerked about in his head. He was signalling to his wife to leave the ward. Edna was unable to understand. She frowned and pointed discreetly at herself. This made the doctor wave in an exasperated fashion. He seemed to cling on to his annoyance with her in order to delay his entry into the room. Amy spotted him and gave him a shy little wave.

'Here he is,' she said. 'My benefactor!'

Mr Marron jumped to his feet with a comic exaggeration of guilt. He dodged his head this way and that like a cornered schoolboy still looking for an avenue of escape. Edna gave him all her attention, anxious to postpone a direct encounter with her husband's exasperation. Mr Marron made motions with his fingers that indicated that he was afraid that Dr Wilson Thomas was being followed by the Matron and that she still lay in wait for him in the corridor.

'What's the matter?' Amy said. 'You don't look at all well.'

The doctor turned to look at Mr Marron, who had tip-toed towards the door to reassure himself that the Matron was not coming.

'Stop fooling about,' the doctor said.

The words were too crude an expression of what he intended to say and he stood rather guiltily in the middle of the floor, looking around his own legs as though longing for some form of protection. The impact on Mr Marron was immediate. He was transformed into the chairman of a board meeting, straightening himself up to repel an unexpected aggression from an insignificant member of the board. He took the lapels of his dressing gown with each hand and brought them closer, like robes of office, about his person.

'You're still on the sick-list,' Dr Wilson Thomas said. 'You shouldn't be running around anyway. Why don't you go back to your room. You should be lying down.'

'Wilson,' Edna said. 'There's no need to be so nasty.'

'You go and wait in the car,' he said.

He was relieved to be able to turn on someone like his own wife towards whom he felt no obligation to wish he had been more polite.

'Go on,' he said. 'I want to talk to Amy.'

'One day he'll be ill,' Edna said. 'And then he'll have to take a dose of his own medicine.'

She looked at Mr Marron who seemed to accept her words as at least a token apology. He noted the doctor's air of worried confusion and this reconciled him to being silent for the time being. He was capable of making a demonstration of strength but his sensibilities showed themselves fine enough to recognize that this was not the time or the place. In any case, whatever the defects of his physical condition his personality was more than strong enough to allow him to reserve his position while Amy observed his embarrassing predicament sympathetically from the piled up pillows.

'I'll see you later,' he said to Amy.

His tone was tender and graceful.

'Maybe we'll have a lesson this afternoon?'

Amy gave him a brief but understanding wave. He left the way he came, through the garden window, and the doctor made an impatient gesture with the letter in his hand to hasten his wife's departure. He walked after her to close the door and then moved across to peep out into the terrace and close the french window.

'What's the matter, Wilson,' Amy said. 'You look so worried.'

He breathed heavily. He tried to stand still at the side of the bed but was unable to do so.

'This is very painful for me.'

He began to speak and then pulled himself up as if he had suddenly realized that he was not entitled to draw on her sympathy.

'You are my patient.'

Once again the approach broke down.

'Tell me.'

Amy clenched her fists.

'Was it malignant after all?'

He looked surprised. His mouth was hanging open.

'No. You're perfectly all right. It's not you. It's Cilydd.'

He raised the envelope in his hand and lowered it again.

'I'm not an insensitive man . . .'

'What's the matter? What's happened?'

Amy was beginning to sound angry.

'He's dead. Drowned.'

The doctor grasped the rail at the foot of the bed. Amy seemed completely unable to take his words in.

'What are you talking about?' she said.

'He must have taken a train to Scarborough.'

'Scarborough?'

She spoke the place name as if her utterance had brought it into existence for the first time.

'He was going to Swansea, surely. He was coming back today. He had a case in Swansea. You know he had.'

She brushed the air with her fingers as though their misunderstanding were a film of cobweb between them. The doctor was shaking his head in a melancholy fashion.

'He was so sensitive,' he said. 'He was born with one skin less than anybody else.'

'What are you talking about?'

'We are going to have to do something about it. I don't want to upset you, Amy, and I don't want to sound callous, but we've got to act quickly and I've got to ask you to keep your head. Do you understand what I'm saying?'

He looked about for something to sit on and occupied the stool on which his wife had been sitting a short time ago.

'The police are making inquiries,' he said 'It's their duty. His body was found on the shore this morning, by a woman and two children who had gone out for a morning ride on the sands. Apparently they saw him from some distance. Washed up by the tide. Now, we've got to be practical about this. Did he say anything to you? Did he leave a note?'

She shook her head miserably and sank down further under the bedclothes.

'I want your permission to search his study. Is that all right?'

She nodded.

'I'm worried you see. I'm very worried. This places me in a very awkward position professionally. I want to spare you Amy. But I've got to tell you. He sent me this note. It looks like the manuscript of a poem. But it is a note. Look at it. You'd better read it.'

Amy held the scrap of notepaper in her cold fingers. Her eyes were too blurred with tears to read her husband's handwriting. Her lips opened and drew apart the saliva that was filling up her mouth.

'Do they mean anything to you?'

The doctor kept shifting his position on the stool. He seemed to be longing for action but uncertain what to do first.

'"*This is the age of iron*" . . .'

He read from the note as though the words were causing him irritation.

'"*I have seen the black sail . . . The son of purity will not come . . . the hero lies under a sea of glass . . .*" Does it mean anything to you? And look at this at the end. "*Never try to find me.*" The thing is, Amy, could this be interpreted as a suicide note?'

She had pushed herself down into the bed and buried her face in the base of the pillows.

'I could destroy it,' the doctor said. 'I expect I should destroy it. But I must have your consent. You can see what an awkward situation I'm in. Amy . . . Are you listening?'

Her head moved slightly and the pillow fell over it. Impatiently the doctor picked it up, glancing towards the door as he did so.

'If you feel unwell, say so,' he said. 'That could be a good thing. The police might insist on sending somebody here for a statement I'm going to put the screen up around this bed. Where is it? Have they taken it out? Amy. Will you listen please. I want to help you. I know it's overwhelming. But it's got to be faced. He's dead. There's got to be a coroner's court. In Scarborough. Do you want me to destroy this?'

He lifted her head gently and put the pillow under it.

'I'm sure you understand the risk I'm taking. The professional risk. We'll say no more about that now. It's for your sake I'm doing it, Amy. I want you to understand that. All I want you to do now is to say that you want me to destroy this note and the poem and anything else that would be used as evidence of suicide. Do you agree?'

His head was close over hers and his face flushed with the excitement of what he was doing. From time to time he took a glance at the glass panels of the door to make sure that no one was watching and that the Matron had not arrived with a police officer in attendance. Amy stared at the ceiling with a blank and hopeless expression on her face.

'You are not a child,' he said. 'I know this is terrible. But it's got to be faced. I don't want to be crude but I'm a doctor and I've got to face things. You weren't all that happy, were you? We're grown up. We're adults and we must face the world in a sensible way. This isn't the time to say it, but we've said it before. You weren't suited. Let's put it like that. Amy, I'm talking to you. Will you let me handle this? Will you leave everything to me?'

She closed her eyes and nodded her agreement.

'I'm taking my professional life in my hands. You realize that don't you? For your sake. But we can talk about that again.'

His glance shot up to the door just in time. The Matron stood there: a stern-looking woman with masculine features under her starched bonnet. Behind her stood an uneasy looking policeman. Dr Wilson Thomas marched purposefully to the door and closed it behind him.

'She's suffering from severe shock,' he said. 'Could you get the nurse in attendance to put a screen around the bed? I'm going to give her an injection.'

BOOK FIVE

1

At half past nine in the morning the sun burst through the thick sea mist. The great cliff at the north end of the promenade was revealed as if by the slow withdrawal of a white curtain, and the neatly painted curve of hotels and terraces facing the western sea shone like rows of polished shoes in the warm September sun. Bedwyr and Keith Evans sat in an observation window of one of the larger hotels. Bedwyr was reading a morning paper and Evans was looking nervously through a series of schedules in glossy transparent folders. Bedwyr dropped the newspapers and glanced at his wrist watch.

'He's a bastard,' he said.

He spoke very softly but Evans looked around with alarm, afraid that he might have been overheard. The lounge was almost empty. A Spanish waiter was passing through, taking the long way round back to the kitchens after the busy session of serving late breakfasts.

'We'll go through the motions,' Bedwyr said. 'But it won't be anything more than a waste of time.'

Evans looked worried and disappointed. He lifted the folders in his hands. He was immaculately dressed to look like an architect with exceptionally aesthetic antennae. His skin was lightly tanned after an August holiday and his eyebrows met easily as though any form of visual ugliness racked him with pain.

'What about all this work?' he said.

'You watch him,' Bedwyr said. 'Sitting next to the Chairman. Pretending to be humble and efficient like some sort of Uriah Heep in modern dress and thick goggles. Pretending to be impartial, feeding the old bumbler with the correct bumble, edging things along and all the time fully committed to the enemy. A bought man if there ever was one. A fixer fixed. Totally corrupt.'

'Well, what are we wasting our time for?'

Evans sounded hurt.

'All this work.'

'It's got to be done,' Bedwyr said. 'You've got to lose just so many times before you can win. Next time or the time after, it will be our turn.'

'How do you know?'

Evans was pale with irritation and distrust.

'J.M.,' Bedwyr said. 'He's got a finger on the pulse. There are changes coming. A new chairman. Two new members on the Council. Democracy works sometimes.'

'But what about . . .'

Evans refrained from uttering the name of the permanent official.

'Nobody goes on forever,' Bedwyr said. 'Even Stalin died. And he was the best there's ever been. Come on. Let's shake a leg. At least we can have some ozone. Now that's a word nobody uses any more. Ever heard of it?'

Evans shook his head, his mind evidently still coping with the view of their situation that Bedwyr had just given him. The sunlight had invaded the hotel foyer and illuminated the thick carpet which softened their footsteps. Outside in the breeze Evans put up his hands to preserve the neat way in which he had combed his hair. Bedwyr, his jacket open, crossed the road and once on the promenade thrust his hands into his trouser pockets. He looked happy to be outside and determined to make the best of the occasion. If any rival should be watching him it would appear as though he was treating the event as an excuse for a brief holiday by the sea, away from the cares of his thriving practice.

'Now cheer up,' he said to Evans, when he had crossed the road. 'And don't go about looking like the Hamlet of the Sirhowy Valley. It's bad for business. You should never look as though all occasions were informing against you. You've got a straight choice really. If you can't cope with people and the daily rub of human contact, you'd better go straight for the money. And that means Warren's way: hustle, computers, know-how, development and no messing about with fancy schemes and public works. If you're coming my way, exciting schemes and scope for fine buildings and social effort, you've got to learn to cope with people. Like a politician. And it is something you've got to learn. And you can't learn it over night. Or on a crash course in management techniques. And it's vitally important. Do you appreciate that?'

They stood still by the empty bandstand. Evans nodded, but looked resentful at the masterful way in which Bedwyr was treating him.

'Now when we go in to that meeting, we go in to win,' Bedwyr said. 'We'll have those designs of yours pinned up on the board so that the whole lot can see them. I'll do the opening flannel and I'll give you the biggest build up since the last presidential election. Then all you have to do is to talk lovingly and with authority about your designs. Not in too much detail for God's sake . . . But in bold outline. The kind of bold outline, the kind of simplification, popularization if you like, that can only be put across by the expert who is so confident of his mastery of the subject that he has no fear at all of being contradicted. You know what I mean?'

Bedwyr had both his hands out like a director in a theatre, sketching a subtle move to an actor reluctantly obliged to listen. The growing warmth of the sunlight

404

brought more people out. Old people hung about considering whether or not to settle in deckchairs and looking for the more sheltered spots to set them up. For some inexplicable reason a group of young women suddenly charged across the promenade and made for the edge of the sea.

'Speak as clearly as you can,' Bedwyr said. 'But don't rush it. And when the time comes for questions don't treat them as hostile. There will be at least three people there who will try to pull the whole thing to bits. Take your time over answering but don't try and score points. Always be rational and objective. And remember that you are the one will have to change if they demonstrate that you are not giving them what they want. They are the clients, after all. This is a scheme based on *their brief*. If they change the brief, then you are entitled to ask for time to change the scheme. And don't lose your cool. That's absolutely vital. Because some of them will be all out to needle you. And you needle easily, let's face it.'

Evans' face went a deep red under his tan. He became conscious of being observed by an elderly couple in deckchairs who took no trouble to conceal their curiosity. He turned to look at the sea. Bedwyr walked on, a certain swagger in his leisured stroll. This was the seaside after all and he was entitled to loiter with his jacket open and his toe-caps pointing boldly at ten to two. If there was any catching up to do, Evans could do it; but he would not make it any more difficult for him. There was something pleasingly majestic about having the time to move at such an unhurried pace and the sweep of the promenade was a curved area obsequiously laid out for his regal progress.

His interest was taken by a shabby figure approaching in the distance at a curious pace something between a limp and a trot. It was a tall thin figure wearing a long dirty mac tied around the middle with binder twine. It was too brisk a walk for a tramp. The man was bare-footed and around his neck was a thin clerical collar and black vest. He was losing his hair but fair curls still hung about his ears.

'Ken,' Bedwyr said.

He stood still with astonishment.

'Ken! Ken Lazarus!'

The bare-footed man hurried on, no more aware of Bedwyr than of anything else in his immediate environment. His mouth was shut tight, thin and shrunken with neglect rather than age and his long nose was blue with cold in spite of the sunshine. Bedwyr saw him sniff as he passed and dash away a dewdrop with the back of his hand. His startled blue eyes were fixed on a distant target which was infinitely small and could easily be lost by a turn of the head or a sudden distraction. Bedwyr stretched out an arm imploringly. Evans caught up with him.

'Who the devil's that?'

He sounded worried. The strange figure had gone by without taking any notice of either of them.

'The most brilliant chap in our school,' Bedwyr said. 'That's who he is. Always ahead of me. And an athlete too.'

He hesitated.

'I must talk to him,' he said. 'I just can't let him pass like a complete stranger.'

'You'd better hurry,' Evans said. 'He's going at a rate of knots.'

Bedwyr broke into a run. A cluster of people standing behind a short row of deckchairs watched him like spectators at the end of a race. Bedwyr ran as stylishly as he could but by the time he was able to touch Ken's elbow he was out of breath and unable to speak. Ken backed away from him like a frightened animal.

'Ken. . .'

Bedwyr managed to gasp his name and smile.

'Do I look as old as all that?'

With the palm of his hand he shadowed the area of baldness on top of his head.

'Bedwyr.'

At last Ken recognized him. Bedwyr held out his hand and Ken took it in his own which was calloused and horny with manual labour. Bedwyr grabbed Ken's forearm and squeezed it delightedly.

'You are as thin as a bloody rake,' he said. 'When did you last eat?'

He felt Ken's shoulder and Ken suffered the examination with mute patience, keeping his eyes on Bedwyr's face as though a long stare would make everything clear to him.

'Well come on,' Bedwyr said. 'What are you doing? Where are you living?'

Determined to be tactful he averted his gaze from Ken's bare feet and smiled at his old friend with concentrated sweetness.

'I manage,' Ken said.

Bedwyr brushed aside the defensive phrase with a sort of friendly ruthlessness.

'I'm sure of that,' he said.

'I don't get asked to preach. They object to my bare feet I think. But I can get six shillings an hour on the farms. I have to wear wellingtons then of course. Depends what I'm doing really. Footwear is a symbol of false divinity.'

'Where do you live?'

'I've got a caravan. In the trees.'

He pointed towards the country beyond the great hill at the end of the promenade.

'It's a good position. Near a stream.'

'What about your music?'

Bedwyr looked concerned but Ken smiled shyly, showing that some of his teeth were missing and had not been replaced by dentures.

'I don't need it,' he said. 'I need very little.'

Evans joined them. He stood behind Bedwyr with his hands in his pockets, curious to overhear their conversation but not anxious to be linked too closely with them. His presence disturbed Ken.

'I'd better be going,' he said.

'Going? You can't just march off!'

Bedwyr turned to introduce his companion.

'This is my colleague, Keith Evans. We're here on business. This is Ken Lazarus, Keith. One of my oldest friends. And one of the most brilliant minds you will ever be likely to meet. And that's not just my private opinion. What's the matter?'

Ken Lazarus was putting a distance between himself and the two men.

'He doesn't want to meet me,' he said. 'I'm just a fool. He doesn't want to have anything to do with me.'

'Keith?'

Bedwyr was astonished. Evans pulled both his hands out of his pockets as if to show there was no weapon concealed in either.

'He doesn't like me,' Ken said. 'Why should he? I'm not entitled to expect anybody to like me. I want to go now.'

His blue eyes stared unwaveringly at Bedwyr who was struggling with annoyance and embarrassment.

'Go? Where are you going?'

'I don't have to tell you.'

'Of course you don't.'

Bedwyr struggled to be reasonable.

'I want to talk to you that's all. Let me walk with you.'

Ken's gaze moved from Bedwyr's face to study his well-made suit in detail, the texture of the material, the number of buttons at the cuff, the cut, the stitching, the width of the trousers and the way they covered the polished dark tan of his shoes. There was nothing envious in the way he examined Bedwyr's appearance, only an objective admiration. In the end he smiled shyly at Bedwyr, who seized upon this brief recognition of friendship of their childhood and youth.

'I don't know where you are going,' he said. 'But I'm coming with you.'

'Now?'

'Well, I don't want to lose you, do I? Not after all these years.'

Ken seemed eager to withdraw again. His thin body shrunk inside the long mackintosh. Evans looked at his wrist watch and this instantly made Ken step backwards.

'I was just thinking,' Evans said, trying to be helpful. 'There's at least three quarters of an hour until we are due to be called in. If you like I'll go back to the hotel and wait. I'd like to do some more preparation.'

Ken raised his right hand and waved it negatively.

'Why should I interrupt a fruitful communication,' he said. 'I never intended to intrude. This isn't the path I usually take . . .'

'Now you wait,' Bedwyr said determinedly.

He turned briefly to Evans.

'That's fine Keith. Take it that you are in charge. It will be good experience for you. There should be two of us. But if I don't get back on the dot, say I've been delayed by personal family matters.'

When his head moved again he found Ken had moved further away.

'I'm coming with you,' he said. 'But don't walk too fast. Remember I lead a very unhealthy life.'

He stood still to pat his stomach tenderly and then looked up with a grin that he evidently hoped his old friend would recognize. As they walked on, Ken looked down from time to time to check that they were in step and making an effort not to plunge on ahead.

'What was wrong with Evans?'

Bedwyr seemed to select at random one out of a flock of questions that floated about in his excited mind like birds on the brink of migration.

'Wrong?'

Ken had a way of pronouncing a word as if it were some rare specimen picked up among the pebbles on the beach that needed careful examination. Without any warning he accelerated to cross the road and trotted down a pedestrian passage which linked the promenade with a street that ran parallel with it behind the imposing houses and hotels on the front.

'He didn't like me. There's nothing wrong about that.'

'He's an ambitious little chap,' Bedwyr said. 'Proper little office pace-setter. He has to be handled pretty carefully.'

Ken stole a surreptitious glance at Bedwyr.

'Where are we going?'

'It's not far,' Ken said defensively.

Ken's pace increased and Bedwyr was obliged to hurry and keep up with him. They were passing a long row of boarding houses and small private hotels. As they turned into a rear lane a Scotch terrier barked furiously at Ken, jumping up against the heavy garden rails, and this made him move at a greater speed than ever. Near a stock of wooden crates in the lane Ken halted suddenly.

'Wait for me here,' he said. 'I shan't be a minute.'

Rather unwillingly, Bedwyr began to pace up and down the lane, while Ken padded in his bare feet to the kitchen door, which was wide open. Out of his mackintosh pocket he extracted a blue plastic bag. He did not knock the door. He coughed and cleared his throat, repeating the operation after a respectful interval and shuffling from the left to the right of the door. A young girl in a housecoat with a great blonde hair-do appeared in the corridor, nodded quickly and hurried to the kitchen to pick up a parcel of stale food which she brought out to Ken. Her manner was patronizing and confident. Ken opened his plastic bag and held it out.

'Mrs H. has gone to Cardigan,' she said. 'But this is what you wanted, isn't it?'

The girl pushed the food into the bag.

'Did she leave any message?'

Ken's voice was cracked and hoarse. He spoke like a man emerged from a month of silence, unpractised in ordinary talking.

'She didn't say anything,' the girl said. 'But she got it ready for you. Never forgets that, does she? She forgets my wages on a Friday often enough but I've never seen her forget this.'

Ken mumbled his thanks nervously and hurried back to join Bedwyr who by now had set the questions in his mind in order.

'It's fantastic meeting you like this,' Bedwyr said. 'I can't tell you how pleased I am. It's something I've wanted for so long. Do you know what I mean . . .'

Ken was staring at his face as if he were straining to hear a second voice that could be dimly heard behind the sound barrier of the words being uttered.

'So many things have happened,' Bedwyr said. 'Have you seen Clem? Do you ever see him?'

Ken shook his head.

'There's something about the friends of your childhood and youth,' Bedwyr said.

He waved his hand in the air, trying to snatch down some lyrical inspiration to express the way he felt.

'To see them again gives you a sense of wonder like the repetition of the seasons. Do you know what I mean?'

Ken looked doubtful.

'Think of old Clem,' Bedwyr said. 'There he is out in Wanstead somewhere, teaching generation after generation of little Wansteaders. Every year he comes

411

to see me. On his motorbike usually. He turns up at the most unusual times and I'm always delighted to see him. A little older, but just the same. Bouncing about like a living proof of something, but I never quite know what. Do you know what I mean? Am I moving, I say to myself, or is he standing still? Does the earth turn at equal speed for both of us? You know I've got three children?'

Ken opened his mouth to show surprise.

'Why don't you come and see us?' Bedwyr said. 'Come and stay with us. You've never seen Sian have you? She's a marvellous girl.'

Bedwyr searched for an aspect of his wife's character that would commend itself to his old friend as he found him standing patiently in the back lane holding a blue plastic bag full of stale food.

'She's religious,' Bedwyr said. 'I tease her about it.'

He smiled to demonstrate sympathetic detachment and loving objectivity.

'I know it's simple-minded of me but I always want people I like to get on with each other. I know you two would. Sian needs to talk to somebody like you, Ken, married to a lump of old materialist like me. She's always having cosmic thoughts that I never seem to appreciate properly. Now come on. Tell me why you came here. What's so special about a place like Aber?'

Ken considered the question carefully before making any reply.

'I must be within walking distance of the sea,' he said. 'But I like to be in the trees too. Specially oak trees. And near a river. It's got everything I need.'

'A simple life, eh?'

Ken smiled absently. He seemed to want to go back now to his retreat.

'Alone?'

'Yes.'

Bedwyr shook his head, mystified.

'I can't understand that,' he said. 'It's not that I'm afraid of solitude. I quite like it. I'm not all that sociable, as Sian would tell you. You remember how I used to be? A bit like my old man. A bit of a loner. It's the work I'd miss. I love work you know. I'm a bit ashamed to admit it, to tell you the truth. It's a drug with me. It really is. I get uneasy after a bit, if I'm not working. I can't live without it. Do you know what I mean?'

Ken had turned away. He was no longer staring at Bedwyr's face. He stood waiting patiently for him to finish talking. Bedwyr made a greater effort to engage his interest.

'You've given it up,' he said. 'Working I mean. I don't blame you, boy. I often think there must be something better to do in this life than staying in the office day in, day out and half the night. Tell me what it is, Ken? I'd like to know.'

He spoke politely, a friend asking for a piece of information as in former times he might have asked to borrow a football jersey or for the use of a bicycle. It was little to ask: something that could pass so easily between friends. Ken considered how to answer.

'I listen,' he said.

Bedwyr thrust forward his right foot and nodded to show that he accepted the statement and was waiting for further elaboration. But nothing came.

'Listen to what?' he said at last. 'Listen musically? Is that what you mean?'

Ken frowned and stared at the green mould at the base of the stone wall separating the lane from the rear of the premises. Bedwyr became jovial.

'Listening to sounds coming in from Outer Space,' he said. 'Quasars. News from nowhere. Come on. Tell me. I want to know.'

'It's not for me to tell you.'

'What do you mean by that? Am I beyond the pale or something? A stinking atheist. A spiritual fascist beast.'

Ken smiled to show he too remembered echoes of their adolescent conversations.

'You are a good man,' he said.

'Thanks very much.'

'You always had the will to do good,' Ken said.

'Never mind about me,' Bedwyr said. 'What about you. You are at it in the woods there casting spells. You've got a cave with a great big laboratory. You are working on the secrets of the universe. And my curiosity is killing me. Come on. Tell me about it.'

'I can't.'

'Why not?'

Bedwyr sounded petulant. He could have been a boy arguing stubbornly in the back lane about a needle sharp point of childish triviality in the long afternoon between being called in to meals.

'You are meant to be active,' Ken said. 'You will do much good.'

'Thank you very much.'

'That is not what you mean.'

Ken's face was long and doleful.

'What do I mean then?' Bedwyr said. 'You tell me.'

'You may have to wait a long time.'

'Wait for what?'

Ken stretched the toes of his bare feet, but did not hesitate to be frank.

'Perhaps when something terrible happens. A cry will escape from your heart.'

'Oh Crikey . . .'

No sooner had the frivolous comment been made than Bedwyr showed he regretted it. Ken began to walk away and he followed him, apologizing.

'Ignore it,' he said. 'It was just a nervous reaction. I didn't mean to be stupid or spiteful. I can't stand people who think everything is a giggle. Ken, I'm not one of those . . . don't take offence . . . for God's sake . . .'

Ken stopped and smiled at him.

'I don't,' he said. 'But we can't use words to talk. Not any more. Words are shadows and smoke.'

Bedwyr pointed at the plastic bag.

'Come and have a decent meal. Somewhere quiet. You need filling up.'

Ken shook his head.

'I must go,' he said.

'You want to leave me,' Bedwyr said. 'Just like that.'

Ken smiled again, too innocent to bother to conceal his intentions.

'Where can I find you?'

Bedwyr was distressed and dissatisfied.

'This is all wrong, you know. I was so overjoyed to find you. It seemed a marvellous thing . . . and yet we are making no contact at all. It makes me miserable. When I think of the old days . . . Doesn't it make you miserable?'

'No.'

Ken's missing teeth seemed to neutralize his smile. Brushing aside the traces of resentment with a little wave of his hand in front of his eyes, Bedwyr came closer to his old friend in order to let his hand rest lightly on his arm. He was a boy again, consciously overlooking the fact that his companion is breaking the rules of the game in order to keep the game going.

'When shall I see you again?' he said. 'Tell me where you live.'

'I don't think you need me,' Ken said. 'If you do, you'll find me easily enough.'

Before Bedwyr could offer his hand, Ken touched his arm and then hurried on his way.

2

Bedwyr sat with Evans at a corner table in the dining room. It was laid out in antique style on two levels and constructed from two rooms at the back of the old coaching inn. He frowned critically at the exposed rafters.

'I vowed I'd never come to this place again,' he said. 'I stopped here with Sian and the children last summer on our way to North Wales. We were still hungry when we went out. You've no idea. They served us with slices of melon as thin as this serviette with half a cherry on top. Half a cherry!'

'It's convenient,' Evans said.

He was making an effort to be at his ease.

'A sort of halfway house.'

'And the service was appalling,' Bedwyr said. 'It's no joke when the kids are starving and they can smell the food on other people's plates. I'm afraid I had to give them a piece of my mind. I don't like making a fuss but if you let things pass, it gets worse. Other people come along and they have to suffer.'

'It seems a lot better this time,' Evans said.

He trod warily, anxious to be more friendly without losing his cherished independence. Bedwyr pushed his soup plate aside and placed his elbows on the table.

'I can't get over it,' he said.

'I was pretty surprised myself,' Evans said.

His chest expanded with modest pride.

'We've broken new ground,' he said. 'It's quite an achievement. Do you think I could order a bottle?'

Bedwyr smiled and said

'You deserve it. You've done very well. I'll just take a glass. Drink an' driv'.'

He pronounced the last phrase as one word with a comic Welsh accent and they both laughed as though he had freshened up an old joke.

'I'm very glad you didn't lead me to expect too much,' Evans said. 'I think it put me on my mettle.'

Bedwyr acknowledged the tribute with a friendly nod. With a controlled excitement that would engender a detailed but shrewd commentary on the event, Evans was prepared to go over the interview with the council step by step. These words would be the solution that would fix the portrait of his triumph in his memory. And the portrait would be easier to reproduce than a continuous painstaking excavation of the original events.

'Did you see him afterwards?'

Evans chuckled happily.

'He didn't say anything but you could tell he was absolutely livid.'

'I can't get over it,' Bedwyr said.

Evans looked surprised.

'You've no idea what he was like,' Bedwyr said. 'I can't begin to tell you. He was handsome, you know. Like a young Adonis. A bit thin in the face but he had this wonderful head of golden hair. And he was so clever and talented. The most brilliant boy in school. We all thought he'd be a great composer. I was a bit in awe of him to tell you the truth. He was more at home with older people, like my father. He set some of my father's poems to music. We were no end impressed.'

Bedwyr fixed his gaze on Evans who did his best to show an intelligent interest. Without moving his head Evans raised his hand to attract the waitress's attention. While Bedwyr continued to speak he asked in a hushed voice for the wine list.

'It's the most unbelievable story really,' Bedwyr said. 'We were very close in a way. The three of us. Ken, Clem, and I. Clem was an orphan brought up by a

417

pair of aunts who lived in our terrace and Ken lost his father in the year we were sitting our School Certs. A sergeant in the police force. Nice old boy. A bit old to be Ken's father. Old-fashioned anyway. He died when he was fifty-three and Ken must have been fourteen or fifteen at the time. Two of them without father. So as usual I felt responsible being the only one *with* a father. I'm not boring you?'

Evans hastily denied the allegation. Two waitresses served them with food. A third brought the wine which Evans obediently sampled. Bedwyr continued to brood over the past.

'I can't tell you the shock I had, seeing him this morning,' he said.

'Is he mad?'

Evans asked the question with casual politeness.

'Good lord no. I wouldn't say he was mad. But he's had a terrible life. I feel so guilty. I should have done something for him. I offered to take him for a meal, but he refused. Imagine it, he's living off the scraps from one of those crumbly so-called private hotels behind the promenade. I can't get over it.'

'He smelt a bit,' Evans said.

He recorded an objective fact, trying not to appear too fastidious.

'Did he? I didn't notice.'

They ate for a while. Evans registered his approval of the food and Bedwyr nodded. But he could not leave the subject of his old friend for long. He persisted in thinking aloud, unable to eat and anxious to bring his reaction to the encounter under some control. He spoke calmly enough, as though he were discussing an office problem with his colleague.

'It's one of those things you can ponder for hours on end and never begin to understand: is it something he brought on himself, or did the circumstances of his life land him in just this one single unavoidable situation?'

Bedwyr was stirred by his own question. He gave Evans a brief opportunity to provide some kind of an answer. Evans looked at the food on his plate and waited for the pause to pass.

'Consider his history,' Bedwyr said. 'Quite extraordinary. He was one of those rare chaps who could have done anything. He was a fine musician. He was first class at maths. He was interested in politics. He was a Marxist in form six. A Marxism all of his own too. Analytical Marxism he called it. He chose to go to Cambridge to read History. He could have gone anywhere. And then something happened. I never really discovered what. My father died about that time and I had troubles of my own. We just heard that he had got married in his final year. The daughter of a pub on the outskirts of Cambridge. He'd got tangled up with her in some way and felt obliged or duty bound to marry her. As I say, I only heard all this at second-hand. Anyway it was a complete disaster. He was doing research on the Fifth Monarchy and people said the stuff went to his head. It all became too real. I remember Clem telling me this. They went for a walk one day in the autumn outside Clare and Ken began to talk about Cromwell and George Fox and Vavasor Powell as if they were still alive. He was quite frightened. Ken didn't get a fellowship and he ended up teaching in a school in Birkenhead. And that was another disaster.'

'Accident prone.'

With his mouth full Evans murmured his subdued humorous comment. Bedwyr looked at him almost threateningly.

'What did you say?'

'I just said "accident-prone". It's the second time you've mentioned disaster.'

'"Disaster"? Is that what you mean by accident-prone? Do you think they amount to the same thing? Is that what you think?'

'I didn't mean anything really,' Evans said. 'It was just something that came to my head. Have some "drink and driv". It's quite "drink an' drivable", isn't it?'

Bedwyr watched the white wine pouring into his glass. His mind was still on Ken.

'You can analyse these things until you're blue in the face,' he said. 'I often do. A fat lot of good it does you.'

'My grandmother used to say that thinking was bad for you.

Eased by the wine, Evans was prepared with the slightest encouragement to embark on some aspect of his own family background. Given the initiative he would uncover a more intimate detail of domestic history than he had ever revealed to Bedwyr before as a prelude to returning to the main theme of the day, their triumph in the council chamber and the unaccountable discomfiture of the permanent official who took his defeat so badly.

'Clem saw his wife. I never saw her. She was an uneducated woman: quite unexceptional according to Clem. Very ordinary. Inclined to whine a little. But she managed to destroy him.'

Emboldened by the wine Evans lifted his eyebrows in mock alarm. Bedwyr accepted his unconcealed lack of concern as an added qualification. It would enable him to listen objectively to events in which he was not emotionally involved and his cool considered judgement would help Bedwyr to put them into a perspective where he could incorporate them into his own reasoned scheme of things.

'Clem visited the school. He ferreted out the full story. He was pretty steamed-up at the time and I imagine he went there breathing fire and slaughter. He's a keen Union man, Clem. The wife had managed to win the ear of the headmaster's wife. They were women from very similar backgrounds. And this woman had her husband well under her thumb. Ken's wife made allegations about Ken's sexual deficiencies. She said he wouldn't sleep with her. Complained I suppose that she was being deprived of her conjugal rights. Now this seeped into the staff-room and as far as Clem could find out the headmaster encouraged a whispering campaign against poor old Ken. He was accused of communism, pacifism, homosexuality, religious mania, the lot. Ken never put a foot wrong. He never complained and he carried out his duties to the letter. Probably the most conscientious teacher in the place. He would sit on a bench by the wall throughout the lunch hour marking books while the rest were playing bridge, chess, table-tennis and reading the *Daily Express*. And the final result was he was sent to Coventry both for being too good and too bad. In other words beyond the pale. Not a single member of the staff, not even the headmaster's secretary, spoke to him for a whole year. He stuck it for a year and then his wife left him and took their only child with her. He thought the world of the kid.'

Evans divided his attention delicately between an unsatisfactory area of gristle in the slice of meat on the side of his plate and Bedwyr's melancholy stare that never moved to watch what he was doing.

'Ken went to a theological college in the North of England. He seems to have been fairly happy there. At least, he was until his wife took the little boy on holiday to one of those massive Butlin-type holiday camps. Somehow she neglected him and one afternoon he was drowned in the bathing-pool. Trodden to death under water. And then of course poor Ken had a nervous breakdown.'

'My God,' Evans said. 'A chapter of horrors.'

'You'd call it that, would you?'

Bedwyr seized on Evans's reaction.

'I should say so. Wouldn't you?'

'I don't think he would.'

Bedwyr was puzzled by his own proposition.

'I honestly don't. It's amazing, isn't it?'

'What is he then?' Evans said. 'Some kind of mystic or something?'

'He didn't want me to see where he lived,' Bedwyr said. 'He didn't want me at all really.'

'He might have been ashamed,' Evans said. 'People like that can live in filth can't they and not notice. But if someone else comes along they start to notice it.'

'Detached from the world,' Bedwyr said. 'I can understand that. That's not what disturbs me.'

He stared at Evans.

'There's no point in running away from these things,' he said. 'I believe in facing the truth and putting it into words. He didn't want my friendship. He just had no use for it.'

Evans looked a little embarrassed, but Bedwyr would not break off his long masterful stare.

'I've always attached the greatest importance to friendship,' he said. 'A friend is a man you can trust. A man who is loyal. Without trust, you have distrust. Without loyalty, disloyalty. And another word for disloyalty is treachery. And that's one of the worst sins of the lot.'

Evans leaned back in his chair, pale and resentful, as though Bedwyr were making a series of accusations against his own behaviour.

'Treachery,' Bedwyr said. 'It sounds awful and it is awful.'

'You're not getting at me are you by any chance?'

Evans folded his arms and tried to stop his voice from trembling.

'He seems to be above it all,' Bedwyr said. 'Completely detached. He doesn't need these things any more. These things we take to be so important. Nothing has become Everything and Everything has become Nothing. Do you know what I mean?'

'Not really,' Evans said.

Bedwyr had not even noticed that he had taken offence at his remarks about treachery. He was too absorbed in his quasi-philosophical musing to give him the minimum of decent, polite attention. Evans was no longer inclined to make the effort to steer their conversation back to his recollections of their victorious interview. He had been denied the pleasure of recording his impressions of his triumph: deprived of the harmless pleasure of setting it out in a pleasing pattern of words. It would be one more item on the debit account he was probably keeping of his personal relations with the firm. The noise of cutlery on plates was a more soothing sound than jagged fragments of uninspired conversation. The remainder of the meal was finished in silence.

3

The gates of Brangor Hall were closed. Gwydion sat at the wheel of the battered Land Rover and pressed his chin on his knuckles as he considered the wrought-iron gates that barred his way. The panatella in his mouth had gone out and he jutted out his jaw until the butt of the cigar touched the end of his nose. On either side of the gate two small lodges built of imposing blocks of stone stood ornamental guard over the entrance. A high park wall protected the interior from the road along which he had driven. Overgrown fuchsia bushes, concealing the side windows of the twin lodges, were still conspicuously in flower. Gwydion threw away the cigar butt and then blew a decisive blast on the horn.

The Land Rover carried a set of wooden tripods for a film camera and a heavy box of lenses and filters. Even when the vehicles was stationary they shook about in the vibrations from the worn engine. Gwydion was about to blow his horn a second time when a man appeared on the inside of the gates. He was in his shirt sleeves – it was a warm day – wearing a waistcoat that was too big for his spare figure: a heavy watch and chain weighed down the front and bunched the panels of grey material together. His face was small and foxy with a moustache covering his mouth. He was frowning at the Land Rover with open disapproval and did not appear to have any intention of letting it in. Gwydion leaned out over the loose door which rattled as he shouted.

'It's all right, Barr,' he said. 'It's me. You can open up.'

Barr still hesitated. He came closer to the gates, chewing and mumbling to himself. He was chewing tobacco and the brown stain made his moustache more youthful. He was much older than appeared at first sight.

'Come on, Barr,' Gwydion said. 'Open up them pearly gates!'

Barr lifted his hand at last as a sign of recognition and guarded pleasure. With wide steps, and yet dragging his feet so much the heavy end of his waistcoat dangled far from his stomach, he slowly opened the gates. Gwydion edged the Land Rover forward a few feet until he was close enough to talk to the lodgekeeper without raising his voice to a shout. The man's hair was cut short. It was still springy and residually ginger, much stronger and more youthful than the rest of his aged body. Gwydion ran his finger over the breast pocket of his shirt.

'Where are your medals?' he said.

Indeed he could have been a man grown old and small and thin on lonely sentry duty.

'People forget, you know.'

His fingers tightened irritably around a wrought iron rail of the gate.

'And I can tell you why too. Because they don't want to remember.'

His accent was a twangy cockney and his attitude was stoic. His chest was bad and it heaved as he claimed the right to be humoured with a little conversation.

'Boer War,' Gwydion said, with a wink.

'Steady on.'

Barr wasn't altogether willing to take the joke.

'How old do you think I am then? Go on. Have a guess.'

'Thirty-nine.'

'No. Be serious. How much?'

'Sixty-four. A year from your pension.'

It was what Barr wanted to hear.

'I'm seventy-seven.'

He spoke triumphantly.

'I was right through the First World War. Came out without a scratch. Just a touch of gas that's all. I'm as fit as a fiddle on a day like this. I told you, didn't I, how Lord Brangor found me working behind the bar in the Constitution Club? Nice little bar it was too. All spit and polish. Billy Barr's bar the members used to call it. I was very popular.'

'Father!'

A woman with protruding teeth and fuzzy hair thrust her head out of the parlour window of the lodge opposite. Barr ignored her call.

'You've heard what she's up to, haven't you? Your mother I mean. It's getting worse up there you know. Since Mister Hubert passed on. Nothing but bloody women. Salter's gone, of course. You heard that?'

'Father! Father!'

His daughter emerged from the lodge, her fat white legs bare and moving at speed to show how busy she was.

'Here she comes. The toast of the bloody regiment.'

His daughter's teeth shone in the sunlight but there was a heavy frown on her face.

'You'd better go in at once father,' she said. 'You can't stand out here in your shirt sleeves in all this unnatural weather.'

'Daughter of Eve,' Barr said.

His tone was contemptuously friendly and he spat tobacco juice on to the gravel.

'Oh Mister Gwydion,' his daughter said. 'I had no idea it was you. Her ladyship will be ever so pleased to see you.'

'D'you think so?'

'Oh I'm sure she will. We all need our nearest and dearest in times of trouble and sad bereavement. Go in now father, will you.'

'Daughter of Jezebel,' Barr said. 'She-Serpent of Satan.'

She bent her plump arm to pat her fuzzy hair, turning her head slightly as if she half expected Gwydion to admire its strength and luxuriance.

'Oh dear,' she said. 'He keeps this up all day sometimes. It can be very trying. Now go in, Father, will you now. How many times do you have to be told.'

'I've got to close these gates,' he said.

'I'll do that,' his daughter said.

'What did I tell you?'

He turned to protest to Gwydion.

'Bloody women doing everything.'

'You must go right indoors or you'll catch something, surely to God.'

'It's my job and don't you blaspheme in my hearing.'

As the Land Rover drove on Gwydion could see in the driving mirror the lodgekeeper and his daughter

426

struggling jealously over the right to close the gates. Seen in silhouette the trees on the south side of the drive appeared to be enjoying a pseudo-spring: needles of sunlight pricked holes in shrivelling leaves and above the engine roar of the Land Rover a robin was singing. Gwydion slowed down and leaned out over the rattling door to feel the air on his face. The road was narrow but the surface was good. It began to wind its way through an uneven landscape. The strong sunlight dispelled the lingering ground mist among the beech trees and picked out the shrubs still in flower closest to the carriageway. It shone on the bare rock where it had been blasted to make the road and showed up the subtle colours and the broken strata. Near a small quarry filled with brambles Gwydion slowed almost to a stop, as if he were tempted to get out and pick the fat blackberries that had been left to glisten invitingly in the sun.

A steeper ascent obliged him to accelerate. The road curved sharply to avoid an outcrop of rock, and then suddenly Gwydion was compelled to slam on the brakes. They were not as efficient as they should have been and the Land Rover came to a grinding stop within six yards of the soles of a woman's feet. The equipment in the back lurched forward noisily. Milly was sitting in the middle of the road with her short legs wide apart and between them a large square basket filled with loaves of bread. She was in the act of breaking a loaf into small pieces and as she lifted her head to stare sulkily at the car which had suddenly intruded into her line of vision her fingers sank out of sight into the sides of the loaf. Her face was smooth and swollen and her small eyes were red. There were a few crumbs still stuck to her face and it was possible that she had just been washing her countenance with bread crumbs. There was fresh soil on her pleated skirt and, because her legs were so short and tapering towards the buckles on her shoes,

427

her woollen stockings were coming down. A length of
red ribbon was tied into a bow in her straight hair. She
continued to stare at the Land Rover with indifference
more than hostility, pushing a piece of white bread into
her mouth and starting to chew.

'Milly! You can't sit there in the middle of the road.
Cars come along here. It's very dangerous.'

She screwed up her eyes against the bright light
above the trees and began to break up another loaf of
bread. She showed no inclination to move or to speak.

'Now come on Milly, love. I can't pass until you move
can I?'

Gwydion switched off the engine. He pushed the
gear lever into a forward gear and pulled hard at
the handbrake. He jumped down and then stood
still for a moment to enjoy the clear air which was
fresh and yet fragrant with the ripeness of the season. Somewhere in the distance a fire of old leaves
and dead wood was burning and yet on a bush of
buddleia near the road butterflies in great numbers
were exploring the white blooms. Gwydion walked towards the trees as though the charm of the season was
casting a spell over him and drawing him away from
his purpose. He sighed deeply and turned to look at
Milly.

'Come on, old girl,' he said. 'Move.'

Milly shifted about on her buttocks and gave a sly
grin.

'Not so much of the "old girl",' she said. 'I'm not your
old girl, am I?'

Her voice was a blurred croak but Gwydion understood perfectly what she was saying. He laughed and
she moved her lower jaw clearly delighted with the notice she was getting.

'Let me put the basket in the Land Rover,' Gwydion
said. 'I'll give you a ride back to the Hall. How about
that?'

'I haven't finished,' Milly said. 'I've got all this to do yet.'

Gwydion walked up to her.

'Let me take it,' he said.

Milly leaned forward and spread her short arms over the handle of the basket. Her voice sank to a soft mumble.

'I want to finish,' she said. 'Don't you touch.'

Her head hung over the basket. Gwydion moved away as if to consider what to do next. He stood with his back to her, looking into the bushes. Milly looked at him and nodded her head towards the shrubbery.

'He's under there,' she said.

Gwydion turned to look at her. Her face was lifted and her mouth was open.

'That's where I found him,' she said.

She was a little nervous, uncertain whether or not to trust Gwydion but too full of pride in the part she had played not to speak.

'Mr Hubert,' she said. On his face in the nettles and the flowers. Gwydion approached her again and knelt down beside her.

'It must have been a shock for you,' he said.

Milly looked down shyly. She swung her head a little to catch a glimpse of Gwydion's knees and then she returned her attention to the monotonous but comforting work of breaking up the bread.

'What about my mother?' Gwydion said. 'Has she got over it?'

Milly lowered her head and examined the surface of the drive very closely.

'He's under there,' she said. 'Like buried treasure.'

She looked at Gwydion's face, waiting for him to agree with her.

'Who told you that?'

'He'll be coming back one day.'

Gwydion held himself back, steady and smiling.

429

'That's what we're waiting for. We're got to be patient. That's all.'

Gwydion looked at the load of stale bread which crammed the basket.

'What are you going to do with it all? For the dogs is it?'

'And the birds. They all come to me for bread you know. It's my job you see. It's a lot of work but I don't mind doing it.'

'Milly . . .'

Gwydion's voice was filled with warm persuasion.

'You are going to move for me, aren't you?'

Gently he placed his hand on her arm. Her head moved to allow her to stare at his hand. She kept perfectly still. She seemed lost in a trance of admiration for its strength and beauty.

'You're awful,' she said.

'Me? Awful? Who says I'm awful?'

'Everybody.'

'Who says I'm awful?'

Milly's face twitched with a smile. It was a question she wasn't going to answer.

'You haven't been on telly for ages,' she said.

She wanted to connect the appearance of the back of his hand with seeing him on television.

'Now Milly,' he said. 'Come on now, Milly. You're going to move for me, aren't you?'

His hand moved tenderly on her arm.

'You're touching me,' she said.

Her breathing was becoming more rapid.

'You shouldn't touch me. It's not nice.'

Her head sank down and he watched her intently. He was on his guard and yet eager to observe her reactions to his close presence in clinical detail. Milly's fingers were sinking deep into the sides of another loaf.

Her smouldering excitement mirrored his curiosity. They both remained in a wordless trance until the warm silence of the morning was broken by the snorting sound of a motor horn. Gwydion looked up to see an old Rover 105 free-wheeling majestically down the gentle gradient towards them. The bonnet looked as ornamentally aggressive as the metal helmet of a medieval war horse. There was a challenging squeal of brakes as the large car came to a halt. May Huskie sat at the wheel. Like a uniform she wore her usual costume of russet tweed with the collar of her pearl-coloured silk blouse worn outside the collar of the jacket. She emerged importantly from the car like a senior police-man just arriving at the scene of an accident or a crime. Gwydion rose to greet her.

'Oh Gwydion,' she said in a deliberately neutral tone. 'It's you, is it?'

She could not altogether disguise the fact that she was pleased to see him behind her attitude of business-like authority.

'Now come on, Milly,' she said. 'Get up. You'll catch an awful cold sitting on the damp ground at this time of the year.'

She held out a hand to help Milly to her feet. Milly clung to her protector's hand and lowered her head guiltily.

'Is she expecting me?'

Gwydion appealed to Miss Huskie for some sympathy and cooperation, while she was trying to adjust the red ribbon in her sister's hair.

'I couldn't say where she'll be exactly,' Miss Huskie said. 'You know how she flashes about. She could be in the greenhouses. You could look there.'

She gave Gwydion a brief but encouraging smile.

'So it's not too bad then,' Gwydion said.

He began to look more cheerful.

'She was very hurt,' Miss Huskie said. 'It's no use pretending she wasn't.'

She looked at Gwydion reproachfully.

'You might have come to the funeral,' she said.

'Yes I know,' Gwydion said ruefully. 'But how could I? I was stuck in Aberdeen or some much place with that awful show on my hands and a million things to set right and no money to do it with . . . you can't imagine the mess I was in.'

'Oh, I can imagine that all right.'

Miss Huskie's grin was like an echo from the past. He accepted it without resentment as the proper level for their present conversation.

'Honestly May,' Gwydion said. 'I don't think you can. Unimaginable! I'll tell you all about it. It will make your hair curl. How's old Frank?'

The question was open and innocent, without any implication of criticism or unsympathetic curiosity and Miss Huskie responded at once to the kind of interest he was showing in her absent brother.

'He's got a very good job,' Miss Huskie said. 'A draughtsman he is really. He was always very good with his hands. The trouble is it's a long way away and we'd like him nearer, wouldn't we, Milly?'

She turned to repeat the words to her sister.

'I said we'd like Frank nearer home, wouldn't we, Milly?'

She did not wait for a reply from Milly, who seemed still under the spell of Gwydion's nearness.

'He's so unlucky that boy,' Miss Huskie said. 'You wouldn't believe it. He does tend to speak out of turn I suppose and the unions rule the roost in that place. You never saw anything like it. They really rule the roost. And I've got a feeling he's said something he shouldn't have said to a shop steward. Or something like that. They're doing their best to keep him down. I know that much. He was here you know when it happened, thank God.'

Miss Huskie dropped her voice to a whisper with the object of preventing Milly from overhearing what she

432

was saying. The decrease in volume in fact had the effect of making her speech more intelligible.

'I don't know how we would have managed without him. He's marvellous with Milly. I've never seen anything like it. Your mother noticed it. In all her grief and agony she noticed it. And I'll say this for Frank too. He always sticks up for you.'

'Does he really?'

Gwydion could have been amused or grateful. Miss Huskie accepted it was the latter.

'I'm not saying I don't stick up for you. Of course I do. But Frank puts it better. You know my trouble. Half the time people can't understand a word of what I'm saying.'

Miss Huskie chuckled at her own shortcomings of speech.

'It's all feeling, isn't it really?'

'What is?'

'Life,' Miss Huskie said. 'It's all feelings and loyalties. People think we're fools I dare say. But we're not, you know. We know what it's about. And we know which side our bread is buttered.'

She came nearer to Gwydion but failed to reach him with her nudge. They enjoyed an outburst of laughter together and Milly turned up her face towards them like an inhabitant of a northern climate turning her face to the rays of the sun. Miss Huskie made a further bid for Gwydion's sympathy and attention.

'You know what I'd like, Gwydion? I don't mind telling you straight out. I'd like him to come somewhere near home and open an antique business. Don't you think that would be a good idea?'

'Um . . .'

Gwydion agreed cheerfully. He stole a quick glance at the Land Rover and then returned his attention to Miss Huskie.

'He's marvellous with his hands. He really is. He's never had a chance, that boy. I don't know what it is. There are always people who are dead set against him. I can't understand it. I really can't.'

'He's had bad luck,' Gwydion said.

'Oh, it's worse than bad luck. It's deliberate. That's what I've found. Time after time. Quite deliberate. I mean . . . He'd been very useful here you know.'

She jerked her head back up the carriage drive in the general direction of the Hall.

'But your mother will have none of him. And I'll tell you what I think. People have poisoned her mind against him.'

'You ought to tell her that,' Gwydion said.

She glanced at him suspiciously but he kept a very straight face.

'And she doesn't like the antique business,' Miss Huskie said. 'It seems to remind her of things in the past she wants to forget. It's a great pity. I keep on telling her. She's sitting on a gold mine up there. But she doesn't want anything to do with it.'

'Look,' Gwydion said, unable to delay any longer, 'May, do you mind awfully? Would you reverse back up to the Park? We can't really pass here and the reverse gear on this damned thing has packed in. You wouldn't believe it would you? It's like a sheep. It can only go forward or turn in a circle but it won't reverse.'

May Huskie felt obliged to join in with his laughter at the deficiencies of his machine.

'It's hired,' he said. 'It was the only one I could get at short notice.'

'Your mother was saying,' she said. 'I didn't get the whole story. Making a film or something are you?'

Gwydion nodded cheerfully and returned to the Land Rover. Miss Huskie went through the business of packing Milly and her basket of loaves into the Rover car with practised ease. Milly looked more contented

once she was in the passenger seat and Miss Huskie reversed the car with noisy confidence until the carriageway reached the open parkland. The car left the drive
and shot back bumpily over the grass.

4

Brangor Hall, approached from the south west, stood
in isolation at the centre of an extensive park. A herd
of deer was disturbed by the noise of the Land Rover
and they fled to the edge of the trees, where they stood
bunched together, the leaders with their antlers aloft,
panting behind the inert dead branches blown down by
the gales of a previous winter. Their pale coats merged
into the foreground of rotting branches and long withered grass, but their wide bright eyes betrayed their
position in the shadow of the trees. Gwydion drove
along the narrow carriageway towards the massive facade of grey granite. He parked the Land Rover on the
gravel outside the broad arches of the heavy portico.
The whole place looked locked up and deserted. He
walked across the mossy lawn and turned in order to
consider the whole shape of the building. Inside every
window the white panelled shutters were closed.

Gwydion walked towards a small door between the
main building and a lower extension built to house a
billiard room and a conservatory. A small door hidden
by a heavy buttress seemed a possible loophole whereby
he might penetrate the great silent spaces within the
house. He pulled the brass knob of the doorbell. It was

an action which demanded a certain physical effort and in response, in a distant corridor inside the house, a bell could be heard faintly clanging. He stood in the chilly shadow of the buttress and waited for some sound inside the house before he pulled the bell again.

The total lack of response made him impatient. He hurried back to the Land Rover, circled in front of the portico, and followed a new drive which led directly towards a thickly wooded slope. Once in the trees the drive, newly surfaced in yellow gravel which was still unweathered, cut its way in a zig-zag up the steep slope. Before the summit of the the ridge was reached a small white sign with the word *Nyth* printed in black letters indicated a new road curving to the right. This led to an unexpected plateau facing west just under the crest of the hill. The Land Rover swept noisily around the curve over the loose gravel and came to a halt in sight of a one storey house of modern design. It gleamed and glittered in the October sun, a small pavilion made of glass and polished metal. The front part of the dwelling seemed balanced on concrete stilts and jutted out where the land fell away with spectacular abruptness. The walls of glass had an uninterrupted view across the fertile valley below, of terraced mountain ranges that now could only be made out in vague outline in the bright haze of the autumn morning. To the north was the expanse of an imperturbable sea.

Gwydion did not stop to admire the view. He was already trying the door of the side entrance. This house too was locked. Long grey curtains protected the interior from the sunlight. He stood briefly by the kitchen window and stared resentfully inside. He was now a man whose time was being wasted. He took a quick glance at the service wing which contained a double garage, a small laundry, the central heating plant, an outside lavatory and a small workroom which had been left unlocked. Gwydion went inside and stood among the gardener's tools and the assorted picture frames and painting materials. There was nothing there of real value. The place annoyed him. He kicked a box near the door and went back to the Land Rover. He attempted to reverse, forgetting the gear was broken and the failed attempt seemed to enrage him. The Land Rover lurched forward and drove over the edge of an eccentric mixture of chrysanthemums and sweet peas supported by a thin bamboo trellis.

He drove down the hill in a low gear at a dangerous speed. Something of the gentler upland landscape that protected the tilted plateau from the east was visible through trees that were half stripped of their leaves by a steady winnowing wind. He drove the car as fast as it would go across the narrow carriage way, passing the massive facade and slowing down to take the road that led to the two courtyards on the east side. As he passed under the arch leading to the inner courtyard he blew the car horn vigorously to draw attention to his arrival.

Once again he tried the doors. There were three possible entrances and they were all locked. Perplexed, he stood alongside a curious pavilion set high upon wooden stilts and with window spaces faced with metal finely meshed to keep out the flies and the light and let in the air. It had been painted many times in some preparation that included pitch and there were ancient black stains on the bare rock beneath the structure.

It was hot in the courtyard, which served now as a sun-trap. He considered his long shadow which pointed towards a barred window in a semi-basement of the main building. He caught a glimpse of an old face looking up. The sunlight showed the face in great detail: the wispy white hair caught up under a net did not conceal the gleaming scalp. The restless red-rimmed eyes worked ceaselessly in the long pallid face.

'Clayton!' Gwydion called out.

The face disappeared immediately.

'Connie! Where is everybody?'

He ran to the window and knelt down, holding the bars to look inside. In a cage on the table just below the window a budgerigar was fussing nervously on his perch. There was no sign of Connie Clayton in the room crowded with Victorian furniture. On the table alongside the birdcage there was a large black family Bible and on it a bilingual book of Common Prayer with plump ornate covers and gilt-edged pages. The prayer book was kept in a torn presentation box for its better preservation. Gwydion pushed his face closer to the bars. The door from the room into the passage opened in two halves. Attached to the lower half was a curved counter where the butler once stood to pay the indoor servants their wages. The top half of the door was not shut. Gwydion tapped the window urgently but she did not reappear.

Gwydion stood up and took control of himself. He thrust his hands in his pockets and sauntered back to the Land Rover. He leaned against the door of the driver's side and studied the exterior of the house. Once again his nostrils caught something of the fragrance in the air. It came chiefly from the garden and the greenhouses. He walked down a narrow shadowed cobbled passage between the outbuildings which led southwards to the greenhouses and the walled garden. He smelt traces of burning leaves and apples freshly stored: ripeness everywhere. Nearing the first greenhouse he caught the first whiff of his mother's perfume mingling with the smells of tomatoes and geraniums. Then he heard her groan.

For a second he stood rigidly in the open doorway of the greenhouse. On the brick floor he saw his mother sitting with her head almost between her legs. Her panama hat was on the ground and her ringed fingers were clutching her skull between the silver roots of her tinted hair. Her head shot up. Her eyes were shut tight and her face was a white mask of pain.

'Amy!'

Her eyes opened and she attempted to smile.

'Gwydion. Oh I'm so glad it's you . . .'

Her face screwed up as she was overcome with another spasm of pain. Gwydion knelt carefully alongside his mother and managed to support her back so that she could relax a little. She covered his hand with hers and opened her eyes, gasping as she spoke.

'There,' she said. 'I'm better already.'

'What is it?'

'I'll be all right in a minute. I'm very silly really. I ought to have them out. But I'm getting to be such a coward as I get older. I just don't fancy going under the knife. Aren't I silly?'

'What is it?'

'Gallstones. And I just can't be bothered with them.'

'Well that's silly, isn't it?'

He chided her gently and offered to help her to her feet.

'Not yet. Just leave me for a minute. Go and stand over there where I can look at you.'

Gwydion sat on a ledge near the door. Amy breathed hard, her eyes closed, enjoying the relief from the pain even as it was passing. Gwydion pushed the shallow boxes behind so that he could sit more securely on the shelf.

'Better?' he said.

Amy nodded and held her head a little to one side as if she were listening to the sound of horses' hooves receding in the distance.

'It's going,' she said. 'It's taking its own time.'

She looked at her son. They kept a silence that was like a tacit agreement to leave a long series of questions unasked and unanswered. She smiled and he knew they would speak with care but without reproaches. Amy

439

was wearing a black armband stitched to her working smock. Gwydion looked at the armband.

'I'm sorry I couldn't come,' he said. 'I really am.'

She glanced at the mourning band, clearly pleased that he should say he was sorry.

'This thing,' she said. 'I'd forgotten it was there. It's time it came off.'

She bent her head again and then lifted it, holding out her hand.

'Help me up,' she said. 'I think I'm better now. I'm sure I am.'

He helped his mother to her feet and then embraced her. She laughed, happily delighted to have him with her.

'Gwydion,' she said, 'I'm sorry too. About that musical thing. What was it called?'

'*Infidel.*'

'Yes of course. No wonder poor Hubert was so much against it. You knew that, didn't you? I'm not trying to pass the blame off on to him, but he disliked the idea more than I did. That's why . . .'

'Quite right he was too.'

Gwydion displayed a prompt cheerfulness which she found endearing. It relieved her of all further explanation and apology.

'It was all an unmitigated disaster.'

'You poor darling.'

She leaned heavily on his arm and then turned to survey the spot where lately she had been sitting.

'I was potting geraniums,' she said. 'Everything is so far behind this year. It's been a terrible time, Gwydion. It really has. Old Roberts died you know. At the end of August. I miss him dreadfully. He was a lovely gardener. A bit slow of course, because of his age. And he was so poetical. You remember Roberts? He used to talk about "the young of the day" and that sort of thing. Don't you remember him telling May Huskie not to drown the miller when she was pouring hot water in the teapot. I remember it took your fancy at the time . . .'

Gwydion accepted the jolt to his memory with dutiful gratitude.

'Well, his son still comes three days a week, but he's not nearly as good. He's a very sulky man. Not a bit like his father. Oh dear. I've got so much to tell you. Where shall we go and sit? Would you like a drink or something?'

'What about you?'

Gwydion was exceptionally considerate.

'I would have thought a brandy or something. After that frightful pain. You ought to see a doctor.'

'I don't like doctors,' Amy said.

'Oh I know,' Gwydion said. 'But they're a necessary evil.'

'Look . . . you must see the walled garden,' Amy said. 'I always think it looks so marvellous in the autumn . . .'

'Fine,' Gwydion said. 'I can see it later. But we ought to get you lying down and sipping hot lemon juice . . . after two spoonfuls of brandy . . .'

She laughed happily, pleased that he should remember one of her home-made remedies. She walked along taking a new pleasure in her surroundings because she was enjoying them in the warmth of her son's presence. In the outer quadrangle he gave her his arm again as she stepped carefully over the uneven surface of the yard. She wanted to draw his attention to the new roof over the saddle room and she gave impatient care to where she was placing her feet. In the centre of the courtyard she turned around slowly to survey the condition of the buildings which were all empty including the cottage formerly occupied by the Salters.

'I think it's so important to keep it all in good repair,' Amy said. 'I don't quite know why . . .'

441

She paused and then smiled at her own hesitations.

'. . . But yes, of course, I do. I've got plans.'

She shook his arm as she made the confession, encouraging him to laugh.

'Aren't I awful,' she said. 'I never give up, do I?'

'I don't see why you should.'

She squeezed his arm. It was what she wanted to hear.

'I'd love to hear,' Gwydion said. 'I really would.'

They walked back to the inner yard.

'You must tell me exactly what you think of it all. Promise?'

'Promise.'

The formula seemed to amuse them both and like an echo of an ancient family ritual they both raised their right hands as if they were swearing an oath.

'Well it's really very simple,' Amy said.

She began to feel about in the pocket of her working smock.

'Bother,' she said. 'I must have dropped my key in the greenhouse . . . Never mind. Just bang the door. Connie's in there somewhere. She's developed a mania for locking everything recently. It's quite alarming. She locks up absolutely everything.'

She smiled affectionately at Gwydion as they waited patiently for Mrs Clayton to come and open the door. Something of the delicacy of their newly achieved reconciliation seemed to bear in upon her consciousness as they waited: the number of subjects that could not easily be brought up until they had reached a more general understanding. She took hold of the door knob and shook it. It was important that the initial impetus of good will should not be allowed to evaporate in the frustration of waiting outside a locked door.

'Would you believe it! I can't get in my own house. She carries this thing to ridiculous extremes.'

Apparently recovered from her attack, she moved quickly along the wall to the barred window of Mrs Clayton's room. She bent down to call out in a loud voice.

'Clayton! Clayton! Where are you? Come and open the outside door. Clayton! Can you hear me?'

Mrs Clayton's white face appeared above the butler's counter. She waved urgently to show that she was on her way. Amy relaxed a little.

'It's getting to be an obsession with her,' she said to Gwydion. 'She prowls around night and day locking every door she sets eyes on. She's like a human watchdog. She thinks more of this place than I do. It's a form of idolatry. And that comes of spending a lifetime in the service of the great. All this "ladyship" business. She insists on it. She loves it. She loves it all.'

They could hear the noise of bolts being drawn in the cavernous interior.

'What a business,' Amy said.

The noise of the old woman's footsteps echoed on the flagstones as she limped towards the outside door. Again a bolt was drawn before the key was turned in the lock and the door opened and Mrs Clayton's worried face appeared.

'I'm so sorry, your Ladyship,' she said. 'I thought you had your key. I saw a strange vehicle driving about the park so I thought it was wise to take every precaution.'

She lisped a little as she spoke, pushing her lips out to overcome some slight maladjustment in her large elegant dentures and then covering her mouth with a lace handkerchief and pressing inwards in the hope that they would slip back into their correct position.

'It's Gwydion, Clayton! There's nothing at all to worry about. Isn't it nice to see him?'

Mrs Clayton shifted out of their way and gave a slight bow.

'Very nice indeed,' she said from behind the lace handkerchief.

She was puzzled equally by his arrival and by the warmth of the reception his mother was giving him.

'He's making a film of some kind. Is that right Gwydion?'

'Well I have to have your permission first,' Gwydion said. 'Just the Old Village and Arthur's Cave and maybe something in the Penygaer . . . would it be all right?'

'Of course it would, my darling. We'll do everything to help him, won't we, Connie dear?'

Amy led the way down the passage and then paused as they reached a row of ageing fire appliances. They were confronted with another locked door.

'Connie,' she said, 'you'd better open or we'll just never get through. I had a bit of an attack when I was potting the geraniums . . .'

'Attack?'

Mrs Clayton uttered the word with bated breath. She was in the process of unlocking the passage door.

'Gallstones,' Amy said more cheerfully. 'Nothing to worry about.'

'I'll bring you some hot lemon right away . . .'

Mrs Clayton was full of concern for her mistress. She opened the billiard-room door and then hurried back to the kitchen to prepare hot lemon for Lady Brangor. The billiard-room was in darkness. Amy switched on a weak light and suggested that Gwydion should lift an iron crossbar and open one of the shutters of the three windows. As the shutter opened a bar of light fell directly on to the face of a full-length portrait leaning against the dado of the billiard-room wall: the fair, fresh, face of a young major in the British uniform of the Crimean war period. The billiard table was shrouded by a large grimy dust cover and two

444

more long paintings lay face downwards on the cover. More paintings and empty picture frames were stacked in depth against the table's solid sides.

'I don't know what to do with it,' Amy said. 'I really don't.'

The carpets and soft furnishings had been removed and her voice reverberated between the bare walls.

'The whole place really.'

She gave a wave of her hand and her rings glittered in the dim light.

'All this locking up is quite ridiculous. We must have some trust in others, mustn't we? Otherwise the whole world will relapse into savagery.'

She was troubled and concerned.

'You know what you should have done?' Gwydion said. 'You should have gone in for politics.'

His tone was just serious enough to underline the note of flattery.

'Weren't you ever tempted? I'm sure you were.'

'It came too late,' she said. 'Like everything else in my life it came too late. And too far from London . . .'

She lifted a finger like a reference mark to an old point of agreement between them.

'I think I could have done it. I was just as capable as that Sally what's-her-name any day of the week and she got a ministerial post for goodness' sake. But she had the right connections and the right start . . . It's quite funny really. I've often heard women say they envy me. But as far as I'm concerned I consider myself a failure . . .'

'Nonsense.'

Gwydion followed his mother into the study beyond the billiard room. He opened the shutters before she asked him to and told her to make herself comfortable on the chaise-longue. The tennis court outside the window was in the shadow of the house. It was sunk two feet below the general level of the ground and the unmown grass was weighed down with dew. The room was cold. Gwydion knelt down to light a neat paraffin stove painted in pale blue which appeared both feminine and contemporary in the dark nineteenth-century surroundings of the room: the black furniture, mahogany bookcases and photographs of rowing men, college societies and sixty year old regimental groups.

'But I want to achieve something. I really do. Before I die. And that's why I can put up with all this. I see it as my opportunity that still has to be taken. Shall I tell you about it, Gwydion? Will you listen?'

'Of course I'll listen.'

Her smile seemed a pardon for all the occasions in the past when he had refused to listen.

'I'm getting old,' she said. 'I may not have much time left . . .'

'Rubbish,' he said. 'You're as strong as a horse.'

'I want to concentrate my energies,' she said. 'I want to be able to look back and say, well, at least one thing I managed to do really well . . . You may not like the idea. You didn't before.'

She became unexpectedly stern and Gwydion looked surprised.

'Didn't I?'

'No you didn't. You made jokes about it. You called it Hen's Castle. Don't you remember?'

He scratched his head until she showed some further sign of forgiveness and then they were able to laugh together.

'Well, it's much more advanced now. Since poor Hubert died I've given it a great deal of thought. What was wrong you see, before, in the earlier plans, what was wrong was they weren't ambitious enough. They really weren't. Now what I'm after is government support. And in order to get that what I have to do is start it all off myself with my own money.'

446

Gwydion became restless. He moved a box full of old letters from a horse-hair armchair and sat down in it. His face was gloomy but he nodded to his mother to show that he was giving her his full attention.

'I'm going to convert the place myself,' Amy said. 'And I'll enjoy doing it. I'm going to turn Brangor into a Centre for the Creative Arts for Women. C.C.A.W. I know initials are silly. I hope in time the name Brangor will be enough. The Brangor Centre. That sounds better, doesn't it? Do you want to see the plans?'

'Plans?'

Gwydion was unable to suppress the note of alarm in his voice.

'I'll turn the chapel into a chamber music room. That will be easy. And the carpenter's shop and the stables will be very simple to convert. I'm not sure whether we shouldn't keep a small museum of the more interesting pieces . . . it's really quite exciting, isn't it? I mean what else is life for, Gwydion, except to get things done?'

He heard the squeak of the wheels of an ancient tea trolley on the bare floor of the billiard room and he jumped to his feet to open the door. He could barely see the old woman approaching. She was bent low behind the large trolley like the drawing of a woman in an early nineteenth-century print, naked to the waist as she pushes a waggon full of coal up a narrow shaft. Gwydion went to meet her, anxious to demonstrate that he could be helpful.

'Let me do that,' he said.

'It's all right Mister Gwydion . . . if you'd just stand to one side. . .'

Connie Clayton was out of breath but determined to prove that the efficiency of her service was in no way impaired by the disabilities of old age. Once inside the study she began to display a practised smile that uncovered the gold fillings in her properly adjusted dentures.

'I've made some refreshment for Mister Gwydion . . . And here's your hot lemon, Ma'am. I'm sure it will do you good.'

'Clayton! How nice . . .'

Amy clapped her hands, delighted that Gwydion should sample some of Connie Clayton's delicious little savouries and cakes with his coffee.

'You are a great treasure, Connie. You really are. I've never seen anyone anywhere who could cook half as well as Connie Clayton and I'm not exaggerating. She is quite superb.'

The old housekeeper warmed herself in her mistress's praise and limped around the trolley in an oddly coquettish manner, delaying her departure until Gwydion had tasted one of her savouries. He made ecstatic noises and Mrs Clayton was ready to be dismissed.

'Don't work so hard,' Amy said, 'for goodness' sake. Take a proper rest now and don't let me catch you scrubbing that scullery floor. You let Beryl Barr do it. She's young and strong.'

Mrs Clayton clutched the doorknob for support.

'I don't want to worry you about it now, ma'am,' she said. 'But I would like a word with you later if you could spare the time . . .'

Her red-rimmed eyes were as exposed and as restless as a bird's, constantly expecting danger. When she left the room Amy whispered softly to Gwydion.

'She's fallen out with the Huskies,' she said. 'I try to ignore it, but it does get very embarrassing.'

She sipped her glass of hot lemon and then spoke in her normal voice.

'I'm not going to ask you what you think of it,' Amy said. 'I know you think I get obsessive about these things. And I suppose I do really. But that's the only way to get things done. I read that somewhere the other day . . .'

448

She looked at her son, openly longing for his approval. He put down his cup as though he had come to a decision.

'I think it's a jolly good idea,' he said.

'Do you really?' You're not just saying that to please me?'

'No. I really mean it. It's something that's genuinely missing in modern life. I honestly do think women have a very raw deal. I've thought that for quite a long time.'

Amy could no longer lie still on the chaise-longue. She jumped to her feet and went over to the large desk near the window.

'I was thinking last night,' she said, 'about forming a Trust for this place. I shall have to get down to that soon. I can't delay it much longer. I was thinking of the word Trust and I suddenly had the image of a medieval castle defended by three concentric things. You know the kind of shape I mean? And in the centre there is Absolute Trust. And then around that Qualified Trust and then around that Necessary Trust. And outside the savage hostile world. Can you see it?'

'Very vivid,' Gwydion said

'I'm not sure, that I didn't dream it,' Amy said. 'It seemed like a revelation, but of course there was absolutely no one I could tell it to so it just evaporated. Or shrunk rather. Not quite the secret of living that it seemed when I woke up. But a good practical method of picking Trustees and seeing that the power is in the very centre: Absolute Trust.'

'You are getting younger,' Gwydion said.

'What do you mean?'

Amy couldn't prevent herself being a little flattered.

'Here you are bubbling away with ideas like a man – I mean a girl – in her twenties. It's quite ridiculous. You make me feel middle-aged and useless.'

'You silly boy . . .'

449

She was overtaken by happiness.

'I'm so glad you've come. I want you three to be Trustees of course. Bedwyr and Peredur and yourself. Wouldn't that be wonderful?'

5

Peredur moved carefully down the steep slope. The ground was slippery with pine needles and sheep droppings. When he stumbled, he saved himself by stretching out the palm of his hand and letting it take the weight of his whole body as it thudded against the gnarled surface of a tall pine tree. He pressed his cheek against the bark and looked downwards first to the bright stream more than forty feet below. The torrent sparkled in the sunshine as it swept around stones and boulders, and near the edge of the water a tramp-like figure squatted, apparently absorbed in staring at the water. Peredur looked up and watched formations of high cloud floating in the blue sky far above the tight assembly of short branches. His nostrils were assailed by the fresh smell of pine as he watched the man below and considered his next move. His best way down was to traverse from the safety of one tree to another until the slope became easier and he could move down to the path alongside the stream. He appeared anxious to avoid disturbing the man sitting on the river's edge by too sudden an approach. He grew over confident as he allowed himself to fall softly from tree to tree. Missing a hold he tumbled unceremoniously down to the path,

450

landing on his back with his feet in the air, unable to prevent himself crying out his alarm.

Ken Lazarus had been eating peacefully from the blue plastic bag which dangled conveniently between his knees. He jumped to his feet startled by the intrusion. His retreat to his caravan on the patch of wasteland the other end of the path was cut off by Peredur, who was getting to his feet, unhurt but flustered by his own clumsiness. He waved his arms about partly to dust himself down and partly to reassure his quarry.

'Mr Lazarus! Wait a minute. Please . . .'

Ken Lazarus was preparing to scramble away over the rocks behind him. As Peredur drew nearer he became truly frightened. He climbed up the rock face out of reach and then looked down at Peredur.

'Please come down,' Peredur said. 'I want to talk to you.'

To prove that his intentions were not aggressive Peredur stepped back slowly to the water's edge and sat down exactly where Ken Lazarus himself had been sitting. To demonstrate that he would if necessary take instruction in the art of meditation, Peredur began to stare at the water. He wanted to show that he was capable of stillness. A small bird of pale green plumage settled for a moment on a stone near his feet. As it flew away a bright light refracted from the surface of the water dazzled among the fine feathers under its wing.

Ken Lazarus came down to the base of the rock against which he had attempted to climb. He sat down, opened his blue bag and resumed his meal. Peredur made an effort not to look at him, to show that he had no wish to intrude upon the privacy of his eating. When he had finished, Ken Lazarus approached the river's edge to wash the plastic bag. When he realized that he was occupying the most convenient position, Peredur moved away to give the solitary his accustomed access to the water. He stood still until Ken had completed washing out the bag.

'I need your help,' Peredur said.

Ken settled back in his usual place and stared at the river.

'How can I help you?'

'Do you know who I am?'

Ken nodded.

'Do I look like my father?'

Ken turned around to study the earnest young man. He shook his head.

'How do you know who I am then?'

'You look like Bedwyr.'

Ken studied him again as if to check the comparison.

'Less worldly perhaps. Less preoccupied with worldly affairs. Less active.'

'Can I sit down?'

Ken looked at the water, not willing to make any sign of encouragement.

'If you wish.'

Together they contemplated the flow of the water.

'Is it wrong to be active?'

He seemed a little moved by the childlike way in which Peredur asked the questions.

'Not wrong,' he said. 'Different. A different mode of living.'

'Does it gather more evil: being active?'

'Not at all. Evil is not the general rule. It is only the exception to the good.'

'Do you believe that?'

Peredur's response became perceptibly more eager.

'I don't believe it,' Ken said. 'I see it.'

'Is that how you spend your time? Meditating?'

'Listening,' Ken said. 'That's what I would call it. Just listening.'

'Listening for what?'

Ken ventured to smile a little.

'Something I can't put into words.'

'Praying . . . Could you call it praying?'

'Well . . .'

Ken closed his eyes and thought hard and long to produce an answer that would satisfy such an urgent question.

'If you could say your prayer was a ship and that you are riding inside it.'

He opened his eyes and looked at the sky above them which seemed confined because of the wooded valley in which they were hidden.

'A ship like a cloud. A prayer like a ship like a cloud. But you can't say such things can you? It's better not to say anything than to say things that can't be said.'

He imposed a silence and Peredur accepted it. He shook out the plastic bag. When it was dry enough he folded it with care and put it away in his mackintosh pocket as though it were an object of considerable value. Peredur stared respectfully at his bare feet.

'You don't need much,' he said.

'That is important,' Ken said. 'You have to keep your needs as few as possible. And even then Time is precious. Time I don't spend listening seems to be wasted.'

'Look . . .'

Peredur burst out impulsively

'Do you think you could teach me?'

'Teach you?'

The idea seemed so foreign to Ken and the word so unfamiliar that he had to repeat it to grasp its meaning.

'I wasn't a success as a teacher. Didn't they tell you about me?'

He stared at Peredur's face in order to gather how much Peredur knew of his history.

'It doesn't matter about that,' Peredur said ardently.
'I think you might be right . . .'

Ken shook his head.

'I'm sorry, I didn't mean "right" in that sense or indeed in any sense. What I meant was I think your way could be the way for me. If you could show me.'

Again Ken studied the younger man's face.

'I don't think so,' he said.

'Why not?'

Peredur sounded indignant.

'You have other things you want to do.'

'Is it because of my father? Is that why you don't want to have anything to do with me?'

'You are not your father.'

'Well, what is it then?'

'I have told you. The urge to action. It's written all over you. More than Bedwyr I would say.'

Peredur looked downcast. He pushed his fingers into the mud under a stone near his hand.

'It's nothing to be sad about,' Ken said. 'I don't think any the less of you.'

'What happened to my father?'

The question came as no surprise to Ken. His answer seemed prepared.

'He gave up too soon.'

Peredur was far from satisfied.

'What do you mean by that?'

'He despaired too soon. He died of despair.'

'Whose fault was it?'

'I don't know.'

'Was he in love with you?'

Ken looked calmly at Peredur.

'I don't want to think about it any more.'

Peredur scrambled to his feet.

'Well I do.'

'He lost hope. That's all it was. He was ashamed of loving me. Loving a man's flesh he called it. He was

454

horrified by that. He couldn't live with it. He thought it was a disease. And he thought he was being punished. Cut off from his family. He thought everything he valued was dying. He said the words he used in his poetry were like dead leaves.'

'I want to find those last poems,' Peredur said. 'I've found some notes. Some of his old folders. In one of the servants' empty bedrooms. Over the old kitchens at Brangor. But you saw them. They did exist.'

'I remember one poem ... His own end, the end of a culture. He was the last of a defeated tribe. He saw his own corpse washed up on a shore of time.'

'You don't sound concerned,' Peredur said. 'It doesn't seem to affect you.'

'Oh it does. I could have been responsible for his death. It was quite a simple thing. He wanted me to go on holiday with him. I refused.'

'Was that all?'

'It was a time of growing apart. A breaking point. He saw I was going my own way.'

Peredur had a further suggestion to make. He sat on his haunches alongside Ken Lazarus.

'If I brought the folders to you,' he said, 'do you think you could help me to piece the bits together ... make sense of it ... there's a great deal of material there. Couldn't we do something together?'

Ken Lazarus stared at the glittering surface of the water and shook his head.

'I wouldn't be any help to you,' he said.

'Don't you care? Don't you feel that some sort of justice should be done? Why else should he have been alive at all? He was a man who loved you.'

'Other people loved me,' Ken said. 'I did worse things to them.'

6

'I like to have some idea,' the focus-puller said. 'I'm not an absolute ignoramus.'

He sat with his short legs on either side of the bar-stool, smartly dressed, recently bathed and ready to relax after the day's shooting. He was a dark young man wearing three tones of green, a pale green shirt, an olive green pullover and dark green trousers. Gwydion was buying drinks for the camera crew, but paying particular attention to the senior cameraman.

'He's been bottling it up for the last three days.'

The cameraman referred to the staff director who sat at a table at the other end of the saloon apparently dictating letters to his secretary.

'A hired crew is a hired crew,' the cameraman said, in a tone of scriptural finality. 'Either you know the job or you don't and that's all there is to it.'

He was a morose Scot in his late forties who dressed his thin hair like a young man and wore a silver bracelet on his wrist.

'As far as I'm concerned he could go home tonight,' he said. 'Or back to his wee office. I'm not bloody-minded by nature but in my book that man is no use whatsoever.'

Gwydion glanced across the room to see if the staff director realized they were discussing him. The man had an ulcer and two lines scored deeply down his sunken cheeks. He was dividing his effort between basking in the unfailing supply of motherly warmth provided by his secretary and sending out hostile glances at Gwydion for fraternizing with a rebellious and uncooperative hired crew. The expression on his face was constantly changing: a winning and grateful smile for the industrious and dependable female and a cold frown for the disaffected elements at the other end of the room. This obliged him to be restless, looking first in one direction and then in the other and it affected the way he smoked one cigarette after another, creating a smoke screen about his own head out of which he reassured himself by making constant signals and gestures with his nicotined fingers, conducting the subtle discords of some imagined symphony.

'Well, I've never worked with a better crew,' Gwydion said. 'And I should imagine I've made more programmes than our friend has had hot dinners.'

'I like to know what it's all about,' the focus-puller said. 'I like to be in the picture as well as on it.'

Gwydion stretched out his left hand to pat the young man on the back and applaud his verbal felicity.

'Did you hear that, Stanley?' he said to the cameraman. 'This boy is not just a pretty face.'

The cameraman sipped his gin and tonic and glanced at his silver bracelet.

'It's not just that he has no idea of film technique,' he said. 'Let's forgive him that. He doesn't know what he wants. And that's unforgivable.'

The stern accent made the verdict sound irreversible. Gwydion glanced with a comic slyness over his own shoulder.

'You know what he's doing now?' he said. 'Behind that ostentatious half-pint? Totting up his mileage and expenses. That's all he really cares about. When I brought him up here on a recce I couldn't get him to talk about anything else. I said, Rithy, this is probably your actual King Arthur's Cave. If we nip in quickly we might even catch him asleep with the bell around his neck. He couldn't care less. He was too busy working it out at ninepence three farthings a mile plus overnight allowance. He's obsessed with it. It's more than a fiddle with him. It's a religion. It's a way of life.'

The camera crew avoided each other's eyes as they showed varying signs of contempt at such a mean concern as the constant totting up of mileage and expenses. They strained their ears above the noise of the saloon bar to show Gwydion the homage of close attention and demonstrate a fuller enjoyment of the privilege of his company.

'Well that's what I'm on about,' the focus-puller said. 'What's fact and what's fiction.'

'Moments of destiny in the history of this great country of ours!'

Gwydion's blithe and open manner won easy laughter.

'Just think, if only that cave had been twice as big, the whole history of the world would have been different.'

'Well, that's where I don't get it,' the focus-puller said. 'It wasn't was it?'

He was inhibited from saying more. The cameraman had looked at his feet accusingly. He blushed and moved them away in case the cameraman teased him solemnly about his fancy boots.

'This is mythological country,' Gwydion said. 'It should set your imaginations all of a tremble. You are creative artists after all. Those are not stones you're photographing, you know. They are lion's heads and the wings of gryphons and eagles.'

'Okay,' the focus-puller said, willing to be reasonable and his feet well tucked in under his stool. 'But what about the history bit?'

'What about it?'

Gwydion set down his beer mug on the counter, prepared to expound at length.

'If that cave had been twice as big,' he said. 'Glyndwr would have held out. Right?'

They nodded obediently.

'I'm not talking about Arthur now. I've talking about Owain. And he was historical. Now if the cave had been twice as big, your Prince Henry, later to be Henry V, would have been defeated. Killed, let's say hopefully. The Tripartite Indenture would have divided your actual England into two and the Cymric state under Glyndwr would have stretched as far as the Trent. Right? Now inevitably the North of England would have become absorbed by Scotland. Ireland would have been left alone. Gaelic and inviolate. There would have been no English Tudors. Because there would have been no widow for Owen Tudor to marry. The South of England might well have become French speaking. Like the whole of North America. No French Revolution. No Napoleon. No Karl Marx. No Lenin. No Hitler. What a lovely world, if only that damn cave had been twice as big!'

'And the moon made of green cheese,' the Scotsman said.

'You are a gross and unimaginative fellow.'

Gwydion wagged a finger at him in mock reproof. The crew laughed except for the focus-puller.

'That's what I mean,' he said. 'When did all this happen. Or not happen?'

Gwydion stretched his arms to touch the edge of the bar and survey the young man in a sad and solemn silence.

'Well I never did history . . . not this kind of history anyway. When was he around? This chap you're talking about.'

'Four hundred years ago.'

'Stone the crows!'

'What's up?'

The focus-puller looked at Gwydion pityingly.

'He's been dead a long time, hasn't he? He's been dead a very long time.'

'Ah!'

Gwydion raised a warning finger.

'But he's not dead.'

'Not dead?'

The focus-puller was polite but openly triumphant. He scratched his freckled forehead.

'If he's not dead, what is he?'

'He's with Arthur,' Gwydion said. 'They never caught him you see. He just vanished.'

'Look,' the focus-puller said. 'It's just like a kid's game isn't it? You know. "Yer dead yer dead" "No I'm not dead" "Yer missed me!" You don't take it seriously do you? It's not right, is it, to go around spreading fairy tales without a word of truth in them?'

Gwydion winked at the cameraman, who was amused by his assistant's burst of indignant eloquence.

'You think so?' Gwydion said. 'Well come on now, Gordon love. Tell me why you think so.'

The focus-puller blushed.

'You're just having me on.'

'Go on,' Gwydion said. 'Tell me. I'd like to know. Seriously.'

'Well you'd never know where you were, would you? Fiction is one thing and fact is another. We can't go through life mixing it all up.'

'Why not?'

'It would be wrong.'

The focus-puller was determined to stick to his ground.

'You've got to have Truth haven't you? You've got to have the Facts. Otherwise where are you?'

'What would happen to your mortgage?'

Gwydion shook his head in mock despair.

'If the never-never really became the Never Never. Oh dear.'

'Well that's what I'm saying.'

The focus-puller began to look genuinely worried. A note of pleading entered his voice.

'It would all collapse, wouldn't it? Like a pack of cards.'

'You may just be right,' Gwydion said. 'Now come on Gordon. Have another factual drink on me.'

The cameraman had taken a further glance at the staff director who was leaning back now in his chair to indicate that the day's stint of administration was over. The secretary had gone to the smaller bar to get them fresh drinks. The cameraman noticed Peredur standing just inside the door. He carried a thin black portfolio under his arm. He was staring in their direction, at Gwydion's back.

'Is that someone looking for you?'

Gwydion turned.

'My brother. Now that's the man to set you right, Gordon.'

He spoke to the focus-puller.

'He'll answer all your questions. And some of mine as well . . . I'll bring him over.'

Cheerfully he crossed the room.

'Come and meet the boys,' he said to Peredur. 'Very nice bunch. Full of intelligent questions that I can't answer. Come and answer some for me. Do your Socratic thing. Do no end of good to my prestige in the business.'

'They're going ahead,' Peredur said.

He looked tense and excited.

'Who are going ahead?'

'Pendraw Town Council. It's been passed in principle. They're going ahead with the Memorial.'

Gwydion pressed his lips together.

'The mayor is enthusiastic,' Peredur said. 'And that counts for a lot there. He's very keen on the idea. What's the matter? Aren't you glad?'

'I don't want the old lady upset,' Gwydion said.

'Why? What's happened?'

'I'm back in favour,' Gwydion said. 'At the top of the class.'

'What difference does that make?'

461

He shook his head slowly, openly moved by his brother's innocence. He decided against answering the question and placed his hand on Peredur's shoulder.

'Come upstairs, Snow White,' he said. 'I've got something to show you.'

He called at the reception desk for the key of his room and climbed up the shallow stairs with giant strides.

'Not a bad place this,' he said. 'They've given me the Bridal Suite. Should have brought somebody with me really.'

He grinned as he unlocked the door.

'I'm very sensitive to the atmosphere of hotels,' he said. 'Must be because they are my natural habitat. Can't see me in domestic surroundings . . . Can you? I'm the kind of chap born to live out of a suitcase. What do you think of that? A four poster. All for little Gwydion. Sit down. And hold on to your seat. I've got something to show you.'

He opened the door of the heavy wardrobe and brought out a suitcase which he laid on the bed to unlock. Under some clothes lay a large folder. He extracted it like a magician anxious to create the maximum effect.

'What is it?'

Peredur's curiosity was easily roused.

'A fortune, among other things. Now don't breathe on them for God's sake . . .'

Gwydion moved the suitcase away so that he could lay out the folder on the bed. With meticulous care he unlaced the bow which kept it closed and opened it out to reveal drawings of various sizes, some protected by tissue paper which had gone brown with age.

'Views of Rome and its environs,' Gwydion said. 'Drawn by one Richard Wilson esquire. The Alban Hills. Lago Albano. Nemi. And the jolly old Golden Bough itself. There they are. If my researches are correct mostly executed in 1753. Probably for Griffith

Pughe, uncle of the third baron Brangor. Now what do you think of that?'

'Where did you find them?'

'In that workroom behind the chapel where the old nut case used to do his carpentry.'

'Who?'

Peredur frowned crossly.

'Your trouble is you've no interest in family history. Uncle Francis. The harmless lunatic. Spent half a life in there making table boxes with inlay patterns on them. He died during the last war with his mouth full of glue and little nails . . . honestly.'

'It's not my family.'

'You mustn't take such a narrow view,' Gywdion said. 'I've been converted. I'm going to help Amy create The Brangor Centre for Creative Women.'

'Rubbish,' Peredur said impatiently.

'That's what I've been doing. Making an inventory of the unlocked rooms. Amazing the stuff you can find.'

'I thought you were making a film,' Peredur said.

'Not all the time. Not every minute. You shouldn't underrate my versatility.'

'What are you going to do with them?'

Gwydion consciously ignored his brother's attitude, which was suspicious and hostile.

'Wait,' he said.

He lifted a layer of the drawings to reveal a rectangular sheet of paper which had been folded in the centre to make it fit into the folder. He opened it with great care.

'What do you think this is?'

It was a series of figure groups in pen and ink. The figures were in biblical dress. There were old men in curious turbans, a Christ-like bearded figure holding a staff, a woman in distress and fishermen drawing their nets out of a boat.

'Unless my old eyes mistake me, you are now looking at a Rembrandt,' Gwydion said.

'A what?'

In spite of himself Peredur was suddenly overtaken by awe.

'A Rembrandt pen and ink that was quite possibly once in the possession of old big-nose Wilson. Can you imagine it? Well you don't have to. There it is in front of you. Worth every penny of £20,000. Probably more. Isn't that nice?'

'What do you mean?'

Peredur's face was white. Gwydion held out his hands.

'This is marvellous,' he said. 'It's more than what I wanted. It solves all my problems. I'm in, Peredur my boy. I'm in the Big League. And you are in with me. We are on our way to controlling a company exercising a franchise in the most powerful medium of mass communication ever invented. Blah, Blah, Blah. Don't you see it?'

Peredur was shaking his head.

'It's alright you fool. I'm not going to pinch them. Although I quite easily could. They belong to Amy now and that means that in the fullness of time and by the law of the land they will ultimately belong to us. It's much simpler than that. They are of great value. Right? What do we do? We pop them in a bank vault. For safe keeping. Where else in this wicked day and age? And we leave them there getting more and more valuable year by year instead of being buried under a heap of Victorian rubbish and photographs of disgusting old men sitting in front of a drive full of dead pheasants. That's all there is to it. I shall be doing everybody a favour. Especially me.'

'How do you mean?'

'Security. Against which I shall raise monies in order to take my place on the board and have my proper say in guiding the future of the imagination of our race. I'm not stupid you know. I know what it's all about. And I want you in with me.'

Peredur went to sit in an armchair in the corner.

'And don't look so bloody doubtful. This is the chance of a life-time. And we've got to take it. If we don't you can be quite sure others will. And you know what that means. I'm a hundred and one per cent behind you in your Welsh lark. I really am.'

'What Welsh lark? What are you talking about?'

'That's what it is really. All this stuff about Cilydd and his Memorial. You haven't realized it yet. Isn't it amazing how we can't see things right in front of our noses? Peredur my son, let me be prophetic for a moment and tell you this. No good will ever come of you until you own up to being a dyed-in-the-wool twenty-two carat, copper-bottomed, Welsh-speaking Welshman.'

Peredur shifted about uneasily in his armchair.

'And that's exactly what I want you to be. Between us the three of us will have it made. And you won't have to worry about poor old Cilydd any more because we shall succeed just where the poor old miserable bastard failed.'

Gwydion held out his hand to forestall any objection.

'And I don't mean that disrespectfully. It wasn't his fault poor chap. He was not only non-practical. The stars were against him. Not to mention South Marine Terrace.'

'He gave up too soon.'

Peredur muttered the words but Gwydion heard them.

'That's right. That's exactly it.'

He sounded delighted to find that they were in such accord.

'So you can see what it means, can't you? What it involves.'

'What?'

'It's like politics really. To get anything positive done you have to compromise. Now what we are after is something pretty big. So we've got to think big. That's essential. It's no use fiddling about on a small scale. And it's no use being constipated by personal integrity. You know, Peredur, when I think of the big-wigs and big-wheels I've seen in this business, in films and in television, and when I compare them to you . . . and I'm not trying to flatter you now . . . or when I compare them to myself for God's sake, and I haven't got a half of your intelligence . . . we just can't allow this opportunity to pass by. It would be a crime in the face of history. We would be letting the old country down just when she needs a helping hand to lift her over yet another technological hurdle. Now you know exactly what I'm talking about. Do I have to tell you? If I go on like this I'll talk myself into a noose. Can't you see it?'

Peredur nodded slowly.

'Well there you are then. No problem. Just mark time on the Old Memorial project. That's all I ask. We'll give him the Albert Memorial one day. And a de-luxe collected edition. I promise you. Just let it ride for a bit.'

'Why?'

'Why?'

Gwydion became suddenly irate.

'You know exactly why. We've got to keep Amy happy. Rub her the wrong way now and God knows what explosions we'll get. You saw what happened to *Infidel*?'

'To what?'

'*Infidel*. My ill-fated musical. I wish you wouldn't behave as if you lived under a glass jar. I've told you before. This academic life is terribly bad for you.'

'What happened?'

'You know what happened. Just because I was a bit rude to poor old Hubert she wouldn't lend me the money. She's like that. She's devilish touchy. So don't upset her. Do I need to spell it out? That's all I'm saying.'

Peredur stood up. He breathed deeply and his hands were trembling slightly as he pulled down his dark double-breasted jacket.

'Well it's too late,' he said. 'The wheels are in motion.'

'Wheels? What wheels? Well, you damn well go and stop them.'

'How can I?'

Gwydion ran his hands through his hair.

'I made a big mistake calling you intelligent, didn't I?'

'Yes, you did.'

Peredur took a last glance at the drawings before walking towards the door.

'Now where are you off to?'

Gwydion was uneasy. Disturbed and puzzled by his brother. Peredur looked distantly at the bed.

'I don't want any part of it,' he said.

'You . . .'

Gwydion was speechless.

'. . . You can't go back on it like that,' he said. 'You just can't. That's no way to behave and you know it.'

'I didn't give any undertaking,' Peredur said. 'I went to see Dr Thomas yesterday.'

'Who?'

'Wilson Thomas.'

'Oh him.'

'Yes. Him. Now it's my turn to remind you of your own family history. I stayed with them for a few weeks after my father killed himself. He didn't like me a bit. I was glad to get away.'

'It was all so long ago.' Gwydion said. 'It worries me the way you behave as if it were yesterday.'

'He was sitting in the Yacht Club. He goes there for lunch every day and then he spends the whole afternoon sitting in the clubroom by himself. Waiting for people to say hello. He's got something wrong with his back. It's like a carapace. He leans forward all the time. He takes a sip of his drink once every fifty seconds. He wanted me to stay with him. He was irritable but desperate for company. I didn't waste any time. I asked him what he'd done with Cilydd's last poems. He quite enjoyed telling me. "I burnt them," he said. "I had to. For your mother's sake." But he was smiling when he said it.'

'You've got this on the brain,' Gwydion said. 'It's like an obsession with you. You're losing any sense of proportion.'

'I'm a very small person.' Peredur smiled sourly. 'I can't afford to have any delusion of grandeur. All I can do is set the record straight. And I'm going to do it.'

7

'You must be absolutely frank with me,' Amy said. 'I want you to say exactly what you think.'

She sat with Gwydion in the arbour at the north end of the walled garden. The sun was shining but she wore a winter overcoat. Estate plans on the bench were kept from blowing about by stones Gwydion had picked up in the flower beds. The five-lobed leaves of small exotic trees had turned red and gold and birds on the paths began to hop closer to them in the hope of being fed.

'I don't see why women with children should be pre-
cluded,' Amy said. 'As soon as you have children you
have a whole range of interesting problems opening up
before you. You realize what we're doing, don't you?'

She raised her hand with the palm downwards and
smiled winningly at her son.

'We are planning a female Utopia.'

She laughed delightedly at her own daring.

'And what is wrong with that may I ask?'

Gwydion was unremittingly affable.

'You must be critical,' his mother said. 'And you
mustn't flatter me. Bedwyr never flatters me.'

'He doesn't have to.'

Gwydion pretended to be jealous.

'I'm very cross with him,' Amy said.

'I can't believe it . . .'

'If he doesn't accept my offer and give me proper
professional attention, I'll engage another architect.
A London man. Somebody at the very top of the
profession.'

'What about the Trust?'

'Well that's what I'll recommend to the Trust.'

'Isn't Bedwyr going to be on it?'

Amy laughed girlishly, delighted to be caught out.

'You told me to be critical and frank!'

'I know I did. But you mustn't tease me. Not too often
anyway. I'm full of ideas you know. Absolutely full of
ideas. That's why I want you all here. There's got to be
a real session of hard thinking. We must hammer out
exactly what it is we want. That's the proper order . . .'

She raised her fingers and began to tick off her
priorities.

'Appoint Trustees. Draw up Articles of Association.
Register as a non-profit-making body under the Act.
Draw up a clear and concise statement of Policy. Appoint a staff. Both full time and part time. And get
the government to collaborate. That's important. Oh

469

you know, Gwydion, I get so excited every time I start thinking about it. It could be something wonderful.'

She gazed at him eagerly and he gave a wise and encouraging nod.

'I keep a pad by my bedside, you know. So that when I get a new idea, I can jot it down at once. I had a wonderful idea last night.'

'Did you?'

'Mini-mundus. The little world of Brangor Hall . . . you don't like it?'

She reacted as if he had winced whereas in fact he had kept his face perfectly still.

'I don't know what it is yet, do I?'

'I mean a giant children's garden. A really big one. In the southern part of the park. Full of scale models of the world's most famous buildings where children can wander in perfect safety. Full of small fountains and ponds and little carriages drawn by Shetland ponies. A whole little world. Don't you think that's a delightful idea?'

'Yes I do.'

'You see how easily we talk to each other,' Amy said. 'That's what I need, you see. Stimulating company. Steel on steel and the sparks fly!'

Gwydion's attention was taken by a female figure occupying with statuesque determination the open doorway set in the high wall at the lower end of the garden.

'When the time comes,' he said, 'we mustn't jump the gun of course; we must do a programme about it on television.'

'Oh Gwydion . . .'

Amy clapped her hands together in front of her face.

'What a splendid idea. Now wouldn't that be wonderful?'

There's no better way of catching the attention and

the imagination of the public . . .'

'No. Of course not.'

'In fact television is a factor you ought to keep in mind.'

She appeared very willing to learn about a field in which she saw him as an expert and to take his advice. Miss Huskie stalked purposefully across the lawn towards them. Her arms swung close to her sides and in her left hand she held a long sheet of flimsy paper. She stood on the paved path a foot below the level of the arbour, her hands on her hips, her feet apart, breathing heavily.

'I'm sorry to interrupt,' she said.

Amy tried to ignore Miss Huskie's grim expression. She spoke light-heartedly.

'Gwydion is going to teach me all about television, May,' she said. 'Isn't that nice?'

Miss Huskie was unable to contain herself any longer. The words gushed out tumbling over one another.

'It's that old woman, Amy . . . She's getting impossible . . . can't count . . . never could . . . what does she know about it anyway . . . gone to her head . . .'

Amy waved her hands to stop her.

'Don't get excited, May, or I won't understand a single word, will I? Now just tell me calmly what it's all about.'

'She says there are three items missing. Clayton says. Well I've been checking.'

'Where?'

Amy was stern and business-like.

'In the Japanese room. You can spend your life doing this sort of thing . . . can you know . . .'

Miss Huskie slipped in an explanation to Gwydion.

'Drive you mad in no time I can tell you. Well, there's been a silver music box missing for over a year. That could be somewhere else because it never belonged there in the first place. And the bullock cart. The ivory bullock cart. God knows where that's gone to. That's been missing for months. But she says there's one of those Japanese sword things, the ceremonial what-you-may-call thing, she says that's missing and she says its worth hundreds of pounds. Is it? Worth hundreds? It can't be far away. But in any case it's not worth hundreds. Is it? Is it?'

'Don't repeat yourself, May.'

'She's making such a fuss,' Miss Huskie said. 'In my opinion it would be a kindness to put her into an old people's home.'

She looked at Gwydion, trying to get him to agree with her.

'Now May,' Amy said. 'Don't be uncharitable. You know that would break her heart.'

'Well, you'd better come,' Miss Huskie said. 'I can't do anything with her. She wants to ring up the police and God knows what . . . she keeps on mumbling and hinting as if it was all my fault in some way. I tell you what I think Amy, quite frankly. Being in there day out is driving her round the bend.'

She stopped when she realized that Amy was not approving of what she was saying. Gwydion rolled up the plans and followed them across the springy lawn. Against a greenhouse wall a row of late tomatoes was ripening in the sun and the smell of chrysanthemums issued richly out of the open doors. Amy lingered there, waiting for Gwydion. The peace of the afternoon was broken by a strange screaming noise that came from the inner courtyard.

'My God,' Miss Huskie said. 'That's our Milly. What's happening to her?'

Her head came down and she rushed down the cobbled corridor, clearly unaware of anything except an urge to protect her helpless sister. Amy touched her son's hand and sighed and shook her head in a silent appeal for his understanding. When they arrived in

472

the inner courtyard they saw Milly sitting on the exposed rock between the stilts that held up the black pavilion. She was bent forward hugging something to her breast. Mrs Clayton was leaning over her, with one hand against a pitch black wooden pillar while she clutched a shawl lightly about her neck with the other. Miss Huskie was marching back to intercept their approach, protesting as she came.

'Amy,' she said. 'That old woman's gone quite mad . . . just look at her! She's frightening the life out of poor Milly. Frightening the life out of her . . . and she's trying to say that Frank's been here . . . Frank's been here. Well that's not true you know. That's a lie you know. A complete lie and she's got absolutely no right to say it . . .'

Amy said nothing. She moved purposefully towards the black pavilion. Milly, when she saw her coming out of the corner of her eye, seemed to judge it wiser to stop howling.

'Now then,' Amy said, as briskly as a schoolmistress. 'What on earth is the matter?'

'She's got a piece of Dresden there,' Mrs Clayton said, pointing at the object Milly was clutching to her bosom. A young man kneeling on a chair reading a book. 'It's that Frank! He's teaching her to steal.'

'Now keep calm,' Amy said.

'I'm sorry Ma'am,' Mrs Clayton said, 'but I have to speak out. I can see right through them.'

She glared at Miss Huskie and her mouth seemed to swell with indignation.

'Now stop it, Connie,' Amy said. 'It does no good to talk like that. No good at all.'

She knelt and held out her hand to Milly.

'Now Milly,' she said. 'Let me see what you've got there.'

Obediently Milly handed Lady Brangor the piece of china. It was broken.

473

Amy held it up.

'It's broken now,' Connie Clayton said. 'But where did she get it and how did she get it? And how did it break?'

'From the laundry room I suppose,' Miss Huskie said. 'Where else? There's a lot of broken stuff there that needs mending.'

'All this fuss over a broken piece of china,' Amy said.

Miss Huskie looked a little apprehensive.

'Well they're worth mending,' she said. 'Some of them anyway . . .'

'And how did she get in?'

Mrs Clayton was not to be put off.

'How did she get in there?'

'How should I know?'

Miss Huskie made herself angry. She wagged her finger at Mrs Clayton.

'It's time you left that poor girl alone. You do nothing but frighten her and it's not right. She can't sleep at nights because of you. And that's not right you know. You are damaging the poor girl's health . . . that poor girl . . . everybody in their right minds, everybody knows that she is as innocent as the day she was born into this world . . . as the day she was born.'

She bent down to help Milly to her feet.

'Come on, Milly love. Get up now, there's a good girl.'

'I'm not blaming her.'

Mrs Clayton carried on while Miss Huskie helped her sister on to her feet and tidied up her appearance.

'I'm blaming a certain somebody who's teaching her bad tricks. And that somebody is a person who has been forbidden by her ladyship to set foot inside the Hall.'

'What are you saying?'

Miss Huskie paused in the brushing of the seat of Milly's skirt.

'Say it out. Go on, say it.'

'He comes back here in the night and he's carrying on a deliberate campaign to frighten me. I know exactly what he's about. And they're all in it, ma'am. All of them. It's a matter for the police in my opinion. I can give a description.'

'Well, call the police.'

Miss Huskie stood erect and her chin pointed first at Amy and then at Connie Clayton.

'Go on, call them. At least it will clear my brother's name. I'll call them myself if you like.'

'They want to frighten me out . . .' Connie said.

Amy stood back and raised her hand, holding the piece of Dresden.

'Now listen to me,' she said.

She waited for their silent attention.

'Now just watch this.'

With a vigorous swing she hurled the piece of china in the direction of the wall of the house. It just reached the base and shattered into many fragments. Connie Clayton groaned and put her hand to her mouth. Milly pulled on her sister's arm as though she wanted to be allowed to collect the bits.

'You must understand this,' Amy said. 'Works of art are absolutely useless if people don't know how to live together.'

Milly sniggered quietly, overcome with her own kind of embarrassment. There was an awed silence while Amy quelled the other women with a thunderous frown.

'You are supposed to be women I can trust,' she said. 'This place has a purpose. And I want you have a place in its purpose. But I will not tolerate this jealous bickering. Is that understood?'

Mrs Clayton limped meekly over to take a closer view of the broken pieces of Dresden on the ground.

'I was hoping to mend it,' she said. 'And put it on the mantelpiece in the butler's room.'

8

'Leave it for God's sake,' Bedwyr said. 'Anybody would think you were in training to become a skivvy.'

Sian was on her hands and knees mopping the block floor of the playroom where Nia had spilt orange juice. Bedwyr's rebuke made her smile. She was pleased to see him home early from the office.

'I can't stand getting up to a mess first thing in the morning,' she said.

'What's Mrs Peace good for?'

Bedwyr seemed bent on continuing criticism of their domestic arrangements. He was tired. Quickly he wetted the tip of his little finger on his tongue and used it to freshen the inner corners of both eyes. As swiftly as he did it, Sian caught a glimpse of the operation, which made her smile at him affectionately.

'As far as I can see you go around cleaning the place up before she comes so that she can have plenty of time to sit in the kitchen sipping tea and smoking her secret cigarettes.'

'She's got varicose veins,' Sian said.

'So have I.'

Bedwyr answered promptly.

'And so have you. I think sometimes the whole world has got them. Come on out of there. I'm going to give you a drink.'

Sian continued with her cleaning.

'No thanks,' she said. 'I don't want one.'

Bedwyr frowned.

'There's nothing wrong with you, is there? You're not . . .?'

Sian laughed at him openly and shook her head.

'I just don't want one that's all. You go and have a big one. You need it.'

In the living room Bedwyr prepared himself a large gin and tonic. He threw his jacket over a chair and carried the telephone to the low table so that he could use it lying down on the settee. He dialled a long sequence of numbers and sipped his drink while waiting for a reply. Sian appeared in the doorway. She raised her arms to tidy her long fair hair.

'Who are you ringing?' she said.

'Amy.'

He spoke his stepmother's name with determined neutrality.

'Looks as if she's out.'

'What does she want?'

Bedwyr listened to the bell ringing in the empty house on the hillside and put down the receiver abruptly.

'I don't know,' Bedwyr said. 'She rang the office this afternoon when I was out . . .'

'She expects you to run at a moment's notice,' Sian said.

'She's got her hands full up there,' Bedwyr said. 'She creates problems for herself. I don't know how she's going to cope quite honestly.'

'Well, let Gwydion take care of it,' Sian said. 'He's on the spot. Why can't he help her for a change.'

'She wants us to go up,' Bedwyr said. 'Next weekend. All of us. We can stay in the Hall.'

'That's ridiculous.'

Sian played nervously with her hair.

'Why is it ridiculous?'

'All that way with three children. And you know what Nia's like on long journeys. Just for one weekend.'

'It's half-term,' Bedwyr said. 'We could make it a long weekend. I would quite like to get away to tell you the truth. Let them get on with it in the office. This is a good excuse. We could take it easy. Make it a holiday.'

'What does she want?'

Sian stared hard at her husband.

'It's this Centre notion. She wants to form a Trust.'

'Something else to waste your time,' Sian said. 'It's a silly scheme anyway. I wouldn't have anything to do with it if I were you.'

'Why is it silly?'

'It's so impractical. A lot of women together. And Amy in charge I suppose. And why has Gwydion suddenly become interested in it?'

'He hasn't,' Bedwyr said. 'He just happens to be up there making a film.'

'What kind of a film?'

Sian sounded profoundly sceptical.

'How do I know? Some kind of television thing I expect.'

'Has he paid you back yet?'

It was more a threat than a question and it made Bedwyr uncomfortable.

'No. But I'm sure he will. We mustn't be impatient.'

'He's certain to be after something. That's what makes me so cross. You'll get all the burdens and all the hard work and he'll blithely walk off when he's got what he wants. Which usually means money. And it's no use you smiling. I can see it happen now. So don't grin.'

'I'm not grinning,' he said. 'I'm just amused at the way you are fighting to protect my interests. Anybody would think I was the kind of naive Willy-wet-leg that anybody could take for a ride.'

'I don't want David to go there,' Sian said stubbornly. 'I'm quite definite about that. It's not good for him.'

'He expects to go.'

'Expects?'

The word angered Sian.

'Why should he expect to go?'

'I told him we might be going . . .'

'She spoils him completely. Buying his affection all the time. And Gwydion's there. He'll be exactly the

478

same. They'll make him impossible to handle for weeks on end. You've no idea.'

Bedwyr sighed deeply.

'Look,' he said. 'We've simply got to try and be sensible about these things. We've all got to live together in one way or another. She's my mother after all.'

'Stepmother.'

'That's just a word. She's my mother to all intents and purposes. I feel a certain obligation towards her. Now you should understand that. You are a Christian. A practising Christian.'

'You know David isn't easy.'

She spoke with a determination to face unpleasant facts.

'With you he is. Because you are his hero. But when you are not here I worry about him.'

'Why? Why should you?'

'He's so silent sometimes. It's quite frightening.'

'Well . . .'

Bedwyr waved a hand dismissively.

'And he holds things against me. And now of course if he doesn't go there'll be one more item to add to his list.'

Sian sat down and bowed her head as if she wanted to show him that she was prepared to bow to the inevitable. Bedwyr moved his hands about with a degree of desperation as if he longed to wave away the thoughts that were oppressing her.

'If you don't want . . .'

The telephone bell rang and he picked up the receiver with swift hostility: any external threat was easy to deal with, compared with the subtle complexities of family relationships. It was Amy who spoke.

'Bedwyr darling,' she said. 'How are you? I'm sure you're working much too hard.'

'I'm fine. Where have you been? I rang a few minutes ago and got no reply.'

He murmured into the receiver with his customary near whisper. It was a sound which demonstrated calm and inspired confidence.

'My dear, I've just been to the Pen-y-Gaer. You never saw anything like it! I've just been trying to write down my impression . . . I nearly got lost on the way down I can tell you. It was dark you see . . . Where is it? . . . Are you listening?'

'Of course,' he said. 'Let's hear it.'

He winked at Sian and she interrupted her worried reverie to give him a brief smile.

'"Mountains, jagged, menacing silhouettes and across the sea molten red gold flowing from the furnace of the setting sun. The sky above, serene and decorated by a row of small shining clouds that hung in rows of tiny pearls inside a vast golden shell about to close over this western world" . . . Do you like that?'

'Not bad,' Bedwyr said.

'It's a bit of a purple patch,' Amy said. 'But I got carried away. I thought I was going to be stuck up there to tell you the truth, I couldn't see the path in the dark.'

'Where's Gwydion?'

'Oh, he stays in the hotel with the film crew. He says he's got to keep them happy. Keep them sweet. That's what he calls it. I can't talk on the telephone.'

'Why can't you? Is your phone bugged or something?'

'We had some trouble here today. Connie and the Huskies have really fallen out. It's most distressing. And Connie is developing the most awful persecution complex. She thinks the house is going to be robbed any minute. And she keeps on seeing Frank Huskie around every corner.'

'She may well be right,' Bedwyr said.

'What do you mean? Frank has a good job in a factory near Rugby.'

'I didn't mean that. There are treasures in that house

and it is extremely vulnerable.'

'That's what I mean,' Amy said. 'Why don't you come and live here?'

Bedwyr shook with silent laughter and Sian looked at him instantly alarmed that he would be influenced by some wild suggestion that her mother-in-law would make on the spur of the moment.

'I've been thinking a lot about it,' Amy said. 'If you come up here the children could have a country upbringing. Think how important it is to bring up children close to Nature. And think of the pleasure I'd get as a doting grandmother, watching them grow up.'

'Haven't you forgotten your Brangor Centre?'

'No, indeed I haven't. I'm thinking big, Bedwyr. That's what you've always advised me to do. You could build a new house anywhere you liked in the Park. Something marvellous and new and easy to run for Sian. With complete privacy. You could live in semi-regal state . . .'

'Amy . . .'

He failed to stop the flow.

'No, let me finish. You could be boss of the whole show and run it anyway you like . . .'

'But that's impossible . . .'

'Nothing is impossible if you really want it to happen. That's what I think. This is a large estate and there's room for all of us. There really is. The Hall and the buildings are quite enough for the Centre. And we'd all be around it to keep an eye on it. Can't you just see it? A thriving creative society.'

'Who's we?'

'All of us. The whole family. All of you near me in my declining years. That's a joke of course. I'm being much more serious. And you wouldn't have to overwork with those selfish partners of yours in that ridiculous office. You could really give all your time to architecture.

481

You always say that is all you truly want. And you could transform Brangor into the eighth wonder of the world, well, of Wales anyhow. Doesn't the idea excite you?'

Sian had been roaming suspiciously about the living room, and now, moving an ornament on the Welsh dresser, she held her head still while she strained to catch something of the crackle of words issuing from the telephone receiver.

'And it's not just for your sake or my sake, you see. But for the children's sake. For the future. I know you agree with me really, don't you? Why don't you just say "yes"?'

Bedwyr murmured softly a phrase which included the word 'kingdom'.

'Did you say something?'

'I'd have to talk to Sian about it.'

Sian could not resist shaping a silent question with her mouth.

'Well there you are,' Amy said. 'Talk it over and we'll discuss it at the weekend. I am so looking forward to seeing you all. I really am. It's all too much for me you know. By myself here.'

'What about Gwydion?'

'He's rather absorbed in his film. I don't like to disturb him. And there's Peredur you see. He really is causing a lot of trouble. I've had a letter from the Mayor of Pendraw. He's that awful Sammy. His father kept an ironmonger's shop in Abraham Street.'

'Why awful?'

'Do you want to hear it?'

'Can't you tell me what's in it?'

'They want me to pay for a Memorial. That's what it amounts to.'

'What are you going to do?'

'It's Peredur,' Amy said. 'He wants to hurt me. I know it's a terrible thing to say, but he must hate me.'

482

'I'm sure he doesn't,' Bedwyr said. 'If he hates anybody, he hates himself.'

'What shall I do, Bedwyr? I've tried to write a sort of polite letter to say I'm not interested. Do you want to hear it?'

'I don't think that would be wise.'

Bedwyr took time to think. His silence disturbed her. She shook the receiver to make sure it was still working.

'Why? Why wouldn't it be wise?'

'You ought to humour him you know. That would be the proper way. Show him you are all in favour of it.'

'But I'm not. I think it's awful the way he goes around digging up the past and scratching around for any little scraps he can find to discredit me! You know he's been to see that Flo Cowley-Jones more than once? Well that woman never forgave me for marrying your father in the first place. She was after him you know. And she's feeding him with all sorts of lies and distortions. And what hurts me more than anything is that he's believing it all. It's disturbing me you know. I can't sleep at nights without a sleeping pill. And I have a horrible nightmare about your father rising from the dead. He wears a huge mask. A sort of Mexican head-dress made of live worms and seaweed. It's all his fault you know. He is being very cruel.'

'Take my advice,' Bedwyr said. 'Say you've no objection. Suggest they form a committee to sponsor the project with representation on it for the family. I'll serve on it if you like.'

Sian moved around the living room as she heard him make the offer of his services. She wanted Bedwyr to see her raise her fist at him and shake it.

'Anyway, that's my advice. He's that kind of character. Oppose him and he'll become even more fanatical.'

'I wish I understood what you are trying to say . . .'

483

'You understand perfectly well,' he said. 'Anyway, you needn't answer the letter until the weekend. Just send a polite acknowledgement and say you want to discuss the suggestion with your sons.'

'Yes. I could do that, couldn't I?'

Amy sounded much brighter.

'How clever you are,' she said. 'You see how much I depend on your advice. Life would be so much easier if you were here on the spot. Let me give this place to you . . .'

'I wouldn't do that if I were you,' Bedwyr said. 'I'd only sell it and emigrate to the Bahamas!'

'Bedwyr! I'm not joking.'

'Of course not . . .'

'Is Sian there? Let me talk to her.'

Bedwyr looked at Sian and pointed a finger at the receiver. She shook her head violently.

'She's upstairs with the kids,' Bedwyr said.

'Is she? Tell her from me, Bedwyr, it's the best time of her life and say that I'm desperately jealous. Tell her that, will you? I won't keep you any longer. And tell her how much I'm looking forward to the weekend.'

He replaced the receiver quietly.

'She wants me to tell you it's the best time of your life,' Bedwyr said.

He folded his arms.

'And that she can't wait to see you next weekend.'

'What was all that about?'

Sian pointed impatiently at the telephone which he had placed back in a recess by the fireplace.

'She wants to give us Brangor Hall. She wants me to turn the whole place into the architectural eighth wonder of the world and she wants your children to grow up in the park living close to nature in semi-regal state.'

'Don't be so silly,' Sian said. 'Tell me what she said.'

'She's worried about Peredur. He's on about that

484

Memorial to Cilydd. It's become an *idée fixe*. I'm sure he should be in Redbatch spouting sociological wisdom to his students. Instead of that he's forever down in Pendraw, stirring things up. Anybody would think he was a politician nursing a constituency.'

'Well, why shouldn't your poor father have a memorial? He was a poet after all. They're quick enough to put up memorials to politicians and industrialists and war-mongers. I think Peredur is quite right. Why shouldn't your children know that their grandfather was a great poet. It's something to be proud of surely?'

'"Great"?'

'Well he might have been. Aren't there unpublished things?'

Bedwyr picked up the evening paper.

'People use the word so loosely,' he said. 'And monuments can be such hideous things.'

9

The top half of the door of Mrs Clayton's sitting room was open. Amy stood in the passage tapping the counter and leaning forward to call out almost playfully.

'Connie! Connie! Is there anyone at home?'

Mrs Clayton emerged from her kitchen, wiping her swollen hands on the coarse apron she had been wearing.

'Goodness,' she said. 'Your ladyship! I'm such a sight! I'm not fit to be seen . . .'

'Can I come in?'

'Of course you can. But you must forgive the mess . . . I haven't had time you see.'

She limped about using her apron to polish any surface within reach.

'Now calm down, Connie dear. Just calm down.'

'I know I should. I wish I didn't get so flustered.'

'Just sit down for a minute. What on earth were you doing?'

'I was scrubbing my scullery floor, ma'am.'

'Connie, you really shouldn't.'

'I like a clean place, your ladyship.'

'Oh I know you do. That floor is never dry. But times have changed, Connie. Nobody scrubs floors anymore.'

'That's half the trouble,' Mrs Clayton said.

She gave a vigorous polish to the brass rail at the top of the tall fireguard in front of the cast iron fireplace. She moved a canterbury music stand stuffed tight with magazines, old menus and other mementoes of social events she had catered for in her heyday so that Amy could sit in the basket armchair she herself considered the most comfortable position in the crowded room. By the window the budgerigar hopped about inquisitively. Amy moved to give him a little notice and the basket chair creaked. Mrs Clayton sat by her work-table. A worn fabric bag hung inside the hexagonal top.

'I'm sorry if I did wrong, ma'am.'

Mrs Clayton had drawn back in her chair like a cat preparing to ward off an attack. Her unblinking eyes watched every move Amy made and yet she managed to preserve and attitude of proper respect by preserving a frozen stillness.

'But I was very alarmed you see, and I didn't want to disturb you so early in the morning.'

'It doesn't really matter,' Amy said.

She spoke forgivingly.

'But I saw a man. Definitely. He was there all right. On the stairs. I definitely saw him. It was the only thing I could do. I rang up the police.'

'Well, it's all over now anyway,' Amy said. 'And there doesn't appear to have been anything missing.'

'But he could have taken something,' Mrs Clayton said. 'He had a key. But he must have seen me, you see, and that disturbed him. I wouldn't say so if you didn't want me to, but I know who it was, you know. It was that Frank Huskie.'

'Now Connie . . .'

'If you don't want me to say a word I won't say a word. But I'm sure it was him.'

'But Connie, he's far away, working. Outside Rugby. Miles away.'

'Nowhere's miles away anymore, is it? Not if you know your way about. And you have a key. Or a set of keys.'

'My main concern is for you not to worry,' Amy said.

'I know, your ladyship. I know that and it's a great comfort to me.'

Amy looked around the room. Mrs Clayton was surrounded by her own personal pieces. In the bureau bookcase there were large velvet-covered Edwardian albums that could only be housed lying flat on top of each other.

'You're not too lonely, Connie? You don't mind sleeping alone in this enormous house.'

'I've spent my whole life in big houses, ma'am. I'd be lost anywhere else.'

'But sleeping alone . . .'

'I love my bedroom It's a beautiful room. And I've got a wonderful view of the stars from my bed. I love to lie there awake and watch them. They make me all calm you know and it's a lovely feeling. They're so pure, you see, and so far away. And I think to myself if I die in the night my soul will fly out straight up there to the stars!'

'Connie! What a nice idea.'

'I've spent my whole life in service,' Mrs Clayton said. 'And I'm not ashamed of it. And I've never missed Holy Communion since the day I was confirmed – except when I was nearly dead with that awful Spanish 'flu. I've always believed in giving all my loyalty and strength to my employer, ma'am, and I've never had cause to regret the path I took.'

'You are quite right, Connie.'

'I don't like to tell you this, your ladyship, and if there's one thing that gets on my nerves it's people who are always complaining, but they want to get rid of me.'

'Who?'

'Those Huskies. I can see right through them. They want to do away with me. That's why that Frank comes in here. Trying to frighten me to death.'

'Connie!'

'They want to move in. That's what they want, you know. You're kind-hearted, your ladyship, and you can't see it. But I can see it.'

'But I thought you liked Rose,' Amy said. 'I thought you got on well with Rose.'

'I never said I liked her, your ladyship. I said she knew how to work. She's the only one of them who really knows how to work. She does a good day's work. And she kept an eye on that dreadful Salter woman. She was good at that. But she's completely under her sister's thumb. May rules her with a rod of iron.'

Amy sighed and her chair creaked. Mrs Clayton looked at her anxiously.

'It's the last thing I would do, to add to your burdens ma'am. But I've seen her, you know, only the day before yesterday. With the man from the Electricity Board . . .'

Mrs Clayton lowered her voice, appalled by her recollection.

'She was giving him the definite impression that she ran the whole place. As if she was the owner. Strutting about, she was.'

Amy laughed.

'You're so kind-hearted, ma'am, as I say. You don't see it happening.'

Mrs Clayton's head was wobbling on her shoulders and her lips twitching with disapproval.

'Now listen Connie: Bedwyr and his family are coming next weekend.'

Mrs Clayton gave her instant professional attention.

'I'll prepare the rooms, ma'am.'

'Get Rose to help you,' Amy said. 'And Beryl Barr. Now you remember. Don't try and do it all yourself.'

Mrs Clayton kept her own counsel. Amy rose to her feet and the housekeeper followed suit, steadying herself by pressing her fingers on the edge of the work-table.

'I think better times are coming,' Amy said. 'I really believe so. Then you will have a much easier time, Connie, and a well-earned rest.'

Mrs Clayton instantly took alarm.

'I don't need a rest, ma'am, indeed I don't. I enjoy my work. I always have done.'

'Yes, but not too much Connie and not too much responsibility. I feel very guilty about it.'

Mrs Clayton put her hand to her mouth and then waved it about to indicate that she had something important to say and had almost forgotten to mention it.

'Alice Hopps,' she said.

Amy looked puzzled. She held open the butler's counter ready to leave.

'I told you ma'am. She was in service with me at Cranforth Royal. Alice, the still-maid. She's always kept in touch with me down the years. Never goes on holiday without sending me a postcard.'

'What about her?'

'She married John, the footman. A very reliable and experienced couple. They are well into middle age now of course. Very experienced. They would be ever such a help, your ladyship. Alice is such a hard worker and never complains. Never. And John can drive a car. He's a good mechanic you see. I'm sure he could repair the old boiler here in no time at all and get the whole system working perfectly. And keep it working right through the winter. Sir George Temple-Holmes offered him a job as his chauffeur in the South of France. But he was courting Alice you see and didn't want to go abroad. They are ever such good people. Church-goers, both of them. Very regular.'

Mrs Clayton's encomium petered out.

'What about them?'

'We keep in touch,' Mrs Clayton said. 'They're due to retire in a year or so, but they are both very fit. John is as strong as a horse. They'd come here very willingly and I've been thinking how nice it would be if they could. They could help me put the Hall back into tip-top shape. As it used to be in the old days . . . I hope you don't mind me mentioning the idea?'

'Of course not,' Amy said.

Alongside the door was a shallow cupboard with many white drawers marked with the names of different spices. Amy opened it while she considered what to say. She opened and closed one of the little drawers holding the flattened head of the brass knob delicately between finger and thumb.

'The old times,' she said. 'We can't go back to them, can we? Not really. We have to look ahead, Connie, to a new and different world. A better world I hope.'

Mrs Clayton already looked disappointed.

'They would never ask for a big wage,' she said. 'I'm quite sure of that. They're not that kind. I always used to tell Alice when she first came to me, "Happiness comes before money, Alice" . . . That's what I always told her.'

'It's not money,' Amy said. 'It's the future of the estate. The future of Brangor. It's a very fluid situation, Connie. There are death duties you see. Twice over.'

'Death duties,' Mrs Clayton said.

She recognized the weight of the phrase without fully grasping its meaning, like the name of some mysterious plague.

'Wicked,' she said. 'It's a terrible thing. Terrible.'

'All I am saying . . . put it like this . . . it would be wrong to raise their hopes. How could you involve a couple looking for a quiet, tranquil, eventide of life in such a fluid volatile situation. Do you see what I mean?'

Mrs Clayton looked a little bewildered but she nodded obediently.

'You mustn't worry about it,' Amy said. 'You know I'll always look after you.'

Mrs Clayton could not conceal her disappointment. She had suddenly been deprived of a particular comfort, something she had been wrapping over her shoulders to keep out the draughts of misery and fear. She shifted about on her feet, bracing herself to meet a new situation.

'Alice likes a quick reply,' she said. 'She always used to say she could put up with anything except not knowing where she stood.'

'You mustn't encourage them.'

Amy pulled the counter into place and turned to face the old woman alone in the room.

'Send her a note,' she said. 'Tell her you'll be writing soon when the situation becomes a little clearer.'

Amy smiled understandingly.

'Blame me if you like.'

Mrs Clayton shook her head. She turned slowly towards the window of her room and the extended wings

of her budgerigar. He was preening himself with simu-
lated urgency in the slanting afternoon light.

10

The south-west wind and the shifting grey pebbles on
the desolate beach made their progress rather difficult.
The Mayor led the way. He wore his bright chain of
office over his thick overcoat and the fitful sunshine
that set patches of the heaving sea gleaming shone on
his polished gold chain. He carried a cigar and he held
it out like an act of sustained public generosity, allowing
the wind to smoke it. He was a short, wide man. His
face was bright red after a public banquet and his eyes
shone excitedly. Bedwyr was a few steps behind him,
his head lowered against the wind. The Mayor looked
back, opening and shutting his dark jaw which was almost ready for the second shave of the day. He waited
until Bedwyr came into close range before speaking.

'What's the matter with them, then?' he said, in a
rasping voice. 'Are they a bunch of cripples or something?'

Peredur had come without an overcoat. The collar
of his dark suit was turned up and he walked sideways,
his shoulder giving him some protection from the wind.
Behind him came a voluble councillor, the borough
surveyor and the town clerk, a tall, melancholy-looking
man with fine dog-like eyes in his weary face. The
councillor was talking strenuously and the borough
surveyor looked at him from time to time with his head

on one side gulping for air against the prevailing wind.
His mouth was set in a curve of permanent scepticism
as though it was his normal practice to disbelieve everything he was told, without full documentary evidence.

'I think your mother was very wise to stay in the car,'
the Mayor said.

He gave a flourish with his cigar towards the large car
parked where the promenade came to an abrupt end.

'And she's got Gwydion with her,' he said. 'He'll keep
her entertained alright!'

He seemed very pleased to renew his acquaintance
with the family.

'I remember him in the old days, you know,' the
Mayor said. 'When we had the bicycle place in Abraham
Street. Proper little devil he was.'

He marched on, chuckling to himself. It was a long
way to the rock but he was determined to get there
first. He was bare-headed and the wind curled up the
ends of his iron-grey hair which was trimmed close, the
top plastered down securely with a strong application
of hair oil. Turning his head again, rather too sharply,
the Mayor lost his balance. He stumbled first one way
and then another. He managed to win support for his
back from the wind. For a moment, while his arms
remained outstretched, he could have been inviting
Bedwyr to dance.

'I'm sorry about the weather,' he said.

Bedwyr was looking anxiously at the rock in the
distance.

'It's not far at all,' the Mayor said, anxious to dispel
any misgivings Bedwyr might have been feeling. 'It
looks further than it is. What's the matter with them,
then?'

The borough surveyor had paused and turned to
point out the broken end of the promenade. They were
three coloured figures pivoted on the monochrome
grey beach and the distance grew between them and

Peredur's struggling black figure.

'He's always on about that Promenade,' the Mayor said.

His prominent jaw was sliced by a curving grin but his voice was full of resentment. The borough surveyor's arms were outstretched and then tilted slowly towards the sea to emphasize his point.

'He says it's sinking,' the Mayor said. 'Sinking slowly under the sea. No foundations. Something like that. But we all know that, don't we? We'll all be under the sea sooner or later.'

The chain of office glinted as his shoulders shook with the seismic force of his own joke.

'We don't want to worry about little things like that, do we?' he said. 'We've got plenty of real troubles to worry about.'

Peredur joined them, his face blue with cold. The Mayor raised his voice to include a second listener. It was hoarse from a lifetime spent in energetic salesmanship.

'As I was saying,' he said. 'This is really one of my most cherished ambitions. It really is. As you both know I never had much education. I've worn myself out expanding the family business. That's my excuse. But I love poetry, you know. I always have done. Even more than music. Now there's that poem of your father's to the *Wood Pigeon*. I know that one off by heart.'

He looked at them both as if he were hoping they would challenge him to prove it.

'And there was that one about *The Hawk*. I know that one too. We make the kids learn them in school you know. What's the use of having a great poet in your midst without knowing his work? That's what I say. It's when you're young you should learn it. That's what I say.'

The approach of the council officials rekindled his urge to be first to reach the rock.

'Onward!'

He called out gaily and once more led the way against the wind. They reached an expanse of wet sand and this gave him the idea of adopting a zig-zag trot to reduce the resistance offered by the wind. He looked back at the others and shouted.

'Tack!'

Nobody followed his example. He slowed down again and waited for Bedwyr.

'There are conflicting views,' he said. 'About the amount the town should spend.'

Bedwyr lifted his hand to shade his eyes and stare at the distant headland.

'Personally I would go to the limit. The absolute limit. The way I put it to Ways and Means was this. "We have here," I said, "very possibly one of our great invisible assets." Those were my exact words. They are surprisingly dull some of them you know and you have to spell everything out. I haven't had any education as you well know, but I'm not dull. Far from it. "What is our major industry?" I asked them. "Agriculture? Yes and no. Fishing? Not any more. Explosives? Only employs a hundred men and due for redundancies when full automation becomes operative. Now our growth industry," I said, "is tourism. There can be no question about it. And we must have our minds clear," I said, "what kind of tourists we want to encourage. Not day-trippers and not caravans. Our party is in power on that very platform. The family holiday? By all means. But above all," I said, "what we want to encourage is a better class of people. I'm a self-made man," I said, "and many of you remember me delivering bread instead of studying in school which is where I should have been. But I think the world of our little town," I said, "and I've got its true welfare in the very middle of my heart," I said, "and everybody know this is gospel."'

He paused for breath and Peredur took the opportunity to march ahead. The Mayor hurried after him. Bedwyr turned to look at the distant promenade. The bonnet of the car in which Amy and Gwydion were sitting glittered above the jagged edge of the concrete which sagged into an accumulation of stones driven into the top corner of the shelving beach by the pounding of high seas. He was overtaken by the town clerk, the borough surveyor and councillor John Artemus who couldn't wait to expound his ideas to Bedwyr. He fastened his eager gaze on Bedwyr's face and spoke with an urgent fluency in spite of his lisp.

'I believe in it,' he said. 'I really do. Pendraw is a marvellous place you know. I mean, you wouldn't believe the number of famous people born in Pendraw. And connected with Pendraw. You wouldn't believe it, if I told you. Since I've been running this campaign I've made a special study of the subject. Did you know that Thomas Jefferson's mother was born in Allt yr Eiryn? Just two miles outside the town! Nobody knows. Think of the Americans coming here every summer and going away without knowing that vital fact. It makes you think doesn't it?'

'You've got to be sure of your facts,' the borough surveyor said.

His sceptical smile was fixed firmly on his face and it drove the young councillor to make his claims with even greater emphasis.

'And there's Bishop Edwards,' he said. 'And Captain Price – Price the Pirate! And the Black Minstrel from Dalar Wen. And the Fair Oriana, the friend of Alexander Pope. And four chaired bards. There isn't another town in the country of this size that can boast of four chaired bards! Four national winners! And the man who invented the first steam motor car. And the Blind Harpist. And Cilydd of course. And the house where . . .'

496

'We'd better move,' the borough surveyor said. 'His worship is waiting for us.'

The town clerk paused to cough with a sad intensity and to wipe away the tears the wind had brought to his eyes. He did not appear to be enjoying the outing. The Mayor and Peredur had reached the rock. The Mayor was examining it in great detail as though it had recently landed and he had never seen it before. Peredur disappeared on the further side. The Mayor came out to meet Bedwyr, his arms outstretched.

'Welcome to Craig Cilydd,' he said. 'Castell Cilydd!'

He stood still and barred the way of Bedwyr's advance.

'I hope you're not getting the wrong impression by the way. It was a unanimous decision. The only question left undecided was how much to vote and that of course would largely depend on the form the Memorial would take. And this is why we value your visit so much and why I have to thank you on behalf of the Town Council.'

Bedwyr nodded and indicated his desire to get closer to the rock. He walked around with a professional look on his face, examining yet another prospective site. Between the rock and the gorse on the edge of the foreshore there was a sequence of worn outcrops fissured by the action of the sea and studded with rock pools. When he returned to the group from the Town Hall he found them standing back to look at Peredur who had climbed to the top of the rock and was facing the wind on the sheer edge, staring out to sea.

'You can understand it, can't you?' the Mayor was saying. 'I was just saying to the others . . .'

He came to stand close to Bedwyr as though he were a favoured customer.

'. . . You can understand it, can't you. He used to be up there for hours. Composing and thinking.'

The borough surveyor had thought of a joke. He

leaned forward and pointed up discreetly at Peredur. He addressed himself in a comradely fashion to Bedwyr as a distinguished practitioner of a kindred profession.

'That would be one way of doing it,' he said. 'Ask him to keep still while we spray him with concrete.'

The Mayor was appalled by the borough surveyor's lack of taste and good sense.

'It's got to be something original and ambitious,' he said. 'That's what I feel. Take Lloyd George's grave as an example of what I mean. Beautifully designed in a beautiful setting. And even Beddgelert and the dog. Where would that place be but for an imaginary grave? It makes a difference you know. It really does.'

He stared at the Town Clerk until he paid him the proper homage of a melancholy nod.

'Well now then,' the Mayor said. 'Ideas. That's what we need.'

Councillor John Artemus was anxious to make his contribution.

'A walk,' he said. 'That's what I think. A really nice walk down past the golf links and through the gorse coming out over there. And then linked by a neat causeway to the rock itself. And a statue perhaps. With little railings around it. That's what I thought.'

The Mayor gave him a nod of approval and encouragement and then glanced at Bedwyr to see how he had taken the suggestion.

'Cilydd's walk,' he said. 'And then Cilydd's Castle. How does that appeal?'

Bedwyr was in no hurry to react. The borough surveyor bustled into the discussion.

'I don't want to be mundane,' he said. 'But we've got to be practical, haven't we? That's going to cost a pretty penny as you can imagine. Now, why not put something substantial at the end of the promenade? It could act as a buttress and stop the sea eating away at the foundations. You could stick something on top of that if you wanted.'

He grinned sceptically at Bedwyr, resolutely unsentimental. The Mayor intervened hastily.

'I tell you what I've been thinking,' he said. 'Why not have a competition? Open to the whole world. To design the most effective and useful memorial. That might delay things a little but it would create more public interest. And we need that, you see. We need it. That's one thing I've learnt from public life. You've got to have public interest.'

The Town Clerk was looking back at the distant promenade.

'It's rather a long way,' he said.

His voice was nostalgic.

'I've thought about that, haven't I?'

The Mayor looked to Councillor John Artemus for support.

'A secluded spot could be a positive advantage. A secluded spot is just what is needed. The whole of this end of the town is a bit of a wilderness. It needs opening out.'

The Town Clerk was gazing dolefully at Bedwyr's face, trying to gauge his reactions.

'Mr More is an architect,' he said. 'He may well have ideas of his own.'

'Well of course!'

The Mayor looked bright and eager.

'You must forgive our enthusiasm,' he said. 'My wife was saying only this morning, "Now for goodness' sake," she said, "get on with your breakfast and stop going on about Cilydd and his memorial." I was trying to tell her, you know, make her realize. "How many people", I said, "when he was alive and living in this town, how many people realized they had a genius in their midst?" It made her think, I can tell

499

you. That's what I call a poet you know. A man of genius.'

He stuck out his chin, determined to stand by his judgement come what may. Bedwyr looked quiet and patient.

'I haven't mentioned the legendary significance of the rock have I?' the Mayor said. 'I've been reading it up, you know. You can't launch these things without being properly informed. Now the question is, did he come here because the legend of the rock had some special attraction for him?'

'Or did he just like the walk?'

The borough surveyor preserved his set smile in spite of the Mayor's frown.

'He came here very often,' the Mayor said. 'Especially when it was raining. I'm sure you'd confirm that, Mr More.'

Bedwyr nodded obligingly.

'Now according to the legend the magician stood on top of this rock and caused a crystal city to disappear under the sea. Either because it was sinful or just out of spite. Nobody knows quite which. Now the question is, could something of that idea be brought out in the Memorial?'

The Mayor waved both his hands artistically.

'I'm just throwing ideas out,' he said. 'I'm quite aware it's not my proper field, as they say, but ideas have got to come from somewhere, haven't they?'

He looked up at Peredur, who still remained a still silent figure challenging the wind at the end of the rock. The Mayor was showing signs of impatience. Bedwyr remained politely calm.

'This wind is getting at my kidney,' the Mayor said. 'It's one of the penalties of office, all these public luncheons.'

He tapped his gold chain lightly.

'Well let's put it like this,' he said. 'It all boils down to

£.s.d. The size of the scheme would depend on the size of the available funds.'

The borough surveyor nodded encouragingly. Discussing costs broughts out his professional interest, but he was still willing to be witty.

'That's what Pharaoh said when he was planning his Pyramid.'

The Mayor showed no relish for the interruption. He pushed Bedwyr's elbow so that he could turn more of his back on the borough surveyor.

'Now what the council would obviously like to know is what extent we could depend on a contribution from the family . . .'

'You've got a committee?'

Bedwyr's question rang out with unexpected force after his long silence. The Mayor was taken by surprise.

'A sub-committee you mean?'

'There ought to be a committee,' Bedwyr said. 'Some kind of an official committee. A memorial committee. All the interested parties could be represented on that committee. And they could take the appropriate steps in the appropriate order. Obviously there are many ideas and many suggestions. They ought to be carefully sifted. And a policy should be laid down. Is there going to be a public appeal? Is it going to be by public subscription? These things need to be carefully considered.'

'Oh I agree,' the Mayor said.

'If you wished the family to be represented on the committee we would discuss it among ourselves, my mother and my brothers, as soon as we received an official invitation.'

The Mayor was looking up at Peredur on the rock as though he wished he would come down at once and join in the discussion.

'We are of course very grateful to the Town Council for initiating the idea. And very honoured. And we are most anxious to collaborate in any way we can. But I'm sure you would agree there is a procedure in these matters. Where there's money involved and the expenditure of public funds . . .'

Bedwyr glanced at the Town Clerk who hastened to nod his complete agreement. He was shivering with cold and anxious to get back to his office.

'It is very necessary to take the correct steps in the correct order,' Bedwyr said. 'You know what I mean?'

11

'My God! What's that?'

Gwydion and Bedwyr stood still on the Jacobean staircase. A powerful burst of soprano came from the direction of the empty chapel, going up and down in echoing arpeggios. Gwydion exaggerated his reaction for his brother's benefit. It always appeared to give him satisfaction that he could make his solemn older brother laugh so easily.

'She's started already,' he said. 'The creative women are among us.'

He made theatrical gestures of horror extending his arms to protect himself from invisible furies.

'It could be Connie of course,' he said in a calmer voice. 'About to exit on the wings of song.'

The soprano began to sing an aria from Purcell. They listened for a while.

'Have you noticed,' Gwydion said. 'With most of the rooms locked there's hardly anywhere to sit in this damned place. Isn't that extraordinary?'

'Shall we go in and listen? It's rather nice.'

Bedwyr was ready to follow his own suggestion but Gwydion shook his head.

'I want to talk to you. Before old Savonarola turns up. Business.'

'Not another Musical, I hope?'

Bedwyr was ready to tease. He was anxious to relax and enjoy himself.

'Now be serious. Let's go down there shall we and I'll tell you about it.'

He pointed hopefully to a long settee set against the staircase below them.

'It's about television,' he said. 'With a capital "T"'.

'I'm an architect,' Bedwyr said. I've got a diploma to prove it. What on earth has television got to do with me?'

Gwydion prevailed upon him to sit down.

'A great deal. Now, first I want to ask you about that chap J.M.'

'You called him an old windbag.'

Gwydion became impatient.

'Well, I dare say he is . . . But from what you told me he's one of South Wales's leading wire-pullers.'

'So?'

'Well that is exactly what we want. What we must have.'

'Who's we?'

Bedwyr became more cautious. He sat sideways on the long settee, his fist under his mouth, watching his brother with critical closeness.

'Our consortium. We need local connections,' Gwydion said. 'Really good powerful local connections. I said so all along and now it's becoming quite urgent. Sir J.M. sounds just right. Do you think he'd be interested?'

'I want to hear more about this,' Bedwyr said. 'I want to hear the whole story. In detail.'

The soprano had stopped singing. The doors leading to the chapel opened and Amy emerged, her voice already reverberating between the pillars.

'I thought it would interest you, Miss Hopkin,' she was saying. 'What do you think of the acoustic? Do you think it has possibilities?'

The visitor looked nervous. Her hands were still clasped together high on her bosom, clutching a small handkerchief, and her round face was glistening with her recent exertions. She was in her early thirties and her beaky nose made the restless movements of her head appear birdlike. She walked with great care, lifting her feet, which were shod in dark blue court shoes, high off the ground.

'Now look who's here,' Amy said cheerfully. 'My two fine sons sitting under the family tree. Bedwyr, Gwydion, this is Miss Maud Hopkin who has just finished my hair. Do you like it?'

She turned around unhurriedly so that her sons could admire her coiffure.

'It always looks a bit stiff at first,' she said, 'and artificial. But it wears out well. Doesn't it Miss Hopkin?'

The hairdresser nodded happily, content to stand by the product of her craft.

'And you heard her sing,' Amy said. 'You heard Miss Hopkin sing! Hasn't she got a gorgeous voice . . . What else can you expect. She comes from Aberdare. A real nightingale. I've been telling her about our plans for the Brangor Hall Centre and I think she's really interested, aren't you, Miss Hopkin?'

'Well . . .'

Miss Hopkin looked modest.

'Miss Hopkin has a brother who teaches at the Comprehensive school. The poor man lost his wife last year and Miss Hopkin keeps house for him, don't you, dear? I'm telling her she is sacrificing herself and her art on the altar of her family duty. Now this is just

504

the kind of problem that the Brangor Centre will be designed to cope with. You could call it a classic case.'

'It's very kind of you,' Miss Hopkin said.

She had become hot and flustered with embarrassment.

'But I must be going.'

'Oh what a shame,' Amy said. 'I was going to show you some more of the house.'

'Well I'd love to,' Miss Hopkin said. 'But it's three o'clock you see and it will take me over half an hour to get back to Llanelw.'

'Of course it will. I'm being self-absorbed as usual. You must come again. And bring your brother with you next time. You say he's interested in history, don't you? Well this place should fascinate him. It's what I call a higgle-piggle museum. Not raggle-taggle, but higgle-piggle! A great junk-shop of history . . .'

Bedwyr and Gwydion watched their mother leading the way down the passage lit from above by a long skylight.

'To the manner born.'

Gwydion smiled ironically as he murmured his comment. Bedwyr's admiration was more unreserved.

'You've got to hand it to her,' he said. 'All that energy and enthusiasm. At her age. After all she's been through.'

'She's collected a new victim,' Gwydion said. 'She'll eat that scraggy soprano for breakfast. Just imagine this entire mausoleum stuffed with them, like battery hens and old Amy gobbling them up one after another!'

'I thought you were sympathetic towards the whole idea?'

'Am I?'

Gwydion raised his eyebrows quizzically.

'You tell me. I'm not a mind reader.'

'She's got a giant appetite for human beings. That's what it is. Some like waffles. Some like strawberries.

505

Amy likes humans. Look at it. Did you ever see a building better designed to be a boarding school for elderly girls and everyone of them with a 'pash' on the dashing headmistress? Of course I'm in favour of it. God willing she won't have any time left to interfere with me.'

Bedwyr frowned, displeased with what he heard.

'What's the matter,' Gwydion said jovially. 'I can be frank, can't I?'

'Oh yes; you can be frank. And so can I. It's time you grew up.'

'I'm doing my best,' Gwydion said.

He was determined to remain good-humoured.

'It always worries me. This attitude you've got towards Amy. As if she was directly to blame for all the deficiencies in your own nature.'

'What "deficiencies"?'

Gwydion was quick to pick out the word.

'Try and be fair to the poor old thing. She dotes on you. But you always want to see her in the worst possible light . . .'

'Hey. Steady on.'

Gwydion held on to Bedwyr's arm.

'Don't be so touchy. I was only trying to be funny. Not with any success.'

Gwydion smiled agreeably and Bedwyr became a little embarrassed.

'She's gone to so much trouble . . . getting her hair done,' he said. 'It's obvious that her heart was set on some grand Family Reunion. Have you seen the dining room?'

Gwydion smiled.

'I've been watching them all week. Old Connie thrashing around like a station-master with a wooden leg seeing off the "Royal Grouse Train". She had Beryl Barr and Rose Huskie chasing about like a pair of demented porters.'

'It's pathetic,' Bedwyr said.

He looked genuinely worried.

'She always expects too much. Have you seen that table laid for six? The chandelier gleaming and a fire in the grate and the silver and the best dinner service laid out . . .'

'I'm sorry Sian couldn't come,' Gwydion said. 'It's nothing serious I hope.'

'A family feast. And a place laid for David. As if his mother would ever allow him to stay up to dine with the grown-ups! But she had this great glittering image of herself sitting in state at the head of the table and her sons and her grandson sitting around the table. It is pathetic. Don't you think so?'

Gwydion gave him a warning nudge. Amy was returning down the corridor. She raised her hands and clapped them together silently when she saw her sons.

'I'm so glad you both saw Miss Hopkin,' she said. 'Wasn't she a dear? And the sacrifices that girl has made. All her life. She nursed an invalid mother for years. And then when she died, her brother's wife fell ill of some awful disease and she came up here to nurse her. And she never complains. And by the sound of that brother of hers she has every right to. Just imagine. Until his wife died he was superintendent of their chapel Sunday school. Now he never goes near the place. I call that typical.'

'Typical what?'

Bedwyr's tone was sympathetic but implacably rational.

'What I call the Welsh sulk.'

Amy spoke defiantly.

'Providence treats you badly and you shrink back into your shell to nurse your grudge. That sort of thing. And that poor girl waits on him hand and foot. There's something so pathetic about it. You know, I think it

507

would be so wonderful if Brangor could help women like that.'

'So do I,' Gwydion said.

His voice rang out cheerfully between the pillars of the Hall.

'Do you really?'

Amy looked moved by his whole-hearted agreement.

'I'm so glad.'

She took hold of Gwydion's wrist and shook it gratefully.

'I don't want the scheme to sound cranky,' she said. 'At the same time I want it to be hugely ambitious.'

She opened out her arms and thrust her hands upwards, laughing at her own enthusiasm.

'Ideas are tumbling about in my poor old head,' she said. 'So I need your help, I really do. And I'm sure that's the modern way. Isn't it, Bedwyr?'

'What is?'

He gave her a quiet smile, obviously designed to calm her down a little.

'I can't help being excited,' she said. 'All my sons home. Poor Connie is in a state. She's trying to prove that she's the greatest cook this place has ever seen. I'm terrified she'll do some damage to herself. There's nothing I can do to stop her. You know how she got that limp, don't you? I think it's such a tragic story. She had the most frightful accident. In 1937 she was icing an enormous cake at Cranforth Royal. For the daughter's twenty-first. Lady Anne her name was. A silly girl incidentally if ever there was one. She died an alcoholic three or four years ago. Poor Connie was quite heart-broken. You would have thought she had lost her own daughter. The fact is she stayed up all night icing this fearsome cake and about two o'clock in the morning she spilt boiling water all down her left leg.'

Bedwyr looked as though he had heard the story before. Gwydion seemed the more interested listener.

'Poor old thing,' he said cheerfully.

'What makes me cross is those Cranforths did absolutely nothing for her. She had all this trouble with an atrophied muscle in her leg and they just took the first excuse they could to get rid of her. And she still idolizes them. They are her Big People.'

'People are incredible.'

Gwydion made his comment obligingly.

'They are, aren't they? I've always felt that. And there's such pride in that old woman. Sheer unadulterated pride. She has to be *the* perfect cook. *The* perfect housekeeper . . . now wait a minute. Will you go to the cellars for me?'

She took out a key from her pocket and waved it under Gwydion's nose.

'I don't know anything about wine,' she said. 'But Connie suggests red Burgundy of one sort or another and white Mosel. Could you bring up half a dozen of each?'

Gwydion took the key. He looked inquiringly at Bedwyr as if to suggest he might like to accompany him.

'Do you mind going by yourself?' Amy said. 'There's a light on the stone shelf at the bottom of the steps, on your left as you go down. You switch on there and drag the lead after you. It's primitive but it works.'

Gwydion still hesitated.

'You won't be afraid of the dark?'

Amy was genuinely concerned.

'You never liked the dark when you were little. Do you remember singing in the lane coming back from Aunty Grace's house? I was coming to meet you and I could hear your little voice piping away in the darkness such a long way away.'

'You were late,' Gwydion said.

He couldn't keep the reproach out of his voice.

'I was such a hopeless mother.'

Amy shook her head and sighed with self-reproof and remorse.

'If there's anything else there you fancy, darling, just bring it up. I'm putting you in complete charge of the fountains of pleasure.'

She laughed engagingly and both men were prepared to respond to her mood.

'It's your gift, you know.'

'What is?'

'Your gift is for dispensing joy,' Amy said. 'You should cultivate it. Never get too bogged down, my dear, in the sordid intricacies of business. Am I right, Bedwyr?'

'You may well be.'

Bedwyr smiled.

'It's obvious really. That's why he's so good at television.'

'Aha,' Gwydion said.

He glanced meaningfully from his mother to his half-brother and back again.

'You want me out while you get down to serious business. Some tiny carve-up?'

'Nonsense, darling.'

Amy slapped his arm.

'Just hurry. We'll be in the Oak Room for tea. Be as quick as you can.'

'You'll hear me singing,' Gwydion said. 'I get scared stiff down there. It's full of hidden dragons.'

In the Oak Room there was a cheerful fire burning. It was a comfortable room. The leather padding on the club fender surrounding the fireplace had been scratched and scored by generations of dogs who had also growled in their sleep on the thick rug. Bedwyr showed some interest in the oak panelling. Designs that were Celtic and vaguely ecclesiastic were carved on isolated panels which were obviously older than the rest.

'I'm so grateful to you, Bedwyr,' Amy said. For

persuading Peredur to see sense about this memorial business.'

'I don't know that he does yet,' Bedwyr said.

He glanced at his wrist watch.

'He's late.'

'I've been thinking,' Amy said. 'He could sleep in David's bed. It's all ready. Then he wouldn't have to leave early. And we would all be together for the first time for goodness knows how long.'

Amy smiled as she stared into the fire.

'Perhaps things are really going to be better from now on,' she said. 'I hope so. There should be a place for each one of you in a proper scheme of things.'

She extended her arms to represent branches.

'Three green branches!'

'What does that mean?'

Bedwyr smiled at her fondly.

'You know how I like to see things in images. I'm the tree trunk you see and you are the three green branches. We've got to arrange things so that you can all burst into leaf and into flower . . . don't laugh at me. I'm being serious.'

He sat down and listened to her obediently.

'I'm not saying I'm rich,' Amy said. 'But I have got wealth of a kind. And I want to put it to good use. I really do. Otherwise it's useless. Just an accumulation of rubbish. And I want you all to benefit from it. So that you'll all have a chance to flourish in the way that suits you best. And I don't want to interfere. In any way at all. I wish you'd tell Sian. Even with the children. I promise I won't interfere.'

Bedwyr nodded uncomfortably.

'I can quite understand her point of view. But you tell her, Bedwyr, just because I'm old I'm not set in my ways. It doesn't mean I'm incapable of making a fresh start. Will you tell her that?'

'Yes I will.'

'Since the children aren't here, we can give all our attention to talking about the place and all the problems that go with it. You won't mind that, will you?'

'Good Lord, of course not.'

Bedwyr was eager to please and to make amends for the absence of his family.

'There's so much to tell you, now I've got you all to myself.'

She seemed encouraged by his serious attention.

'I've been thinking about this Trust. It could be a much bigger affair altogether, you see. Not just the centre. It could be a sort of Foundation. And you three could administer it between you. I wouldn't want any part of it. Three brothers shouldn't find it too difficult to cooperate. I've always thought, you know, that if only we could learn to cooperate more how much more creative and successful we would be. Don't you agree?'

'It's idealistic,' Bedwyr said.

'But of course it is. Why shouldn't it be? Apart from ideals what other good reason is there for living?'

With a gesture of his hand he gave in gracefully to the force of her enthusiasm. There was a knock on the door and Rose Huskie, her eyes wide with alarm and her goitre moving in her neck, pushed in a tea trolley. Amy thanked her but Rose's hand was already beckoning nervously in the air. She always seemed uncertain how to address Amy. Unlike her sister May, she did not have the confidence to use her Christian name, but as a very old acquaintance she could not bring herself to say 'Lady Brangor' and she was even less able to say 'Your Ladyship'.

'Could you come?'

She gobbled her words.

'Mrs Clayton's upset Beryl Barr. I wonder if you'd come. She says she's spoilt the trifle. She's made the cream curdle that's what Connie says. Could you come and settle it?'

512

Amy rose to her feet but Bedwyr stretched out his arm to prevent her leaving.

'No,' he said. 'You just leave them. Sit down, Amy. Sit down please.'

Reluctantly she obeyed him as far as sitting on the arm of a chair.

'Now look,' Bedwyr said. 'I want my mother to have her tea in peace.'

He glanced authoritatively at his wrist watch.

'In exactly half an hour I suggest you see each one of them. In the old study behind the billiard room. Make it a proper interview. I see no reason why you should have to go running every time any little thing goes wrong.'

Amy was still inclined to go to the kitchen.

'I have to keep the peace, don't I? It's part of my function.'

She tried to make light of the problem. Rose's mouth was shut tight as she pushed the trolley into position and her head seemed to be swaying slightly on her long neck. Amy watched her with some concern.

'It won't take me a minute and then you'll be easier in your mind, won't you, Rose?'

Rose was by the door. She nodded rather self-righteously and then stood to one side as Peredur came in. His hair was wet and he was mopping his face with a large, dirty-looking handkerchief.

'Peredur!'

Amy was immediately anxious.

'You are soaking wet. Where have you been? Take your jacket off.'

He seemed unaware of his condition until it was pointed out to him.

'Rose, could you put this on a hanger, dear, and put it up somewhere in the boiler-room. I'll be along as soon as I can. Sit by the fire, Peredur. I'll pour you some tea. Where on earth have you been?'

'Exploring.'

Peredur smiled frostily but he was not inclined to say any more. Amy complained about the weather and Bedwyr tried to ask Peredur questions about his work at the university. He gave monosyllabic answers which were like press-studs keeping down a black cover over his thoughts and intentions. Gradually his unwillingness to converse imposed an uneasy silence on the room. They listened to the flames roaring in the chimney and rain water pouring from a gutter above the window which was choked with autumn leaves. Both Amy and Bedwyr were greatly cheered and relieved when Gwydion arrived carrying a half-bottle of German wine covered in cobweb and dust.

'Just look at this,' he said. 'This is either nectar or poison, probably the latter. There's a whole row of them. All half-bottles. And they've been there since 1930.'

'Older than I am,' Bedwyr said. 'It must be sour by now. I know I am.'

Together he and Gwydion went to the window. They wiped the label and Bedwyr held up the bottle to the light to examine the contents.

'You'll have to open it tonight,' Amy said. 'Before dinner. And if it's any good we'll get up the others.'

'I thought we were going to discuss the Memorial,' Peredur said.

They all turned to look at him. He sat on the leather fender in his shirt-sleeves, sipping his cup of tea.

'I wouldn't have come here otherwise.'

'Charming.'

Gwydion moved nearer to him as though to indicate to the others that he was adept at handling the difficult member of the family.

'There's no point in concealing the truth.'

His blunt attitude distressed his mother. She looked at Bedwyr as though asking for help. Gwydion walked over to the trolley and poured himself a cup of tea.

514

'I thought we could do that later,' Bedwyr said. 'After dinner perhaps. We could have a proper discussion.'

'Why not now?'

Peredur looked at three empty chairs in turn as though he were suggesting they all sat down and got down to business.

'No reason at all. But there are other things to talk about.'

'Such as?'

'The Trust. This is obviously an ideal occasion to hear about it and discuss it. While we are all here.'

'That doesn't concern me,' Peredur said.

'Of course it does. It's a much bigger concept now. Amy would like it to concern all of us.'

'I'm all for it,' Gwydion said.

He was sitting down carefully in a low armchair balancing his cup and saucer with both hands. Peredur looked at him suspiciously.

'And I'm sure you will be. It's not just a centre for creative women now, is it?'

Gwydion looked at Amy for confirmation. She nodded her head gently.

'It's something much bigger.'

'Does it include a television consortium?'

Peredur was openly sarcastic. Gwydion took the remark as a joke.

'No, by George,' he said, 'but you never know. It jolly well could.'

The cup rattled in the saucer as his shoulders shook. Amy smiled faintly, unable to appreciate the joke but glad that Gwydion was succeeding in forcing back the pall of gloom that seemed to exude so persistently from her youngest son. Peredur concentrated his attention on Bedwyr.

'What do you think of the plans?'

'The Memorial?'

Peredur nodded impatiently.

515

'There seemed to be so many of them . . .'

Bedwyr was unwilling to be rushed.

'The Mayor's,' Peredur said. 'That's the one that really counts.'

'What did you think of it?'

'Expensive,' Bedwyr said. 'And vulgar.'

'Why vulgar?'

Peredur put down his cup on the fender and folded his arms.

'It's very difficult to define vulgarity,' Bedwyr said. 'That Walk for example. It would have to be some kind of a concrete path ending in a sort of slipway in front of the rock. Nearly two miles long. What's the point of it? There's already a rough path; why go messing about at such expense when you'd get better results by just leaving nature alone. And then the idea of a statue on the rock looking out to sea. That seems dreadful.'

'Why?'

'Why?'

Bedwyr's voice was pitched up to indicate that he believed the truth of what he was saying to be self-evident.

'He was a poet to begin with. Not Christopher Columbus or Henry the Navigator. And that idea of a garden grotto on the sheltered side of the rock! You can see what he's after. He wants us to pay for some crazy expansion scheme he's got for tidying up the West End of Pendraw, a job which needs doing I've no doubt, but no part of our terms of reference.'

When he saw that Bedwyr's reasoning was making Peredur uncomfortable, Gwydion hastened to put forward his own point of view.

'It's a dreadful idea,' he said. 'I must say I'm all against it.'

Peredur turned on him.

'You didn't bother even to get out of the car,' he said.

516

'Well, somebody had to stay and keep Amy company,' he said. 'Anyway, Bedwyr's the expert. If he says it's a rotten plan, it's a rotten plan and that's all there is to it.'

'This is exactly what I suspected.'

Peredur's face was flushed with anger.

'And I am pretty sure it was all worked out carefully beforehand. And it was your idea.'

He pointed at Bedwyr who remained professionally calm.

'Pretend to accept the idea. Go along with it nicely. And when the appropriate moment comes sabotage it.'

'You always dramatize everything.' Gwydion said. 'It's a sign of immaturity.'

'Is it?'

Peredur showed his teeth.

'Is it really? You must think I'm very stupid.'

'No, of course I don't,' Gwydion said in his cheeriest manner. 'It's a well-known fact that you are the brightest person in this exceptionally bright family. In this particular case I just think you are making much ado about nothing.'

'Nothing?'

Peredur seized on the word. He moved away from the fire, wiping his blotchy forehead with his large handkerchief.

'I'd like to know what you mean by "Nothing". I really would.'

His calm was more menacing than his anger and Gwydion became suddenly uneasy.

'Nobody's against it,' he said. 'I just happen to agree with Bedwyr's criticism. Something much simpler would do very nicely. It would be more dignified and much cheaper and far more sensible.'

Bedwyr waved Gwydion into silence.

'Look,' he said, addressing Peredur. 'I don't know what we are arguing about. We accept the idea of a

Memorial in principle. That's fine. You've won your campaign. Let's put it like that. You've made your case. All that remains to be settled is the most effective form the memorial should take. You can't really take exception to my criticisms. They are objective. The kind of criticism any reputable architect and designer would make. Specialist criticism you could call it. To a certain extent, as it should be and indeed has to be, impersonal. Do you accept that?'

Peredur looked at the carpet and then stuck out the hand which held the handkerchief.

'What's your alternative?'

Bedwyr's raised his eyebrows.

'Your alternative plan. What do you suggest?'

'Nothing yet,' Bedwyr said.

'"Nothing" again?'

'It needs thought,' Bedwyr said. 'And it needs discussion. I would have thought this was an excellent project for the Trust. We could initiate a whole series of decent monuments for neglected artists and men of letters . . .'

'What Trust?'

'Well, there you are. That's exactly the point I tried to make at the beginning. Amy is forming a Trust, a Foundation. It's an exciting concept and it needs serious and extended discussion. That's why we are here.'

'It's a fine idea,' Gwydion said. 'And it's just the kind of thing to interest you. Isn't it, Amy?'

'I hope so.'

Amy sounded uncharacteristically subdued. Peredur was shaking his head.

'It's a very simple thing,' he said. 'And I won't be put off. The town where he lived wants to put up a memorial to a man who was your father, and yours, and mine, and your husband. But you are so ashamed of him, you want him to be forgotten. And the kind of world

518

and the kind of culture and the kind of language he represents. You want to forget that too. Not a word, not a book, not a stone. Nothing. That's the "Nothing" I'm making a fuss about.'

'Oh really . . .'

Gwydion groaned.

'Peredur,' Bedwyr said.

He spoke urgently.

'Listen to me. You are getting this whole thing out of proportion.'

'Am I? I don't think so. Too expensive you said. Too much money. And yet you talk about forming some grandiloquent Trust. What with and what for? He was too small I suppose. Too insignificant. He wasn't even worth a wooden cross.'

'Don't get excited,' Bedwyr said. 'And stick to the point.'

Amy stood up and extended her arms pleadingly.

'Please don't quarrel,' she said. 'Please don't. I've been so looking forward to today. I've been so looking forward to having you all home.'

Peredur waved an arm.

'You call this home! You know what I call it? I call it the House of Plunder and I want nothing at all to do with it.'

'He's raving,' Gwydion said. 'Don't take any notice of him. He's been crossed in love again, or is it the same one. Now come on.'

Peredur went white. Gwydion laughed and waved his hand as though to rub out an incautious reference to something told him in confidence. A note of open begging came into his voice.

'Please stop acting like a prize bloody prig. Is this what you call your thing-a-me moral imperative?'

'Yes. It is.'

'Now Peredur! Just listen. Amy's turning the whole place to good use. She's doing the right thing by

519

anybody's standards including yours, I hope. So stop beefing like a delayed adolescent.

'You can't build anything worthwhile on rotten foundations.'

'What's that supposed to mean?'

'You can't buy yourself into a television consortium by filching a Rembrandt drawing from this place and kidding yourself that it isn't stolen property!'

Gwydion flopped back his chair.

'Oh my God,' he said. 'What can you do with him?'

'What's all this about?'

Bedwyr began to show a new interest.

'You can't do anything with him,' Gwydion said. 'It's something to do with that University, I'm sure. He's been buttoned up by persecution. All by himself. And they've turned him in to a jet-propelled fanatic. I don't know . . .'

He ran his hands through his hair.

'I was going to tell you about it anyway,' he said. 'In the fullness of time. I found a folder in old Uncle Francis's work room. A folder of drawings by Richard Wilson. Views of Rome. And there was a Rembrandt drawing folded down the middle.

'But that must be worth thousands.'

Bedwyr sounded shocked.

'Of course. All I was going to do was deposit the lot in a bank and raise capital on the security.'

'How much?'

'I was going to tell you all about it tonight. Now old Periwinkle here has jumped the gun and spoilt my story. I was going to buy my way on paper on to the board of a television consortium. And I was going to see everyone of you were all right. That's why I wanted you to knobble old J.M. for me. It's the only way it can be done. Perfectly legitimate. What's the matter? Have I suddenly developed the plague or something?'

Peredur looked out through the window at the rain, pressing his handkerchief against his lips. Bedwyr stood with his hands in his pockets staring at the carpet and frowning heavily. Amy moved to the door. Gwydion held out his arm towards her.

'Now wait,' he said. 'Where are you going?'

'There's been trouble in the kitchen,' Amy said. 'I must go and settle it.'

'Well, it looks like trouble here,' Gwydion said. 'Look at those two. They are horrified at the thought of having a thief for a brother. I just needed the security. Nothing more. Look at them standing. Dying of their own perfection.'

'Connie will be so upset.'

'Never mind about Connie. I'm upset. They just don't begin to understand what it's all about.'

'Tell us.'

Bedwyr's stare was full of accusation.

'I can't just operate in the open,' Gwydion said. 'Not on the scale I'm aiming at. Not at that level. Haven't you ever heard of merchant bankers having secret meetings in the air? In specially hired executive jets. Or on two yachts that meet at a secret rendezvous? That's the kind of area I'm operating in. On your behalf as well as my own.'

'No, thank you.'

Bedwyr was cold and polite.

'Oh no,' Gwydion said. 'You can't opt out. Like little brother there. And if it comes to that, he can't opt out either. If you want to survive as a recognizable entity in the modern world, brother, you've got to fight for whatever piece of the future your good fortune will allow you to grab. Now that's what the Past is really for. To give you your grip on the future. The first law of economic growth.'

'I'm going.'

Peredur spoke. Gwydion turned on him quickly.

521

'Where?' he said. 'To print Cilydd's last poems on a hand press? You know what the trouble with you is? With both of you? You're not really up to it. If you are so unwilling to relinquish your father's ghost, Peredur, you should take it with you and tuck yourself away in a cloister.'

He turned to Amy.

'You can have the Rembrandt back,' he said. 'And the Wilsons.'

'I'm worried about Connie,' Amy said. 'She's been doing too much all week.'

'Amy.'

Gwydion kneeled on his chair and appealed to her over the back.

'I wasn't going to steal them. You understand that. I wouldn't have shown them to him if I was going to steal them, would I?'

She looked at him sorrowfully.

'You can have them,' she said. 'If they're any help to you.'

'Amy!'

Bedwyr was deeply shocked.

'Have you any idea what they're worth?'

She was silent for a moment, apparently willing to attempt a calculation and then she shook her head to show her lack of interest in the question.

'They're two against one,' she said. 'And Connie is so old and so cranky.'

With nothing more to say, she left them.